IT WAS LIKE SEEING HIMSELF—
THROUGH THE EYES OF SOMEONE ELSE . . .

Jonathan was not just imagining seeing himself. He was actually looking down at the bed from a place near the ceiling; looking down with real seeing eyes at himself while his body lay outside his mind and eyes. And his vision was sharp, sharper than it had ever been.

It was no dream. It was terrifying, yes: yet the power was so thrilling that his heart leapt into the night sky . . .

NIGHTFLYER

CHRISTOPHER FAHY

A JOVE BOOK

NIGHTFLYER

A Jove Book / published by arrangement with
the author

PRINTING HISTORY
Jove edition / August 1982

ISBN: 0-515-06217-0

Jove books are published by Jove Publications, Inc.,
200 Madison Avenue, New York, N.Y. 10016. The words
"A JOVE BOOK" and the "J" with sunburst are trademarks
belonging to Jove Publications, Inc.

PRINTED IN THE UNITED STATES OF AMERICA

To Harris Dienstfrey and William G. Thompson
Thanks, Harris
Thanks, Bill

CHAPTER ONE _____

From the spot where Jonathan Petrie sat on the hill he could see the highway, hundreds of cars and trucks flowing by, and far away in the brooding gray March light he could see the Midvale skyline murky and dark. He thought of that gigantic darkness beyond his sight, New York City, and the ocean beyond New York three thousand miles wide. He closed his eyes and leaned against the slender oak that marked his spot; he listened to the steady rush of traffic and he sighed.

Jon was fifteen years old but looked more like twelve; he was short and thin, and his skin had the smooth unblemished clarity of childhood. He wore strong, expensive, wire-rimmed glasses that gave him a comical, bug-eyed look, and his hair stuck up in tufts like unruly grass. His posture was poor, his shoulders slumped, and on this damp March day he had a runny nose. He sniffed and coughed, and his glasses slid down his face. He shoved them into place again and again he sighed, a deep quiver this time, then put his hands behind his head and dreamed.

The roar of the trucks and cars on the highway was like the roar of surf. His eyes still closed, he pictured that ocean beyond New York, he saw himself skimming across the water, dancing like a butterfly, a monarch butterfly orange and black, he watched himself sailing three thousand joyous miles, free from worry, free from pain. A band of weak light bled through the clouds and bathed him in feeble warmth, and he flew on its rays to the very sun and was warm and happy forever.

1

A truck shifted gears with a violent groan and he opened his eyes. The colors and shapes flowed past far down below. So many cars. So many people, all that metal, all that speed. The noise never stopped, the speed never stopped; it went on all day and all night, on Sundays and holidays, summer or winter or spring or fall. *Full of sound and fury,* he thought, *signifying nothing.* All that hurry, hurry, hurry—and every so often, death.

The year before, he had seen an accident here. He had heard the squeal and the crash, had seen one of the cars slide into the tractor trailer as if it were skidding on ice, though the road was totally dry and the month was June. From his perch he saw it all in miniature: the police, the ambulance, the tiny bodies placed on stretchers and carted away. It was all unreal, an insect drama, so small it didn't matter. The next morning he read in the paper that one of the insects killed was a girl his age. He thought a long while about that death, about his own death, about pain and freedom from pain. Killed instantly, the paper said. Well, that was not so bad.

The clouds closed over the wound in the sky and blotted out the warmth. Jon shivered. He pulled a crumpled handkerchief out of his pocket and blew his nose, stuffed the handkerchief back, pushed his glasses up again. Then suddenly a shock flashed through him and he froze.

A noise like a twig snapping—somewhere behind him. Furtively he turned and looked through the trees, the stand of thin maples and poplars and oaks that shielded his hill from the swamp and the field next to Evergreen Row. There was nothing. No one. Yet he thought he had heard—

He stood up, brushed off his pants. He had better be getting home. It wasn't smart to sit here too long; they might find him here and his spot would be ruined forever. It was getting cold now anyway, the sky was low and dull, the sun a thin red streak on the edge of the world. And there were things he wanted to do before dinner, things he wanted to study. Yes, he'd better get home.

He made his way back to the path and walked along it, walked beside bottles and beer cans and cigarette butts, beside crumpled, snot-caked tissues and wrappers from candy and gum. He walked through the scraggly trees by the oily swamp—and saw the butterfly.

It was a mourning cloak, and it sat on the thick black mud at the edge of the slimy water, slowly opening, slowly closing its wings. Jon stood there motionless, watching it. He had never seen a mourning cloak so early in spring. This must be its first day—possibly even its very first hour—out of hibernation, it was so bright and new.

He watched the maroon velvet wings fold up and down, and a thin beam of sunlight glowed through a crack in the clouds and lighted the dark rich scales: the wing tips crisp and yellow, the bands of black with dots of brilliant blue. A perfect specimen! If only he had his net and his jar! Its beauty took his breath away. He stared.

Then he heard the laugh. He turned. It was Carl and Bruce—both of them—and his heart contracted with fear.

The two boys came down the path. Bruce Hodges laughed again, his mouth in an ugly sneer. "Hey Pee-Tree, what are you doin', playin' with yourself?" Carl Renniger, tall and bony with sharp pale slits of eyes and high cheekbones, said, "Thinkin' of going swimming, dingbat?"

Jon's words were caught in his throat. He forced them out: "I thought I saw a quarter in the water. It was just a reflection." He felt his pulse race into his neck, thick, full. "I have to get home for dinner now. We're eating early tonight."

Bruce looked at Carl, then back at Jon. He stuck his heavy forearm across the path, right under Jon's chin. "Hold on a minute. We want to talk to you."

Jon's knees went weak. "What . . . what about?"

"About that homework I gave you to do."

"It's finished," Jon said. "I finished it this morning."

"It's a good thing, Petrie, a damn good thing."

Carl Renniger said, "What are you doin' here, Petrie
—lookin' for Headquarters?"

Jon shook his head violently. "No! I swear I wasn't,
no!"

The mourning cloak took off with a flutter, danced
across the swamp. Jon saw it in the corner of his eyes,
and soon it was lost in the trees.

"He was watching a butterfly," Carl said. "A butterfly! Can you believe this faggot?"

"How can he watch anything with eyes like that?"
Bruce said. "Let me see your glasses, Pee-Tree."

"No!" Jon said. "Bruce, please—"

Swiftly Carl grabbed Jon's arms and pinned them
behind his back and Bruce snatched the glasses off.
Everything was a blur as Bruce's voice said, "Nobody
can see out of things like these, they're no damn good.
What the hell are you keepin' 'em for?" Jon saw a fuzzy
arm sticking up in the air, saw the arm make a sudden
sideways movement and Bruce said, "Up, up, and
away!" He snickered and said, "You didn't really want
those goofy things, did you, Pee-Tree?"

Panic rushed to Jon's chest. He struggled against
Carl's wiry arms. "What did you do with my glasses?"
he screamed. "Give them back, give them back!"

"Nah, you don't want them," Bruce said, spitting on
the ground. "They were really ugly. Let him go, Carl,
let's see how he looks without those stupid things."

Jon's arms were suddenly free, and he made his hands
into fists. "Give me back my glasses!" he shouted
again. "Give them back, you . . . you—"

"You *what*?" Bruce Hodges said in a voice like ice.
"Come on, Pee-Tree, say what you wanted to say.
Bastards? Motherfuckers? What was it you wanted to
say?"

Bruce seemed to be staring, but Jon couldn't tell. All
he could see was an orange blur where a face should be
and a dark brown blur of hair. He saw sharp swift
movement but didn't see knuckles until the split second
before the jolt, when he felt his nose explode with
stinging pain, the bones in his head crack into each
other, and felt himself falling backward, backward, into

the freezing swamp. The shock of pain and cold and surprise—he couldn't breathe—then he felt the scum on his hands and head, felt the flow of blood down his lip and chin, felt the hot numb throbbing begin in his nose and he couldn't hold back the tears.

"Hey, you *did* want to take a swim," Carl said. His laughter burst like rockets in Jon's ears.

"We'll see ya, Pee-Tree," Bruce said. "Don't spend too much time lookin' for your glasses, you might miss dinner. You want to know where they are, you can ask the trees." He laughed. Two orange blobs moved through gray and bright green and were gone.

Sobbing, Jon crawled on his hands and knees, soaked, dripping with slime from the swamp. If they're broken, he'll kill me, he said to himself. If they're lost. . . . His throat was swollen and choked. If they're lost! Oh God, they can't be lost! "Father, I don't mean to be this way," he said aloud through his tears. "I can't help it, that's all! I can't be tough and strong like you, I can't help it, I can't!"

It took him over an hour to find the glasses. They were stuck on a maple branch and moved gently back and forth in the cold spring wind. He grabbed them eagerly, held them close to his feeble eyes, examined them quickly—and found they were whole. "Thank God," he said with a heavy sigh of relief, and he put them on. One earpiece was bent and the world was a little crooked, but he could see again; they weren't broken, it would be all right.

Quickly he wiped the slime off his jacket, his pants, and his shoes, then went to the edge of the swamp and threw water on his bloody mouth. He hurried along the path and out of the trees and walked through the field that bordered Evergreen Row.

His lips throbbed dully as he crossed the matted grass. Fresh sprouts were pushing their way through the previous year's dead growth. Soon the field would be full again, the daisies would flower, followed by black-eyed susans and thistles and goldenrod. And the butterflies would come, the swallowtails and fritillaries, and maybe even the metalmark. Maybe this would be

the year he would catch a metalmark. Next to the
monarch it was his favorite butterfly. It wasn't at all
spectacular, just small and brown, but it was rare, so
rare that he sometimes only saw one specimen all summer. The only place he'd ever spotted one was in this
field, his field. His father's field, really. His father had
built the Evergreen Row development and owned this
land, all seven acres of this place where the metalmark
made its home.

Jon's heart sank again as he thought of his father. He
took his glasses off and squinted at them, tried to
straighten the earpiece further. The world was still
crooked when he put them back on. His father probably
wouldn't notice the glasses, but his lip, it felt bad, and
he'd see that for sure. His mother would see it too unless
she was . . . *that way*. If she was *that way* she'd be
oblivious, but his father would see it. Maybe he would
be out somewhere. He could only hope he was out.

Jon came out of the field and onto the path that
wound past the backs of the houses of Evergreen Row.
He checked his face in the side-view mirror of the first
parked car he saw. His lip was swollen, there was still
dried blood near his nose. He dabbed at it with his
soaking handkerchief. He winced from the sting. He
dabbed at the blood until it was gone, then took his
glasses off and worked on the earpiece again. He
couldn't get it exactly right but he managed to make it
better. He put the glasses on again and hurried home.

He slipped cautiously into the foyer. The blare of the
TV muffled the sound of the door as it shut behind him.
The house was heavy with Sunday dinner, the smell of
potatoes and beef.

He glanced through the kitchen doorway and into the
family room, saw the huge color image: Two men in
shorts were attacking each other savagely. "A hard
right hook to the jaw and Crews is stunned! He's back
against the ropes, now Watkins will work on his body,
it's a right to the ribs, another right . . . ." Jon's father's
voice, gruff, harsh above the din: "Throw the left!
Come on, the left! Now. NOW!" "Crews is hurt! He's

cut above the eye!'' And Jonathan watched the torrent of blood flow over the boxer's cheek, watched him flailing in helpless confusion as his enemy hammered his face. He looked away, sick, as his father shouted: "Come on, Watkins, finish him off! *Kill* the bastard!"

Jon started up the stairs. His legs felt weak and watery, tears flooded his eyes. He steadied himself on the railing and took a sharp breath. They'll never understand, he thought. I'll never be able to make them, never, never. Aching, he stared at the foyer floor, the dull hard quarry tiles, then forced himself to get moving again. He had to get cleaned up before—

"Jonathan?"

He gripped the railing hard. His mother was in the foyer, staring up.

"Jonathan, come down here and let me look at you."

His heart in his throat, he turned. Slowly he walked back down the steps and stood before his mother, eyes averted.

"*Jonathan*." His mother's voice was whining, soft and sad. "Have you been playing in that swamp again?"

Jon still did not look up. "Yes, Mother."

"If I've told you once to stay out of there I've told you a hundred times."

"Yes, Mother, you have. But—"

"Oh Jonathan, look at your clothes."

Jon stared at his shoes. He saw the slimy algae there, the scum on the legs of his pants. "I'm . . . sorry, Mother, I slipped."

"So clumsy, so clumsy," his mother said. Her tone was filled with despair.

Jon glanced at her, saw her soft yellow hair, her sad face resigned to his hopelessness. He smelled the sweet perfume of liquor on her breath. She'd been drinking, but not enough to be *that way*. He avoided her watery eyes and looked at his shoes again.

"It looks like you've been *swimming* in that mess. Look at me. What happened to your lip?"

"I . . . fell. There was a butterfly . . ."

"A butterfly." His mother sighed. "Well *that* explains it.'' Gently she touched his mouth. His face flushed hot with embarrassment. "What a nasty cut. You really have to be more careful." She took her hand away and his lip felt cool. "All right, get washed and changed. We're going to eat. And put those filthy clothes in the hamper."

Jon hurried up the steps and went into his room. He closed the door and sat on his bed and wept, crying into the pillow to muffle the sound. He cried for five minutes, sobs racking his body, the long deep ache reaching down from his throat to his lungs. Then he cleared his throat and blew his nose and rolled over onto his back.

He was safe again in his very own world, his room. On one wall were his mounted butterflies, bright splashes of ragged color; against another wall was his train layout—with his very own mountains and streams and trees, and houses where everyone smiled and no one was mean; and across the room's center the planets hung on a string: There was hot little Mercury, huge cold Jupiter, colorful Saturn with all its rings. He wished he could live anywhere but on this earth. He wished he could fly far away and far up in the wind like a butterfly, but no, he was trapped in this town, this neighborhood, he was trapped under glass like the butterflies on his wall. He would live here and live here in daily pain; he had done it for years. There was nothing else he could do.

He took a hot shower and changed his clothes, then sat on the edge of his bed and looked out the window, looked at the line of trees beyond the pool. All his life he had spent long hours staring through windows, daydreaming into the sky: the winter sky, the summer sky; the evening sky, the morning sky; the sky red, yellow, purple, gray, the sky bright azure blue. When he was very small his mind had flown into the wide expanse, the sky had been a magic universe of endless possibility. The years had dulled that wonder, but a part of him still clung to that early vision.

On the top of the bookcase across the room sat a battered gray stuffed animal, a donkey with drooping ears.

His Eeyore, a baby toy he'd never thrown away. As a little child he'd spent hours talking to Eeyore, and sometimes when things were very bad, he remembered those childhood days.

"It wasn't so bad back then, was it, Eeyore? I was different, but they let me alone. But now . . . . How much more can I take? Father and Mother, they don't understand. I can't even tell them about it." He looked at the toy with wet eyes and said, "*You're* the one I tell. Not Chuckie or Meg or anybody real, I talk to *you*, a piece of cloth, that's how bad it is. Fifteen years old, and *you're* the one I tell." He smiled sadly and said, "Good, old Eeyore, still with me through thick and thin—and isn't it ridiculous?"

He thought about Carl and Sonny and Randy and Bruce. They hated him so much, and why, what had he ever done? Not a thing. He had just been himself, that's all, like the guidance counselor, Miss Weller, had said you should do in that talk she gave. Oh Yes, Miss Weller, it's fine to be yourself as long as you aren't different. Meg can be herself without any problems. But what about Chuckie? Chuckie doesn't have any choice but to be himself and every day of his life he's tortured for it. Tortured because he was born a certain way, born with a damaged brain that won't work his muscles right. People think that's *funny*, Eeyore. They *laugh* at him.

He stared at the toy on the shelf and shook his head. A terrible despair washed over him. "Eeyore, it won't always be this way," he said in a whisper, "I swear it won't."

He saw himself flying again, soaring over those ominous trees past the swimming pool, soaring high into light, into sun, so high that no one could touch him. He sat there and stared at his babyhood toy, then suddenly his chest was filled with pain. Pain rushed to the back of his throat: It was swollen and burning and red, he choked on pain, it was hot and salty and wet and raw and it hurt when he tried to swallow. "I try, I try," he said, his eyes blurred. "I do, you know I do, Eeyore, I try . . . ." Then tears overwhelmed him, his throat closed up. The salt of his tears hurt the cut in his lip and his thin chest heaved up and down in short bursts. "If only . . . if only . . ."

"Jonathan, it's dinnertime." His mother's weary voice from the foyer.

Jon swallowed hard and choked back the pain and answered, "I'm not hungry now. I don't want to eat right now." His butterflies in their case, pressed flat, dead, beautiful in death.

"What, Jonathan?" The voice unfocused, soft, preoccupied.

"I said I don't want to eat!" And the pain welled up from Jon's chest and filled his throat and the tears rolled over his cheeks and he sobbed to the battered donkey in quick hot breaths: "I want to kill myself, that's what I want! I want to die!"

CHAPTER TWO _____

Bruce Hodges swung. The fist screamed at him, huge, made contact, hit his eye, and his eyeball shattered like glass. He tilted his head and brown transparent splinters fell into his open hand. He was too amazed to cry, to even feel pain. Then he woke with a start, the crack of the fist fading out of his ears and he knew that the sound had been real.

It had come from across the room, from the window. He slipped his glasses on, got out of bed, the fragments of nightmare dissolving (bright glittering splinters, black socket of useless eye), and crossed the room.

There on the window pane in the early sun was a dull gray smear. A tiny black feather adhered to its center. Jon put on his robe and slippers, left his room, and ran down the carpeted stairs.

The bird was on the concrete in front of the pool, completely limp, eyes closed. It was black, with glitters of red and blue and green on its shining feathers. A starling. An ugly bird, a mean dirty bird, that's what his mother said, but to Jon it looked beautiful. He picked it up and felt its warmth; he felt it quiver in his hand. Quickly he ran with it into the house, took it up to his room, and placed it on the carpet under his bed.

In the garage he found a small cardboard box and filled it with grass. He took the box to his room, put the limp bird in it, stuck the box on a shelf in his closet, and closed the door.

He wasn't allowed to have any pets because of his mother's allergies. All his life he had longed for a cat or

11

a dog or a bird, but no, his mother would get a rash, she would sneeze, she couldn't breathe, and all he had was Eeyore, a make believe pet, a baby toy. He smiled. But now a pet had come to him out of nowhere, out of the sky. "A real pet, Eeyore. A bird, a real—"

The alarm clock rang. He jumped. He turned it off and got ready for school.

His father was sitting at the breakfast table, sipping his coffee, smoking, staring out at the pool. The small TV in the corner was on and the newsman said, ". . . Cut off his father's ears and nose and flushed them down the toilet . . ." Jon got the milk and the Cheerios, the bowl and spoon and sat down.

"Good morning, Father."

Doug Petrie squinted. Steel-gray hair, dark eyes. He said, "What happened to your face?"

Jon looked at his cereal bowl. "I, uh . . . I fell."

"You look like hell."

Jon poured himself some cereal as his father smoked. He thought of the bird in the box in his room and a thrill went through him. Then he looked at the clock and his stomach tightened. Monday again, the start of another week of school. The thought of it made him feel sick. He forced himself to swallow the Cheerios. " . . . In a Bergen tavern," the TV said. "The victim was stabbed a dozen times in the throat and chest . . ."

Doug Petrie tilted his head back and gulped the last of his coffee. Without a word he crushed his cigarette in the ashtray, stood, slipped his jacket over his rugged shoulders, walked through the laundry room and into the garage.

Jon ate as the Cadillac Eldorado purred to life. He heard the garage door squeal, heard the car move out, heard the door grind down again. Then he pushed himself away from the table, snapped the TV off, and ran upstairs.

He packed his briefcase: his books, his homework, the homework he'd copied by hand for Bruce, and his special projects. He went to the wall and took down one of the walnut-framed, glass-covered butterfly cases and put that in his briefcase too. He checked his wallet to see that he had enough money, then opened the closet door.

The bird lay motionless on its side. He touched it gently. Again he felt the feeble shiver, as if it were freezing to death. "I'll make you better, bird," he whispered. "Don't worry, I will." If only he could stay home with it, take care of it all day. But now it was really late, and he had to go.

As he hurried along the sidewalk that bordered the woods below the school, the heavy briefcase straining his arm, loud angry cars roared by. Every so often a shout was directed his way, but he stared straight ahead and kept walking, pretending he didn't hear.

"Pee-Tree, you pisser!" The growl of headers and out of the side of his eye Jon saw the car. Sonny Richardson's car, the painted fire flaring over the hood. A head of long red hair torn wildly by the wind, Randy Hankins's hair, and a hand sticking out of the window, a hand clenched into a fist. Jon's knees felt weak, an acid belch rose to his throat. But the car didn't stop this time and, skinny shoulders slouching forward, he kept on walking, walking up the hill.

Springdale Elementary School hadn't been so bad. At least it didn't seem so bad compared to Aronson High. He hadn't really had any friends there and here he had Chuckie, Chuckie and . . . Meg. Yes, Meg was a friend, he told himself, not just an acquaintance, a friend. But while he hadn't had friends at Springdale he hadn't had enemies either. Not enemies like those at Wallace Aronson. Even when he had skipped fourth grade it hadn't been so bad: the older kids had picked on him for a month or so but then they had left him alone.

Then his father had built the new development, Evergreen Row. He had picked out the choicest piece of land in the whole twelve acres, a half-acre lot on a knoll that bordered the woods, had built the first and most elegant house, and they had moved. Ever since then, life for Jon had been hell.

It had started right from the very first day at Aronson High with the kids from Russelville, the neighborhood at the foot of Evergreen Row. That first lunch period still burned in Jon's mind: Randy Hankins grabbing him by his shirt and smashing him up against the wall and sneering, "Your old man built houses on our ball-field, creep! We gotta get a new field because of you!" Jon's heart had pounded so hard he had thought it would burst through his chest. And Randy had grabbed his hair and twisted it and made him kiss his shoe, and then they had taken his money. And he had lived with the fear of Randy and Sonny and Carl and Bruce at least five days out of every week, at least forty weeks out of every year, and sometimes they got him on weekends too and sometimes they got him when school was out in the summer. Three years of their torture. It seemed like a lifetime. He shifted his briefcase, sighed, continued to walk.

Sonny Richardson stood at the foot of the rope, flexing his powerful hands, his flat, hard face expressionless. Just looking at that face sent bolts of fear through Jon's heart. Of all his enemies, Sonny scared him the most.

Mr. Bondino looked at his stopwatch and then yelled, "Go!" and Sonny was rapidly pulling himself up the rope with his bulging arms. He reached the top, slapped the iron bar, slid down again. "Four seconds," Mr. Bondino said. "Okay, Richardson, not bad." Sonny's face remained bland. He sat on the floor again, not even breathing hard. Mr. Bondino looked at Jon and said, "Okay, Mr. Universe, your turn."

Jon walked up to the rope, the whole class watching. Somebody snickered. Mr. Bondino looked at the stopwatch and shouted, "Go!"

Jon grabbed the rope and jumped. He tried to pinch the rope between his legs as he'd seen the other kids do but he couldn't get a grip, it kept slipping away. He clenched his teeth and pulled with all his might. Far above in the glare of the lights he saw the iron bar impossibly distant and pulled and pulled, arms aching, sweet drenching his skin, and he simply hung, he dangled there skinny in white gym shorts and shirt, went nowhere at all.

"Come on, Petrie, *try*!" the gym teacher shouted, and Jon clung desperately, his hands beginning to slide. Suddenly the rope whipped through them, burning them red, and he dropped to the floor, stunned, gasping for breath. Everybody laughed, Jon's face flashed red and Mr. Bondino said, "Good going, Mr. Universe. Do twenty laps."

"But Mr. Bondino—"

"Move it out!"

The other kids played basketball while Jon ran. Around and around he went, his thin ribs heaving, his undigested breakfast sloshing in his stomach. He had tried as hard as he could and it wasn't fair, he just wasn't as strong as the other kids. He had a terrific memory, was born with it, but he hadn't been born with muscles, and Mr. Bondino shouldn't make him do laps because of the way he was born. As he ran he thought of the ads in the comic books. *BUILD MUSCLES FAST! STRONG ARMS MAKE ALL THE DIFFERENCE!* He almost sent away for those courses a couple of times, but never did. They wouldn't work for him, he just wasn't meant to be strong. Sonny had never taken those courses and he was so strong he could fly up the ropes without using his feet. It was how you were born, that's all.

He kept running around the gym. Sometimes they tried to trip him but he avoided them, panting, sweating, his thighs in pain, his stomach cramped, and Mr. Bondino, ex-college football star, now bald and paunchy, yelling, "Move it, Petrie, move it!" Till after the sixth lap he ran through the doors at the end of the gym and into the locker room and puked the Cheerios into the toilet and sat on the bench in front of the lockers, dizzy, gasping for breath and shivering. Soon Mr. Bondino came in with the others and said, "Petrie! Who told you to quit? I said twenty laps." And Jon said weakly, "I can't. I'm sick." Jim Bussington laughed but Matt Wilson said, "You want me to take him up to the nurse's office, Mr. Bondino?"

"No . . . I'm all right," Jon said as he swallowed hard.

Mr. Bondino shook his head and sneered and said,

"Okay, Mr. Universe, take a shower."

Jim Bussington said, "He don't need no shower, coach—he ain't even got any hair!" and all the kids laughed.

Then Jon had to take his shorts off, his underpants off since he had no jockstrap, hurry naked—still bald down there although he was fifteen—through the slimy dark showers, his stomach beginning to heave again in the humid heat, his glasses steamed, eyes blind, and they finally tripped him and down he fell in the slime and cracked his elbow on the concrete floor. By the time second period started the hurt place was aching sharply and starting to swell.

Alice Petrie woke up after nine with a headache. She usually had a headache when she woke up, but this one was worse than usual: a throbbing that started in the back of her neck and branched out into her eyes. Her throat was dry and her nose was running. She felt absolutely miserable. It was almost as bad as that time in the hotel on Lake Champlain.

They came to the hotel late after driving twelve hours, went right to sleep, and two hours later she woke in the dark unable to breathe, chest tight, nose running, throat sore. She sneezed so hard and so often she thought she would never stop. It had been the pillows, pillows stuffed with down. And from then on she took her own pillow on trips, a Dacron pillow, nonallergenic.

Yes, she thought, lying there, staring out of her window, it felt like that. A lot like that. All at once she sneezed. She reached for a Kleenex and blew her nose, eyes throbbing. There wasn't any down in this house, no feathers at all in this house, so it couldn't be that. Hay fever? Awful early for that. But the buds were swelling, the grass was tinged with green, and that must be the answer, it must be hay fever.

She stared at the sun on the window sill, at the Swedish ivy hanging in front of the glass, then slowly slid out of the bed, slipped her feet into fluffy pink slippers, and went to her bathroom. She sneezed again, and took two antihistamines, two aspirins, and a Valium.

She spent a long time in the bathroom, showering, putting on makeup, preparing herself for the day. The days were long and she had so much to do. This morning she had to have her hair done, and then in the afternoon the grocery order would come and she'd have to put it away. She would have to start planning the next order too and work on the decorating scheme for the living room. She'd been working on those living-room plans for the last six months. It was an exhausting job.

In the kitchen she saw her husband's empty coffee cup and Jon's half-eaten Cheerios, the milk now caught in a ring of bright morning sun. He never eats enough, she thought. You just couldn't get him to eat enough. She had tried and tried to get him to eat, but it was impossible. She stared at the bowl and thought of Jon, her only child, the only child she would ever have. He was a good boy, a sweet boy, but he had grown so fast, had grown away from her these last few years. She thought about this as she sat at the breakfast table and stared across the empty swimming pool. When she checked the clock again, she was amazed to see how the time had flown.

She sneezed again. The antihistamines had helped but she didn't feel well at all. She stood up slowly, sneezing fitfully now. She blew her nose, the headache thick in her temples. She cleared the dirty dishes off the table, rinsed them, put them in the dishwasher. So much to do today, God only knew where she'd find the strength to get through it all. It was already ten of eleven. She had to be at the hairdresser's soon. She sighed and sneezed again and blew her nose. She opened the cabinet above the sink and poured herself a Pernod.

At Aronson High, the second period was coming to a close.

CHAPTER THREE _____

"While technically the range of the giant swallowtail extends through southern New England, its appearance is rare even here in the Middle Atlantic States. I felt very fortunate to be able to capture a specimen here in New Jersey. Especially one as nice as this." Jon propped the glass covered case, the Riker mount, on Mrs. Blaylock's desk and pointed to the butterfly.

Meg Hale was watching with a little smile. Jon's heart skipped a beat. For a moment his elbow didn't hurt, he forgot about Randy and Bruce and Carl—who sat in the back of the room with bored expressions, slouching down—and he smiled, too, tentatively. Meg's eyes met his; he looked down.

He slipped the Riker mount into his briefcase and said, "My favorite butterfly is the northern metalmark. It's indigenous to this area but it's very rare. I've only seen it twice, and I've never even come close to catching it. Here it is." He held up a book for the class to see.

"Doesn't look like much," Ann Gelman said.

"Oh, I've seen those," Joan Sanders said.

"I doubt it," Jon said. "There are several other butterflies that look like this, but the northern metalmark is very hard to find."

Mrs. Blaylock looked at the Seth Thomas clock on the wall and said, "That was a fine presentation, Jon. Any questions, class?"

Dave Schubert, frowning, said, "Yeah. How do you kill them?"

18

Jon wet his lips. "I saturate some cotton with a chemical fluid, drop the cotton in a jar, stick the butterfly in, and screw on the top. In two or three minutes the insect's unconscious. In fifteen minutes or so it's dead."

"Oh, gross," Linda Blanksby said. Paul Robinson, under his breath said, "Petrie's a . . . *murderer*." Several kids snickered, and then the bell went off.

Jon hurried out of the classroom and into the first-floor locker room and waited there for Bruce Hodges. Bruce came, and Jon gave him the carefully copied sheets of homework. Bruce said, "Okay slave, you'll live for another day." His heavy face broke into a grin. Now he wants money, Jon thought. Now he'll ask me for money. But instead Bruce said, "Hey, let me see those butterflies."

"I . . . don't have time," Jon said, breaking into a sweat. "I'll show them to you later."

"Let's have the briefcase, slave, or—"

Then Mr. Turnbull, short and thick with a fat red neck, was there. In a less enlightened age he'd been called the disciplinarian, but now he was called the vice-principal in charge of discipline. He looked at Bruce with his sharp little eyes and said, "Let's go, get moving, no hanging around in the lockers."

Bruce sniffed. "We'll make it later then, Petrie," he said, and moved casually out the door.

They were walking slowly down the long hill that led away from Aronson High to Evergreen Row and Russellville: Jon, Chuckie Palmieri, Meg.

"You sure do know your butterflies," Meg said.

Jon smiled. "I guess I ought to know a lot," he said. "I've been collecting for five years."

He walked, the briefcase tugging at his arm. He couldn't wait to get home. All day long he had thought of his bird, the starling, wondering if it had lived or died. Through all of his classes, through lunch and study hall he'd thought of it, and he wanted to run. But he had to go slowly because of Chuckie, who walked with a slow sort of shuffling limp because of his cerebral palsy. Everything Chuckie did was slow: He moved his arms slowly, spoke slowly, thought slowly. But he was a good kid, Jon's best friend. Jon's only friend . . . besides Meg.

He was thrilled to be walking with Meg. He almost never did, she usually walked with one of her girl-friends, and even when he had the chance he chose to walk by himself or with Chuckie. It was painful to walk with Meg, he loved her so much.

Her soft blond hair caught the light of the sun. She looked at him with her hazel eyes and he felt as if he would melt. He'd loved her since the day she had moved into Evergreen Row two years ago. He would never dare tell her, but someday . . . someday when he was older, when things got better, when things straight-ened out. . . .

"But don't you feel bad when you kill them?" she said.

"Well, yeah . . . a little. But I don't kill that many, just one of each kind."

Chuckie's face had a sunny smile. "He puts them in the jar and screws on the lid and before you know it . . . they're dead!"

"It's quick," Jon said. "And painless, I'm sure."

"How *can* you be sure?" Meg asked.

"Well, think of the butterfly's nervous system. How much pain can you feel with a limited nerve network like that?"

"Well . . . I don't know. If you say so, Jon." She smiled again and again his heart dissolved.

They were quiet a while, just walking along in the sun, and Jon thought about killing the butterflies. No, they didn't feel pain. He talked to them gently, calming them, then screwed on the jar lid tightly and that was it, they were dead within minutes. No pain, he was sure. Then he thought of when he had started collecting but-terflies, that bad mistake he had made. He hadn't known what to use to kill them then. The first thing he'd ever caught was a moth, a huge cecropia moth that had come to rest one night on the sliding door in the family room. The book he had read, his first butterfly book, had said to use carbon tetrachloride in the killing jar. Excitedly he'd put the moth in the jar and screwed on the lid. And the moth had banged against the glass for hours, trying to escape, until its wings were shreds and it lay there trembling feebly on the cotton, weak and sick. Finally Jon had stepped on it to put it out of its pain. He had felt bad for days after that, and didn't start collecting again for over a month.

He glanced at Meg as they walked along. He pretended that Meg was his girlfriend: that she loved him as much as he loved her. Kids whipped by in their cars. Some of them shouted and whistled at Meg. She seemed not to hear, but Jon knew she did, and with each shout and whistle he flushed. She shouldn't have to put up with that. Not her. She was special, the nicest girl in the world.

"Huh . . . hey, wow, look!" Chuckie suddenly said, bending over and picking up something that lay in the street, and Jon looked up. Chuckie wasn't too bright, but he sure had a sharp pair of eyes. He found more stuff on the side of the road than Jon could believe: coins, rubber bands, screws, marbles, paper clips, and all sorts of junk that only he would want: bottle caps, rusty nails, bolts—nothing escaped him.

"This fits my bike!" Chuckie said, holding up a large six-sided nut. "It's just what I need!"

Jon laughed. "You're incredible, Chuckie."

"And here's a quarter!" Chuckie dipped down again, came up, the coin in his hand.

"That's amazing," Meg said. "Every time you need some money you just come out and pick it up, is that it?"

"The . . . that's about it," Chuckie grinned.

They were walking past the heavy woods that stretched to Evergreen Row. Suddenly a muffler's roar, the scream of brakes, and there was the car, the black Nova SS with the flames on the fenders and hood. Randy Hankins was smoking, grinning, Bruce Hodges beside him, Sonny in the driver's seat. The door came open. Randy and Bruce got out. Jon's heart contracted with sudden pain, his knees went soft. He stood there trembling, Meg on one side, Chuckie on the other.

Randy sucked on his cigarette, then flipped it at Jonathan, missing his face by inches. He reached in his denim jacket, took out a wad of paper, and gave it to Jon.

Jon opened it. The English assignment due Friday, the topics that Randy and Bruce were to write about.

Randy stared, his freckled face cocky, smug. "Okay, Petrie?"

Jon quickly folded the paper and put it away. "Okay," he said.

"And one more thing—I need a loan. Three bucks."

Trembling, Jon put down his briefcase and reached for his wallet. He took out three dollars and handed them over.

Randy's snide smile. "Thanks, Petrie. I knew I could count on you."

Jon picked up the briefcase and started to walk.

"Hey Petrie, wait a second," Bruce Hodges said. "You forget what I said in the locker room? I want to see those butterflies."

Jon tensed; he gripped the briefcase tightly. "Look, I gave you the loan and I'll do the other thing . . ."

"I just want to get a better look," Bruce said. His smooth, full face, small brutal eyes. "It's hard to see from the back of the room."

Jon swallowed. He started to walk again.

Then Bruce ran up and grabbed his hair and Jon cried out and the briefcase fell out of his hand. "Hey, we been treating you too nice or something, slave?" Bruce bent Jon's head back, forced him to his knees.

Chuckie's eyes went wide. He stammered, "Duh . . . duh . . . don't you . . . duh . . . do—"

"Aah, shut up, Crip," Randy said.

Jon's scalp was blazing. Tears formed at the rims of his eyes. He heard Meg say, "You leave him alone! Take your hands off him!" and he felt so mortified he wanted to die. He gritted his teeth and swore he wouldn't cry. No matter how much they hurt him he wouldn't cry, not in front of Meg.

Bruce yanked Jon's head down hard and said, "Okay, slave, kiss your master's foot."

Jon's face was inches from Randy's shoe. The pain consumed him, the tears began to trickle down his cheeks. He heard Meg screaming, "Pigs! You animals, you pigs!" and his head went down and his mouth was touching leather.

"Good going, slave," Bruce said. Then Randy's shoe was gone and his voice was saying, "Whoa, the chick's a boxer," and he laughed, and Bruce yanked Jon to his feet and pushed him away. As stars of pain dissolved, Jon saw Meg punching Randy's arm with small hard fists and Jon screamed, "Stop it, stop it! I'll give you what you want, just stop!" He grabbed the briefcase and opened it up and took out the butterflies.

He handed the Riker mount to Bruce. Bruce took it and said, "You shoulda done that in the first place, Petrie—save yourself some trouble. All I want to do is get a better look."

He tilted the box and frowned. "I can't really see too good with this glass on here. Take it off."

Jon took the box, unhooked the cover, stuck it in his briefcase.

Randy snickered. "You think we were gonna break the glass on you, Petrie?" He shook his head and looked at Sonny sitting in the car. "Still doesn't trust us—after all these years."

Jon's throat was tight, his body quivered, his scalp was raw and itching.

"Now which one was it you said you were lucky to find?" Bruce said, the mount in his hands again.

"The yellow one," Jon said quickly. "This one here." He pointed to the tiger swallowtail, the most common butterfly in the collection.

"This one?" Bruce said. "Hey, I see lots of them around, I think it must be this big one, this brown one here." He lifted the giant swallowtail out of the box.

Jon's heart stood still. The giant swallowtail, the only one he had ever seen, was there in Bruce's huge hand.

"What did you call this again?"

"A . . . giant swallowtail."

"I bet you're good at that, huh Petrie?" Randy said. "Swallowin' tail?" In the car, Sonny laughed. Jon looked around, confused.

"Let's see if the sucker flies," Bruce said, and he thrust his arm forward quickly.

The swallowtail flipped backwards, up, then nosedived into the ground.

"Huh . . . hey, be . . . be . . . be careful!" Chuckie said, his features writhing.

"Don't let it get you, Crip," Bruce said. He picked the giant swallowtail up again and said, "You try it, Hankins, I can't make her fly too good."

He tossed the butterfly to Randy. Randy grabbed it—and half of a wing came off. Jon was shaking, trembling, flooded with rage.

"Oh hey, that's really funny," Meg said. "Leave him alone, you animals! Give it back!"

"Just want to see how good it flies," Randy said. "Of course, we can't expect too much with a broken wing. Jesus, it's all dried out, it must be *old*." He frowned intently at the crippled wing—then snapped it off the body.

A stinging sensation rose to the back of Jon's nose. He clenched his fists and fought back tears.

"Hey, Petrie, you don't want this, it's too old," Randy said. Slowly, smiling, he crushed the giant swallowtail into dust.

The particles blew away on the wind. Jon's mouth was trembling, his eyes were wet. *I will not cry*, he told himself. *I will not cry in front of Meg.*

Meg suddenly wrenched the Riker mount out of Bruce's hands. Two butterflies fell out, rolled down the sidewalk. "Hey," Randy said, "the prisoners are trying to escape." Sonny laughed again from his seat behind the wheel. Randy pinned the tumbling monarch with his foot, picked it up and tore it apart. "Bugs!" Bruce

Hodges cried. He crushed the spicebush swallowtail under his heel.

"Get out of here!" Meg screamed. "Get out of here!" She set the Riker mount on the grass and ran at Bruce.

"Hey, we're goin'," Bruce said with a laugh. "We're going, don't get so upset." He and Randy jumped into the car, Sonny started the engine. The three of them drove off, laughing wildly.

"Those pigs!" Meg said as they disappeared. "What a rotten thing to do." She picked up the butterfly case again and gave it to Jon and said, "I'm sorry. I was trying to save them, I didn't know they'd fall out."

Jon could just about talk, he was shaking so hard. "I can get more of those, it doesn't matter."

"But the big one. The giant one."

Jon shook his head, taking the Riker mount's cover out of his briefcase. He hooked it in place, slipped the mount into his briefcase again. "Maybe I'll be lucky this summer and catch another one," he said.

They started walking again, Chuckie frowning, limping along. Jon was so embarrassed he wanted to crawl in a hole. His enemies had treated him that way a hundred times, but never in front of Meg. To be so powerless, humiliated, while she watched. . . . It was horrible, horrible. He tried to think of his bird again, block his enemies out of his mind, but it didn't work.

"Those creeps," Meg said. "What do you lend them money for when they treat you like that?"

Jon shrugged. "I just do," he said.

"I bet they never puh . . . pay it back," Chuckie said. "Do they, Jon?"

Jon blushed bright red. "Of course they do," he lied.

Jon got an allowance of fifteen dollars a week, and every week he gave a dollar here, two or three dollars there, to Randy and the rest. By the end of the week there was almost never anything left for himself. He'd been doing this for so long that it seemed the natural order of things.

"Crushing your butterflies, pulling your hair, you

shouldn't let them get away with that," Meg said. "I don't mean fight them, but you ought to do something."

Jon reddened again. Meg had fought them, had actually punched them. But she was a girl. If he tried that, they would kill him.

"I mean, why don't you tell your father?"

He shook his head. "My father doesn't want to hear about it, Meg."

They were quiet a minute, then Chuckie said, "When they tease me in school it makes me stutter. And the . . . the . . . then I get so mad!"

"There ought to be *something* you can do," Meg said.

Jon thought of the comic books again. *STRONG ARMS MAKE ALL THE DIFFERENCE.* Or maybe karate lessons. Sure. It was so ridiculous he almost laughed. Staring straight ahead he said, "They could kill me and nothing would happen to them."

Meg shook her head. "That isn't true."

"Oh no? Well, what would happen? Maybe they'd go to Jamesburg or someplace like that for a while and then they'd be free again. I'd be dead and they'd be free! And they'd start all over again with somebody else."

They were walking up the hill to Evergreen Row. Chuckie went very slowly now, his breathing loud, face pale. Oddly enough, no matter how much he exerted himself, he never seemed to sweat. "You know what you ought to do?" he said, eyes wide, chest heaving, puffing hard, "You ought to blast 'em! Just blast 'em!"

Jon sniffed. "Yeah, Chuckie. How do I do that?"

"You know . . . like on TV."

"TV," Jon said. "TV is garbage, it's nothing but crap, it has nothing to do with life!"

Chuckie frowned, a pained expression on his face. "I duh . . . didn't mean to make you muh . . . mad," he said.

"You didn't make me mad," Jon said. The anger

welled in him again, again he felt tears form.

"I just don't understand why they hurt you like that," Meg said.

Jon glanced at her, then quickly looked away as she caught his eyes. Good Meg. Good, beautiful Meg. Someday when all this horror of school was over and he was on his own, he would marry Meg. Just one more year of Aronson High. That's all, just one more year and he'd go off to college, get away from here, and never see Randy and Bruce and the others again. He sighed. A year was a long, long time.

I don't understand why they want to hurt you like that she had said, and he thought: I'm different, Meg, that's why. I'm not one of them and they know it. I see things they'll never be able to see and they hate me for it. I'm not part of their world. They are made for the world as it is, and I'm not. He glanced at Meg shyly again. You're made for my world too, Meg, not theirs. You may not know it yet, but you are.

At the top of the hill, at the start of Evergreen Drive, they stopped. Meg said, "Did you understand that math homework? Sharkey lost me today."

Sharkey was Mr. Pensack, the math teacher, whose face was pointed and sharp. "Yes, I understood it," Jon said.

"Do you think you could help me with it tonight?"

Jon's heart leaped up. "Well . . . sure."

"Hey, that would be great. You want to come over to my house after dinner?"

"Yeah. Sure I do."

"Terrific. Look, I'm going down to Fogle's to get a soda. You guys want to come along?"

"I do," Chuckie said with his sunny smile.

Jon thought of his bird. He said, "I have some work to do, but . . . I'll see you tonight. About six, six-thirty, something like that?"

"Great, Jon." She smiled and his chest felt weak.

He hurried up Evergreen Drive. He thought of Bruce and Randy, how they crushed his butterflies, and his stomach hurt again. He told himself not to think about any of that, to just think about Meg, about Meg and his bird, good things.

He went in the usual way, around back, through the garage and the laundry room, and his mother was there in the kitchen, working at the sink in her slow, deliberate way. Her pale blond hair was stiff and gleaming, artificial as a wig. Her face was puffy, bleary. The TV was on. The program was "The Edge of Night."

"Hello, Jon. Have a nice day at school?"

"Fine, Mother."

"Would you like some Oreos?" Her eyes were watery, red.

"No thank you, Mother, I have work to do." Quickly he went upstairs to his room and locked the door.

He opened his closet and looked inside.

The bird wasn't on its side anymore. It was sitting up and its eyes were open. Jon carefully picked up the box and set it on his desk. The bird still shivered; its orange eyes looked dull. Jon hurried into the bathroom, filled a jar lid with water, set it on the grass in front of the bird. The starling blinked. Jon held the water up to its beak, but it didn't drink.

Gently he put his hand on the starling's back. The bird quivered with fear. "No, no, you're going to be all right," he whispered. "I'm not going to hurt you, I'm going to make you better. You're already better, so much better than you were." He looked at the yellow beak, the glazed eyes. "I have to think of a name for you," he said, "I can't just keep calling you Bird."

He looked at the toy on his shelf and said, "Hey Eeyore—got any ideas?" He looked at the bird's black feathers and frowned. Then suddenly it came to him. Black as the devil, fallen from heaven, "Your name is *Lucifer*," he said. "Now come on, Lucifer, drink some water." He held the jar lid up to the beak. "Come on, I know it still hurts, but you have to drink and eat if you want to—"

A sneeze outside his door and he stopped. He waited, not moving.

"Jonathan?"

His breath was loud in the quiet. "Yes, Mother?"

"Who are you talking to?"

"Oh—nobody, Mother. I'm practicing my French. We have to say the verbs out loud."

"You know how your father feels about talking to Eeyore."

"It isn't Eeyore, Mother, it's only my French."

She sneezed. He waited. She sneezed again.

"My hay fever's acting up. I'm going to rest for a while. If the phone rings, answer it, please."

"Okay, Mother, I will."

He waited; heard her close her bedroom door. He looked at the starling again and whispered, "Okay, Lucifer, back you go in the closet. And drink some water while you're in there, will you?" He ran his hand across the feathers; the starling ruffled its wings. He smiled. At last, a pet of his very own.

CHAPTER FOUR_____

Fogle's Fountain sat on the corner of Main and Trent in Russelville. It was an ancient place with a marble counter, eight booths, and two pinball machines. It had sold its sodas, ice cream, sandwiches, Life Savers, gum, and cigarettes to generations of Russelville residents and was practically an institution. Pat Fogle, the fountain's founder, had been dead for twenty years, and Jack Falcetti, his former helper, had run the place for a quarter century now.

Matt Wilson had worked at Fogle's for over two years. He had started shortly after his sixteenth birthday, and in those two years Falcetti had come to depend on him more and more. Matt was the most responsible kid Falcetti had ever hired, and Falcetti couldn't figure it. A kid from Brewery Hill, from a family like that, and he turned out to be a gem. Pleasant to customers, worked his tail off, honest as they come. And to think he almost hadn't hired him because of what people said.

Matt's mother had died when he was ten. He lived with his father and younger sister in Brewery Hill, a tough blue-collar section of Midvale on the other side of Russelville. His father was a thin, dark, nervous man, a cabbie, working nights and sleeping days, always in a hurry, never smiling: except for that bitter, tight, sardonic smile when things went wrong. Matt hated him.

Matt was a serious kid, more serious than most his age. He was saving his money for college, was going to be a chemical engineer. He didn't have a car, it cost too much to run, and he walked the three miles from Fogle's to home every night. He had seen a lot in his eighteen years and the worry was there, was buried there hard and deep in his brain, but he swore that no matter what happened he'd never let life defeat him. He swore he would never end up like his father, bitter and beaten, hating life, no matter what came his way.

He and Meg had been going together for over six months—if you could call it that: a few minutes' talk in the hallway at school or during lunch or over a soda at Fogle's when Matt was working; meeting in secret at night every once in a while, or down in the park near the golf course on Sunday afternoons. Nothing out in the open, because Evergreen Row girls didn't go out with boys from Brewery Hill—at least according to Meg's parents they didn't. And this wasn't just *any* boy from Brewery Hill, it was one of the crazy Wilsons.

Meg went to Fogle's no more than twice a week after school, though she wanted to go every day, because somebody—Mr. Falcetti, her father, one of her classmates—would put two and two together, and that would be that.

She was lucky today: When she and Chuckie got to the store it was uncharacteristically quiet, the after-school rush of kids having already left. Two boys about ten years old were playing at one of the pinball machines, and a pair of old ladies she didn't know were eating hot fudge sundaes in one of the booths. Chuckie ordered a Coke and went to watch the little kids play pinball. Meg drank her Coke and talked to Matt.

"Grabbed him by the hair and shoved his face to the ground. Made him kiss his shoe. Then crumbled up his butterflies."

"They're just creeps," Matt said. "Nothing better to do with their time."

"I don't understand why they hurt him like that."

Matt wiped the counter with his sponge. "He's weird, that's why. He's out of it. He doesn't know about sports or girls or cars—for god's sake, he carries a briefcase. And the *clothes* he wears. And he's weak. He's a perfect target.''

"But other kids are weak." She glanced at the pinball machine, where Chuckie was drinking his soda. "Shrimp, Chicken Cindy . . ."

"Hey, come on, don't call her that'."

"Well that's what they call her."

"I know, but it isn't nice."

"But why don't they do stuff to them?"

"They get their share. But Jon's not only weird, he's smart. He's useful to them." He ran some water into the sink. "I heard Hankins makes him do homework for him."

"So that's what was going on," Meg said. "He gave him this piece of paper. . . ." She sighed. "I asked him to help me with mine tonight. With my math."

"Since when do you have trouble with math?"

"I don't. I asked him because I felt sorry for him, I thought he could use some company."

"I hope he doesn't get the wrong idea."

She laughed. "Who, Jon? You're kidding. All he cares about is butterflies and stamps and planets, stuff like that."

"Hey, you got to watch out for the quiet guys."

She smiled. "Jealous?"

"You better believe it." He washed the stuff in the sink. "So what about Sunday?"

"I'd love to."

"Down by the creek. Around two o'clock."

"Sure." She frowned, stirred the Coke with her straw.

"What's wrong?"

"Poor kid," she said.

Matt shrugged. "It's sad, but what can you do? He'll just have to learn to deal with it."

"I worry about him sometimes. The look on his face when they crushed his butterflies . . ."

The door burst open, four kids came in, two boys and two girls, laughing and teasing each other. They sat at the counter and spun on the stools, their faces bright with privilege. Evergreen Row kids, the kids with pools. "Give me a black-and-white shake." "Give me a banana boat." Some Russelville kids came in and took over the other pinball machine. Then Sonny Richardson came in.

The laughing kids on the stools grew quiet. The only sound was the nervous ping of the pinball machines. The little kids still chattered and laughed, oblivious, but the older ones were silent, intent on their game. Chuckie Palmieri's face wore a worried frown.

Sonny sat at the counter next to Meg. The day was cool, but he wore a blue T-shirt rolled up at the sleeves and over it an open black leather vest. His jeans were spotted with dirt and splotches of grease. He brushed his long black hair away from his forehead with grease-stained hands and stared at Meg with hard gray eyes. "Hey, fancy meeting you here, doll."

Matt wiped his hands on a towel. "Okay, Richardson, what do you want?"

"Hey, what do you think I want?" Sonny said, still grinning at Meg.

"Order something or get out."

Sonny narrowed his eyes. "Hey, Wilson, what's your problem? You two got something going?"

Meg flushed.

Matt tried to calm the sudden anger that rushed up. That anger was trouble for Wilsons, had always been trouble: for Pete, Denise, the old man, all of them, and he had to control it. He stared at Sonny, tense as a coiled spring. "You don't bother the customers in this store," he said calmly. "Now order something or leave."

Sonny stared, eyes diamond hard. He sucked on his teeth and said, "Seven-Up."

Even by Brewery Hill standards, Sonny was tough, but he wasn't about to take on Matt. Matt was older than Sonny by more than a year, and bigger, and the Wilsons—Pete, the high-school football star who wrecked Dan's Tavern with a crowbar and had to be put away for a while, crazy Denise, the old man—no, you didn't mess around with the Wilson family.

Matt yanked the lever, the seltzer rushed into the glass. Meg slid off her stool and said, "I have to leave. See you later, Matt. Chuckie, you walking back?"

"Oh, yeah," Chuckie smiled, "I'm ready."

Matt said, "I'll see you, Meg."

Sonny stared at her tail as she left. "Hey, later, baby."

Matt's gorge rose hot and hard. It was all he could do to keep himself from punching Sonny's face.

"And that's all there is to it," Jon said.

"You mean like this?" Meg said, writing the figures down.

They were sitting at the breakfast table under the Tiffany shade and Mrs. Hale was working in the bright fluorescent kitchen. The air was filled with delicious baking smells. "That's perfect," Jon said.

Meg smiled. "That wasn't so bad after all. You'd make a great teacher, Jon."

Jon blushed, and his glasses steamed up.

"How about some cookies, kids, fresh out of the oven." Mrs. Hale scraped at the tray with her spatula, slid the steaming cookies onto a wire rack.

As they ate the cookies and drank the milk, Jon wondered what it was like to have a mother like Mrs. Hale. She seemed so pleasant and so . . . capable. So different from his own mother. Everything was so hard for her, took so much effort. Tonight they had eaten frozen fishcakes, instant mashed potatoes, and frozen peas—and it had taken her a full two hours to get the meal on the table. She was always tired, always complaining about one thing or another. Hay fever time again and now she was sneezing. And drinking a lot again. As far back as his memory of her went, it was linked to the smell of alcohol.

Meg's mother cleaned up from her baking. It took her ten minutes. His mother would have taken at least an hour, or, exhausted from making the cookies, would have let it go till tomorrow and had a drink. Jon couldn't remember the last time his mother made cookies.

When the cookies and milk were finished and Mrs. Hale had gone upstairs, Meg said, "Jon, I know this is none of my business—but what was that paper Randy gave you?"

Jon wet his lips and smiled nervously. "Just something stupid," he said.

Meg frowned. "Do they really pay back that money they borrow from you?"

"Of course they do." He felt she could tell he was lying, and it hurt.

Looking at him with her soft, clear eyes she said, "I keep thinking about what they did to you. Why do people do such horrible things?"

Jon looked at her, expressionless, his lips a line. "Because that's the way people are," he said. "That's how they are and always will be, Meg. The history of the human race is a history of horrors. People drawn and quartered, skinned alive, thrown to the lions, tarred and feathered—the disasters of war, the holocaust. . . . It never changes. Turn on the TV and watch the news. Tonight, any night, any morning, it never stops. Stabbing, shooting, stealing . . ." And raping, he thought, too embarrassed to say it. His face was flushed and he took a deep quivering breath.

Meg shook her head. "Oh, Jon you shouldn't feel that way. Most people are good. Some people are bad, but most are good. At least the ones I know."

He looked at her. "You really think so?"

"Of course I do. I believe that God created a basically decent world." She frowned. "Your family doesn't go to church; do you believe in God?"

Jon sat there, staring at his hands. He took a deep breath and said, "My mother used to go to church when I was small. I guess she'd still go but she's . . . so tired so much of the time."

"And your father?"

"I never talked to him about religion. I think he's Episcopalian like my mother, but I never remember him going to church. He plays golf on Sundays—when the weather's right.''

"And you?''

"I used to believe. When I was a kid. I used to believe in ghosts and witches and the tooth fairy, too.''

"So now—?''

He shook his head. "It's just another myth. I don't believe in God or heaven or life after death, a soul apart from the body, any of that.'' He looked at her, eyes serious and sad. "One man thinks that God will punish him if he eats pork, another one thinks that eating beef is bad. Others are sure that God wants them to kill the people who think in different ways or wear different clothes or speak a different language. If God exists, why doesn't He tell us what He wants and straighten us out? For good. I mean once and for all.''

Meg said, "Maybe we're not meant to know all that.''

"Well, it doesn't make any sense. Sonny Richardson's a Catholic—he wears a medal around his neck. Does that make him a better person? Has religion ever helped? The human sacrifice of primitive tribes, the Crusades, the Inquisition. . . . In ancient India the kings used to sacrifice themselves to the gods by cutting off their ears and nose and lips and . . . everything, and keep on cutting off flesh until they died.''

"Oh, gross,'' Meg said.

"In 1600, the Spanish Inquisition burned Giordano Bruno at the stake. Burned him alive in public for ideas that were later proved right.''

"Jon, how do you *remember* all that stuff?''

He looked at her as if waking out of a dream. He smiled oddly. "Eidetic imagery,'' he said.

"Eye what?''

"I have complete recall of anything I see.''

"You're kidding.''

"Give me a book. Any book.''

Meg took *The Joy of Cooking* off the shelf behind her.

"Open it to any page at all," Jon said.

She did. Jon looked at the page for no more than a minute, then shut his eyes and recited the page, word for word.

Meg stared at him. "That's *amazing*," she said. "How did you ever learn to *do* that?"

Jon laughed. "I didn't. I've always been able to do it, I was born that way. I remember everything—everything people tell me, whole conversations, math formulas, everything."

"Wow, I guess that comes in handy in school. That's terrific, Jon."

He shrugged. "It's a gift, that's all. I didn't practice it or anything."

"You're so modest. I know other people who would brag their heads off about something like that."

"Why should you brag about what you were born with?"

"I guess you're right," Meg said. "But still, I think it's super of you not to." She smiled. "You're a pretty super kid, you know that, Jon?"

Jon cleared his throat, smiled weakly, pushed his glasses up his nose. "Well . . . thanks," he mumbled, looking at his hands again. It was quiet a minute and then he said, "I guess I'd better get home. It's pretty late."

Meg walked him to the door. He felt flushed, excited, warm, both weak and strong. "Goodnight, Jon. Thanks again."

When he was out of sight of the house, hidden by the thicket of trees that separated Fairfax Mews—Meg's mews—from Mulberry Mews—he spun around in a circle, laughing, and whispered to himself, "She called me super. 'A super kid,' she called me, she really did."

The TV was screaming, shots rang out, Jon said goodnight to his father, who didn't respond. He went upstairs, checked Lucifer. The bird was sleeping. Still warm, still alive. He closed the closet door and sat at his desk.

Over and over on a sheet of lined paper he wrote in his cramped handwriting, Meg loves Jon, Meg loves Jon, Meg loves Jon. He spent nearly fifteen minutes writing, then looked at the toy on the shelf and whispered, "Oh Eeyore, Eeyore . . . if only it was true!"

CHAPTER FIVE _____

In the morning, Lucifer looked much better. His eyes were brighter and it seemed that he'd drunk some water, though he might have just splashed it around. It was clear what was wrong with him now: He had hurt his wing. He would stand up briefly and stretch and his left wing would unfold slightly, trembling, then close up tight against his body again.

Jon slipped downstairs and took the jar of honey out of the kitchen cabinet, then sneaked back upstairs. In her bedroom his mother sneezed. Jon poured some honey in the jar lid, mixed the water into it, and gave it to the bird. Lucifer cocked his head but didn't drink. "But look at him, Eeyore, he's standing up. He's going to be all right. Once he starts eating again he'll be . . . he'll be super!"

He dressed and went downstairs to eat. He heard his father in the den: "I don't give a damn *what* Rouse says! He pulled this shit the last time, and I'm sick of it! Steadman's not going to have to wait another week to do that sheetrock, I want them out of there Friday!" A pause, then: "Terrific. My heart bleeds for him. And how the hell am I supposed to *eat*?"

Jon looked at the empty pool, at the grove of trees beyond it, the pale blue sky. The TV in the corner said, ". . . . In an argument over a raincoat. The victim, Arthur Stefanick, of 248 Oak Street, was shot eight times in the head. . . ." Upstairs a fit of sneezing. In the den his father yelled, "Friday, Kelleher! And no more

39

crybaby shit out of Rouse, you tell him that!'' and the phone slammed down.

Jon picked up his briefcase and headed out the door. He thought about school and the same old queasy feeling hit him once again. His elbow still hurt from yesterday's fall in gym and his scalp was sore. But today first period was art, that wasn't so bad, and Meg was in that class. If he hurried he might be able to walk to school with her.

Doug Petrie came into the living room in time to see Jon walking down the driveway, briefcase in hand. He lit a cigarette and stood there, watching, anger from the phone call burning his stomach like acid. Rouse and his goddamn tricks. The second straight time he'd been screwed by that son-of-a-bitch electrician. Twenty thousand extra bucks in his pocket if he met the schedule and that bastard put him behind.

He watched Jon turn the corner and disappear. Candy-ass kid, he thought. A *briefcase*, for Christ's sake. Always up in his room, always off in a world of his own. So goddamn out of it. Like somebody else I know, he thought as he heard his wife sneeze upstairs. Fifteen years old and his mother still buys his clothes. He took a deep drag on his cigarette. When he was fifteen he'd been working two years, his mother was dead, he had plenty of girls. Life is a goddamn battle, he thought, and Jon had better start to shape up. He'd had it too goddamn easy, that was the problem. Everything handed to him. Fifteen bucks allowance a week and look how he'd turned out. No girls, no sports, no friends—except for that freaky Palmieri kid.

He thought of the time a few years back when he'd taken Jon to Shea to see the Mets. The game had baffled Jon. Not the rules, but the purpose of it. Why did people want to spend their time throwing and hitting balls—especially grown men? He had always been that way, questioning the things that other kids took for granted, fascinated by the things that other kids ignored, frightened of the things that other kids enjoyed.

Just weird as shit. He still even had that goddamned baby toy, that donkey, in his room, and sometimes he still *talked* to it. Enough to drive you up the wall. He'd always thought that once the hormones started flowing things would change, but so far nothing. Maybe they hadn't started flowing yet. But Jesus, at fifteen?

He took another drag. Alice said he went over to the Hale girl's house last night. First time he'd done that. First time he'd gone to see any girl, and maybe things would be different soon. Jesus, he hoped so, he'd had it up to the gills with the goddamn kid. Upstairs, Alice sneezed again. The telephone rang. He crushed his cigarette out in the ashtray on the coffee table, cursing under his breath.

Jon had a good day in school. They tied his laces together in history class and he tripped into Mr. Worthington's desk, but that wasn't too bad, and as he walked home with Chuckie he was in a good mood. Meg walked ahead of them with Diane Haney. Jon watched her, sick with love.

As they walked up Evergreen Drive he decided he'd let Chuckie know about Lucifer. He took him home and they went to his room.

"Wuh . . . what kind of bird is it?" Chuckie said loudly, staring into the closet.

Jon winced. "Ssh, quiet! My mother's right down the hall." He could hear her sneezing. She had just come back from a trip to the allergist and was resting in bed.

"Oh," Chuckie whispered, eyes wide. "Wuh . . . what kuh . . . kind of buh . . . bird is it?"

"A starling. Introduced into New York State by a Shakespeare lover in 1890. He wanted the United States to have every bird mentioned in Shakespeare's work."

"Oh. That was nice."

"A lot of people don't think so," Jon whispered. "Including my mother. She says starlings are dirty and selfish and ugly."

Lucifer ruffled his feathers and tried to extend his hurt wing. It had slightly more range than it had in the morning. "Lucifer, you're going to be just fine—right, Eeyore?" He turned and looked at the toy on the shelf, and Chuckie laughed.

"Eeyore," Chuckie said. "Does Eeyore know about birds?"

"Eeyore knows about everything," Jon said.

"Does he know about fractions?"

Fractions. Chuckie had been trying to master fractions for about eight years. "You need help with your *fractions* again?"

Chuckie shrugged apologetically. "Well . . . just a little bit."

"Okay," Jon said, "let's see if Lucifer will eat. Then we'll work on your fractions."

He got fresh water, stirred honey into it, put it in front of the bird. And wonder of wonders, Lucifer drank. "Eeyore told me you'd drink today," Jon said with glee. "Look at that, Chuckie, he loves it! Now you'll get your strength back fast, that wing's gonna heal up fast, you wait and see!"

Chuckie grinned his slow grin. "I thought birds ate worms."

"Worms, bugs, plants, all kinds of stuff. I'll try him on that tomorrow. Look how bright his eyes are now."

"Jon?" Chuckie frowned, his head cocked to the side.

"What, Chuckie?"

"Do you love Meg?"

Jon blushed bright red. "Of course I don't!"

Chuckie nodded. "Oh. I just thought maybe you did. She's a real nice girl."

"Don't ever ask me that again," Jon said, his face stern.

"But why?"

"You want me to help you with your fractions or not?"

Chuckie blinked; his features twisted. "Sure," he said.

"Then don't ever say anything foolish like that again."

* * *

He had done his own homework in study hall. He helped Chuckie, ate, and after dinner he worked on assignments for Randy and Bruce and Carl. When he finished he played with Lucifer. He held a raisin in his palm. The bird pecked at it sharply.

"Jon."

His father in the hallway. Needles of shock went through him. Quickly he closed the door to the closet and answered, "Yes?" Lucifer, he thought, don't make a sound. Oh *please* don't make a sound or we're in terrible trouble.

"Come out here, I want to see you."

Anxiously, Jon opened his door. His father never had a talk with him unless something was wrong. "Yes, Father?"

"Come with me."

Jon followed his father down the stairs, through the family room, into the den. His father sat at his desk. "Sit down."

Jon sat in the leather armchair. An interview, he thought. He hadn't had an interview in a long time. What had he done?

Doug Petrie lit a cigarette and leaned back in his chair. "Why the hell do you spend so much time in your room?" he said.

Jon shrugged, the answers racing through his mind. Because that's where I'm safe. That's where no one will beat me up. Because I have to do homework for four other people besides myself. He shrugged. "I . . . have a lot of stuff up there that interests me," he said.

His father nodded, frowning. "Yeah, Jon, I know that, but it's spring. Kids are playing ball, I saw some down at the field this afternoon. Christ, when I was your age I worked in construction. Hauling concrete, cutting studs. Jesus, I would've killed for the chance to play ball. And here you could be outside in weather like this and what do you do? Hang around in your room."

Jon wet his lips. "Well, uh, when the weather gets warmer I'll be out catching butterflies." When school is out and I don't have to spend half my life doing homework for bullies, he thought.

Doug Petrie smoked. "Butterflies," he said. Exhaling a stream of smoke he said, "Jon, I bought something for you." He opened the bottom drawer of his desk.

Jon frowned. Bought something? Why? It isn't my birthday. His heart leaped up as he thought it just might be the ten-cent Columbian Exposition stamp, mint, that he wanted so badly. He'd been trying to save enough money to buy it for over a year, but Randy, Carl, Bruce, and Sonny made it impossible to save.

The legend on the large bag read MALONEY'S SPORTING GOODS.

Jon took it gingerly. He reached inside—and pulled out the baseball glove.

His father smiled. "What do you think?"

Jon turned the foreign object over in his hands. "Oh . . . it's . . . beautiful," he said. "Thank you, Father."

"A Rawlings, made in the U.S.A., none of that cheap Korean crap."

"It's very nice."

"Now *use* it, for Christ's sake."

"Yes, Father." Jon squinted behind his owlish spectacles. "Is that all?"

Doug Petrie sucked on his cigarette. "I think you ought to try to make more friends," he said. "I mean Chuckie's a good kid, I guess, but . . . you know . . ."

Jon blinked. "Know what?"

"Well, come on, Jon, I mean . . ." He shook his head. "Forget it." He smiled. "Your mother tells me you saw a girl last night.

Jon's cheeks flushed furiously. "It was only Meg Hale," he said. "She needed help with her homework, that's all."

"What the hell are you so embarrassed about? That's what you have to do, get out, see different kids."

Jon looked at the glove. "Yes, Father. Are we finished now?"

"I also wouldn't mind if you did some work around here. I give you fifteen bucks a week. You could wash the cars, you could clean the garage every once in a while.''

"Yes, Father.'' He got up from the chair. He smiled weakly. "Thanks for the glove. It's very nice.''

Doug Petrie nodded. "Yeah.'' He sighed and crushed out his cigarette as his son, his only child, left the room.

CHAPTER SIX _____

All week long, Jon was obsessed by the bird. Soon
Lucifer was drinking honey-water greedily. He opened
and closed his beak as if silently squawking. His eyes
had a cocky malicious glint, and he stretched his
damaged wing more every day. Pretty soon he would
fly. He would need a cage. Closet door open, the bird
peering out, Jon sat at his desk and drew plans for hours
on end: round cages, square cages, rectangular cages,
triangular cages, octagonal cages. He'd taken two years
of shop in junior high and knew how to use tools, and
once he got the plans just right he'd build the cage himself.

On Friday the sky was overcast, the air was cool. For
the first time since Monday, he wore his jacket. He was
in the locker room before he discovered the wad of
folded paper in his jacket pocket.

He felt suddenly weak. The English assignment for
Randy and Bruce! He had finished his own assignment
in study hall Monday and left it in his locker, and hadn't
even thought about it till now.

He'd promise to work on it at lunch, that's what he'd
do. But no, they wouldn't have time to copy it out in
their own handwriting, no, they'd have to turn it in late.
He broke into a sweat.

He walked to the row where his locker stood—and
Randy Hankins was waiting.

"Okay, let's have it, Pee-Tree," Randy said over the
clatter of voices, the slam of metal doors.

Jon stood in front of his locker, cold with sweat. "I

. . . forgot it," he said. "I'll do it at lunch."

Randy grabbed his arm hard. "What the hell do you mean, you forgot?"

Jon's briefcase fell out of his hand as the pain tore through him. "Randy, please—"

"Please bullshit!" Randy said between clenched teeth. "When I give you an order you do it, slave!" Down at the end of the row of lockers, somebody laughed.

"I'll do it at lunch!" Jon said. "I swear, I'll do it at lunch!"

"And how the hell am I supposed to copy it before sixth period? You fucking creep, I ought to—"

Suddenly Matt Wilson had him by the shirt. With one powerful thrust he smashed Randy into the lockers. The row of green-painted metal quivered with shock. Matt held him tight against the steel, eyes blazing, the cords in his neck taut. "Leave him alone, Hankins! Understand? Just leave the kid alone!"

The color had drained out of Randy's face. His lips were almost gray. With a gasp he said, "Hey, come on, Wilson, it's none of—"

Matt smashed him into the lockers again as Jon watched in awe.

"Hey, he owes me—"

"Leave him alone!" Matt said. "Or I'll break your goddamn neck!"

"All right, all right, I'll leave him alone!" Randy said. His mouth was trembling, but defiance shone in his eyes.

Matt took his hands away. Randy brushed his hair back, smoothed his shirt. He shot Jon a glance that could kill, and left the locker room.

Matt went to his locker, the one next to Jon's, turned the dial, jerked it hard. It didn't open. He dialed again, muttering under his breath.

Jon's heart was still racing. He wet his lips and said, "Matt?"

Matt pulled on the lock again. It opened. He looked at Jon. "Yeah?"

"Thanks."

Matt grabbed his sneakers and gym suit, jaw tight. "Those rotten punks," he said. He stood there, breathing heavily, staring into his locker. Then he pressed his lips together, slammed the door and said, "Come on, let's go to gym."

Last period was chorus. As soon as the bell rang ending the day, Jon started for the door.

Chuckie was in chorus too, and as Jon left the room he said, "Huh . . . hey, wait up!" But Jon said, "Chuckie, I can't today. I have to go."

He had packed his briefcase earlier so he wouldn't have to go back to the locker room. They might be waiting for him in there, he couldn't take the chance. He had finished Randy's essay at lunch, too late for Randy to copy it, and he didn't work on Bruce's essay at all. They were angry, very angry, and he had to get away fast before they could catch him.

He was out of the building before almost everyone else and hurried down the pavement toward the woods at the foot of the hill. In the woods was a path through the trees. He would take the path and hide in the brush till the coast was clear.

He half walked, half ran. The briefcase jerked at his arm, his thin chest heaved. Nervously he looked over his shoulder as cars rushed by on the street. He forced himself to go faster and his thighs ached from the strain. A sharp pain tore at his side, sweat ran down his face.

Now the trees were about a hundred yards away. The cars sped by. He began to run. A spasm ripped his right thigh, his ankles hurt.

Then behind him he heard the muffler, Sonny's muffler, roaring closer, heard the motor growling darkly, and a horrible weakness hit him. The squeal of brakes, the smell of exhaust and burnt rubber—and they were there, all four of them.

Bruce Hodges's heavy arm leaned out of the window. "In a hurry, Petrie? You got an appointment?"

Jon's chest felt rubbery and light. He continued to walk, staring straight ahead. The briefcase suddenly weighed tons.

"Hey dink," Carl Renniger shouted, "we're talkin' to you!"

Jon licked his lips. Salt taste of sweat. His heart was pounding so hard he thought it would break.

Doors opened, slammed. In panic Jon started to run and they had him, God, they had him, Carl had him by the collar, lifted him off the ground.

Jon wriggled and squirmed in the air. His face was flooded, hot, he couldn't breathe. They laughed.

Bruce narrowed his eyes and shook his head. "You shoulda done the essay for me, Pee-Tree. I don't like to get zeros, dink."

"I'll do it . . . tonight!" Jon said, his voice strangled and thin.

"I'm real glad to hear that, Pee-Tree. But now it's gonna be late. You know that Robards doesn't like late papers, dink. The best I can get is a B, and I wanted an A."

Jon dangled there in Carl's hard hands. Cars on the street slid by and people stared, but no one stopped. Jon stammered, "Bruce, it won't happen again, I swear. The paper was in my jacket and I forgot it."

Bruce nodded. "You forgot. And the best I can get is a B, because you forgot." He smiled his loose, cruel smile. "When people forget important things, they need memory lessons, Petrie."

"Please," Jon pleaded, "put me down. *Please* put me down." His shirt was starting to tear, he could hear it, a brand-new shirt a week old.

Then a car went by that he knew, the principal's car. As it passed, Jon saw Mr. Diedrick glance in the rear-view mirror as if to get a better look at what was happening. But the car kept going, didn't even slow down, because they were off school grounds. Once they were off school grounds they ceased to exist in the minds of the faculty and administration. Crossing property lines automatically turned them into ghosts.

Carl put Jon down, then held Jon's arms behind his back while Sonny tied his wrists. There were kids on the sidewalk across the street but nobody stopped, nobody seemed to see. "Petrie, we'll have to give you some memory lessons," Randy said, and Jon was in the car, his briefcase still on the sidewalk, he was jammed in the back of the car between Randy and Carl: pressed against their muscle and smell, and the fear was so great that he thought he would faint.

The car peeled out with a scream. "You were looking for Headquarters, weren't you?" Carl said in the rush of wind. His face was inches away. Gunmetal eyes. The smell of smoke, of sweat, stale beer and gasoline.

Jon shook his head quickly. "No! I swear, I *wasn't*!"

"Don't give me that shit."

Then Carl took Jon's glasses off and Randy quickly tied the blindfold over his eyes.

"My glasses," Jon whimpered. "Oh please . . ." Tears sprang to his eyes, wetting the cloth that bound them. In the darkness he thought, Oh no, not again. Not the blindfold again. He couldn't take it, he'd die. He gagged. A small, pathetic moan escaped his lips.

"We're going to take you to Headquarters, Pee-Tree," Carl said. "We'll give you your lessons there."

Wind whipped Jon's hair and Randy said, "Where's your buddy Matt Wilson, Petrie? Lets you down when you need him the most. See what happens when you count on crazies?"

The muffler growled. Jon's arms were cold as ice, the tang of terror filled his mouth. The blindfold pressed against his eyes. He thought: They can't do anything as bad as last time, they can't, oh God, they just *can't*. . . .

It was back in December, the week before Christmas, the weather bitter cold. They had bound and gagged him and driven away, and the next thing he knew he was walking on something rough, small stones. They forced him to his knees.

"Put your head down!" Sonny said, and Jon obeyed.

"I mean *all* the way down, slave!" He grabbed Jon's collar, choking him. "Now stick out your tongue."

He did. His head was thrust sharply lower, his tongue was suddenly freezing cold, so cold it burned, and it was stuck, stuck to the ground, to the smooth cold surface of—

The railroad track. That's where he was, the railroad

track. And they let him go and laughed and laughed as he struggled to free himself. His throat blazing with pain he slobbered and gagged, made inarticulate animal grunts and cries, his heart banging violently in his chest. Then the track was humming, tingling with a powerful vibration and the warning alarm went off with a clang, and he pulled so hard he thought he would rip his tongue right out of his head. He cried and wet himself. Then his stomach spilled, hot vomit washed the tracks and broke the bond and his tongue was free.

In a frenzy he ran, falling over the track and slashing his knee and crashing into the brambles beside the road as the train's incredible power thundered by. And they pulled him out of the brambles, laughing like mad, and tore off the blindfold, jammed his glasses on and jerked his head around and said: "The joke's on you, asshole—the train was on the other track!" And they laughed and laughed.

And now as he sat in the back of the car and remembered, he thought he would die. His pulse triphammered in his neck, his head, and he thought of his mother. She was watching "General Hospital" or "The Edge of Night" in her cottony world so far away from this real world where mufflers throbbed and roared, the radio blared.

Carl repeated a phrase from the song with a coarse deep laugh and said, "You a muff diver, Petrie?"

Jon barely had the strength to answer. "A . . . a what?"

"Come on, Petrie."

"I don't know what you mean."

"Hey, Richardson—tell Petrie what a muff diver is."

"You oughta know, Renniger," Sonny said from the driver's seat. "—You're goin' with Ellen Murphy."

"Hey, you're real funny." Then something hard and cold was shoved against Jon's lips. "Here, Petrie, have a drink."

The bitter smell of beer, a thin cold slime on Jon's cheek. He twisted his head away.

"Hey, what's the matter?" Carl said. "Pabst not good enough for you? I guess all your old man drinks up there in his castle is Lowenbrau, huh?''

"Petrie, you gotta learn to loosen up," Bruce said, "You'll never be any fun."

"Come on, Petrie, have a swig. Just a taste." The rim of the bottle clicked against Jon's teeth.

And then that other time came back: blindfolded on his knees and, "Suck on it, Petrie. Stick it in your mouth," and they yanked his hair till he did it and whimpered and gagged. When they took the blindfold off Carl said, "You shoulda told us you didn't like hot dogs, Pee-Tree." And that's all it was, a hot dog, raw, and he covered his face and wept. And the time when they dangled the contraceptive in front of his face, the condom they found on the side of the road, and they screamed at him, "Kiss it, Petrie, kiss it!" twisting his arm till at last he obeyed. And he vomited into the bushes, ran home in hysterical panic and washed his mouth out five times with Listerine while his mother downstairs in the family room watched "Days of Our Lives."

"Come on, drink up," Carl said. And Randy had him by the hair and yanked his head back. The beer poured over his lips and down his shirt. He gritted his teeth against the bitter taste as Randy said, "That's better, dink," and gave his head a shove.

"Throw that bottle away," Carl said, "it's got Pee-Tree on it!" Bruce made a gagging sound and Randy laughed.

The radio sang loudly, and then the car was lurching, bumping along on one of the old dirt roads that cut through the woods behind Evergreen Row.

They stopped. The engine and the radio went dead, doors opened. "Okay, Petrie, end of the ride," Randy said, and yanked Jon out of the car.

They dragged him through the woods. He stumbled over roots and rocks, blind, choking with fear. He was totally in their power, beyond all help, hopelessly trapped in their world. The world of adults, of law and reason, had ceased to exist, there was only this moment of terror. He would have to endure whatever torture lay ahead, there was no way out.

They stopped. The smell of damp woods soil, a smell like the spot where he watched the highway. The creak of rusty hinges, a flight of rude steps, then sound was muffled, the air was close. They tore the blindfold off and shoved his glasses on.

The room was dark and damp. The floor was paved with wide, flat stones. From the floor to the height of four feet the walls were dirt; then logs for another three feet or so to the dark rough ceiling. A chrome-and-formica kitchen table sat beside one wall with well-worn copies of *Hustler* and *Genesis* on it. On the floor there were piles of rope and a couple of six packs of beer. In the dirt of the wall at one end of the room was a small wooden door. At the other end of the room was a fireplace lined with stone, and Sonny was stuffing it full of paper and wood.

"So here's what you've been looking for," Bruce Hodges said with his slack, malicious grin. "Headquarters. It's a little damp, so we'll warm it up for you."

Sonny sneered. He struck a match and the paper caught smokily, slowly, then started to blaze. "What do you think?" Bruce said, "You like it?"

Jon stood there, breathing hard, mind dazed.

"I asked you a question, Petrie."

"What?" Jon said with startled eyes.

"I asked you if you like Headquarters, dink."

"Oh . . . yes," Jon said, nodding quickly.

"Right out of *House and Garden*, isn't it?" Bruce said. "I'm glad you like it—since we're going to leave you here for a while. Want to look at our magazines? Go right ahead, just don't beat off too much. Want a beer? Go right ahead. Stay as long as you want. Enjoy yourself." They walked out, laughing, slamming the door behind them.

Jon ran after them, flooded with sudden fear. The door was locked. He pulled it as hard as he could, but it didn't budge. A soft, pathetic moan escaped his lips and he slumped to the damp stone floor defeated, quivering, filled with dread.

Then suddenly he smelled the smoke.

They had blocked the chimney off and smoke was

pouring into the room in thick gray clouds. For the first time, he realized the room had no windows. He scrambled to his feet, smoke stinging his nostrils, choking him. He rushed to the door in a wild panic; he pulled and kicked and banged.

"Let me out!" he screamed. "Let me out!" The room was lost in gray, and huge tears poured from his burning eyes, his throat and lungs were seared. He attacked the door again, tore at it, cut his hands. He beat at the door with bloody numb fists, fell backwards, gasping, clutching his throat and tripping, crashing into the table, eyes blind.

With one last reflexive burst of self-preservation he dug at the wall with his bleeding hands, clawing into the clay and rock, his fingers numb, chest tight, the world a dying blur.

And the door came open. With the last of his strength he burst for the light and clambered up the steps. Eyes watery, smeared, he crashed into a huge oak tree and fell, rolled over and over in pain. On his back, the sky and the treetops spinning, he sucked huge gulps of air. He coughed, gagged, moaned, shook uncontrollably. The sky had been gray all day and now it was starting to rain. He lay there, rain spotting his glasses, tears flooding his eyes.

He could hear them laughing, but he didn't care. He was out in the air again, he could breathe again, the smoke was gone and that was all that mattered. He lay there panting, his thin chest heaving, his heart exploding in his ears.

Then Randy was standing above him. "Hey, Petrie, what happened, I thought you *liked* Headquarters."

"You shoulda hollered louder," Carl said, "we could just about hear you."

"Too warm in there for you?" Bruce said. "You shoulda put the fire out." Sonny just stood there, smoking, with narrowed eyes. The rain was coming harder now.

Randy grabbed Jon's arm and pulled him up. He shook him like a broken doll and said, "You gonna forget my assignments again?''

"No, no!" Jon said, quickly shaking his head. There were crumbs of dirt on his lips.

"You think we fixed your memory—or you need another treatment?"

"No, Randy, I swear! I'll never forget again.''

Randy held him, staring with ice-cold eyes. He let him go with a shove and Jon fell to the ground. "Get up!" Randy shouted. "Get up, you fucking pussy!''

Jon got to his feet again, legs rubbery. Sonny took his glasses off, blindfolded him again, and once again he was dragged through the woods. Then the car was bouncing, the radio blaring, they were laughing, the car roared onto the smooth road, picked up speed, the wind rushed in. And now the wind felt good to Jon, it was life itself, he breathed it gratefully.

At last the car jerked wildly to a stop. The blindfold was torn away, Jon's glasses were shoved on his face, he was thrown out into the street like an old beer can.

He was blocks from where they had kidnapped him. Slowly he walked, bedraggled, in the rain. He found his briefcase open in the grass, its contents scattered in the brush: his books, his pens and pencils, homework—and his plans for Lucifer's cage.

The plans were soaked and runny, ruined. He picked up all his stuff, his torn hands burning in the rain. As he put the ruined plans in his briefcase he screamed, "You'll pay for this! I'll get you for this, I swear to God I will!''

But he never would. They were just too strong. Aching, burning, soaked to the skin and exhausted, he started home.

It was raining hard by the time he reached Evergreen Row, and nobody was outside. His shirt was torn, his hands were bleeding, his hair was disheveled, his eyes were swollen and red. He walked slouching, head down, ashamed. If Meg saw him like this he would die.

He couldn't let his mother see him either. She would be in the kitchen making dinner, she started about four-thirty when "The Edge of Night" was over, and now it was quarter of five. He would go in the front and sneak upstairs before she could see him.

He took the key out of its hiding place next to the mailbox, slipped it in the lock, hand shaking, turned the knob. He stepped inside—and his mother was standing right there.

She was wearing her baby-blue robe. In her hand was a yellow handkerchief, loosely folded. She brought it to her nose and weakly blew, sneezed twice, and looked at Jon with watery eyes. "Oh . . . is it raining out?"

She was *that way*. Very much *that way*. "Yes, Mother, it is."

"Why didn't you take your umbrella, Jon? You're all wet."

And half dead, Jon thought. They almost killed me, Mother, while you were watching TV and drinking. But he was grateful that she didn't notice his bloody hands, torn shirt, and said, "I'll wash up now." And leaving her staring, smiling vaguely, he hurried up the stairs.

He locked his door, put his briefcase beside his desk, and sat on his bed. His hands throbbed and stung. He looked at the toy on the shelf and said, "They could have killed me, Eeyore. They actually could have *killed* me—and what would have happened to them? Not a thing. They'd say they didn't mean it, they'd say it was an accident. Or maybe they'd put them away for a while, and then they'd be free again and I'd be dead. And nobody would care."

He stared at his wounded hands, the horror he'd just been through replaying itself in his mind. He blocked it out and thought of Lucifer, and quickly went to the closet.

Lucifer peeped loudly as the door came open. Jon winced. "Ssh, no, be quiet, Lucifer!" But his mother was very much *that way* and probably wouldn't hear. The bird cocked its ebony head, stared with glittering eyes. It stretched its wings—full length.

"You're almost well!" Jon said. "You're almost ready to fly again! I have to get a cage for you—fast!" He thought of his sketches, soggy and ruined. A flash of anger set his teeth on edge. And he had no money to buy a cage either—because of *them*.

He would work on the cage tonight. He would draw a new set of plans and tomorrow, Saturday, he'd build it in the garage.

He closed the closet door, the starling peeped again, again Jon cringed. He held his breath and waited, but heard nothing from downstairs. He took off his clothes, shoved his ruined shirt under his bed, put his robe on, and walked to the bathroom.

In the shower the water stung his hands, and afterwards he bandaged them with Band-Aids—eight of them. Then he went to his room, got dressed again, gave Lucifer some honey-water. The bird drank eagerly. When it finished, Jon petted it gently. Lucifer sat motionless as he ran his hand over the feathers. Then he closed the closet door and started drawing his plans.

As he worked, he smelled nothing cooking. When his mother was *that way* she often forgot about dinner, cleaning, the wash, appointments—everything—and sometimes it lasted for days. Jon didn't care about dinner, he wasn't hungry, and he worked on his sketches painfully, hands puffy and tender now. The work went well. Then shortly after eight his father came home and he heard it begin:

"Goddamn it, Alice, I'm hungry! Sick, my ass." There was banging and yelling, the front door slammed, and his father was gone again. Soon afterward he heard his mother in the hallway, weeping softly, then she started to sneeze again and shut herself in her room. Jon tried to finish the drawings but couldn't concentrate and he went to his mother's door and gently knocked.

"Mother, can I get you anything?" No answer; she had fallen asleep. So he went to the garage and looked for wood with which to build his cage, then made himself a peanut butter sandwich. And shortly after ten o'clock, exhausted, hands burning and raw, he fell asleep.

CHAPTER SEVEN _____

The next day he woke up after ten. The sun was shining. He slipped out of bed and winced from the pain of his hands. He started across the hall to the bathroom, his penis erect.

He heard the dryer rumbling softly down in the laundry room. It was a gorgeous day, a perfect day to hang out clothes, but the dryer was going, because hanging out clothes took energy, it took time. But even if his mother had the energy and time, she wouldn't hang out clothes, because nobody in Evergreen Row did that. That was for people in Russelville or Brewery Hill, not for people in Evergreen Row.

In the kitchen his father coughed.

". . . Couldn't sleep . . . was having a sneezing attack," his mother said.

"Attack," his father said.

"I was *sick* when you came home."

"You were shitfaced when I came home."

Her voice was full of hurt. "Don't you dare use that kind of language with me—and Jonathan's upstairs."

"Fuck Jonathan. You think he doesn't hear that kind of talk in school? Jesus Christ, stop babying that kid. . . ."

Sighing, Jon closed the bathroom door. He urinated, watched his erection die. No hair. The only kid in the whole gym class without any hair. It had to come, he was fifteen years old, but when? He washed, he brushed his teeth, he put new Band-Aids on his hands. He dressed, then waited till his parents were out of the kitchen before going downstairs.

As he ate his Cheerios, he thought of the cage he would build. The door would have leather hinges, the floor would be mesh so the droppings would fall through into a tray. It was based on a cage from Madagascar, one he had seen in the natural history museum. The roof was octagonal, tricky to build, but beautiful, elegant, right for a royal bird like Lucifer. He ate quickly, excitedly, pushed his chair back, picked up his bowl with the splash of milk and leftover floating cereal and started out of the kitchen. He'd give the bowl to Lucifer, give him a *meal* for a change.

"Where the hell are you going with that?" His father, there at the foot of the stairs.

"With what?" Jon said, eyes wide with sudden alarm.

"With *what*? With that *cereal*."

"Oh . . . I forgot. I got up from the table and just . . . forgot."

"Jesus Christ, you're as bad as your mother."

Jon hesitated, went back to the kitchen, poured the cereal into the sink. How stupid of me, he thought. My God, how careless of me.

He went up to his room. And there was his mother, in front of his closet, two freshly washed shirts in her hands. Jon's breath stuck in his throat as she reached for the doorknob.

"Good morning, Jon." Her voice was distant, soft. She sniffed gently and started to sneeze.

Quickly, frantically, Jon said, "Mother, give the shirts to me, I'll put them away."

His mother dabbed her nose with her handkerchief. "I'll do it, Jon I'm right here."

Jon wet his lips. "I . . . I have some rearranging to do in the closet and I'll only have to take them out again. Here, give them to me. *Please*."

His mother stood there, frowning. "I've been thinking about this closet too," she said. "It *does* need rearranging. Her hand was on the knob again. Don't you think if—" She turned the knob, the door came open, a numbness spread through Jon's chest.

A quick black blur, a rush of wings—and Lucifer was in the room.

Jon's mother shrieked and dropped the shirts on the floor. She stumbled backward, crashed into the bureau. Lucifer circled, dived, banged into one of the windows beyond Jon's bed. He beat his black wings frantically against the glass.

"Doug!" Alice Petrie cried. "Oh my God! Doug!"

"Mother! No!" Jon said. "It's all right, I'll take care of it!"

But the sound of his father's feet on the stairs, and his father was there in the doorway, face livid, eyes blazing. "Jesus Christ!" he shouted. "How did that get in here! Filthy son-of-a-bitch! Get out of here, Alice! I'll get the broom and kill it."

"No!" Jon shouted. But his father had gone, was running down the stairs.

His mother left the room. Jon ran to the window. "Lucifer, why did you *do* this?" he cried. He undid the catch on the sash, threw the window up, and frantically opened the screen. "Lucifer, hurry, get out!" But the bird still banged against the upper pane, oblivious to the freedom just inches below. Jon tried to shoo it down, it flew up to the ceiling, circled, dipped, and Jon's father was there with the broom. He swung. He missed. He cursed and swung again. Jon screamed, "No! Stop! It won't hurt anything. Please stop!"

Then Lucifer squawked and dived and flew outside.

Panting, shaking, Jon watched the bird rise up in the shining sky. It landed on a distant tree, perched there a second, shook itself, was gone.

Doug Petrie's face was flushed with rage. His hands gripped the broom so hard his knuckles were white. Then he threw the broom on the floor and shouted, "You mean to tell me—" He stared at Jon with cold gray eyes, then went to the closet. In the hallway Jon's mother sneezed and sobbed. Doug Petrie grabbed Lucifer's box, thrust it under Jon's nose. Dry grass and excrement. "How long have you had this filth in this house?" he screamed.

Jon trembled all over. In a quavering voice he said,

"Only since Monday. That's all."

"That's *all*! You've made your mother sick the whole goddamn week. Do you realize that?"

Tears blurred Jon's eyes. "I'm sorry. I didn't mean to do that, really I didn't. I'm *sorry*. It was hurt, it banged into my window, it needed help. Oh please—"

"A filthy goddamn *starling*," Doug Petrie cried. "Look at this, goddamn it, a box of *disease*. Get this shit out of this house!"

Jon took the box, shaking so hard he almost dropped it. His mother sneezed again. The doorbell rang.

"Who the hell is that?" Doug Petrie said, his jaw muscles bulging with rage. "Alice?" No answer. He turned and left the room and went downstairs.

Jon hurried out through the garage and dumped the contents of Lucifer's box in the bushes beyond the pool. Tears stung his nose as he thought of Lucifer, the only pet he'd ever had, gone out of his life forever. He put the empty box in the trash can and hurried back inside to hear Chuckie say "Cuh . . . can he come out later, then?" And his father said, "No, he'll be busy. We're going out."

Jon stood there in the kitchen. Out? he thought. Out where?

The door slammed shut, his father called, he hurried into the foyer. His father said, "Get your glove."

"My glove?"

"The baseball glove I bought you. Get it. Hurry up."

Jon went to his room, got the glove, returned, his heart beating rapidly, lightly. "Are we . . . having a catch?"

"Come with me."

He followed his father to the garage. "Get in," his father said. Jon did. His father sat behind the wheel and started the engine. He pressed a button on the box in his hand; the garage door opened behind them.

Jon's mouth quivered so hard he could barely speak. "Where are we going?" he said.

"To the baseball field," his father said. "You're going to act like a normal goddamn kid. I'm sick of this hanging around in your room, never doing shit around this place. I'm taking you to the baseball field and you're going to play."

"But, Father!" Jon cried. "I don't know how! I can't just go out there and play, they won't let me, I'm not any good! I don't know how!"

"Learn how," his father said. He pulled the Cadillac Eldorado out of the garage.

They rode. Sun gleamed on the Eldorado's long black hood. Jon slouched in the front seat, the baseball glove in his lap. He thought he would suffocate, thought he would vomit. Trapped. Trapped again, no exit—and he thought of the day before, of how he had clawed at the door, at the rocks and dirt, as the smoke had filled his lungs.

His father looked at him. "What the hell did you do to your hands?"

Jon swallowed. "I was trying to make a . . . make something. I cut myself."

"That goddamn bird did it, didn't he?"

"No!" Jon said quickly. "Lucifer would never hurt me, never!"

"Lucifer," his father said. "You even had a name for the goddamn thing!" The muscles in his jaw worked back and forth, he stared through the windshield with narrowed eyes.

The car turned left, went down a block, turned right. Then it slowed, pulled up to the curb.

In the distance Jon saw the screen behind the plate, the blur of players. His father turned the engine off and looked at him. "I'll wait here," he said. "Get over there and play ball."

Jon fought the nausea that rose in his throat. Without a word he opened the door and stepped into the gleaming sun.

His legs were shaking as he walked toward the field. For an instant he thought of running, just running as fast and as far as he could. But he would have to stop sometime, he would have to come home sometime, and then it would all be twice as bad. No, he had to keep going, go through with it. Again, again, go through with it again.

He could see that they were already having a game, and he thought that maybe he'd be in luck and they wouldn't let him play. He slowly approached the field, and as he came into their view the action stopped. The kid at the plate stepped out of the box and everybody stared as Jon walked toward them, slouching, holding his glove with both hands.

Jon's stomach plunged, cold fear shot through his heart. The kid at the plate was Sonny Richardson. "Jesus —Pee-Tree!" Sonny said, and everybody laughed.

The pitcher was Carl Renniger and the catcher was Randy Hankins. Bruce Hodges was out near second, a leer on his bloated face. Randy spit in the dirt. "Hey, Pee-Tree—since when are you a jock?"

"You're just in time to hit," Sonny said.

Jon looked at him with alarm. "Hit? No, I—"

"Pinch hitter!" Carl yelled from the mound. "Pinch hitter," the kid at third said laughing, and then it was a chant: "Pinch hitter, pinch hitter, pinch hitter . . ."

Sonny snatched Jon's glove away and threw it into the dirt. He shoved the bat at Jon.

"Pinch hitter, pinch hitter, pinch hitter!" The cry rose like the shriek of angry insects in Jon's ears. He took the bat from Sonny, quaking so hard his teeth were clicking, and stepped up to the plate.

The bat weighed tons, was hot in his sore, raw hands. Carl looked small, unreal, and far away. The image of Lucifer flashed through Jon's mind—how he flew out the window to freedom, soared into the trees. Gritting his teeth, Jon swore he would do his best. He would try just as hard as he could and not show them that he was afraid. He stood there, shaking, the bat cocked oddly behind his ear. Then Carl reared back and the ball, a blur, came screaming at his head.

In terror he dropped the bat and fell. When he dared to look up the ball was in Randy's mitt and Randy hadn't moved, he was still right there in his spot behind the plate. Everyone laughed and Randy said, "Hey Petrie, what's the matter—didn't you ever see a curve before?"

Jon stood up, breathing hard. He clenched his teeth

and brushed the dirt off his clothes. So that was it, another one of their tricks. He picked up the bat, not feeling the pain in his hands this time as Randy tossed the ball back to Carl. "You want to be a pinch hitter, Pee-Tree, you gotta get used to the curve."

The chant began again, "Pinch hitter, pinch hitter, pinch hitter . . ." All right, he was ready. They wouldn't fool him again. He held the bat tightly, his knuckles white. Carl glared, leaning forward, one hand on his knee. Then he straightened up, went into the windup, threw.

At his head again, and fast, unbelievably fast, in sudden panic he flailed the bat—

And his face exploded. Everything went red, then black, he knew he was on the ground, then rockets of white and yellow streamed into the dark and the pain began. He rolled over and over, moaning, Randy's laughter far away in his ears. "Jesus, Petrie, they aren't *all* curves, you gotta learn the *spin*."

Then blood on his hands, the blood that was pouring out of his nose, he pressed his hand against his face to stop the flow. The pain stabbed out in jagged wheels from the center beside his nose and he started to cry. He couldn't help it, he started to cry, the blood running over his hands as he kneeled on home plate.

Randy said, "Time out, I think we got an injury here."

Sonny said, "Hey Petrie, don't take it so hard, you just need practice."

"About two hundred years of practice," Randy said.

Some kid Jon didn't know said, "Here's your glasses."

Jon groped for them in the blur, held them close to his eyes. The wire frames were mangled beyond recognition.

For a second his shock and dismay were so great that the pain disappeared. "My glasses!

And Bruce, who had come in from second, grinned and said, "He's okay, it's only a flesh wound."

Numbed, horrified, his mouth a mix of mucous, spit, and blood, Jon stumbled off the field, their laughter echoing in his ears. "My glasses, oh no, oh God . . ." he sobbed.

He walked down the fuzzy sidewalk, his face stinging angrily now. A black blob gleamed in the sun ahead, his father's car. The pain was huge as he opened the Cadillac's door. He slid onto the front seat squinting and gasping.

"Jesus Christ, what *happened* to you?"

"They hit me with the ball."

"You *let*,them hit you with the ball?"

"I couldn't help it."

"You could duck for Christ's sake, couldn't you?"

"I tried, but . . ." He started sobbing, his face in his hands.

The Eldorado growled to life, moved away from the curb. Jon took his hands down, wiped his eyes. Be brave, he told himself. Stop acting like a baby. He took his handkerchief out of his pocket and dabbed at his nose.

"You broke your goddamn glasses," his father said.

Jon nodded numbly.

"They cost a hundred fucking dollars, do you realize that?"

Jon nodded again.

"You'll pay for them," his father said. "You'll *pay* for them."

Jon mumbled, "Yes. I'll pay."

The Eldorado's engine surged. The blur rushed by. "And where's your glove?"

"My glove?" Jon said. He'd completely forgotten about it.

"You mean to tell me you left it there?" Doug Petrie screamed. "A fifty-five-dollar Rawlings glove and you *left* it there?" He swung the wheel sharply, put the car in reverse. "You're gonna go back there and get it," he said.

The car retraced its route, pulled up in front of the field. His father said sharply, "Get out and get that glove."

Jon opened the door. The field a blur, the players blobs, and everything totally quiet. He tripped on something, caught himself. A laugh. "Pinch hitter!" someone yelled.

There were kids in front of him but he couldn't tell who they were. "My glove," he said. "I left it here."

"Glove?" Carl Renniger's voice. "I didn't see any glove, Pee-Tree."

Jon wet his lips. His nose and cheek were laced with sudden pain. "Please, Carl, give it back."

Behind him the car door slammed. He turned, he saw the huge shape of his father storming closer. His father was there beside him then and said, "Give him the glove you snot-nosed creep, or I'll break your fucking head."

The blur that was Carl hesitated. Silence. Nothing moved. Then slowly Carl walked off, his colors blending into the sky and trees. He reappeared, and the glove was in Jon's hand.

Doug Petrie walked back to the car. Jon followed, stumbling, blind. He got in beside his father and they drove away.

The engine purred. His father said, "You let those bastards get away with shit like that? When the hell are you going to learn to stand up for yourself? Christ, what do you think, I'm going to fight your battles for you?"

"No," Jon said, holding onto the glove, his nose hot and thick with pain.

"You're goddamn right I won't. And you better learn to fight them yourself—damn fast—or I'll send you away to a place where they'll teach you."

Jon looked at him, stunned. "What? What do you mean?"

"I mean Harrington Academy. Military school. A few years there will straighten you out but good."

"You mean . . . I'd *live* there?" Jon said.

"Jesus Christ, you're fifteen years old. You have to cut the apron strings sometime."

Jon shook his head. "Oh Father, please, don't send me there. I'll try to fight my own battles, honest I will."

"You damn well *better* try." He lit a cigarette, sucked smoke. "You should see what you look like," he said. "It's goddamn *disgusting*."

*   *   *

When they reached the house, Jon ran to the bathroom, bladder aching. The pent-up urine streamed out. He sighed, he put his face so close to the mirror it almost touched the glass. His right cheek was puffy and red, his nose was slashed. He splashed cold water on his wounds and gently wiped the blood away, then went to his room and lay down.

His books were a band of merging color, his butterflies bright splotches on the wall. The planets were furry blobs overhead, the window panes were watery, indistinct.

High on the shelf he saw the gray blur that was Eeyore and whispered, "Lucifer's gone forever, Eeyore, it's just you and me again." Holding his head in his hands he said, "How will Meg ever like me when I'm so weak? If only I were strong, like Matt." Looking back at the donkey he said, "Father wants to get rid of me now, wants to put me in military school. To learn how to fight my own battles. I'd love to fight my own battles, Eeyore; but how?" He clenched his fists and said, "I swear to God, I'll kill myself before I let him send me to that place."

He lay back on his pillow and thought: I'd be better off dead. I'd be better off if they hadn't unlocked the Headquarters door and I'd choked to death. It isn't just for another year that I'll have to put up with this torture, I'll be tortured my whole life. I'm different, odd, the misfit, no one will ever like me. Meg likes me a little, Mother likes me—but nobody *really* likes me, nobody *loves* me. Father hates me, the kids at school hate me too—except for Chuckie, who's weird himself.

Carbon monoxide was not a bad death, he thought, you just went to sleep. Not smoking choking death like yesterday, you just went to sleep.

He'd do it in the garage, in his mother's car. That would show them. And if they didn't care, so what, he would finally be free of the pain. He turned onto his side and winced, his cheek swollen and hot.

He lay there breathing heavily, his weak unfocused eyes on the window, and thought of Lucifer. It already seemed so long since he'd flown away. How good it must be to fly, he thought, to go anywhere that you wanted whenever you wanted—to be free! Lucifer was free now. That was good. He'd miss him terribly, but it was good he would not be caged. It wasn't right for anything to be caged. He stared at the smeary window and thought of Lucifer, his mind drifting downward, one thought blending into another, his eyelids gently closing. . . .

He lay like that for a long time then, his mind at ease after all the pain; lay hazy in that half-world just above sleep, his bruised cheek throbbing, his heart slowly pulsing in his ears.

And time went by, his thoughts flowed on in shades of gray, his body faded into his jumbled thoughts. He pictured Lucifer, saw him high up in the tree, then watched him soar down into the darkness of the woods. His thoughts seemed to shift abruptly then and he saw himself on the bed and he said to himself: I'll never change. I'll be this way my whole life. Just look at me—lying there curled up like a fetus. Look at that miserable spindly chest, those matchstick arms, that stupid hair. I *am* ridiculous. Seeing myself like this I understand why they laugh, I understand why they tease. Seeing myself like this—

Like what? he suddenly thought. Seeing myself like *what*? And he thought: seeing myself through the eyes of somebody else.

For he was not just imagining seeing himself, he was actually looking down at the bed from a place up above, a place near the ceiling, looking down with real seeing eyes at himself on the bed. Watching himself with his mind and eyes while his body lay outside of his mind and eyes. And his vision was sharp, sharper than ever, though he didn't wear any glasses.

It was a dream, he thought. A strange sort of dream in which he was awake, where nothing was odd and distorted, where nothing suddenly changed into something else. It was so real!

Then *was* it a dream? He looked out the window. Everything outside was as it should be, the trees were in the right places, the grass was the right shade of green, the clouds moved lazily across the sky.

He looked back at the room and the room was the same as ever. And yet it was different, too, had changed somehow, was somehow more vivid, more real, more beautiful—and terrifying in its beauty. A dream so real it was a new reality! The window light catching in scratches and sparkling, the sun a shining disc at the edge of space. Terrifying, yes: yet so thrilling his heart leapt into the sky.

An airy lightness, a blissful calm possessed him. For the first time in his memory he felt really good: no aches in his muscles, no aches in his joints, no headaches. He felt powerful! Was this how Matt felt? Or Sonny, or Bruce, or Meg? It was wonderful! He floated in this terrific state, detached from the life of the boy on the bed, free of care for the first time ever.

What a delicious dream! He dipped and whirled above his prostrate body. If only he could *really* fly, get out of himself like this! He held out his arms, closed his eyes, and smiled, wrapped in a soft warm cloud.

Then panic seized him. This dream was *too* real, too pleasant, this dream was—He opened his eyes and looked at the boy on the bed. "Wake up!" he said. "You've had enough, wake up!" But nothing happened. He continued to float; his body still lay motionless below. "Wake up!" he cried again. But the body lay unmoving, the room stayed the same.

He dropped down close to the bed. He didn't know how he did it; it just seemed to happen. He looked at his scruffy hair, his puffy face, and thought: Suppose it *isn't* a dream? Suppose this body before him was not in his mind, but real? He watched its frail chest slowly rise and fall. Breathing, alive, and—not part of his thoughts at all, but *out there, real*, alive in another dimension!

It *wasn't* a dream! He was actually out of his body! Suddenly he remembered—astral projection, that's what they called it, the mind and the body existing on different planes. He had always considered it fantasy, nonsense—but now it had happened to him! He was sure of it! Amazed, he watched the oblivious body sleep on. Confused and dazzled, he closed his eyes. His head swam in sparkling brown light, he opened his eyes again.

His body was still on the bed. His eyes belonged to the body on the bed—yet he could see. It wasn't logical, didn't make sense. He could hear; in the distance a dog was barking. He could think, he could move . . . yet he had no substance, was invisible. Invisible! He could see other people but they couldn't see him! He could hear other people—but they couldn't hear him!

Exhilaration seized him as he rose to the ceiling again. He looked down at his donkey on its shelf, its head cocked comically to one side, and laughed. "Eeyore, look at me! Look! Up here! I'm flying, Eeyore, I'm flying!"

The donkey sat there, its chewed gray ear hanging over one eye. "He made me get rid of my bird and now *I'm* a bird! I'm a bird, I'm a butterfly, Eeyore, I can *soar*!"

He shrieked a shriek of pure delight that he alone could hear. He was as insubstantial as air, was less than fog or smoke or wind—and infinitely more. He was vision and hearing and motion and thought set free of the prison of flesh. Set free of that other Jon, that feeble earthbound husk of fear and pain that lay curled up, defeated, on the bed.

That Jon didn't matter now. That Jon was as good as dead. Trapped all these years and now, at last, the inside Jon, the spirit Jon, the *real* Jon—free!

Then all at once he felt himself falling—and he and his body were one again. He sat up, dizzy, his mind in a whirl. Had it actually happened—or was it a dream after all? His vision was blurry, his cheek was hurting again, while just a minute ago . . . .

Confused, mind spinning, he held his head in his hands; then looked up, dazed, to the small gray blob on the shelf. "Eeyore—you saw me do it, didn't you? I really did it, didn't I?" Then he laughed. "Of course you didn't see me—all you could see is what I saw, a body curled up on a bed. But the real me, Eeyore, the real me was"—he whispered it—"up *there* by the ceiling."

That doesn't make sense, he told himself. That can't really happen, it isn't . . . rational. How could part of you split away from the rest of you and fly through the room? But it really happened, he *felt* it happen, he *knew* it did.

He calmed himself and lay there, trying to find the feeling he'd had before, but it wouldn't come. He got up and sat at his desk for a while, he heard his mother sneeze downstairs, and then she was asking, "Jon, do you want any lunch?"

"No thank you, Mother, I had a big breakfast, I'm not hungry now," he said.

Frustrated, confused, he lay down on his bed again. If he could get some sleep, things might sort themselves out. He lay there, cheek throbbing, and thought of Lucifer again. The sadness came over him once more, he drifted into a vague half-sleep, saw Lucifer, a jet black dart of feathers flying out the window and into the tree, then gracefully spreading his wings and drifting down, down into the woods and out of sight.

And the feeling began again. Excited, he jerked awake and the feeling died. The image of Lucifer was the key! If you thought too hard about him though, were too aware of it. . . . He lay back, pictured Lucifer again. But now his heart was beating quickly, he was wide awake, the feeling wouldn't come. All afternoon he stayed in his room and tried to find the feeling again, thinking of Lucifer high in the tree, but nothing happened.

CHAPTER EIGHT

The next day, Sunday, he woke excitedly. He stayed in bed and thought of Lucifer over and over again but nothing happened, and again he thought: It was only a dream.

His father went out to play golf as he did every Sunday in spring and summer and fall, and Chuckie came over. All they could do was talk. Without his glasses Jon couldn't play games, or read, or ride his bike. His cheek was tender and looked like a purple balloon. "Cuh . . . Carl did that to you?" Chuckie said. "You ought to blast him, Jon!"

On Monday his mother let him stay home from school. There really wasn't much point in going when he couldn't read. After breakfast he tried to find the special feeling again, but it didn't work. Without his glasses he was sulky and bored: no books, no stamps, no butterflies. He had homework to do for Bruce and Carl, too, and of course he wasn't able to work on that. By lunchtime he was in a bad mood.

His mother looked at his swollen face and said, "What a dangerous game. You'd think they'd make the ball softer. I never knew you cared for baseball, Jon."

Jon stared at his tunafish sandwich, wondering how his mother had gotten to be that way. Her younger sister, Aunt Edna, was so on top of everything. If only his mother could be like her. He said, "I'm sorry about the bird. I didn't know it would make you sick. I hope you're better."

His mother smiled softly. "Thank you, dear. Yes, I'm much better now." She took her handkerchief out of her robe and gently dabbed her nose.

"It banged into my window, that's all," Jon said. "It was hurt, it couldn't fly. I was scared it would die."

"I understand, sweetheart, but you should have told me. We could have found a place for it outside. My allergies . . ."

"I know. I'm sorry, Mother."

She stood up, came to him and kissed his forehead. The spot where she kissed him tingled and he shivered, smelling alcohol. "I have an appointment with Dr. Reyburn this afternoon. Do you want to go along for the ride?"

"I guess I'll stay here," Jon said.

"He could take a look at your cheek."

"My cheek's all right. It's just a bruise."

His mother spent two hours showering, dressing, putting her makeup on. Jon listened to classical music, brooding, wondering. Maybe I'm going crazy, he thought. Maybe I just imagined it—like people who say they see UFOs or think they can talk to the dead.

His mother was finally ready. She took fifteen minutes to warm up her car, even though the day was mild. It was a wonder she'd never been in an accident, Jon thought. She made turns without signaling, went through stop signs, raced through yellow lights—it was terrifying to drive with her—but somehow she never smashed up.

When she left, Jon sat on his bed and said, "Well, Eeyore, what do you think? Did it happen or not? Blake said he saw God press his head against the windowpane. Next thing you know, I'll believe in God. I'll be crazy like . . . Matt Wilson. They say he's crazy, anyway, but he seems all right to me."

He went to his desk and tried to do homework for Carl and Bruce, the paper two inches away from his terrible eyes. Soon his temples throbbed from the strain and he stopped, lay down, and stared at the watery window.

The house was quiet. Outside, an occasional trill of a bird, and that was all. He thought of Lucifer. His eyes were heavy, closing, as he thought of him in the tree, watched him spread his wings and sail down. . . .

Then smoothly, without any effort at all, he was floating again. A thrill went through him—and he felt his body pulling him magnetically, calling him back. He closed his eyes, breathed easily, and banished the excited thoughts. The pulling stopped. When he opened his eyes he was still outside his body—not far from it, just a yard or so away, but he hadn't merged again.

He forced himself to stay calm. He looked at his body on the bed dispassionately and thought: I was trying too hard. You have to let it come. Relax, find Lucifer and let it come.

The pull began again. He breathed steadily, slowly, and then, without thinking, he kicked his legs—as if swimming—and found he had moved himself farther away from the bed.

The excitement welled up again and the pull was suddenly strong. This time he couldn't find the calm. Before he knew it he was back in his body again.

He sat up, his heart pounding quickly, the room all fuzzy again. He'd done it, no doubt about it now, he'd done it, he'd traveled outside of his body! "Eeyore, it's real! I can actually get *outside* myself! I can *fly*!"

His mouth was dry. He went into the bathroom, drank some water, then stood there frowning, staring at his out-of-focus image in the mirror. Something wonderful was happening. A magical thing, a miracle. He went back to his room and lay down on the bed again.

He let himself go limp and thought of Lucifer. Then felt himself—the essence of himself—split away from the ache of his body and drift up. He kicked his legs and again the kicking carried him higher, farther away from the bed.

He looked at the body below him, his mind completely calm this time. Stay calm. That was the key. As soon as he got excited, the flying would end. He floated, light as the air itself, his senses incredibly keen. He looked at the toy on his shelf. He could see every fiber in Eeyore's fur, saw splinters of light in the animal's plastic eyes. He had never been able to see that well before, not even with a brand-new prescription.

He felt the pull again. He relaxed, breathing slowly, evenly. But his breathing was thick, there wasn't air enough, he opened his mouth to take more in—and then in a panic he started breathing faster, faster, gasping, and then he was tired, and down he went to the bed again and merged with his body.

He lay there, sweating, exhausted. His sore cheek throbbed, his blurry eyes were wet. He panted, catching his breath, staring dizzily up at the ceiling. He'd pushed himself too fast, stayed out too long. His heart was beating quickly in his ears. He took a huge breath, let it out, felt better. Then he smiled.

He knew how to do it now. It was real and he could do it whenever he wanted to, he was sure of that. It was just a matter of practice now, of building up strength. "Hey Eeyore," he said with a grin, "you looked terrific. Your fur, your eyes, you almost looked—*alive*." He laughed, rolled over onto his side. Within minutes he was asleep.

His mother's voice cut through his dream at six o'clock. He had slept three hours.

As was often the case on weekdays, his father wasn't home for dinner. Jon ate Stouffer's macaroni and cheese while his mother drank a Pernod. When she finished the drink she went to her room. She had had a big day, and needed rest.

Jon was wide awake from his nap. He lay on his bed and thought of Lucifer. Again he felt that airy calm, that sense of total well-being, and again he was floating above his bed. He kicked and sailed across the room. I'm getting stronger, he thought, I'm gaining more control.

His excitement was muted by curiosity now. What would happen, he thought, if . . . ? He scissored his legs and thrust, sailed gently toward the wall. He winced, expecting impact, but the next thing he knew he was standing out in the hall.

He had gone right through the partition. He reached for the wall, felt nothing. Reached farther: his hand and wrist disappeared. He jumped and poked his arm through the ceiling, then got to his knees and poked it through the floor; he passed his hand through a vase that sat on the polished mahogany table there in the hall.

I'm a phantom, he thought. I can see, I can hear, I can feel emotions, but I can't touch anything—and nothing can touch *me*. He kicked, thrust hard this time, and sailed back into his room.

He was enjoying this! He kicked again, laughing, winked at Eeyore—and sailed through the outside wall of the house.

And now he was floating above the swimming pool in the dying light. The trees beyond the pool were crisp and clear. He could smell the trees, could hear the song of a bird. Far off some kids were shouting and he heard a car go by.

The world was fresh with incredible beauty, incredible promise, and he felt terrific: alert to every movement, smell, and sound. He was so alive, so filled with energy, so strong, that he wanted to fly all night. Just yesterday he had thought of killing himself, and now he had been reborn: No feeble eyes! No aches and pains! No headaches, no runny nose! Alive! He kicked for joy and soared up over the house.

And saw the Eldorado winding up Evergreen Drive.

He broke into a sweat. He had no body, and yet he broke into a sweat. His father would see him, see him floating there above the roof! Then he laughed. Of course his father wouldn't see him, he was invisible. And he danced and dipped and said, "Hey Father! Look at this! What do you think of me now? Pretty neat, don't you think? Let's see if *you* can do it!"

The car went into the garage, the door slid down behind it, and suddenly Jon was tired. He felt his body's pull begin. It wasn't strong, he could resist it if he wanted to, but it was time to get back anyway, he thought. He twisted and dived through the roof.

He was in his own room again and there was his body, lying there on the bed. A sudden apprehension seized him. Suppose he couldn't get back in? The other times he'd had no choice, his body had pulled him back. This time he'd have to do it on his own.

He floated close to his body, stretched out next to it—and *pushed*. Just pushed with his mind somehow—and suddenly spirit and flesh were one again.

He sat up on the bed. A powerful feeling of fatigue washed over him and he was drenched with sweat. He heard his father enter the kitchen. "Alice?" Silence. "Alice?"

That was all he could hear through the door, but he knew the rest: the muttering, cursing and angry drinking, the TV going on in the family room. Always the TV. How would his father survive without it?

Soon he heard it: shots, explosions, frantic music. He thought of his father, drinking, staring at the TV set, tense, bitter. He thought of his mother across the hall in the bedroom, asleep by now for sure, although it was only eight-thirty. And he thought of himself above the house, flying high like a bird, like Lucifer, feeling wonderful, happy and free. The shots and shouts and music faded, and he slept.

He stayed out of school on Tuesday, too. He was going to get his new glasses. After breakfast he flew again. He was all the way to Chuckie's house before he felt the pull, returned, reentered his body. He rested an hour, then flew once more.

It was getting easy now. All he needed to do was find the feeling, picture Lucifer up in the tree, see him pause, glide down—and there he was, out of his body again.

In the afternoon they went for his glasses. His mother had drunk some wine with lunch and she made a right turn from the left-hand lane, but no one was there and she got away with it. Jon toyed with the idea of leaving his body and flying alongside the car as his mother drove. But what if the car could move faster than he could fly? Or what if his mother asked him a question while he was gone? Would she think he was sleeping—or dead? He figured he'd better not chance it.

At home again, wearing his new glasses, he went out to his spot in the woods. Hiding in some brush, he thought of Lucifer, left his body, and flew over the highway.

He hung above the rush hour traffic, light as air, invisible—and totally invulnerable. He could pass through objects and objects could pass through him. A car, a train, a plane could go right through him and wouldn't hurt him a bit.

Nothing could hurt him! He laughed exultantly. If only Bruce and the others could see him now! And Meg. If only Meg could see him! "Meg, I can be with you any time I want. I'll be right there with you and you'll never even know it. I won't bother you, I'll just be *with* you. Me and you together, Meg—forever!" He laughed and spread his arms and dived, did a loop in the air.

The cars below, bright colored dots, were clotted, snagged. Jon cruised above them, filled with joy. That petty world of anger, competition, and worry seemed small and far away. And he suddenly knew that he didn't have to live in that world anymore. Oh yes, he would eat and sleep in that world, brush his teeth in that world, tie his shoes in that world, but his real existence would be in air, away from the curse of the body, the weight of material things. *This* was real, this floating and flying. That other world of pain and fear and evil, that was the dream. He closed his eyes and dived. He felt so good, so wonderful, so strong, so . . . in *control*—in a way he had never felt before in his life.

The tiredness started; he drifted toward the trees. He floated down to the spot where his body lay, and the trees and grass were beautiful and magical. The pull was strong. He let it take him, merged with his body. He blinked, adjusted his glasses, smiled.

He would come out here every weekend. He would

say he was going out to see friends and he'd hide in this spot and fly. He would be happy and his father would be too.

He looked at the highway again, the angry mesh of steel, and headed home.

CHAPTER NINE _____

In school he couldn't concentrate. All of a sudden it all seemed boring, meaningless. The colors looked dull, the kids seemed dumb. Carl threatened him about the homework—and he knew he should be concerned, but he couldn't be bothered.

Macbeth might not have been boring if Jon hadn't already read it three times on his own: The witches, Duncan, Banquo's ghost. . . . He sat there in a reverie as his classmates read aloud. Ghosts, the old superstitions. Yet when he flew what *was* he? Two people, one made of spirit, one made of flesh. The spirit part was like a ghost. The Holy Ghost. The part that kept on living after death? He had always thought that was nonsense, but now. . . . The religious people who spent their lives preparing for the life beyond—were they really so crazy? The ancient Egyptians—

"Jonathan?"

He blinked, coming back to the room. Miss Robards came back into focus, her face prim, severe. "Oh . . . yes?"

Kids laughed. Miss Robards glared. "*The earth hath bubbles as the water has . . .*"

"What?" Jonathan said. More laughter. He flushed and said, "Oh . . . you want me to read?"

"It wouldn't be a bad idea," Miss Robards said sarcastically. "—Since it *is* your turn. Page nine, line seventy-nine."

Jon cleared his throat.

> The earth hath bubbles, as the
> water has,
> And these are of them.
> Whither are they vanished?

Rich Edwards said.

> Into the air; and what seemed corporal
> melted
> As breath into the wind. Would they
> had stayed!

Jon frowned. He hesitated, licked his lips.

> Were such things here as we do speak
> about,
> Or have we eaten on the insane root
> that takes the reason prisoner?

He stared at the page as Rich Edwards went on with his part. *Or have we eaten? . . . The insane root, the insane root. . . .* A silence, snickers, and Miss Robards said, "Jonathan, is something wrong with you?"

Jon's forehead was covered with thin, cool sweat. "Oh no, Miss Robards, nothing's wrong." He looked at the book again. "To the selfsame—"

"Your children shall be kings!" Miss Robards said.

Jon frowned. "My children?" he said. The class roared and he turned bright red.

"Yeah," Randy Hankins said, "Your kids, Petrie."

Miss Robards said, "Cathy, maybe you're more alert than certain other members of this class."

The back of Jon's neck burned. The room was suddenly unbearably stuffy, and for a second he thought he might black out.

At last the day was over. At the foot of the long hill Chuckie said, "Do you think he'll ever come back? I mean, dogs come back."

"Lucifer was a *starling*," Jon said, lugging his briefcase. "They don't have the same instincts as dogs."

"Oh," Chuckie said. "That's too bad. So now you don't have any pets."

"Just Eeyore," Jon said.

Chuckie smiled and said, "Eeyore. You're crazy, Jon."

Jon turned to him quickly, eyes sharp. "Don't you ever say that to me!" he snapped.

Chuckie stammered, "I'm suh . . . sorry, Jon. I didn't mean anything, it was just a joke."

"I don't like jokes like that."

Chuckie hung his head. "I'm sorry."

They walked. Jon couldn't wait to get home. . . . *What seemed corporal melted As breath into the wind.* He laughed to himself as he thought of what Chuckie would think. I can step right out of my body and float in the air. You think that's crazy? Well I don't blame you, I don't blame you at all. He would love to share his secret with Chuckie but that was too risky, impossible. And anyway, he'd never understand.

Then all at once a sound in the distance—*that* sound—and his stomach plunged. Oh not again. Not now, not today, oh *please*.

He broke into a slick, dead sweat. The muffler's angry threat, the engine's roar, too late to run to the path that led through the trees—then brakes, the smell of exhaust, the slam of doors, and Sonny and Carl were there.

Carl stared. High cheekbones, narrow slits of eyes. "Get over here, Petrie."

Sonny smoked unsmilingly. Chuckie's thin face went gray.

"The math assignment, Petrie. I gave you a math assignment last weekend. Where is it?"

Jon swallowed. "My glasses," he said. "I couldn't see, I didn't have any glasses. I'll do it tonight."

Carl shook his head. "But it's gonna be *late*. I thought we refreshed your memory, Petrie, but I guess you need more lessons."

"No!" Jon said. "I'll do it, Carl, I'll do it right now, as soon as I get home! I couldn't *see*!"

"You see okay now, Pee-Tree?"

Jon quickly nodded yes.

"Then take a good look at this," Carl said. He made a fist and shoved it at Jon's face.

Jon's legs began to shake. "Take a real good look," Carl said. "Because if you ever get your old man on me again, this is gonna be down your throat—taking every goddamn one of your teeth along with it. You understand?"

"I understand."

"What?" Carl said.

"I . . . understand," Jon said.

Carl's mouth was a hard, cruel line. "I don't think you do. Like Miss Robards said today, I don't think you're payin' attention." He gave Jon a shove and Jon stumbled backward.

"He don't understand," Sonny said. He tossed his cigarette away. "We'll have to teach him all over again."

"No," Jonathan said, his heart beating fiercely. "Please!"

Chuckie's face was twisted; the words burst free. "Wuh . . . why don't you just luh . . . leave him alone!"

"Keep out of it, Crip," Carl said, and he shoved Jon again.

Jon dropped his briefcase and fell to his knees. He crouched, protecting his head with his hands. Carl laughed. Cars passed on the road and nobody stopped. Jon's stomach was water, his chest ice cold. He felt a sharp jab in his ribs, squeezed his eyes shut tight, tensed his body, thought of Lucifer high in the tree. . . .

—And drifted up and away from his cowering form. He was up in the air looking down at himself, and Chuckie was standing there, jaw working back and forth in agitation, and Carl shouted, Answer me, Petrie! Will you ever forget again?" And he kicked the crouching body square in the ribs.

Jon felt no pain. He floated calmly, watched as Sonny brought the flat hard edge of his hand down hard on the body's neck.

Again no pain. Jon smiled. Then a thrill went through him and he laughed. Carl shouted and cursed. He kicked again. Chuckie said, "Stuh . . . stop, stop it, go *away*!" Sonny spit between his teeth and yanked Jon's hair. No pain, no pain. He would never have to endure the pain again!

He floated, fascinated, watching them punch and kick his body, and he thought: How weak I am. What a coward I am. I hate it, I hate it, I hate it!

Then Sonny kicked hard and the body fell down. Fell onto its side, still curled in a fetal position, hands over its head. Chuckie screamed, "*You're killing him*!" The body lay there, motionless, and Carl said, "Get up! Come on, Petrie, get up!"

He looked at Sonny with sudden alarm. "He passed out or something, he's throwing a fit or—Jesus Christ, look at his eyes!"

Jon looked. The hands had come away from the face and behind the new glasses the eyes were white, had rolled up into the head.

"All I did was tap him," Sonny said. "Get up, you son of a bitch!"

"He's dead!" Chuckie screamed. His body was shaking, his arms flailed away from his sides.

Sonny grabbed his collar. Through gritted teeth he said, "You shut your goddamn mouth, Palmieri! And keep it shut, you hear?" Cars passed on the street, kept passing, and Chuckie began to cry. "You tell anybody, Crip, and you're next—you understand?"

Chuckie nodded as best he could, his face a blur. Then Carl and Sonny jumped in the car and were gone.

Jon drifted down. Chuckie wiped the tears from his face and went to the body. He kneeled, bent over it, and said, "Jon? Jon? Oh Juh . . . Jon, are you dead?"

Jon entered his body again. As he did he cried out in pain. His back, his neck—sharp stabs tore through him. He rolled over, biting his lip.

"Jon! You're alive!"

Jon moaned, rolled back and forth on the ground,

eyes closed. He struggled to his knees. The pain stabbed his back again, he buckled, caught himself.

Chuckie helped him up. "Duh . . . do you need a doctor, Jon? I could get my mother . . ."

"I'm all right," Jon gasped. "No, don't tell anybody. . . . I'm all right."

"But what happened? You didn't move. I thought they *killed* you."

"That's . . . what I wanted them to think," Jon said. He adjusted his glasses. Brand new glasses, and now the right earpiece was bent. He brushed the dirt off his clothes, his neck throbbing sharply.

"Oh," Chuckie said, smiling slowly, "now I get it—playing dead!"

"Yeah . . . playing dead. But don't ever tell them that. They can't know that, they'll get so mad they really *will* kill me next time."

"I'll never tell them, Jon, I swear."

Jon picked up his briefcase. He started to walk, aching with every step. What a fool he had been to leave his body like that. If he'd stayed in his body he would have screamed and they would have known when to stop, but to leave, to expose himself like that. . . . He would never do that again, never fly in the open, only from his bedroom now and never in the woods.

As they started up Evergreen Drive he thought, I can do something nobody else can do, but what good is it? I'm still at their mercy. My flying is wonderful, fantastic—but it can't keep me safe from them. If only I could use it to protect myself. There ought to be a way. . . .

At home he shut himself in his room and left his body and stayed out till dinnertime. He went past the pool and into the trees and floated down Evergreen Drive. He drifted, letting the flying heal him, and when he entered his body again the pain was not so bad.

The next morning he didn't hear the alarm. He awoke to bright sun, heard the family-room TV say: ". . . Pushed his son in front of the car, hoping to collect in-

surance for the injuries, but the boy died instantly.
. . .'' Quickly he dressed, wolfed down a piece of toast,
and went to school.

In the locker-room confusion he handed the
homework to Carl. "Here's Bruce's copy too." Carl
took the papers, sucked his teeth, said nothing, and
turned away.

They didn't hassle him or give him stuff to do. I
scared them, he thought. They thought they really hurt
me, maybe *killed* me, and now they'll leave me alone.

For a while, he thought. And then in a week or so it
will start all over again.

On the way home he told Chuckie no, he couldn't
come over today, he had work to do. He went in the
house and his mother was drinking and watching
"General Hospital." He told her he wanted to take a
nap, and he went to his room, lay down on his bed—and
flew.

It was so easy now: He just had to picture Lucifer and
get the mood. He flew down Evergreen Drive, saw Meg
walking home with Sue Greely, dived down close. "He's
so *conceited*," Meg said. "I think he's sickening."

"It's all an act," Sue said. "Did you see that new car
he has?"

"I saw it, so what?"

They stopped in front of Meg's house. Sue said,
"You going to the dance?"

"I don't know yet. I'll give you a call."

"Okay. I'll see you, Meg."

"See you, Sue." She turned and went into the house.

Jon went in after her, just walked through the wall.
He followed her into the kitchen. Her mother was there
at the sink.

He quivered, thrilled. He was in Meg's house, right
next to her! He could see her, hear her—and yet he was
invisible, completely safe.

He stood there and listened as Meg and her mother
talked. They talked about school, the dance, her
cousin's wedding. It wasn't important talk, but it was
real. He would love to be able to talk to his mother like

that but she never had time, she never felt right. She was so wrapped up in her problems that she never seemed to hear.

He listened, soothed by the conversation, mind drifting, calm. Then suddenly it hit him.

He could be with anyone at any time without their knowing it. He could see what they did, hear what they said, know all their secrets, all their plans. Meg's plans. His parents' plans. His enemies' plans! He could spy on them whenever he wanted, know every move they were going to make. If he knew their plans, he could stay out of their way. His flying *could* help him fight them after all! He laughed with excitement, jumped in the air.

Meg shivered. Her mother said, "Is something wrong?"

"I just had a funny feeling."

"What kind of a feeling?"

"A creepy one. Like someone was watching me —through the window or something."

Jon tensed. He felt suddenly trapped, hemmed in, exposed. He kicked, flew out through the wall.

In the trees behind Meg's house he looked at himself. Invisible, of course—his body was back in his bed. But was it possible—under cetain circumstances—for his body to rematerialize wherever his spirit was? He thought about it for a while and told himself that no, that couldn't happen. But then, his flying couldn't happen either, was just as fantastic—and yet it was real.

He flew through a tree, felt nothing. I am less than a shadow, he told himself, I am less than air. Yet Meg had felt him, felt his presence, felt his . . . mind? He thought about it, puzzled.

For a long time he weaved in and out of the trees along Evergreen Drive. He stood in the road, arms spread, letting cars pass through him. He spun in circles, laughing. Invincible! he shouted to the sky. They think they're strong, but I am . . . invincible! I'm stronger than all of them put together!

Then Chuckie was coming along on his bike and Jon lay down in the street and let the wheels roll through him. Hey, what's the idea, Palmieri, he yelled in his silent voice, I thought you were my friend! He laughed as he watched Chuckie pedal awkwardly home.

Then suddenly that claustrophobic feeling hit him once again: a tightness in his chest, a lack of air. The way he had felt at Meg's. Danger, danger, something was wrong! He kicked with all his might and hurried home.

As he went through the bedroom wall he froze in shock.

His mother was standing over his bed and saying, "Jon, wake up, what's wrong with you?" And with horror he saw that his body's eyes were open, rolled back, white.

Quickly he slid back into himself and blinked. "Oh . . . hi, Mother. . . . I fell asleep."

"I was calling and calling," his mother said with a worried look. "I just had to come in." The alcohol smell was strong on her breath. "You looked so . . . strange."

"Just tired, Mother. Are we ready to eat?" He had no appetite at all.

"Frozen pizza, one of your favorites."

"Great, I'll be right down."

When she left the room he broke into a cold, slick sweat. "My God, that was *close*, Eeyore. What if she'd called the doctor? My pulse and my breathing would be okay, and what would he think? I was having a seizure? I was in a coma? I have to remember to lock my door. Remind me, Eeyore, don't let me forget."

He ate with his mother, forcing the pizza down. It made him gag. When he finished he said, "Have a lot of homework to do," and he went to his bedroom and this time he locked the door.

He flew past the pool, through the trees, down the street. He was flying too much and he knew it. But it felt so good, so wonderful, and he couldn't help it, he *had* to do it. High, high up he went and saw his father's car turning into the Drive. He flew home again, watched his father come into the house, rip off his tie, pour a drink.

Some words with his wife, then he sat in the family room and turned the TV on. The Mets. Jon sighed and went back to his room.

"Doug, please, I'm tired."

His parents had gone to bed early. Jon stood in the dark of their bedroom, listening, the windows on the opposite wall aglow with dull gray light.

His father growled, "Goddamn it, you're *always* tired. Or drunk, or sick, or on some kind of pills."

"I'm not *on* pills, I take prescribed medication."

"Seconal and Valium? For illnesses in your head."

"I have allergies, Doug. *Real* allergies."

"Real shit."

Jon's heart was beating quickly. He should leave their room, he didn't know why he'd come in. But he stayed, as if transfixed.

"Come on, Alice, give me a break."

Jon knew what was happening then and felt suddenly sick. He knew all about reproduction—cell division, the growth of the fetus—but sex was a different thing entirely. Still prepubescent, he found sex sickening, terrifying. He knew it brought pleasure, knew it was nature's trap to continue the species, but what kind of pleasure could be so great that anyone would want to do ... *that*? To think of his mother and father doing it. ... They did, of course, or he wouldn't be on this earth, but to actually *think* of it. ... He shuddered.

"Goddamn it, Alice, do I have to *beg*?"

"I'm tired. I don't feel well. I already took two Seconal."

A pause. He heard his father's breathing, hoarse and ragged, saw the covers shift in the feeble light. His father said, "Goddamn it, always tired, always an excuse. You and your goddamn kid, you're two of a kind."

Another pause, then his mother said, "*My* kid? I suppose you had nothing to do with it."

"Alice, you know damn well we would never have had any kids if it wasn't for you. And look what the hell it did to you. You've been sick ever since."

Jon's stomach contracted hard. His body was lying across the hall, yet the pain was as sharp as ever.

"Could I have predicted how sick I would be?" his mother said. "Was I supposed to know that I'd never be well again?"

"You don't want to be well."

"Oh Doug, what a horrible thing to say." A deadly stillness, then his mother was softly weeping.

"Alice, for Christ's sake, listen. . . ."

"Go to sleep! Go to sleep and leave me alone!"

Jon went back to his room. In his body again, small pains assailed his shoulders, his ribs, his chest. He lay there confused, gasping in the darkness. He turned toward Eeyore's dim shape on the shelf and whispered, "I was the one who made Mother sick. I'm the reason for all the pills. But I couldn't help it. How could I—by not being born?" He lay there staring at the slash of window light on the ceiling above his bed and whispered, "Father never wanted me, he never wanted me at all. . . ."

CHAPTER TEN _____

Again they didn't bother him in school. He was tired in English class again, lost his place in *Macbeth*, and got scolded by Miss Robards, but his enemies left him alone.

If only it could last, he thought. His mother was always feeling bad, his father despised him, and yet if the enemies left him alone it would not be bad at all.

School ended, Sonny passed him in the hall and barely looked at him. No one had given him any assignments to do on the weekend. It was hard to believe, seemed wrong somehow, and he started to worry about it.

He hurried home as fast as he could, went up to his room, and flew—right back to Aronson High.

And he wasn't too late, the Nova was parked in the street behind the school. Randy and Sonny were leaning against it, talking to Linda Raggini and Sandra Jones. He hovered there as they smoked and laughed and fooled around, then Linda said, "I'll see you tonight at the dance," and both girls left. Then Randy and Sonny got in the car and took off.

Jon followed. He had no trouble keeping up with them: They turned, he turned; they slowed, he slowed; they raced, he followed just as fast. In a week he'd extended his powers remarkably. He didn't know what the limits were, how far or how fast he could go, but following Sonny's car was no problem at all. When they stopped at the end of the rutted road in the woods, he felt fine.

They left the car and walked down the narrow path. Jon followed them, flying high. Up ahead he could see the clearing and the huge oak tree—the tree he'd smashed into the day they had locked him in and started the fire. He knew where he was. In the distance he saw the quarry, the small rope bridge that spanned the gorge—the bridge that Bruce and Randy had built. His secret spot was only about ten minutes away from there.

At the edge of the clearing Randy stopped, kneeled down as Sonny stood watching. Jon descended to see what was up.

Randy looked at a cluster of mushrooms that grew near the roots of a tree. He picked them, laughing. The mushrooms were white, with dark brown gills, a lot like the mushrooms you'd buy in the store, but larger, with pointed caps.

"I don't believe this!" Randy said.

Sonny spit between his teeth. "Shit, I got better stuff than that."

"Oh yeah, but this ain't bad. Right *here*!"

He picked the rest of the mushrooms and laughed again. Jon watched intently, fascinated.

Randy and Sonny crossed the clearing. "Remember when we did this stuff last year?" Randy said. "I was high for two days."

"You have to chew 'em for two days too," Sonny said. "Not like my dust."

"How much you got?"

"Plenty, man."

They went down the steps to Headquarters and opened the door. Jon followed. Something glittered above the door jamb, in between the branches there. Jon flew in close. The key to the door, in its hiding place. How interesting, Jon thought, and dived through the roof.

Bruce and Carl were already there at the table. Carl put down his copy of *Chic*. "What took you so long?"

"We were lining up pussy for tonight," Randy said.

"Real stuff, not paper shit."

"Ha-ha," Carl said.

Randy opened his hand. "Look, man."

Bruce smiled his heavy smile. "So where'd you find that shit?"

"Outside the door."

"Come on."

"You fuckers must be blind."

"That's beautiful stuff," Bruce said. "Remember that time last year?"

"I was high for two days," Randy said with a laugh. "You want to try some?"

"Hey, I just want to mellow out for the dance, I don't want to *fly*."

Jon laughed as he thought, Fly? *He* was the one who could fly.

Carl looked at Sonny and said, "So what do you got?"

Sonny reached in his pocket and brought out a plastic bottle filled with coarse dark grains. "This smoke is dynamite," he said. "Get the papers."

Bruce crossed the room. He lifted one of the paving stones and came up with a key, then fitted the key in the lock that hung on the door of the cabinet recessed in the wall. The door came open, Bruce reached inside and brought out a plastic bag full of cigarette papers.

"Hey, stick this in there," Sonny said. He reached in his vest, came out with another bottle. This one held small squares of paper. Bruce raised his eyebrows, grinned.

"Best dust you ever did," Sonny said.

"Something for a rainy day," Bruce said.

"I hear it's supposed to rain tomorrow," Randy said, and they laughed.

Sonny rolled the joints with expert skill. The four of them sat and smoked.

"That asshole Diedrick," Sonny said. "Doin' away with the cigarette break, just because a couple of kids smoked joints."

"Diedrick the prick," Randy said.

"I'd love to get his ass," Carl said.

"Hey, wouldn't we all," Bruce said. "But how?"

Sonny stared at the tip of the joint. "There are ways," he said.

"You got something in mind?" Bruce said.

Sonny smiled.

They finished the first joint, started the second. "*Mellow*," Randy said. He leaned back, stretched his legs, and laughed. "Now he's gonna get silly," Bruce said, and then he was laughing too.

As Sonny lit the third joint, Bruce said, "Hey, I gotta go home and eat, don't paralyze me."

"You'll eat all right," Sonny said. "You'll demolish the fuckin' refrigerator." They sat around giggling, staring, and Randy said, "I'd love to give Palmieri some of this stuff. The fucker would soar."

"How about Petrie?" Bruce said. "No, give him the angel dust, that would blow his tight little ass to the moon."

Carl stared at the floor and said, "You shoulda seen the bastard. He fell over—just like he was dead."

Bruce grinned. "Hey man, don't kill him, he's the franchise."

"*Was* the franchise," Carl said. "He scared the piss out of us."

"Scared the piss out of who?" Sonny said, voice flat.

"Come on, Richardson, you almost shit yourself."

"The fuck I did."

Carl took the joint and sucked it, passed it on to Bruce. "So you let him fake you out," Bruce said, still grinning broadly.

"If that was an act, I really *will* kill him," Carl said. "That prick. We got that biology paper to do."

"He'll do it for us," Bruce said. "He'll do it or else."

"And what if he has another fit? I tell you, man, he looked *dead*."

"You let me handle it," Bruce said.

Randy sneered. "Pee-Tree," he said. "I bet the dipshit doesn't even jerk off."

Jon flushed. They were right about that. He had tried

to do what he'd heard kids talk about at school, pull on himself that way, but it hadn't worked. It had brought a vague, unsettling irritation every time he'd done it, and he'd given up. It seemed stupid and revolting anyhow. He thought about Meg. When they lived together, would he have to? . . . Probably so, most people did. But not all people. He had read a book about George Bernard Shaw when they studied *Major Barbara*. Shaw was married for years and years, and he and his wife never did it. If you wanted children. . . . But he didn't. He wouldn't want anybody to go through the pain he'd gone through. To bring children into a world of bombs and missiles, pollution and killers was cruel, just cruel. He was sure Meg thought so too.

"Linda Raggini," Sonny said, "what a piece of ass."

Bruce said, "You think she'll make it with you, Richardson?"

"She's already made it with me," Sonny said. "She's good, man, she's *real* good."

Bruce grinned again. "You don't have to tell me, man."

They all laughed.

Sonny leaned back, his eyes half closed. He said, "The one I'd really like to make it with is Meg."

A jolt tore through Jon's heart. How dare he dirty Meg's name like that! She'd never go out with Sonny, never in a million years. She'd never go out with anyone who lived on Brewery Hill.

"Old Megsy won't go with anybody," Carl said. "Especially a scuzzball like you."

Sonny tensed. His face was hard and set. "You watch your goddamn mouth."

"I'm kidding, you asshole. Jesus."

The joints were gone. The giggling stage had passed, and they were quiet. Jon stood there, smelling the dregs of the sweet, rich smoke. Carl stared with narrowed eyes. "This shit makes me feel weird," he said. "I feel like somebody's watching me."

"Yeah, me too," Randy said. He turned to Sonny.

"Where'd you get this stuff?"

"This is the best shit around," Sonny said.

"Well it makes me feel weird," Carl said again.

That horrible fear hit Jon again: the fear that somehow his body would suddenly coalesce around his spirit and he would be there, right there in the flesh, in front of them. Quickly he kicked, went up through the roof, rose up to the tops of the trees, flew home.

Enervated, he toyed with his food, ate practically nothing. After dinner he flew again and hovered in the woods beyond the pool.

They were going to start again. First it would be the biology papers, and then it would be more math, more English, history. . . . He didn't have time for that now. He didn't have time for anything but flying. But he'd have to do their work or they would punish him.

He floated there in the darkening trees. His flying could let him *know* their plans, but how could he *stop* their plans? How could he use his power to end their control over him? There had to be a way, there just *had* to be.

CHAPTER ELEVEN _____

Chuckie came over the first thing on Saturday morning. Jon was still eating breakfast when the doorbell rang. He was eager to fly again and didn't want to see Chuckie. He had some important things to think about, the things he had tried to figure out the night before.

But Chuckie was there, so instead they went up to his room and played Stratego. Jon played quickly, nervously, distracted, and won three games in a row. When he saw that Chuckie was getting upset, he threw a game.

Chuckie smiled his ingenuous smile. "I beat you, Jon. Buh . . . bet you didn't think I could."

"Hey, Chuckie, you're really improving."

Jon acted as dull and unenthusiastic as possible, hoping that Chuckie would leave. He wondered again what Chuckie would think of his flying, and thought; How neat it would be if Chuckie could do it too. Always trapped in that clumsy body, unable to run or jump or talk like other people—how great he would feel to be able to sail in the trees. He was picturing Chuckie flying down Evergreen Drive when Chuckie said, "I told my father—about what they did to you."

Jon looked at him. "You *what*?"

"I told muh . . . my father," Chuckie repeated, struggling with the words. His eyelids seemed to stick shut a second as he said, "Meg too."

Jon shook his head. "Oh Chuckie, no! You shouldn't *do* those things!"

97

"But why?"

"I don't want people to know. You tell your father and Meg and the word gets around, and . . . it only makes things worse. If they think I'm telling people, it makes things *worse*."

"Oh," Chuckie said. He stared obtusely. "Oh, I'm sorry, Jon."

Jon shook his head. "I know you didn't mean anything, but *please*."

Chuckie blinked. "I thought they really hurt you, Jon. I mean hurt you bad, and—"

"I was only pretending, Chuckie. I told you that. Playing dead."

Chuckie smiled. "Oh yeah, that's right, I forgot—like on TV."

"Like on TV. Now look, I have things to do. I guess you better leave."

"Are you mad at me, Jon?"

"I'm not mad at you. But please—don't tell anyone else about what happened, okay?"

"Okay."

Chuckie left. Jon went back to his room. He sat on the edge of his bed and thought: Now Mr. Palmieri knows. For Chuckie to know and Meg to know was bad enough, but for Mr. Palmieri to know wasn't good at all. If the day ever came when something happened to one of his enemies. . . .

Well, that was just a fantasy, he thought. All the things he had thought about last night were fantasies—except what he'd thought about Meg. He had made up his mind about that, and he'd do it. He'd do it today. "I will, Eeyore," he said looking up at the toy. "I won't be scared, I'll do it, I really will."

His heart beating fast, he lay back on his bed and thought of Lucifer high in the tree.

Meg checked her pocketbook, slung it across her shoulder, and went to the door.

Jon quickly flew out of her house. He'd been waiting there, invisible, for over an hour. He flew over the rooftops, dropped into his room, entered his body, and ran down the stairs. His mother was there in the kitchen as he hurried through. She said, "Would you like some soup? Split pea."

"Oh, not now, Mother. Later. Thanks."

He ran behind the Mitchells' house and down the path near the trees. His side hurt sharply from the strain. Gasping, he reached the end of the path, stepped out on the sidewalk—a scant ten seconds before Meg came into sight at the end of Evergreen Drive.

She walked closer, didn't see him yet. He took deep breaths and tried to calm his heart. She looked up and smiled. "Hi, Jon."

"Hi, Meg." He stared at her, melting inside.

"What were you doing, jogging? You're all out of breath."

He smiled nervously. "Yeah . . . jogging," he said. "I thought I'd give it a try."

"Well, have fun, Jon."

His heart seemed to stick in his throat. He forced himself to say her name. "Meg?"

She stopped and looked at him.

"Meg, I . . . wanted to talk to you."

She smiled. "Oh?" Light splintered her hazel eyes. "What about?"

Jon swallowed, wet his lips. "I wondered if you . . . could go to a movie with me."

His heart was pounding. His skin was hot, his nose was covered with sweat. He'd practiced this and practiced this, had thought about it all morning while he was with Chuckie, and now he had done it. He'd actually *done* it!

Meg smiled. Her face was radiant with sun. "Oh Jon, I'm not allowed to go out on dates. I thought you knew that."

Jon licked his lips again. "Oh . . . no. No, I didn't."

"My parents are really strict. They're nice, but they're really strict."

"Oh."

"But thanks for asking me."

"Oh . . . yeah. Well, maybe when you get older."

"Sure, Jon. Maybe then."

"Well . . . I'll see you, Meg."

"See you later, Jon."

Slowly he walked up Evergreen Drive, dejected, sad. But still, he thought, she hadn't turned him down, it was just that she wasn't allowed to go out on dates—with him or anyone else. "Old Megsy won't go with anybody," Carl had said, and now he knew why. Well, that was fine. It was great. When she *was* allowed to go out, she would go with *him*.

His depression started to lift, and he smiled. He had actually asked her out. He was changing, he was, it had something to do with the flying. You couldn't do something that special and stay the same. He was becoming more decisive. Bolder.

He went back in the house and his mother was at the breakfast table, staring into her bowl. "There's some soup left," she said. Jon said, "I'm still not hungry, Mother," and went to his room. And now he was tired, completely exhausted, and lay on the bed and slept.

Two hours later an argument woke him up. He could hear his father shouting, ". . . Final, Alice! Every goddamn time . . ." then he couldn't make out the words. He got out of bed and opened his door and he heard his mother softly crying and his father yelled, "I asked you a question!" Then silence except for the crying. "Are you going to answer or not?" Jon pressed his hands over his ears and shouted to himself, "Stop it, leave her alone! She's sick!"

The laundry-room door slammed shut, the garage door too, then his mother was coming up the stairs, still sobbing gently. Jon closed his door and sat at his desk and breathed quick shallow breaths and stared at the yellow blotter.

He took his U.S. stamp album down from the shelf, looked through it. He mounted his new one-dollar stamp in Crystal Mount. The stamp had a picture of an old-fashioned lamp, and around its edge it said,

"America's Light Fueled by Truth and Reason." He licked the Crystal Mount, put the stamp in the book.

He leafed through the album again, looking at all the spaces that would have been filled if it hadn't been for his enemies. If it hadn't been for his enemies taking his money, stealing it week after week. His father had cut his allowance five dollars a week to pay for the broken glasses—because it was *his* fault the glasses got broken, not Carl's fault. No money in the bank, no money in his pocket—because of *them*.

He thought of that sweet fantasy he'd had the other day, the one where he used his flying to—

No, that would never work, he would have to live with their demands, there was no way out. And now he had five dollars less to give them every week, and that was very bad.

Then he thought of the day before, of Randy picking the mushrooms, and had an idea. If he could find mushrooms like those, he could use them as money. Whenever they asked for money, he'd pay them with mushrooms. It just might work. He hurried downstairs, took a bunch of plastic sandwich bags from the cabinet under the sink, and went outside.

He searched along the path near the swamp, looking under the trees. There were mushrooms all over the place, but none of them looked like the kind that Randy had found. He picked them anyway, putting the different species in separate bags. There were white ones, brown ones, yellow ones, pink ones—amazing the number of different kinds, amazing he'd never noticed them all before. It was interesting, a new hobby—a hobby introduced to him by *them*. He laughed to himself as he thought of it.

He'd been searching for almost an hour when he found what he wanted. They were growing in a clump of rotted hay at the edge of the field. It was quite a cluster, enough to fill a bag. He searched for another half hour but found no more.

He took the mushrooms home and put them away in his drawer. Then he got on his bike and pedaled to Henderson, to the library there, and took out a book called *Mushrooms of North America.* At home he carefully identified and labeled his collection. The mushrooms that Randy had gathered were *panaeolus separatus.* He had boletuses, chanterelles, amanitas. . . . Some of the mushrooms were edible, some gave you visions, some made you vomit, some could . . . kill you. It was all very interesting, and he worked a long time.

Just as he finished he shook his head and looked at Eeyore and said, "How stupid I am. I can't use these as money. They'll ask me how I know they eat mushrooms and what can I say? That I spied on them?" He sighed, held his head in his hands. After a while he closed the book and put the mushrooms away in the back of his drawer.

His father had never returned and the house had been quiet all afternoon. There would be no dinner tonight, he knew that. His mother was so absorbed in her pain that he'd ceased to exist in her mind. It was after eight when he crossed the hall and tapped on her door and said, "Mother? I'm going to make a sandwich, would you like one too?" Receiving no answer he went downstairs, ate, drank some milk, then went back to his room. He looked at the mushroom book again, and pretty soon it was dark.

Spotlights shone on the houses of Evergreen Row, on doors and windows and patios, defense against thieves. Jon flew over swimming pools, wide lawns of smooth thrim grass, over Shadowline roofs and genuine redwood siding. Down the hill and across the trees in the dark and into Russelville.

Very little was open on Main Street: the laundromat, the newsstand, the movie, and Fogle's Fountain. Kids hung out in front of Fogle's under the streetlight, leaning against the wall, smoking cigarettes. Jon almost never went to Fogle's because of the kids. If he went, he went early, never at night.

Behind Main Street was High Street, and a row of well-kept colonial homes. Bruce Hodges's neighborhood. Jon passed High Street and Franklin Street and Phillips Street and the houses were smaller and closer together. He crossed the railroad tracks, flew over the sweater factory, started up Brewery Hill.

Here the houses were drab and jumbled together on narrow steep streets. Battered cars, and glass on the asphalt paving. A shout—three toughs in leather jackets coming along the sidewalk. Invisible, high above them, safe, Jon shivered all the same. He would never go to Brewery Hill while he was in his body, not even in broad daylight. This was where Sonny Richardson lived, and hundreds like him: rock-hard people raised in the streets who knew from the start that only the tough survived, who thought that tenderness was worthless and pain was funny. He flew faster, higher, away.

On he sped, through neighborhoods he'd never seen before: row houses, bars with red neon Miller and Bud signs, playgrounds littered with trash, dark factories, dead stores. He thought of his body at home on the bed, safe, lying on flowered sheets as its essence soared. A glow ahead, a shine in the air, and he headed toward it.

The glow was downtown Midvale. He'd traveled all that way! It took fifty minutes by bus from Evergreen Row, and how long had it been since he'd left the house? Twenty minutes? Half an hour? He zoomed close to a luncheonette and peered through the window. The clock on the wall said five after ten. About forty minutes, then. It didn't seem that long at all. He continued down the main street, Payson Avenue, past gleaming movie marquees, restaurants, bars, past darkened offices, closed stores. There was his ophthalmologist's building, there was the store where his mother took him for lunch when they went into town, and off to his right two streets away was the concrete tower that housed his father's office.

He dived down closer. People looking at window displays of summer suits and dresses, TV sets, books, records, candy, shoes. An optician, windows dark, a jewelry store with screens across the glass. A bargain outlet, an auto supply, a furniture store, a gigantic hardward store. A tobacco shop, a newsstand—door open, lots of browsers—and a movie called *To Love Forever.*

Jon hovered in front of the bright marquee and read the title again. Yes, that's what he would have with Meg, a love that would last forever. Once she was old enough to date, they would go out together and that's what they'd have. He passed right through the marquee into darkness, kept going, was in the theater.

Here was something he'd never thought about: He could see any movie he wanted and not have to pay. Just fly right in, invisible, and watch the show, then fly out. He felt funny about it. In a way it was stealing. Then again, he wasn't taking up a seat.

Not that that mattered tonight; there were plenty of seats. It couldn't be much of a movie with so few customers. He floated, watched the screen.

He couldn't make out anything. It was all just a writhing jumble of orange, pink, and red, curved bristles of yellow and brown. Then suddenly he saw, and caught his breath.

His heart was lodged in his chest as hard as stone. Slick surfaces, a man was groaning, "Love me, baby, love me," in a ragged gutteral voice. The camera backed away and Jon saw—everything. The hairy buttocks pumping away, the woman's legs in the air, the sudden withdrawal, the viscous fluid streaming out. The woman's hand was rubbing the fluid across the skin between her breasts. "Oh love me, love me, love me," she cried, and she grabbed the man's red organ and put it, put it in her—

Jon's stomach heaved. He looked away. Whistles screamed in his ears, bright rings of yellow sparkled in his mind.

A sudden scream, a cry of pain. Reflexively he whirled to face the screen.

The man was naked, tied to the bed at his ankles and wrists, face down. The woman, naked too, except for long black leather boots, was slashing at him with a whip. The whip cut whistling through the air and landed on the streaked and bleeding buttocks of the man, who jerked in pain and screamed, "More! Harder! More!"

The whip came down. Jon cringed in terror, panic-stricken. He whirled in darkness, darkness falling, closing over his mind. He had to get out of here, had to get out of here fast! He kicked with all his might and went through the theater's roof.

His heart was pounding wickedly, his throat was dry, he couldn't breathe. His body was miles away in his bed and completely safe, impervious to harm. But his chest was weak, his arms and legs felt feeble, and he had a horrible thought: What if I'm wrong? What if our bodies exist inside our minds? Not mind in body, but body in mind! What then? If that was true and something happened to your mind—

You would die. His body, safe at home in his room, would die.

Payson Avenue. Turn right at the corner. Up two blocks. He fought for breath, lungs heaving. Faster, faster, he told himself, he had to get back, get away. . . .

He kicked, but his legs were jelly. Slowly he drifted, his chest collapsing in on itself. He thought of his body home on the bed and told himself, You're safe! You have to be! Your mind is in your body, it *is*, you're safe! He let himself drift, he rested, calmed himself. Slowly his strength began to return and he coasted home.

When he entered his body he groaned, rolled over, turned on the light by his bed. His planets, butterflies, his books, his Eeyore on the shelf—he stared at all the familiar comforting things of his private world. He lay there, the scenes from the movie replaying themselves in his mind. Over and over and over again, the woman, the man, the whip, and at last he went into the bathroom and vomited hard.

His parents were sound asleep, heard nothing. Back in his room again, shaking and pale he said, "It was horrible, Eeyore, *horrible*! It has nothing to do with love, it doesn't, it doesn't!" He put the light out and turned to the pillow and wept till he fell asleep.

CHAPTER TWELVE

The next day, Sunday, he slept until noon. His mother's knock woke him up.

"Jonathan, do you feel all right?"

He shivered. A wave of dizziness passed over him. He thought of the movie, he thought of his parents in bed, his father's demands, the woman in black boots wielding the whip. "I'm . . . fine, Mother. I'll be down in a couple of minutes."

He gazed out the window, toyed with his Cheerios, stared at the pool's false blue. He'd been safe all along last night. The pain he had felt had not been dangerous, he was sure. He ate, tasting nothing, and thought; If the mind was a thing in the body and could *leave* the body, could it be destroyed? When they kicked and punched him that time that he flew, he felt nothing until he went back. And what if he stayed out forever? If he stayed out forever his body would not be able to eat and drink—and would die. But would his *spirit* die?

"Always Cheerios," his mother said as she watered the spider plant in front of the sliding glass door.

"Yeah, Mother, always Cheerios." Jon put his bowl in the sink and said, "Well, I have a paper to do."

"On such a nice day. Your father is playing golf, and you're writing a paper."

"I'm afraid so, Mother. Maybe I'll get a chance to go out later."

She frowned. "Are you sure you feel all right? You slept so late. And you look rather pale."

"I'm fine, Mother. Really."

It *was* a nice day, a glorious day. And he soared above lush grass, bright flowers, burgeoning magnolia trees. The darkness of the night before was banished; he felt restored.

Lawns sparkled, perfume filled the air. People worked on flower beds, mowed the grass, read the Sunday *Times* on their patios. Everything just fine in Evergreen Row—or so it would seem. To see his mother tending her plants, his father driving off to the golf course, you'd think everything was fine with the Petries too. Jon blocked the thoughts of his parents out of his mind, rose up and up, coasted over the swamp, came down in the acres of field that his father owned.

Green spears of grass stuck out of last year's dead brown. The field was fragrant, radiated soothing warmth. Jon closed his eyes and held out his arms and drifted across it, absorbing its heat and smell. This year, he thought, he'd catch the metalmark. He'd come like this—invisible—and see where the metalmark lived, and then he'd come back with his net and capture it. They were very rare, and it was a shame to take even one, but how great it would be to have a metalmark to look at whenever he pleased. He hoped he could find another giant swallowtail to replace the one that Randy had ruined, but he'd have to be very lucky to come across one of those.

At the edge of the field a lilac was blooming. On one of the purple blossoms a tiger swallowtail drank busily, wings fluttering. And there was a monarch, fragile and pale, returned from its winter down south. Jon loved the monarchs. At the height of summer when the milkweed bloomed they were everywhere, their brilliant orange and black wings dotting the fields. The one on the lilac would be dead by then, its new brood hatched, its life work done. It sat there, wings open, body shivering. Jon watched it, feeling sad for it. Then the tiger swallowtail took off in a jagged swoop and Jon flew after it.

He flew all afternoon, and he felt much better. The horror of the night before, that terrible film, was drowned in the brilliant color and light of the day. He flew in the woods, across the quarry—where the rope bridge stretched like a spiderweb over the gorge—flew up to the golf course, and then turned back.

His father was on the course today. His father was on the course every Sunday. Golf was his religion. To see him would wreck Jon's mood, and he flew back over the quarry, the woods, the field, the trim expensive houses of Evergreen Row, and entered his body tired and happy and slept three hours.

In the woods on the other side of the golf course, Matt and Meg were sitting on a log.

"Chuckie thought they *killed* him," Meg said quietly.

Matt shrugged. "But you know Chuckie. Always going off the deep end. He's just like a little kid."

"But he said that Jon's eyes went up into his head and all you could see was the whites." She shivered.

"It must be hell to live like that," Matt said.

Meg frowned. She picked up a twig that lay at her feet. She toyed with it, snapped it in half. "I met him on the sidewalk yesterday," she said with a sudden smile. "He asked me to go to a movie."

"Hey," Matt laughed, "I told you—watch out for those quiet guys. You think he's in love with you?"

Meg blushed. "Come on, he's lonely, that's all. What a life. Chuckie's his only friend. He really surprised me when he asked me out, I didn't know what to say. I told him I wasn't allowed to date."

"Which is almost the truth."

"Really. If my father ever found out I was here—"

Matt took her in his arms and kissed her hard. He held the kiss a long time there in the ray of sun that streamed through the trees. He looked at her and said, "Your father won't find out. And if he did it wouldn't really matter. Nothing will ever mess us up, Meg. Ever."

She leaned against him, her head on his chest and

said, "I talked about Midvale Community College last night. He was really against it. Radcliffe, Smith, he won't listen to anything else."

"Of course he won't." Matt stroked her hair and said, "Miss Weller wants to see me tomorrow."

"About the loan?"

"The loan—and something else. A scholarship."

Meg sat up, looked at him. "A scholarship?"

He laughed. "Yeah. Something one of the chemical companies gives." He shrugged. "Don't get excited, I don't have a chance."

Meg looked at him sternly. "If Miss Weller wants to see you about it, I guess you *do* have a chance. Why do you always put yourself down?"

Matt looked at the ground. "Meg, listen—your parents are college graduates. You live in Evergreen Row. My old man's a Brewery Hill cabbie. Midvale Community College will be a big deal for me."

"You're as smart and as capable as anyone in your class."

"Hey, a real objective opinion."

"Well, you are. So what's this scholarship?"

"Frazier told us about it in class. You do a paper and the chemical company reads it, they judge it—it's competitive."

"Who's trying for it?"

"Betty Lowry's the only other one."

"Well, that's terrific!"

"The only other one from Aronson," Matt said. "It's a state-wide competition."

"You're *good* in chemistry, Matt."

"I'm good, but where am I ever going to find time to write the paper? It's due a month from now."

"You'll find the time."

He kissed her hair. He looked at her and said, "God, would I love to win it. Then I could use the loan for room and board and wouldn't have to stay home and go to Community. And I could get away from *him*." He looked at the ground, the muscles in his jaw working back and forth. He said, "He killed Mom and he killed

Denise, but I'll be damned if he'll kill me.''

Meg brushed a lock of hair away from his forehead.
"Matt, please—your father didn't kill anybody. Your
mother died of pneumonia, and Denise—''

"Why do you think she did it?" Matt blurted,
looking at her sharply. "Because of him! He wouldn't
give her a goddamn dime! Not a dime! Mom died of
pneumonia, yeah, and why? Coughing up blood, and he
didn't even take her to the doctor!''

"Matt, you're shouting. . . ."

He shook his head. High in the trees, birds sang.
"I'm sorry, Meg. But I have to get out of there before
. . ." His lips were trembling; he stared at the ground.

She held him tight, caressed his hair. "Oh Matt,
there's nothing wrong with you,'' she whispered.
"There isn't, there isn't, you're fine.''

That night there was chicken for dinner, but the meat
near the bone was slimy and pink and his father went into a rage. He took a drumstick and threw it across the
room while his mother, dazed with alcohol, just sat
there with tears in her eyes. Jon choked on his instant
mashed potatoes and Durkee's gravy and went to his
room.

He sat on the edge of the bed, fists clenched in rage.
"I hate him, I hate him!" he said in a whisper to Eeyore
up on the shelf. He thought of his mother's bleary face
and he wanted to take all the bottles of liquor and pour
them down the drain. Small aches assaulted him: his
back, his neck, his ankles, his ribs. . . . God, what a
mess he was. He let himself go limp, fell back on the
pillow.

He lay there, thinking about his parents, his enemies,
Meg, his mushrooms, the metalmark. The little pains
jabbed into him. Time passed and darkness came. He
thought of Lucifer.

Flying was the only way to feel good. As he raced
through the dark night streets he was strong again and

the pains were gone. He dived through a speeding car.
He passed through living rooms, kitchens, bedrooms,
bathrooms, laughing at what he saw. He flew even farther than he had the night before, past Payson Avenue
and down the hill beyond the business district. Old
people stared from the windows of battered row houses,
music blasted into the street from rooms that were
lighted by stark bare bulbs. Down he went to abandoned factories, the river, streets with broken bottles
and smashed-up cars, dark people on corners in front of
bars, tough kids moving quickly along, drinking beer
out of bottles and looking for fights.

In his separate invisible world, Jon laughed. He flew
above the sounds of shouting, bottles breaking, tires
squealing, immune. It was all a show—like on TV—but
a *real* show, really happening. And he was above it all,
outside it all, completely safe.

Three hoods came swaggering down the street,
sharing a bottle of wine. They wore jeans and T-shirts
and denim vests; in the light of a streetlamp their vests
shimmered orange and black. Caught by the color, Jon
dived. He flew behind them, came up close.

And he saw that the back of each vest was adorned
with a shining butterfly, and above each butterfly was
the word MONARCHS in orange script. He followed them
closely, entranced by the gleaming design. If only he
could have a vest like that! The three of them passed the
bottle around, talked softly in clipped sharp sentences.
Their hair was long and black, their skin was olive, their
shoes made a sharp clicking noise in the empty street.

They turned into an alley. Jon followed. Down steps
and into a cavernous darkness with pillars and peeling
paint—the cellar of an abandoned factory. A pale line
of light where narrow, high windows faced the street. A
quick turn right, then left, a door—and one of the
Monarchs knocked four times on the splintered wood
and said, "*Vida!*"—and the door came open.

A large room lighted by candles. In its center was a
wooden table painted bright green. In the shadows,

sagging couches, mattresses, old chests of drawers, a stack of boxes, TV sets and stereos that looked brand new.

Two girls were at the table; both wore Monarchs vests. One of the girls was small and pale, with a face that made Jon think of a mouse; the other one was slender, dark, and beautiful. She said, "You get it, Carlos?"

One of the gang reached into his vest and pulled out a package. He was short and muscular, with wide thick shoulders and heavy arms. His features were sharp, his cheeks were hollow, a long white scar stretched all the way from his right ear to his throat. "Hey, Rita, of course I got it." He gave the thin dark girl a kiss, then put the package on the table, opened it. Red cylinders and copper tubes with wires sticking out.

The guy who had opened the door said, "Carlos Medrano strikes again."

"Hey, Manuel, you're goddamn right." Everyone looked at the stuff on the table and Carlos said, "We'll blow the Scorpions all the way back to Puerto Rico, man."

Manuel said, "Where'd you get it?"

A thin small guy whose right eye twitched said, "Down by the tracks—where they buildin' the tunnel. They got tons."

"You check the mail?" Carlos said to Rita. She shook her head no and he said to the mousy girl, "Tiny?"

"No."

"Hey, what's goin' on aroun' here? Felipe—go check the mail."

The guy with the twitch left the room and Rita looked at the table and said, "Hey, maybe we oughta forget about this."

"Yeah, maybe so," Carlos said. "Maybe we oughta let the Scorpions take over all our territory, hey? Or maybe I should give it up and do like my old man did an' get a job." He laughed. "Loadin' trucks an packin' fish an cuttin' wood ten hours straight six days a week in the pallet mill for minimum wage. Get a good American job like that an' die at fifty-one like my old man, all wrinkled up with no teeth in my head and half blind. —An' leave you here alone in the land of the free an' the home of the brave to live on welfare with your kids. Maybe I oughta do that." He sniffed. "The land of the free an' the home of the brave. I'll tell you somethin'—they don't look so brave with a knife at their throat."

Everyone laughed except Rita. Felipe came back into the room with a note. "Hey, Turk says two o'clock at Eighth and Cumberland."

"Yeah, we'll be there," Carlos said. He smiled and looked at the table; his scar caught the light. "But first we take care of the Scorpions."

Rita said, "You're crazy, Carlos. Someday you gonna get killed."

"Someday, someday. Someday you gonna die too, you realize that? Come on, we got work to do. Skiv, where's the wire?"

Jon watched, enthralled, as they built the bomb. Time flew as he stared, absorbing each detail. When the bomb was finished Carlos said, "Hey, Rita, Tiny, hold your ears, you gonna hear this blast all the way from Newark Avenue."

Felipe said, "We gonna get back late. "We gonna meet Macho an' Turk at Eighth an' Cumberland an' get paid."

"Be careful," Rita said.

"Hey," Carlos said, "you know the future president gonna take good care of hisself. He don't wanna blow his chance to rule the Land of Opportunity. Manuel, grab that wine. . . ."

Jon followed as they walked the black streets. They crossed the railroad tracks, went under a bridge, climbed a long flight of steps on the side of a rocky hill. Down another dark street and behind a half-demolished stone wall, they stopped in the shadows and drank and talked too low for Jon to hear. Then Carlos was running across the street, the black-and-orange butterfly vest a flash in the slant of the streetlight, and then he was gone in the dark.

He came back breathing heavily, leaned against the wall, and drank some of the wine. He grinned. "Fifteen minutes," he said. "Twelve o'clock on the dot." He passed the wine to Felipe.

"Nobody there?" Skiv said.

"Don't know. If there is, they ain't gonna be there long." His face grew hard. "Try to cut in on the Monarchs, hey? Well, they gonna learn."

Jon hovered close as they passed the bottle. The smell of wine and grease and sweat excited him. "You sure this gonna work?" said Manuel.

"Hey, trust me," Carlos said.

"Any minute now," Skiv said. He drank, then turned the bottle upside down. "Hey, perfect timing." He set the bottle down. The air was thick with quiet.

Suddenly the world was gone in a yellow deafening roar. Panic struck Jon like a lightning bolt; and then he was speeding after them as they ran, the image of shimmering window glass and glowing brick in his mind. Down the steps on the hillside, through the tunnel, across the railroad tracks. And they threw themselves into the weeds by the side of the tracks and laughed hysterically and punched each other and Manuel said, "Hey, man, I hope they had insurance."

"You're in good hands with Allstate," Carlos said. "Hey, jus' like the Fourth of July."

"Yeah—independence from the Scorpions," Skiv said.

Sirens screamed in the distance. The Monarchs were running again, across the tracks and down the grade, then through deserted streets. Jon watched them go. He flew up high and saw the orange glow in the sky. Stunned, strangely thrilled, he headed home.

Safe in bed again, the house totally quiet, a dim light coming from the spotlight down by the pool, he lay staring up at the ceiling, all he had witnessed rushing through his mind. "It's a real gang, Eeyore," he whispered to the shadowy lump on the shelf. "—Like you see on TV. But they're real, they're not invented. You should have seen the *explosion*." Again he saw the yellow flash, the way the street had turned day-bright; again he felt the rumble, heard the roar. And now that he was home again he marveled that he'd had the nerve to go there, stay with them, and wait for the bomb to go off.

But there was nothing to fear, he thought. If his spirit self had been caught in the blast, it wouldn't have mattered at all. If cars could run right through him, nothing—no matter how dangerous—could ever cause him harm. He thought of the night before, the movie, the horrible feeling he'd had that he was going to die. It had been in his mind, it was all in the way you thought about things—he had really been safe all along.

Then he looked at Eeyore again and saw something strange: The donkey's fur was infused with a dim pale blue—like one of those plastic dinosaurs that glow when you turn out the light. He blinked, stared harder. He really *was* glowing, wasn't he? Yes, yes, of course he was, he . . . was. But how? And . . . why?

He stared at the donkey fascinated, puzzled, the blue light shining steadily. He felt odd, uneasy, afraid. He thought of the bomb, the Monarchs laughing and drinking wine, that beautiful girl in the candlelight. Everything kept spinning through his head. At last, still staring at glowing Eeyore, he fell asleep.

CHAPTER THIRTEEN _____

Sue Weller sat on the couch in the principal's office, picking at the cuticle of her right ring finger. She didn't get along with Diedrick—that's all there was to it. Her first year in the guidance department at Aronson High and she had to have a rotten relationship with the principal. Well, it wasn't her fault. Diedrick was simply a jerk.

She picked at her finger again and said, "I can't be effective if I can't go into the home."

Stan Diedrick said, "I've told you this a hundred times, Miss Weller—the community does not want us going into its homes."

"No wonder."

Diedrick ignored the comment. "School is where kids are *educated*. If a family needs counseling or social work or psychotherapy or whatever you want to call it, it's not up to us to provide it."

"So we have Diane Corson who's fifth in her class and the star of the track team, and all of a sudden she's failing two subjects and quitting sports, and I can't even go see her mother."

"Get her mother to come see you."

"I've tried. I've talked to her on the phone three times. She won't come in."

"Then you've done what you can with Mrs. Corson."

"Mrs. Holt."

"All right, Mrs. Holt," Diedrick said with irritation. "All you can do now is work with Diane."

"I'm just not *getting* anywhere with her," Sue Weller said. "There's something going on in that home, and unless I find out what it is, I won't be able to help her."

The principal looked at her sternly, as if she were one of the students he'd caught smoking dope. "Miss Weller, you may *not* go into her home."

Sue Weller picked her finger, looked at it, stood up, and smoothed her skirt. "Thank you, Mr. Diedrick," she said, and thought, The kids have you pegged right, mister: Diedrick the Prick. She left the office, closing the door behind her.

The bell had already rung for the start of first period; there were only a couple of stragglers in the hall. One of them was Mike Curcio, a kid she saw on a regular basis for counseling. Mike was a sophomore, good-looking, bright—and practically always stoned. He was flunking everything but gym. His father, a lawyer, had threatened everything short of tearing the roof off the school if his kid's grades didn't improve, but he'd never kept one appointment with Sue Weller. Not one.

Sue Weller had just about had it with Evergreen Row and Cardinal Village and Oak Hill and all the rest of the fancy suburbs that fed their kids to Aronson. They were great at making demands, those people, but try to get them to see that they might have something to do with the problems their kids were having. Yeah, lots of luck.

"Hey Mike—better speed it up."

Mike grinned. His eyes were streaked with red. "Little slow getting off the mark this morning, Miss Weller."

"Yeah, Mike. I'll see you this afternoon."

"Oh right. Is that today?"

"One-thirty, Mike."

She watched him walk slowly away, the only kid left in the hall. She shook her head and went into her office.

Matt Wilson was waiting there.

"Oh Matt, hi—sorry I'm late, I was talking to Mr. Diedrick." She went behind her desk, looked through some papers, pulled out a sheet, and gave it to Matt. Then she sat at the desk as he looked at the paper, a frown on his face. "It's a good deal, Matt."

Matt shook his head. "I'll say it is."

"You and Betty are the only ones who've shown any interest. I'd get the application in as soon as possible."

Matt stared at the paper in silence, then looked up and said, "You really think I have a chance?"

"Of course. You get all A's in chemistry and math."

"I know . . . but there are other things."

"Like what?"

He shook his head. "Nothing," he said.

She sat there, wondering how to proceed. "Do you understand the form? You want me to run through it with you?"

"I understand it," Matt said.

A silence, and Sue said, "If there's anything I can do for you, just let me know."

Matt nodded. He stood up and stuck the application blank in one of his books. "Thanks a lot, Miss Weller. I'll see you later."

As he walked down the hall her words ran through his head: "If there's anything I can do . . ." Yeah, turn my old man into Santa Claus, Miss Weller, that would help. Bring Mom back, bring Denise back; make Pete well. He laughed sardonically to himself. I'll fill out the form, he thought. I'll fill out the form and I'll win the goddamn thing, I swear I will.

After Matt left, Sue Weller sat there, frowning. What was it about him that made her think of Mark? Not his looks, not his voice, but something in his manner: his earnestness, and . . . a certain diffidence. Dear Mark, she thought, and told herself no, please, no, don't think about that.

Then suddenly a squeal of brakes outside, and the wall in her mind fell down. She tried to block the memory but there it was again: "You're turning down a ride in a Porsche 928? Hey Sue, come *on*." But she stayed there in the restaurant while he went with the nameless stranger and the silver car sped off. She waited with a cup of coffee and as soon as she heard the sirens she knew. Before the state police came in and said, "Freak accident . . . went off the road and hit a tree . . . the driver and the passenger killed instantly." The passenger her Mark, the only man she'd ever loved, the man she was going to marry in two more months. Gone. Dead. Killed.

She turned, looked out the window. Two years ago, and just like yesterday.

The car with the squealing brakes roared away from the light. A Chevy Nova with flames on the fenders and hood. Sylvester Richardson's car. "Sonny" Richardson, late for school again. He'd been sent to her office six times already this year. Someday he'd kill somebody too—in that car or another car. As long as it didn't hurt, as long as Mark hadn't—

The fire alarm went off with a deafening clang. Sue Weller sighed, stood up. What nasty surprises you get when you don't check the daily schedule. She thought of Diedrick again and shook her head and said under her breath: "What a jerk."

Jonathan had gotten up early, after a few hours sleep. He had to use the bathroom, and out in the hall he heard the TV set in the kitchen say, ". . . Gang feud. The fire completely destroyed three vacant buildings in the 2800 block of Newark Avenue . . . Continue to investigate . . ."

He stood at the top of the stairs and listened breathlessly. That was the Monarchs' bomb they were talking about. And he had been there, had actually seen it happen. The Monarchs were famous. They were on TV. The thought electrified him. Back in his room he whispered, "I know the guys who did that, Eeyore. They're friends of mine. I was there last night when they did it. You thought I was lying right here, but I was *there*." He laughed to himself, then eyed the donkey curiously, remembering the glow he had seen. He wasn't so sure anymore that Eeyore had really glowed like that.

He seemed the same as ever now, an old stuffed toy, and yet last night. . . . He thought about it, thought about Carlos, the Monarchs. . . .

The next thing he knew, his mother was at his door. He had fallen asleep again, and now it was eight-thirty-five. He was sick, he said. His stomach felt bad, he was tired, no, he couldn't go to school. When she left, he slept again. He was still asleep when the fire alarm went off at Aronson High and the kids had to stand outside for an hour while the building was searched for the bomb.

He got up after ten. Still playing sick he made himself a cup of tea and a piece of toast. He was so excited by all that had happened that he couldn't finish the toast.

His mother watered her spider plant and said, "You look so *pale*. You never used to take naps every day. I think you should see a doctor."

Jon said, "I'm all right, Mother. My stomach is just a little funny—it's been going around at school."

He thought of school, so glad he wasn't there. How incredibly dull it was. He already knew most stuff before they taught it, and as for important stuff—like leaving your body and flying—they wouldn't even believe it could happen, let alone teach you about it.

"You'd better go up and rest some more."

"Yes, Mother, I will."

Fifth period was almost over by the time he flew past the school. Kids crowded around the soda stand across the street, walked aimlessly up and down, some holding hands, some hanging on the chain-link fence above the athletic field. Down on the field in the softball game two kids chased after the ball as the runner rounded the bases. Jon laughed. How stupid it looked from up here. Well, he would have none of that nonsense today.

Chuckie was sitting alone on the step where he always sat, just staring into space. Hey Chuckie, look—up here! Want to fly with me? Bruce and Carl were walking together. They stopped and turned as a couple of girls went by. So small, a pair of bugs. He kicked, flew up, away.

Over houses, factories, parks, and playgrounds, schools where the children were black. Down the railroad tracks and over the site of the blast: the yellow warehouse gutted now, roof sagging like icing on a cake, the two adjacent houses smashed and charred.

Jon shivered with excitement. Bruce and the rest were nothing compared to the Monarchs. If they ever met up with the Monarchs—his gang—they'd be scared to death.

He flew to the Monarchs' hideout, flew through the giant cellar, weaved in and out of the huge flaking columns, muted sunlight playing on piles of trash. Around the bend to the door. It was locked. He flew through it and no one was there.

Stereos, TV sets, clock radios—stolen, of course. Beer bottles, wine bottles, cigarette butts on the wooden table, a jar lid with something burnt and brown. The smell of the room sharp, sour.

Disappointed that no one was there, he flew through the ceiling, cruised four cavernous floors: of peeling walls and ceilings, mounds of trash, abandoned rusted machines. He flew out of the building and into the sky.

He drifted aimlessly for a while, and then as he looked at the tops of the buildings downtown, he thought of his father.

When he was a little boy, his father used to take him to his office now and then. Those visits were only dim memories now. He had seen the new office suite only once, though his father had been there three years. Time to see it again, he thought—as a phantom.

As he flew down the fourth-floor corridor, his father stepped out of his suite. A sudden irrational panic, a flash of sweat—then Jon relaxed in his invisibility. His father stepped into the elevator, Jon flew in beside him.

Down they went, his father holding his attaché case and wearing his usual frown. Always cooking up deals, inspecting sites, holding meetings with bankers, lawyers, realtors. Busy, busy, busy, wrapped up in his mind. Jon flew to the underground garage, watched his father get into the car. Saw him check himself in the rearview mirror, comb his hair and straighten his tie, and drive the Eldorado into the street.

He only went five blocks. He parked where it said, "No Parking 9 to 5." That didn't apply to him, of course—he had money and friends. They went to the shore for the weekend once, his father was going 85 in a 35 mile an hour zone, and he handed the trooper fifty dollars and that was that.

Not an office building, an apartment house. Jon rode the elevator with his father, strangely anxious. Was this one of his father's buildings? A building he wanted to buy? Did a lawyer live here? A friend? The elevator door slid open, his father stepped out, Jon followed him down the hall.

He stopped in front of a door and rang the bell. Jon waited, filled with curiosity.

The door came open. A woman, no older than thirty, with flaming red hair. The smell of lilies of the valley and she smiled and said, "Hi, Doug." His father stepped into the room and closed the door and set his attaché case down and said, "Hey, baby, good to see you."

And then they were kissing. An electric current of shock shot through Jon's chest. He stared in disbelief. "Mmm, baby, you smell so *good*," his father said, and he pulled the zipper on the back of her dress and the dress fell away from her shoulders, her breasts were naked, his father leaned over . . .

Jon gagged. Again the choking rush of panic, noises in his ears, no air, no air! The two of them were on the couch, the woman's dress was at her waist, his father's hands were pawing at her flesh. The woman's head was leaning back, her eyes were closed, she moaned, "Oh Doug, oh Doug . . ."

Staggered, Jon turned away. He gritted his teeth. "No! No!" he screamed, and the world was whirling and dim in his head, his chest was burning with pain. He flew through the door and into the hallway and screamed, "Oh Mother, no!" sobbing there in the empty hall.

The elevator numbers flashed, the door came open, a stranger walked out. Jon drifted weakly down through five apartments—someone cooking, someone showering, the other apartments empty—and stumbled into the street. He stood there, hating his father and that strange woman, hating everyone, and wiping the tears away. After a long time he gathered his strength and flew home.

Eeyore was glowing again. It wasn't dark, but the toy was glowing. "I hate him, Eeyore," Jon whispered harshly. "I *hate* him."

He shook uncontrollably, sat on the edge of the bed, and thought, Meg thinks most people are good. She's wrong. If she could see through things the way I can, she'd know. It's just like the dirt in the walls. The house looks perfectly clean but the walls hold filth and trash. "That's the truth of it, Eeyore, people are just like that."

He stared at the toy, at that curious silver blue, and thought: Maybe it's all in my head. The insane root . . . No, no, it isn't that, he *does* glow! He wet his lips and stared.

Some Indian tribes believed that all objects had souls. But *toys*? He'd read a book about Japanese archery once. The archers said their bows absorbed the spirit of their users. The bows started out as mere pieces of wood, but after years of dedicated use the bows and the archers merged. Became one spirit. Could that be happening to Eeyore—and to him? He took the donkey off the shelf and turned it in his hands and felt . . . vibration. Something flowing, energy. At least . . . at least it *seemed* that way. He shook his head, confused. The toy still buzzed and glowed. Was it . . . alive? He had laughed when he'd read the archery book, but now as he looked at Eeyore he felt awe.

"It was sickening, Eeyore. He was kissing her and . . . feeling her and . . . it was *disgusting*." He closed his eyes. "How can he do it to Mother? How? If she knew, oh God, if she knew. . . ." He tightened his hands into fists and said, "He won't get away with this! I swear—"

"Jonathan?"

He stood there paralyzed, the donkey hot in his hands.

"Jon, who are you talking to?"

Quickly he set the toy on the shelf. "Just homework, Mother. My French again."

"How are you feeling, sweetheart, all better?"

"Yes, Mother, I'm fine."

"Would you like some soup? Some Coke?"

"I'll get some Coke in a minute, Mother. Soon as I finish this exercise. Thanks."

He sat on the bed, exhausted. A storm of thoughts rushed through his mind. He held his head, blood pounding at his temples. He sighed, breathed deeply, stood, went downstairs and drank some Coke.

His mother was on the couch, a Pernod in her hand. She was watching "The Edge of Night." Jon stood at the door of the family room and looked at her. Betrayed and suspecting nothing, living in her hazy dream world, numb, apart from everyone. Maybe it had been different once—a long time ago, before he'd been born. Maybe if he had never been born— Tears came to his eyes. Oh Mother, I'm sorry, it wasn't my fault. He thought of his father again and thought, It's his fault, not mine. Flooded with pain and anger he turned away, stood staring at the trees.

His father was home for dinner. Jon couldn't bear to look at him. He left half the meal on his plate and went up to his room. A short while later he heard his father leave the house again. To . . . fuck? he thought. Is that what you're going out for—to fuck some more? Didn't you get enough this afternoon? Do you have a different woman at night? A different woman for every day of the week? He clenched his hands into fists and banged them on his thighs. In the family room, he heard the TV go on.

* * *

Carlos brought the chain down as hard as he could. It caught the Scorpion across the forehead, knocking him over the garbage can. Links of blood bloomed near his hairline and he lay still. Again Carlos swung. Another Scorpion cried out, and the knife flew out of his hand. "You bastard!" Carlos screamed. Felipe, Manuel, and Skiv and Macho and Turk swung chains and baseball bats, blades flashed in the streetlight, a window smashed. Somewhere inside a house somebody screamed.

The sirens whined in the distance and Carlos said, "Let's go!" And the Monarchs ran down the street, jumped over a fence, crossed a lot filled with papers and broken glass, went down another street, kept running. Jon flew above them effortlessly, thrilled. They reached the factory, went down the alley, through the dark cellar, into the room. Carlos, laughing like mad and out of breath, fell down on a mattress and rolled around. Rita fell on top of him.

"Hey, baby, you shoulda seen it. Ricardo not gonna be so pretty now, his face gonna look like a ad for a chain-link fence."

"Hey, Tiny—wine!" Skiv said.

They drank. There were other girls this time, and everybody shouted, joked around, and poked each other. Felipe rolled a fat joint and they smoked it hungrily. They all lay back on the mattresses and laughed in the feeble light.

"You see it on TV this mornin'?" Carlos said. He grinned. " 'The investigation continues.' "

"Like a empty warehouse an' two empty houses was important," Macho said. He was heavy and dark, with long, black, stringy hair.

"Like a buncha dumb spics was important, man," Skiv said.

"Hey, private property," Carlos said. "Somebody owns them buildings, man. Somebody nice an respectable maybe who lives in maybe Oak Hill."

Jon started, surprised. Oak Hill was near Evergreen Row. He had never imagined the Monarchs knew about neighborhoods like his.

"Hey, yeah," Skiv said. "Maybe some lawyer with a closet fulla silk suits an' a white Mercedes. Or maybe a real-estate developer. Nice respectable people."

"Another tax loss," Macho said, and everybody laughed.

"Hey, someday I'm gonna live in Oak Hill," Carlos said.

"Before or after you president?" Rita said.

"On my way up, baby." He squeezed her hard. "Afterwards I'll live in San Clemente."

Carlos had cuts on both his arms but paid no attention to them. Jon wondered what it was like to be tough like that, so tough that nobody—not even Sonny Richardson—would dare to bother you. He would never be like that, and yet he had a different power, one that even Carlos didn't have. If only he could use it. Not just play with it, *use* it.

They rolled more joints. The room was sour, close. Carlos said, "Hey, blow those candles out," and everybody sank into liquid darkness. Jon flew through the roof of the factory, headed home.

CHAPTER FOURTEEN _____

He was terribly tired on Tuesday and stayed home again. His face was pale and his eyes were dark, so it was easy to convince his mother that he still wasn't well. He slept most of the day, then flew to the field and drifted around in the lazy sun among tiger and spicebush swallowtails and red-spotted purples. And suddenly he saw—the metalmark.

He was lucky to see one metalmark a year. They were getting rarer all the time as progress destroyed one breeding ground after another. They were fast and flew in a jagged path and never stayed still for long. That's why he had never caught one. Now he wasn't even sure that he *wanted* to catch one, the species was so depleted.

He loved the metalmark. He flew across the field beside it, laughing, overjoyed, till it darted off into the woods. Once it was gone, he could hardly believe he had seen it.

He ate little again that night. His father was out and his mother was sneezing again for some unknown reason—probably some new grass or wild flower had bloomed—and he went to bed early and slept.

On Wednesday he went to school. Even though he had slept ten hours he felt worn out. Everything was boring, drab; it was all he could do to keep awake. Carl, Bruce, and Randy would ask him to do the biology papers soon. The thought of it nagged like a pain.

He daydreamed his way through math and French, thinking about the Monarchs, reliving their dark excitement. When the math teacher, Mr. Pensack, called on him, his answer was so far off that everyone laughed, but he didn't care.

At lunchtime, Chuckie talked about Monday's bomb scare.

"It was only a trick," he said. "But wouldn't it be neat if it was real? Blam, no more school!" He laughed.

The Monarchs' bomb, the street as bright as day, the roar. "Yeah, Chuckie, neat," Jon said.

"Huh . . . how you doin', Jon? You better now?"

"I'm fine."

"Can I come over after school?"

Jon shook his head. "I have to catch up on my homework."

"Oh." Chuckie stood there, earnest, dense. "Well what about tomorrow?"

"I'm kind of busy, Chuckie. I'm involved in a . . . scientific experiment."

Chuckie grinned. "Are you making a bomb?"

Jon looked at him, startled. "What? Oh, no, of course I'm not making a bomb. It's nothing like that. I can't tell you now, but maybe someday."

"You're not still mad at me for telling Meg and my father about how they beat you up?"

"I'm not still mad. Just don't ever do it again."

Again Jon thought how great it would be if Chuckie could only fly. To escape that tangled brain that tied his muscles into knots and be able to soar like a bird above the trees. Maybe someday he would know how to teach him that. But he wasn't ready to teach anybody, he had so much to learn, so much to see and do. And school was boring, boring, boring; he just couldn't wait for the day to end.

In English he nodded off in a daydream. He sat blinking, confused, as Miss Robards said, "You haven't answered a question correctly in over a week. If you're still not feeling well, you'd better go see the nurse."

Jon said, "I'm sorry. No, I'm fine."

"Continue then."

Jon found the place and read:

Give me the daggers. The sleeping and the dead
Are but as pictures. 'Tis the eye of childhood that
fears a painted devil . . .

His voice trailed off. He frowned.

" 'The sleeping and the dead are but as pictures,' "
Miss Robards said. "What does that mean?"

Jon blinked at her and said, "The spirit lives."

She hesitated. "What?"

"In sleep or death. The spirit lives."

She looked at him oddly, frowning, and then said,
"Jane, what's your interpretation?"

Jon didn't hear Jane's answer. He was staring
strangely at the chalkboard, squinting, blinking, lost in
thoughts of his own.

". . . As the record shows," Mr. Worthington droned
on, his paunch almost touching the face of Steven
Boggs, who sat in the front row grinning, "no other
country offers such opportunity for advancement or
personal freedom as America. . . ."

The bell rang, jolting Jon out of his dream. History
class was over. In the jumble of noise—kids' voices,
chairs scraping the floor, books slamming shut—he
rose, went out the door. One more period, hygiene. He
could sleep through that.

As soon as he entered the locker room the hand grabbed his collar, yanking him off his feet. Carl Renniger:
his cold gray eyes.

"Hey Pee-Tree, you better start drinking coffee or
taking Geritol, man. You're falling asleep all the time.
Miss Robards doesn't like it. I don't like it either. I
didn't like it at all when you fell asleep last week during
memory lessons."

Kids opened lockers, stashed books, took gym suits
out, ignoring Jon, who choked, turned red. "That was a
nasty trick, Pee-Tree. Real nasty."

Sonny Richardson came out of nowhere, face like
steel. "You ever gonna pull that shit again?"

Jon shook his head. "No, never! I promise!"

Carl loosened his grip and Jon's feet were back on the

floor. "You get tomorrow's math to me by nine o'clock."

"Okay," Jon gasped. "Okay, I will."

"And me and Bruce and Randy want biology papers. They're due in three weeks."

Jon swallowed. "Okay . . . all right."

"And history papers too."

"History!" Jon cried. "But I can't—"

Carl tightened his grip again. "You will," he said through harsh, curled lips. "Or else."

Jon prayed that Matt would come. They were scared of Matt, he'd make them stop. But even if Matt came he'd still have to do the papers. But he couldn't, he didn't have time, he had to fly!

Sonny Richardson stared, his face so close Jon felt his breath. "We missed you at the dance the other night."

"I . . . can't dance," Jon said. "I don't know how."

"Can't dance, falls asleep. We gotta do somethin' about that, Renniger."

Carl grinned. He held Jon tight, Jon smelled an odd burnt smell and quickly Sonny's hand was down his back. Then Carl let him go.

And his back was burning. In panic he slapped himself, jumped up and down, yelped, ran in circles.

"Hey," Sonny said, "I thought you couldn't dance."

Jon beat at his back, shirt snapping and squirming with fire. Kids laughed. Jon's left hand stung, and a smoldering scrap of black fell onto the floor.

Carl clapped. "Hey, all right, Petrie, the Firecracker, a brand new dance."

The bell rang loudly, kids walked off. Carl said, "You think you're awake now, Petrie? You think you'll remember what I told you now?"

Back stinging, hot, Jon said, "Yes. Yes!" His eyes were wide and wild.

"Hey, don't get all steamed up," Carl said. "Just do what you have to do." He sucked at his teeth, then he and Sonny left.

Jon went to the boys' room. The firecracker had burned a hole through his shirt; the skin through the

hole was red and raw. He went to hygiene, the pain stabbing into the hollow between his shoulder blades. He sat
there gritting his teeth against the pain and thought, It
starts again. As I knew it would. But I can't afford to
work for them now; I have too much to learn! I have to
fly. He squinted, pressed his lips together. They think
they're tough. If they had to fight the Monarchs. . . .

But the Monarchs had nothing to do with this world,
the world of Aronson High. Two more months of this
world and he would be free for the summer. He had to
keep thinking that. Stay out of their way, do the work
that they wanted—and then he'd be free.

But at home, instead of doing work for them, he flew.
The pain in his back was instantly gone, he felt powerful, calm again, in complete control of his fate. He
knew it was just an illusion, and yet it sustained him.

But he couldn't live on illusions. He had to deal with
harsh reality, with *them*, had to stop them from
wrecking his life. But how? When he flew he was
nothing but air, a ghost, a shadow boy without arms or
hands or legs or even voice. How could a shadow stop
anything real? That fantasy he'd dreamed about came
back again. He flew, and thought and thought.

Back in his body he took his burned shirt off and hid
it in his drawer. He would never mention the incident to
his parents, his father would have a fit.

After dinner he flew again, sat next to Meg in her
living room as she watched TV. Oh Meg, he thought, I
love you so much. Why do you watch this nonsense?
You're much too good for this. When she went to bed
he flew to the Monarchs and watched them drink and
joke and spar with each other, watched Carlos and
beautiful Rita go off upstairs together and—no, he
didn't want to watch that, and he turned away, flew
home.

He took his burned shirt out of his drawer and spread
it across his desk. Then he took his Magic Markers and
drew a butterfly—bright orange and black—on the
yellow cloth. Above the butterfly he wrote in orange,
Monarchs, then slipped the shirt on. A thrill went

through him. He picked up a pencil and parried with Eeyore. "I'm a Monarch, Eeyore, an' I gonna *stick* you, man." The donkey sat there, ear over one eye, emitting its strange blue glow. "I gonna break you *up*." He laughed a sad laugh, tossed the pencil down, then sat on his bed, his head in his hands. "Oh Eeyore, help me, help me. . . ."

CHAPTER FIFTEEN _____

He slept right through the alarm. He woke up groggy without any appetite, washed hurriedly, got dressed.

He couldn't say he was sick again; his mother would take him to the doctor. While she drank her coffee in the family room, staring out through the sliding glass doors at the freshly filled pool, he noiselessly slipped through the kitchen, sneaked through the laundry room, went out through the garage.

First period was underway, and the locker room was empty. He opened his locker, reached for a book—and remembered: the math assignment for Carl! He hadn't even looked at it. There wasn't any time to do it now, he had to be in art. But Carl was in art too, would ask him for the math—and he'd be dead. He looked at the clock on the wall. Fifteen minutes till the period ended. He had to think of something—fast!

An idea came to him. It was kind of crazy, and yet. . . . He searched under lockers, searched in the trash can next to the wall. If he could find a piece of string, used chewing gum, some wire . . .

A paper clip, one of the big kind. Straighten it out and it just might work. He picked it out of the trash and went to his locker.

Quickly he took his sneakers and gym suit off the locker floor and crammed them onto the shelf. He lifted the latch on the door, put his padlock through it, clicked it shut, and let the latch down again. Then he crawled inside the locker and closed the door.

In the light that came through the vent he wound the paper clip around the latch. If somebody gave the door a pull it might give way, but that ought to hold it for now. He leaned against the back of the locker, closed his eyes, and thought of Lucifer—and flew through the locker door.

Invisible now, he examined the padlock on the latch. If you looked real hard, you could see that the door wasn't locked. Well, nothing he could do about that, he'd have to take his chances. He wished he could give the door a yank to see if the wire would hold, but he was a shadow again with no worldly power. The bell went off. Doors opened in the hall. Loud voices, then the herd of kids.

Matt Wilson had the locker next to Jon's. Jon watched him work his combination: 32-4-8. Matt yanked, the lock didn't open. He dialed again—32-4-8—and pulled. The lock gave way.

How interesting, Jon thought. I can know everybody's combination. Matt Wilson, 32-4-8. He watched Bruce Hodges, memorized his combination too. He did the same for Sonny Richardson and Randy Hankins, flying over them, laughing, shouting, "Hit me. Come on, just try, I dare you to! Hit the shadow boy! Go on!"

Carl Renniger slammed his books in his locker and cursed. "That Petrie faggot son-of-a-bitch! Third day this week he didn't show up, and now I don't have any math."

Bruce Hodges said, "You give him the word about biology and history?"

"He does those papers or he's gonna *die*."

"He'll do them," Bruce said with his slow cruel grin.

The locker room emptied. Jon flew back into his locker and entered his body and crouched there, sweating, his heart beating quickly. When all was quiet he opened the door, took down his books, crawled back in the locker, and fastened the door again, and holding the work to the light that came through the vent, he did the math assignment.

He went to math class, waited outside the door for Carl, slipped him the homework. "It's a damn good thing," Carl muttered between his teeth. "First thing in the morning from now on, faggot, you understand?"

When lunchtime came, Jon was much too excited to eat. He hid in his locker again, wound the wire around the latch. For once in his life he was glad he was skinny and short. Bruce and the others would never be able to hide in their lockers like this, they wouldn't fit. The thought of Bruce attempting to wedge his bulk through his locker door made him smile.

He flew down the hall above everyone's head, saw Meg, saw Chuckie limping toward the cafeteria, toward lunch, the only part of school he really liked.

Miss Robards hurried down the hall. She went into Mr. Diedrick's office and closed the door. Impulsively, Jon flew in after her. She walked up to Mr. Diedrick's desk. He stood, came around to her.

And then they were holding each other and kissing each other hard. Jon gasped. Miss Robards and Mr. Diedrick! Mr. Diedrick was married and had three children; one of them, a little girl, had come to school one day. Jon hung there, motionless, as Mr. Diedrick's stubby hands caressed Miss Robards's back. They kissed again.

The dirt in the wall, Jon thought. Again, the dirt in the wall. He sniffed derisively, flew past Miss Robards and Mr. Diedrick, flew out the window.

There was Sonny Richardson down on the sidewalk, eating a cherry Tastypie and drinking a Coke. He swaggered along, stuffing his mouth, walked quickly, turned the corner. Went another two blocks and was on the edge of the Henderson business district. He tossed the Coke can into the street and lit a cigarette, stepped into the phone booth outside Gordon's Drugs.

Jon swooped down close so he could hear. Sonny dialed, eyes half shut, the cigarette loose in his mouth. He waited there, receiver to his ear, then said in a threatening voice: "There's a bomb in your school. It's set to go off in an hour."

He hung up, smiling, stepped out of the booth, muttered under his breath, "Have fun, Diedrick—you prick." He smoked, inhaling deeply, started back to school.

By the time Jon got back, all the kids were lined up outside. He flew to his body and waited there in the locker. The terrible thought went through his mind that Sonny really *had* planted a bomb and he would be blown to pieces along with the school, but he forced himself to stay calm.

There had been no bomb before, he told himself, and there wouldn't be one now. It was all a hoax, it was Sonny's way of driving Mr. Diedrick up the wall, of paying him back for doing away with the cigarette break. He remembered them talking about getting Diedrick for that, and Sonny had said, "There are ways." This was one of those ways.

He waited, and finally the bell went off bringing everyone in again. He opened his locker, stepped out, and hid at the end of the row, blending in with the crowd.

"No Miss Robards—you're wrong."

It was odd to hear himself say the words. He had never talked back to a teacher before. But he'd never been as angry with one before as he was with Miss Robards. Mr. Diedrick was just like his father. Yes, just like his father, a cheater, deceiver, and with Miss Robards. Just look at her there, so smug, as if she were innocent. If the rest of the class had seen what he'd just seen, she'd never teach again. Over the years his teachers had said a thousand foolish things and he'd never dared talk back, but he would with Miss Robards, oh yes, he would with her. Kids stared.

"Lady Macbeth is a monster. She thinks human kindness is a quality to be despised."

Miss Robards was clearly annoyed. She said, "What she's obviously doing is reacting—maybe overreacting—to her husband's weakness. She says those things to convince him to kill the king.''

''She has no *conscience*,'' Jon insisted. Just like you, he thought. Do you know how Mr. Diedrick's wife and children will feel when they learn the truth? Do you care? ''A person without a conscience can do all kinds of horrible things—betray, cheat, even''—his eyes turned dark—''even *kill*.''

Miss Robards looked at him strangely. The bell went off. In the noise Jon muttered again, ''Even kill,'' and nobody heard. Miss Robards said, ''We'll continue this discussion tomorrow, class—if we feel it's worthwhile.''

Jon flew during history class. The first two classes he'd cut—biology and art—were the first he'd ever cut in his life, and now he was cutting history. He was just too tired to listen to boring Worthington. He flew down the hall to the principal's office. To the office of Diedrick the prick, the traitor supreme.

A meeting was going on. Mr. Geasly, the administrative vice-principal, Mr. Turnbull, the vice-principal in charge of discipline, and Miss Weller, the guidance counselor, were sitting there with serious faces and Mr. Diedrick was saying, ''He's making us look like fools. Every time he threatens us we hop like monkeys on a string. I'll be damned if I'll empty out this place again for a practical joke.''

Sue Weller said, ''But how do you know he's not setting us up? He calls in a couple of phony threats, then really plants a bomb and we don't evacuate—and then there's tragedy.''

Mr. Turnbull, gray-haired, thick and rugged-looking, said, ''If he's really going to plant a bomb, he's not going to call.''

''How do you *know* that?'' Sue Weller said.

Mr. Diedrick said, ''At Riverside and Wilksboro it followed the same pattern. The principal comes down on the kids for something and the bomb scares start. I take away the cigarette break, some clown decides this is how he can get me. As long as they can keep us jumping, they'll do it. There were six bomb threats in

Wilksboro before they wised up.''

"And stopped evacuating the school?" Sue Weller said.

"Exactly."

"I can't go along with it, it's just too risky."

Mr. Geasly, a weary-looking, paunchy man with rings below his eyes, said quietly, "I don't think we're dealing with building policy here, I think we're dealing with district policy."

"I agree with you, Bill," Diedrick said, "but the board hasn't *set* any policy. This is the first time we've ever *had* a bomb scare in this district. The board's supposed to take it up at their meeting, but that won't be for another three weeks. That's what I hear from Steinberg." Steinberg was superintendent of schools.

Sue Weller picked her finger. "I think the situation's important enough to warrant a special meeting of the board," she said.

"If you'd like to try to convince Steinberg of that," Diedrick said with a tight, snide smile, "be my guest."

Jon stayed for another ten minutes. They hashed the whole thing over again and decided nothing. Bored, he flew back to his locker and entered his body.

In study hall he did his math, then sat there, washed out, staring at his books. He thought of the meeting again and a wild, amorphous fantasy began to unroll in his mind. He was still in this dream when the bell went off, ending the day.

CHAPTER SIXTEEN _____

Every night for the next two weeks, Jon flew. He ate little, lost weight, his face became sallow and drawn, dark circles ringed his eyes. In school he was worn out and often confused. When his enemies asked for homework or money he gave it to them passively. Bored, he neglected assignments, cut classes, and flew from his locker.

He and Miss Robards got into an argument practically every day. It was now a game, a game he often won. He started quarreling with pompous-ass Worthington too. School was stupid, the teachers were narrow-minded fools. He failed a history test, two math tests, and an English test, and he didn't care. He just wanted the term to be over. Seven more weeks and it would end, and then he would fly all the time.

The world from the air was the real world now, the only world that mattered. Chuckie and Meg, his teachers, his enemies, his mother and father—they were the ones in the dream, the nightmare of flesh.

He watched his father with the woman—Joanna— again, watched to the point of vomiting, a cold dark hatred smoldering in his chest. He flew to the Monarchs night after night. They fought the Scorpions again, they broke into stores and stole TVs, they took the wallets of careless drunks and con men in the late-night streets, made "love" in the factory's shadows. They did terrible things: Broke the legs and slashed the cheeks of those they robbed, but Jon got used to it, and afterwards he

would fly to his bedroom and put on his Monarchs shirt
and tell Eeyore all he had seen.

In the darkness Eeyore always glowed, glowed
brighter as the nights went by. Or at least he *seemed* to
glow, Jon could never be sure, his eyes were funny now
sometimes. He wondered again if the donkey shared his
soul—absorbing it as the bow absorbed the spirit of the
archer till at last it could hit the target with a will of its
own. He thought long and hard about death. Did it
really exist? Or did only *change* exist? If he was a spirit,
then where were the spirits of those who had died? Why
didn't he ever see them when he flew? Maybe the dead
were ghosts forever and lived on a plane his shadow self
couldn't reach. Or maybe their spirits dissolved, were
gone for good. Jon couldn't imagine that. His spirit
seemed so safe, so immune from harm, so . . . per-
manent.

His early travels had been tentative, cautious, but
now he was unafraid, went everywhere: into houses in
the city's toughest sections, into hotel rooms on skid
row, into brothels, hospitals, bars—even into the
morgue. He saw everything, grew used to everything.
Things he had only heard about or read about he saw
firsthand: robbery, arson, murder, rape—all real, all
real and horrible, the world was just as horrible as he'd
always thought. The dirt in the walls, yes, the dirt in the
walls. Human nature was hopelessly flawed, diseased,
the world was beyond redemption. Someday he would
teach Meg to fly and they'd live in a different world.

He sat on the couch in Sue Weller's office, looking at
his hands.

"Jon, how can you say things are fine? You missed
four days of school last week, you cut class after class,
you argue constantly with Miss Robards and Mr.
Worthington and your grades this term are terrible. You
always did excellent work, you never had problems
before, what's happening?"

Jon stared at his index finger. Wouldn't you like to
find out, he thought. "I . . . don't know," he said.

Sue Weller sighed. "Jon, I'm going to have to call your parents in."

Jon looked up quickly, eyes wide. "Oh, please, Miss Weller, don't do that."

"I have to, Jon."

Sweat bloomed on Jon's nose. He pinched it away. He wanted to speak, but he didn't know what to say.

The day his father came, Jon hid in his locker and flew. As his father talked with Miss Weller, he listened to every word.

Doug Petrie said, "He's *always* been a quiet kid. Ever since he was born. Too quiet, in my opinion." He checked his watch. His meeting at Morgan Title Company was less than an hour from now and he couldn't waste much more time.

Sue Weller said, "Okay, but have you noticed any changes in him lately? Is he acting any differently?"

"Pretty much the same, as far as I can see. Still spends most of his time in his room. I've tried to get him out with other kids, but I can't spend my life on that."

Sue Weller frowned. "Do you and Mrs. Petrie do things with him? Go places? Enjoy any kind of activities together?"

Doug Petrie almost laughed. What the hell am I supposed to do with him? he thought. Go running around in some field with a butterfly net? "My wife has all she can do to take care of the house," he said. "She's not . . . in the best of health. As for myself, I work long and irregular hours. It's the nature of my job. I don't have a whole lot of time to spend with the kid. I tried to interest him in ball games but he didn't take to it." He checked his watch again.

Sue Weller picked her finger, looked up. "Mr. Petrie, I think it would be a good idea to have Jon see a psychiatrist."

He glared at her, face hard. "What? Why?"

"We see a *dramatic* change in him, Mr. Petrie. He's like a completely different kid. He talks back to teachers, he's failing tests, he's cutting classes. . . . And he just doesn't *look* good. He seems so *pale*."

"He's *always* been pale," Doug Petrie said. "Pale and quiet."

"Mr. Petrie, we're concerned."

A silence. Doug Petrie finally said, "I'll take him to the doctor, then."

"And what about—?"

"A psychiatrist? I don't know what the damn kid's up to, but I doubt if that's the answer. What Jonathan needs is some toughening up. I've been thinking of sending him to Harrington."

"Harrington Academy?"

"It's what he needs. He lets kids walk all over him, always has."

"But a military school for Jon. . . . I think he'd really be out of place in a setting like that."

Doug Petrie snickered. "I'm sure your years of experience have made you an expert, Miss Weller. You'll have to excuse me, I have an appointment." He grabbed his attaché case and stood up. "I'll find out what's going on with his schoolwork and take him to see the doctor."

Jon flew back to his locker quickly, anxious and afraid. The military school again. He thought his father had given up on that. He'd have to be very careful from now on, really watch his step. Act normal, that's what he needed to do, act perfectly normal.

It was horrible at dinner that night. Still not over her latest sneezing attack, his mother sat sniffling, picking at her steak, which she'd burned to a charcoal crisp. His red-faced father said to him, "I had to waste forty-five minutes because of you, do you realize that? My time is valuable, goddamn it! You just shut up in those classes and do what your teachers tell you!"

Jon had eaten one piece of burnt steak. It was lodged near his heart like a bullet.

"You always did your work before. What the hell's going on?"

"I . . . don't know. I got behind."

"Got *behind*? Well you damn well better get ahead, or you're going to Harrington! That school lets you do what you damn well please, no discipline!"

Jon wet his lips. "But Miss Weller said she didn't think that Harrington would be right for me."

"Miss Weller." His father sneered. "The expert on child psychology. Unmarried and what? Twenty-five years old?" He stared at Jon and said, "How do *you* know what she thinks about Harrington?"

Jon's face was suddenly hot. "She . . . talked to me," he said. "She told me her recommendations."

His father's steely eyes. "What are they?"

"A . . . psychiatrist," Jon said.

His mother looked up, a piece of charred meat on her fork. "A psychiatrist?" she said. "Whatever for?"

"That's what *I* want to know," his father said, his cheek bulging with food.

The meat was still poised on the fork in his mother's hand. "But I would agree with—" she looked at Jon vaguely "—what's the young lady's name?"

"Miss Weller."

"Oh yes. I'd agree with Miss Weller that Harrington is not the right place for Jon."

Doug Petrie slapped his utensils down on his plate. "Oh would you?" he said. "You're too sick to go to the school and talk to the guidance counselor, I have to take off from work, you can't even cook a goddamn steak without burning it, and you'd agree that Harrington isn't the place for Jon." He stood up angrily. "Well I say it *is* the place, and that's where he's going if he doesn't shape up damn fast! *Damn* fast!" He stormed out of the dining room and into the den. The door slammed shut.

Dr. Goss's schedule was full for the next three months. Jon was greatly relieved. He would not talk back in class anymore, he would get his homework in, he would make an effort to eat. Only a few more weeks of school to go; he'd force himself to act normal, and things would be fine. By the time the appointment with

Dr. Goss rolled around, it would still be summer and all this mess with school would have been forgotten.

But Wednesday afternoon something terrible happened.

Tuesday during study hall he had worked on the take-home test for Miss Robards's class. Bruce and Carl and Randy demanded copies, he just didn't have the time to copy it all three times by hand, he needed the time to fly, so after school he made three copies on the post office Xerox machine.

As the kids filed in at the start of English class, Bruce Hodges said, "Where is it, Petrie?" His back to Miss Robards, Jon opened his briefcase, reached inside, and handed the papers to Bruce. Bruce said between clenched teeth, "Not *here*, you asshole," then: "Hey, what the hell—? *Xeroxes,* what are you trying to pull?" Then the class was totally silent and Miss Robards was saying, "Bruce and Jonathan—bring those papers up here."

They went to the front of the room. Miss Robards took the papers, looked at them, and said triumphantly, "You two can meet me in Mr. Diedrick's office at two forty-five."

In the locker room after class Bruce grabbed Jon's arm and said, "You little prick! What's the big idea?"

"It'll be all right," Jon stammered. "I'll make it all right, I swear!"

"You better," Bruce said. "You damn well better, Petrie—or you're dead."

After school in the principal's office, Bruce sitting beside him, Jon explained his plan to make money by selling homework. The scheme had been entirely his idea. He had sold the test to a number of kids, but he wouldn't say who they were. Bruce was just one of many.

When he finished his story, the principal gave him a long, sanctimonious lecture on honesty and integrity, punctuating the air with his stubby hands. As he spoke, Jon pictured him kissing Miss Robards, running those hands down her back. Miss Robards sat there officiously, primly, nodding her head in agreement with what Mr. Diedrick said, as if he were just her boss and not her lover. She said she'd prepare a new test and discount the one she had given, and after another reprimand, Bruce was allowed to leave. Mr. Diedrick assigned Jon two weeks of detentions and then Miss Robards, wallowing in self-righteousness, told Jon he had to write a twenty-page paper on *Macbeth,* due the day the detentions ended.

So Jon didn't fly that afternoon or night but worked on the paper instead, his mind filled with anger and desperate wild thoughts. No afternoon flying for two weeks now because of Diedrick's detentions. Miss Robards's assignment would limit his night flying too, and he'd still have to do work for Bruce and the others, make all the extra copies by hand, and if he got caught they would call up his father and he would be sent to Harrington.

Too much to do, too much to think about, and everything so complex. But he knew one thing: He would run away before he would go to Harrington. He would die before he'd go there.

He worked late on the paper and after he finished he just couldn't sleep; his mind kept turning over, over, over. Half dreaming and half awake he saw the witches, saw Macbeth kill Duncan, saw the blood-smeared grooms, who looked like Bruce and Carl. *"Had he not resembled/My father as he slept, I had done't,"* said Lady Macbeth with wild eyes; and her father was his father, Douglas Petrie. Jon tossed and turned in a sweat, the images burning, burning. Then all was blood behind his eyes, and darkness fell.

He went through the next day half alive. They were laughing at him, angry with him, talking behind his back. Not just his enemies but others too. They had to do their *Macbeth* papers over again because of him. Selling Xerox copies of tests, how *weird.* Yes, I *am* weird, he thought—weirder than your narrow, regular real-world minds can imagine. He despised them all. As soon as school was over today he'd leave their world and fly. And fly tomorrow afternoon and all weekend too, because Monday the detentions began.

After school he was walking home impatiently and Chuckie was tagging along. Chuckie scoured the side of the road and came up with a baseball card. "Luh . . . Lee Mazilli!" he cried in delight. "Look, Jon."

Jon paid no attention, lost in thought. Chuckie shoved the card in front of his face and Jon snapped, "Do you think I care about stupid baseball players?" Then Meg was there.

He squinted at her, blinking, tried to smile. She said, "They take your money, don't they? Bruce and Randy and the rest. They aren't loans, they steal it. That's why you sold the test—because they take all your money."

He looked at her, in love, embarrassed. "It's not important," he said. "It's over now."

"Except for two weeks of detentions and an extra paper."

"I got caught doing something wrong," Jon said, "and I have to pay."

"But you did it because of Bruce and the others, and nothing happens to them. It isn't fair."

Jon smiled oddly. "The wrongdoer has to pay," he said.

"Buh . . . Bruce," Chuckie said, his face contorted, the baseball card tight in his hand. "I'd like to—*blast* him!"

Jon looked away. His face was sober, dark.

Meg said, "Hey Jon, I'm going down to Fogle's for a soda. Why don't you come along?"

Jon looked up, suddenly alive. He was dying to fly, but that could wait. Shyly he said, "Well, I have the paper to do."

"Come on, you can spare half an hour."

"I'll come along too!" Chuckie grinned.

Jon looked at him, then smiled at Meg. "Okay, I guess I can come."

The three of them walked past Evergreen Row and into Russelville. Jon practically floated. Soon he would ask Meg out again. After the English paper was done. If he had to, he'd get her mother's permission and they would go out on a date. He grinned.

Meg glanced at him, at his pale thin face, his odd smile. She thought of the afternoon before—at Fogle's, with Matt.

"He's been acting so *weird* these last few weeks. He falls asleep, he doesn't do his work, he looks so *tired*. And Xeroxing tests to sell them, he's just too smart for that."

"He's always been weird," Matt said.

"But something's happening."

"And how am I supposed to help?"

"Just talk to him," Meg said. "He likes you, Matty, he'll listen to you."

"Yeah, great, but what do I say?"

"Just let him know you're his friend, that you're willing to listen. Okay?"

Matt shrugged. "Hey, anything for you."

Jon wet his lips. This wasn't working out at all. He had come here to have a soda with Meg, and Matt was asking him all kinds of questions. Why didn't he mind his own business and just do his job? As if he could help. His mother and father and sister were crazy and he was a little crazy himself, that's what kids said. He was smart and nice and worked hard, but something was wrong with his mind. That's why Bruce and the rest were scared of him.

"It's Bruce and those other animals, isn't it?" Matt said. "You want me to talk to them?"

"No," Jon said quickly. "I can handle it myself."

"You sure?" Matt ran some water onto his sponge and squeezed it out. "There was a time in my life when I needed help," he said, "—and no one was there."

His sister. That terrible story. "No, really, Matt, I'm okay."

It was tempting to think of Matt talking to *them*, but it wouldn't help. It would only make things worse—like last time. As soon as Matt wasn't around they would punish him even more.

Meg said, "Jon, you can't let them push you around. You can't live that way."

Again, Jon felt embarrassed. He mumbled, "I'm all right," and thought; I'm more than all right, I can do things nobody else can do. Somehow you sense that and that's why you—

The door opened and Sonny and Bruce came in. They looked at Jon with snide smiles and Bruce said, "Petrie," with a sneer. They went to the pinball machines and Chuckie and Meg and Jon drank their sodas and Matt went back to work.

Jon finished his soda and ordered another he didn't want and sat there and waited till Sonny and Bruce had gone. He waited ten more minutes, then left with Chuckie, scared to death that somewhere ahead they would jump from the bushes and grab him.

But nothing happened. He made it home safely. Chuckie asked to come in but Jon said he had his English paper to do. Once in his room he said to his donkey: "She asked me down to Fogle's, Eeyore. It was almost a *date*. It would have been great if Matt wasn't there. I guess he only wants to help, but he ruined everything. And then *they* came." A dark cloud passed behind his eyes.

He thought about Meg through the silent dinner with his mother—Stouffer's macaroni and cheese again— then went back to his room and got nothing done on his paper.

He flew that night and Friday night and flew all weekend too. On Monday the detentions began. He swore to himself that he wouldn't fly till the two weeks were up and his English paper was finished.

But try as he would he could not keep his promise, and he flew every night, slept late, faked illness, and stayed out of school. Or he went to school late and dozed in class, flew from his locker, quarreled with teachers. He picked at his food, lost even more weight. At home he was in a daze, ignored his father until he screamed. Act normal, I have to act normal, he thought. But then he would fly and forget the normal world.

Every night after his travels he talked to Eeyore. I might not be exactly normal, he thought, but I'm . . . *all right*. There's nothing really wrong with me, no matter what anyone says. He no longer had any doubt that his donkey was charged with power, alive, he could feel it in every nerve. And now he would ask him things and listen patiently for his advice, strange thoughts crisscrossing in his head, strong images of Carlos and the Monarchs, city streets, the homes of strangers, flashing in back of his eyes.

CHAPTER SEVENTEEN _____

He didn't hand his *Macbeth* paper in on time. He had a terrible fight with Miss Robards and called her a toad and she sent him to the guidance office again.

Sue Weller was shocked by the way he looked: eyes dark, skin sallow, clothes disheveled, hair in tangles —and so *thin*. She spent over an hour with him and all he would answer was "Yes," "No," "Maybe," "I don't know." He sat there blinking, smiling oddly. She called his father again.

The psychiatrist's name was Schlosser. He and Doug Petrie had been in the army together. He was short and heavy with shiny, black, wavy hair, and a mole the size of a raisin graced the bridge of his nose. Jon stared at it as the doctor looked through the papers and said, "Dr. Musser found a mild anemia, otherwise your tests were normal. Are you taking the iron tablets?"

"Yes," Jon said, still staring at the mole.

"They'll turn your stool black, so don't be concerned." He smiled.

Jon mumbled, "Okay," embarrassed. He wondered what Dr. Schlosser had found amusing.

The psychiatrist leaned back, frowning, and said, "Jonathan, what do you see as the problem?"

Jon sat with his hands on his knees. He stared at one of them a long time and finally said, "I don't know."

"Well think for a minute. Things aren't going well at school. Why not?"

"They pick on me," Jon said without looking up.

"Who does?"

"A lot of people. But mainly four kids."

"How long have they been doing this?"

"Three years. Ever since I moved to Evergreen Row."

"What kinds of things do they do?"

"All kinds of things. Awful things."

"Such as?"

Jon shook his head and said, "I don't want to talk about that." He looked out the window, out at the buildings, saw himself flying, wished he could be out there.

The psychiatrist rubbed his chin with a hairy hand. He was smiling again. "All right, we don't have to talk about that. But why do you think they pick on you?"

"Because I'm weak," Jon said. "They think it's fun to pick on people who are weak."

"They pick on other kids too?"

"A little. But they pick on me the most."

"How come?"

"I guess . . . I'm weaker than the other kids. Or it must be more fun to pick on me." Or I'll do their homework for them, he wanted to say, but he couldn't tell him that. Dr. Schlosser knew his father, and he couldn't tell him anything he didn't want his father to find out.

"So you think it's more fun for them to pick on you than it is to pick on other kids."

"Yes."

"Why is that?"

"I don't know."

"Could it be because of the way you respond to their teasing?"

"Maybe so."

"So it isn't just them, would you agree?"

Jon looked up, dark eyes squinting. "What?"

"If you learned to respond in a different way, perhaps it wouldn't be so much fun for them anymore."

Jon continued to squint. He didn't say anything for a

while, then said in a soft voice, "Maybe not." He looked out the window at freedom again. He hated Dr. Schlosser.

"If they know they can get a rise out of you, they'll keep it up."

"Yeah."

"Would you like to work on that?"

Jon squinted harder, stared at the mole on the doctor's face. "On what?"

"On learning to respond a different way."

"Oh. . . . Yeah, I guess so."

Dr. Schlosser leaned forward again. "Good," he said with a horrible smile. "When something gets to the point where it makes you feel tired and lose your appetite and interferes with your schoolwork, it's time to do something about it."

Jon stared at him and thought: And what am I supposed to do—learn how to laugh when they're twisting my arm or making me kiss their feet or sticking firecrackers down my back?

"We'll have to talk about what your classmates actually do, then see how we can cope with it. Maybe we'll find that it's not such a terrible problem after all." Again that ugly grin. "It's how we respond to our pain that counts, how we handle it. We can learn from our pain, it can teach us to grow."

Jon simply sat there.

"Of course, if the situation is really bad—so bad you can't learn to cope with it—we'll have to think about alternatives. Your father mentioned Harrington. It's an option we'll have to consider."

The light from the window hurt Jon's eyes. Sharp jolts of fear shot into his arms and chest.

"I'll see you once a week and we'll see how it goes." He stood. "Nice meeting you, Jon."

Jon shook the extended hand. It was pudgy and soft and hairy and slightly damp. "Okay," he said, and dazed, he went to the door.

On the ride back home with his father he thought, So that was it—it was all a trap to get him into Harrington. They had been in the army together and now they were plotting to put him in military school. He would not be able to learn to respond in a different way to the torture, they knew he wouldn't, he'd fail, and they'd send him away.

He stared out the window, watching people and stores and cars go by in a blur. He would never go to Harrington, never, he'd find a way to keep Dr. Schlosser from sending him there. He would learn what he needed to know about Dr. Schlosser, and then. . . .

After school the next day he went home and flew downtown.

He hovered next to Dr. Schlosser, looked over his shoulder. The woman who sat in the chair he'd sat in yesterday went on about her husband, the terrible things he did to her, how he beat her up and pushed her down the stairs. Jon checked the calendar on the desk. Three more patients on the schedule, the last one, Meara, at eight. Under that, at the bottom of the page, was written "Marie."

Jon flew back home and entered his body, went to the bathroom, went downstairs for dinner.

He ate with his mother while his father screamed on the phone, "I want those people *out* of that goddamn place! It's coming down in two weeks, and that's *it*! I'm not having the whole goddamn project held up because two old farts won't move their asses! You get them out if you have to drag them out yourself!"

Jon left most of his meal on his plate and went to his room before his father sat down. He waited until eight-thirty, then flew downtown.

Dr. Schlosser came out of the building at nine-twenty-five. He walked to a restaurant called The Carriage Inn, ordered wine and a meal. Jon watched him, loathing the way he sucked at his food with his heavy lips, the way his pudgy hand held the glass of wine.

Dr. Schlosser finished his dinner, walked to the parking garage, got into a forest-green Mercedes, drove away. He went about a dozen blocks and parked on the street, checking the car doors twice to make sure they were locked. Jon followed him into the building, into the elevator, walked behind him into the apartment.

Marie was dark, with long black hair and dark brown eyes. She looked something like Rita, Carlos Medrano's girlfriend, but was older, quite a bit older, and her face had a hard and frightening quality that Rita's lacked. She was wearing a black shiny robe whose hem touched the floor. The door was no sooner shut than Dr. Schlosser dropped to his knees in front of her. Passionately and repeatedly, he kissed her feet.

Marie opened her robe and let it fall to the rug. She was wearing a tight black leather corset; at its border her breasts protruded, nipples red and hard. She was nude below, crotch dense with bushy black hair. She wore black leather boots that came to the midpoint of her ample, rippled thighs.

Dr. Schlosser held Marie's left leg and kissed its calf, kept kissing, moving higher, higher, as Marie said, "Lick, slave, lick!" Jon thought of Bruce and Randy and the rest: "Get over here, slave! Get down, slave, kiss my shoe!" Dr. Schlosser's stubby tongue was licking the band of thick flesh at the top of Marie's left boot. Then she shouted, "Enough!" in a voice that chilled Jon's blood. Dr. Schlosser stood up meekly —and Marie took off his clothes.

They went to the bedroom. Jon followed. "Down, slave!" Marie commanded, and the doctor fell onto the bed face down and stretched out his arms and legs spread-eagle fashion. Marie tied his wrists and ankles to the bedposts with strips of leather. He squirmed and softly moaned, his fat white buttocks writhing. Marie went to the closet and took out the whip.

Jon remembered the movie *To Love Forever*. It seemed so long ago. It had sickened him then, but he'd seen so much these last few weeks that now he watched emotionlessly as Marie brought the whip down again and again and again.

Dr. Schlosser cried out and begged for mercy. Red welts appeared, then blood. But his cries were not cries of pure pain but of pain and pleasure both. His words came back: We can learn from our pain, it can teach us to grow. Rage congealed in Jon's gut. Marie threw the whip aside and ran her long white fingers over the raised and swollen flesh as the doctor whimpered, "Yes, oh yes, Marie," and then she was in the bed and straddling him with her leather-clad legs and riding him like a horse as he writhed and groaned.

Jon flew through the wall, went home.

Eeyore was glowing brightly when he arrived; the room was bathed in blue. Jon smiled, laughed a little as he said, "He will never send me away. Not him, not Dr. Schlosser, never." And he lay in the blue light, whispering plans to the donkey that sat on the shelf, his childhood toy, his soul mate, his dearest friend. Hours passed; still babbling, he fell asleep.

He was wrecked the next day. He argued again with Miss Robards, but managed to keep himself from calling her names. In the locker room he nodded absently when Matt said hi. The hours were long, so terribly long, and he fell asleep in hygiene class. At last the final bell went off.

He was leaving the building when Bruce Hodges grabbed him and dragged him into the boys' room.

The bitter smell of urine was strong in his nose. Bruce said, "Remember what's due tomorrow, Petrie?"

Jon squinted. "No," he said, shaking his head.

"Biology paper, asshole. *Three* biology papers."

Cold sweat broke out on Jon's brow. "But . . . I can't," he stammered. "I *can't.*"

"What the hell do you mean you can't?"

"If they catch me doing work for you I'll be expelled!"

Bruce tightened his grip on Jon's arm. His beady eyes glared. "Just do it, slave. Do it or you're dead."

At home Jon worked in a furor, slamming books around and grinding his teeth and staring at Eeyore through squinting dark eyes. He had to do his own biology and history papers too, he had to finish his paper on *Macbeth*, and here he was working for *them* again. He read, he wrote, he crossed it out, he crunched it up and threw it in the trash.

He sat there, desperate, dull with fatigue and said,

"Eeyore, it isn't fair and I'm just not going to *take* it! I can't do this, I have to fly. I'm missing so much, I can't afford to waste my time like this." He pressed his lips together, said, "They don't understand. Father and Mother, Miss Weller and Dr. Schlosser, they all just think—"

Then his door came open and his father was standing there.

Doug Petrie's face was furious. "What the hell's going on in here?"

Jon choked. He hadn't even heard his father come home. He swallowed hard and said, "Biology paper. I'm working on . . . biology. Sometimes I talk to myself."

His father's eyes narrowed. " 'They don't understand?' Is that the kind of thing you say when you work?"

Jon's heart was in his throat, the words were gone.

"You were talking to *that*!" Doug Petrie shouted, pointing to the shelf. "Talking to a baby toy like a goddamn two year old!" He stood in front of Jon, face livid, hard, and said, "Let me give you a piece of advice: Stop feeling sorry for yourself. And never *never* let me catch you talking to that baby toy again—or you'll pack your bags for Harrington that *minute*, do you understand?"

"I . . . understand," Jon stammered.

"You damn well better. And you listen to what Dr. Schlosser tells you and do what he says. Shape up, goddamn it, shape up!"

When his father left he lay down on the bed. His pulse beat quickly, softly, his temples throbbed. He thought; Yes, listen to Dr. Schlosser. He saw Marie, the whip, the lacerated flesh. Yes, Father, I'm sure he can teach me some wonderful things, the kinds of things you know about. Is that what makes him normal, makes you normal? Is that what keeps you out of Harrington?

He sat at the dinner table in total silence, forcing himself to eat. The food seemed gross and sickening; he left half the steak and all of the mashed potatoes and nearly all of the peas. He said he didn't want dessert and his mother frowned, his father cursed, he went to his room and flew.

The Monarchs broke into a warehouse and stole five color TVs. No alarms went off, no cops came, it was dull. Afterwards they sat around, smoked dope, joked quietly.

Jon followed Carlos and Rita upstairs. Rita told Carlos again he'd get caught someday; she was scared. Carlos shouted, "You want me to buy the U.S.A. false dream!—The dream my old man bought, the land of opportunity. You know what the land of opportunity gets you? It gets you an early grave! Poverty and an early grave, that's all!" He said some terrible things to her, she cried, and Jon felt sorry for her. She wanted the best for Carlos, he shouldn't treat her that way. Then Carlos was calling her *pajarita* and other words Jon didn't know, and soon they were down on the floor and kissing, Carlos was on top of her, and Jonathan flew back home.

He got back after 3 A.M. The room glowed blue. He thought of that afternoon, his father storming in, invading his sacred space. He saw the biology books on his desk and felt sick. He would finish the paper for Bruce—he had to. Exhausted, he turned on the lamp and worked, worked hard till he fell asleep, his head on the desk, the light still on, and Eeyore staring down from the shelf above.

CHAPTER EIGHTEEN _____

Half awake and his mind a blur, the kids in the locker room swirling around him, he handed the paper to Bruce, who took it without a word. He went to art and dozed through the lecture, scrawled a drawing, went to biology class.

Bruce stopped him before he got there and said: "What the fuck are you trying to pull?"

Jon looked at him baffled, frightened. "What do you mean?"

"That goddamn paper's no good."

"No . . . good?"

"Don't try to play dumb with me, Pee-Tree."

Jon wet his lips. "I'll fix it," he said. "I . . . wasn't feeling well last night. I didn't mean anything, I'll do it over."

"I have to copy it tonight, she wants it tomorrow. It's gonna be late because of you!"

"I'll fix it at lunch," Jon said. "I swear I will."

Bruce smiled. "Slave, you're gonna *die* at lunch."

Jon went through the rest of the morning dazed with fear. The eyes of Bruce and Carl and Randy, watching, watching. In spite of his terror he fell asleep twice. He gave two wrong answers in math, then went to history class instead of French, where he sat for five minutes before Mr. Worthington pointed out his mistake.

In French he asked to be excused, then hid in his locker so Bruce couldn't find him. When the shouting and slamming of locker doors died, he flew.

He found Bruce out in the park, near the luncheonette, talking to Sonny. Bruce said, "I don't know where the bastard went, but I'll get him for this. I'll teach him a lesson he'll never forget."

Sonny sucked on his cigarette with sleepy eyes. "Got any ideas?"

Bruce smiled. "I think we ought to go out to the quarry this afternoon."

"What for?"

"Bridge inspection. And a dress rehearsal. You've heard of walking the plank?"

Sonny smoked. "When we gonna take the creep out there?"

"Tomorrow. We'll give him a lift after school. He's gonna shit himself."

"It's a long way down, man," Sonny said.

"Hey, Petrie's an expert on the ropes," Bruce said. They both laughed.

Jon hovered beside them, listening to every word. They were going to make him walk across the rope bridge. They would kidnap him and force him onto the bridge. Once he was out there—

They would shake it, cut it, wreck it, and he would fall. He shivered, sick.

He would stay home tomorrow. They wouldn't get him, he just wouldn't come to school. Then he thought; If it isn't tomorrow it'll be some other day, sooner or later they'll take me there, there's no escape. His mind was filled with desperation and fear. I have to stop them, I *have* to, he thought.

Destroy the bridge. Today. Before they can get there, destroy the bridge, and they'll have to change their plans.

He had a dentist's appointment after school. He would cut last period, study hall, go to the quarry and wreck the bridge, then go to the dentist. Tomorrow, Friday, he'd stay out of school and do their biology papers. He'd work on their history papers all weekend and maybe by Monday he'd have enough done that they wouldn't still want to punish him. If they did, the bridge scheme would be out, they'd have to try something else—unless they wanted to build a whole new bridge. He'd hide in his locker on Monday, fly again and learn their plans. He'd fly every day from now until school let out, keep one step ahead of them, always. The thought of it exhausted him. He couldn't let them waste his time like this! But he had no choice.

Suddenly a vague apprehension seized him. Not fear of *them*, but a sense of immediate danger, a feeling like—

That time his mother came into his room when he was out of his body. A feeling just like that. Something was wrong in the locker room! He had to get back!

While Jon was spying on Bruce and Sonny, Matt Wilson arrived at school. Like Jon, he had stayed up late. He had worked on his chemistry paper three nights in a row, going right to his room after finishing up at Fogle's. Last night he had stayed up till three, had forgotten to set the alarm, and had slept until almost eleven.

Fifth period was halfway gone by the time he got to school. He checked in at the office, got permission to go to his locker.

In the empty locker room he worked the combination, pulled. The lock didn't open. He dialed again, pulled harder. Nothing happened. He muttered under his breath and tried again. Again no good. This goddamn lock had given him fits all year! In frustration he yanked it viciously. It opened with a snap, the row of lockers quivering. And the door to the locker next to his, Jon Petrie's locker, slowly opened too.

Matt stood there, numb.

Jon slumped against the wall of his locker, limp, jaw loose. A line of drool ran down his chin and neck and onto his shirt. His eyes were rolled up into his head so only the whites were showing.

A strangled sound escaped Matt's throat. He whispered, "Oh my God!" and then in a flash it was back. . . .

"I can get you the money in a couple of weeks. I'll save it up from my paper route."

Denise smiled sadly. "Hey, it's okay, kid. I'm all right now." "You sure, Denise?" "I'm okay, kid, don't worry." And after school he ran upstairs to change his clothes and there she was, the dark blood soaking into the splintered wood, the gun still there in her hand. And her eyes: rolled back in her head like that, all white—like these eyes, Jonathan Petrie's eyes.

Matt choked the memory back. The room closed in. He ran.

Jon saw him racing down the hall. He saw the open locker door and gasped. Quickly he entered his body, stepped out of the locker. The wire that held the latch shut was there on the floor. He cursed himself. How stupid, still using that paper clip after all this time! In anger he threw the wire across the room. Then Matt was there with Miss Weller.

"Jonathan! Are you all right?"

Jon feigned a puzzled look. "All right? Why sure, Miss Weller."

"Why were you in your locker?"

"*In* my locker?" Jon said frowning. "I wasn't *in* my locker."

"Matt said, "I *saw* you there!"

Jon's knees were shaking. "*In* my locker? I just got here, I just opened my locker, I wasn't *in* it."

Matt's eyes were wild. His breath was coming hard. "Jon, you were in that locker and you know it!"

"Matt, I wasn't, I swear!" Cold sweat coated his forehead. "I just came in to get my English book!"

Sue Weller said, "You know you're supposed to get permission to go to your locker when class is in session, don't you?"

Jon's heart was pounding, pains attacked his chest. "I'm sorry. I won't forget again."

"You're sure you're all right?"

"I'm fine, Miss Weller—honest I am."

"You don't want to see the nurse?"

"Oh, no."

"Well where should you be?"

"At lunch."

"You better get there then."

Jon hurried down the hall.

Sue Weller said, "And where do you belong now, Matt?"

Matt stared at nothing, wet his lips. "In English," he said. He looked at her intently, said, "Miss Weller, I swear to God—"

"He says he's all right. If he doesn't want to see the nurse it's up to him."

"All you could see was the whites. . . . He looked *dead*." A look of terror crossed his face, his eyes were glazed. He stood there staring, motionless.

"Matt?"

The memory snapped. He looked at her.

"How's your scholarship paper coming?"

"Oh . . . okay, I guess."

"Why don't you stop by and talk about it sometime?"

He nodded. "Yeah, maybe I will." He wet his lips again and said, "I better get to class. Sorry I bothered you."

Mr. Worthington sprang a surprise quiz in history class. He handed out paper twenty minutes before the end of the period, and everyone got to work. Jon's mind was obsessed with the quarry, the bridge. He quickly scrawled the answers and looked at the clock. Its second hand turned slowly and he read the manufacturer's name, Seth Thomas, over and over again. "Time's up," Mr. Worthington finally said. "Pass your papers to the front of the room."

Mr. Worthington straightened the papers. Feet shuffled and voices snickered, hands reached under seats for books. Seth Thomas, Seth Thomas. The bell rang shockingly. Chairs creaked, the room was alive with sudden talk, and clutching his books Jon hurried out of the room.

Near the boys' room Matt Wilson grabbed him,

squeezed his arm. "What's going on?" he said. "Tell me what's going on and tell me fast!"

Jon's throat was swollen, stuck. He quivered. "Let me go!"

Matt glared. "I saw you in that locker, Jon. That wasn't my imagination, I *saw* you there!"

"Let go of my arm!"

Matt tightened his grip. He shoved Jon up against the wall. "Listen, Jon, I'm not kidding around!"

Time ticked away. Sweat rolled down Jonathan's face. Soon study hall would start. "I have to get to class!" he cried.

"I don't want to hurt you, Jon, but—"

"Here comes Geasly," Jon gasped.

The vice-principal, sad-faced, slow, was coming down the hall. Matt let Jon go and stood there glaring, dark eyes filled with bitterness.

The vice-principal, blandly, softly, said, "All right, Petrie, get to class. Wilson, you come with me."

Jon hurried around the corner, went outside.

Quickly he went down the sidewalk, away from the school, certain a hundred eyes were watching him. Again he cursed himself for his stupidity: using that foolish paper clip to keep his locker shut, how *dumb*, and now he had Matt Wilson mad at him. Mad and confused, mad and worried. He wished he could tell him the truth, but that was impossible, out of the question. It would ruin everything.

Once he was out of sight of the school, he began to run. Soon he was out of breath, his side hurt sharply, he stopped.

His body. How clumsy and fragile it was. If he flew he could make the quarry in no time at all and without any effort. How stupid to be tied down by muscle and bone and blood. But only flesh could do what he had to do now.

He cut through the path at the foot of the hill, he ran through brush and trees, a field. The air was hot and dry. He was sweating profusely, the sun burned into his skin. He stopped for a second, gasping, heart pounding, and checked his watch. Forty minutes left in last period. He thought of time ticking away in school, the bell going off and Bruce and Sonny jumping in Sonny's car and heading for the quarry. He forced himself to run again, down a hill through jagged brush, around a marsh, across another field. Then down the narrow path to the quarry, and then he was at the rope bridge.

He stood there, gasping, faint with heat. Last period was almost over now. He was due at the dentist's in half an hour. He had to hurry. God, there wasn't time!

Ropes anchored the bridge to trees. He would undo the ropes on this side of the gorge and the bridge would collapse. He wished he could take the path around the gorge, untie the other ropes, and send the bridge to the quarry floor, but there wasn't time.

He hid his books in the bushes and hurried to one of the anchor ropes. It was thick, the knot was hard and tight. He pulled with his feeble fingers, cursing his body's weakness.

He worked on the knot for ten minutes, getting nowhere. School was over, they were in the car, they would be here soon! If only he had a hatchet, a knife!

The rope made angry red marks on his skin. He pried at the knot with a stick, pulled back with all his might. He felt the rope give just a little, pulled again. Felt movement again. He forced his thumb into the space that the stick had made. Come on, come on. . . . Yes! It was coming loose! His shoulders ached, his face was red, a hard hot pressure pounded at his skull.

Something gave and he fell back hard. The end of the knot was free! Quickly he got to his knees, set to work again. Now it was easier, now he could get it. But another knot as hard as this to untie before the bridge would fall—and no time, no time!

Suddenly he held his breath. He thought he'd heard—

Voices! He listened, fingers frozen on the rope. Someone was coming down the path! Cold needles of fear stabbed into his chest. Like a fox pursued by hounds, he ran and flung himself behind a boulder near the quarry's edge.

The voices, loud, twigs snapping under boots. It was them, it was Sonny and Bruce. They were already here! He pressed himself against the boulder's hard rough face. Oh no, oh God, they would catch him, he was finished. He closed his eyes and swallowed hard, sweat salty on his lips. He heard Bruce say: "Make everything happen quick. Don't let him think. I'll be first, he'll be in the middle, you'll be last. We'll just keep walking fast and keep on talking to him, see? Keep telling him about the butterfly, where we saw it and all that shit. Just keep walking along, then we get to here."

Slowly, every muscle tensed, Jon turned his head. Out of his blurred left eye he saw them. Not twenty feet away was Sonny: his shaggy hair, his biceps hard and smooth below his turned-up sleeves. Beside him was Bruce—heavy, lumbering, leering, hands stabbing the air as he spoke: "I cross the bridge first, he's right behind. When I get to the other side, I turn around real fast and block him off. You block him off at your end and he's trapped. Then we start rocking him—just a little, then more and more."

Sonny grinned. "We'll make the creep turn green. But what if he falls?"

"If he falls, he's dead."

"You're goddamn right. Then what?"

"Then we untie one of the ropes and it looks like an accident. He was out here looking for a butterfly, he walked across the bridge and one of the ropes came loose. Hey, we'll just shake him up a little, he's not gonna fall. Okay, you ready? Let's run through it."

Sonny squinted. "Wait a second."

"What?"

"I heard something—over there."

Jon flattened himself against the rock. Its edges dug into his back. The sweat on his face was suddenly slimy, cold.

"Over where?" Bruce said.

"By the rock."

Silence. Jon's heart was pounding at his ribs, his breath roared through his ears.

Bruce said, "I don't hear anything."

Again, dead silence. Suddenly a squirrel ran past Jon's feet and scurried into the brush. Jon's heart seemed to swell and stop.

"A squirrel," Bruce said, and he laughed.

Jon closed his eyes and swallowed hard, almost in tears. He kept himself rigid against the rock.

"Okay, let's try it," Bruce said.

Jon slowly turned his head again, the rock pressing into his skull. Out of his burning moist left eye he first saw Sonny's arm, then all of Sonny, then Bruce.

Bruce said, "I'm first, he's in the middle, you're last." Walking forward quickly he said, "I go out on the bridge—"

The loosened knot unraveled. The bridge dipped sharply, Bruce's eyes went wide. Off balance he clawed the air—then noiselessly he fell.

Jon whirled to the other side of the boulder, stared into the gorge. Bruce's skull hit ledge, splashed blood on stone. His body bounced, it hit again, it rolled, turned, twisted, flew, sent dust and gravel into the hot dry air, and then lay still.

Sonny stood on the edge of the gorge, his muscles taut, his features paralyzed. His wide eyes stared. Then quickly he turned and ran.

Jon hid in the bushes and flew. He dived to the quarry floor. He hovered over the mangled body, examined the gashed, contorted face, the shinbone sticking out of the flesh of the weirdly angled right leg. He watched thick blood ooze slowly out of the crooked mouth and over the dusty rocks.

He couldn't believe it. It had happened so fast. One minute Bruce was alive and now he was dead. And . . . I killed him, Jon thought. I loosened the knot—and killed him! But I didn't mean to! I was only trying to save myself, I never meant—

He turned away, flew up to the bushes, and entered his body again. He sat there, staring at nothing. It was all an accident, an accident, I never meant for him to die.

Then a shiver of gladness went through him. Bruce Hodges dead! He'll never bother me again! He braced himself against a tree, stood up. The broken bridge swayed gently in the breeze. His mind was jumbled, jagged, thoughts merged, burst. He blinked, he checked his watch. The dentist, he thought. I have to get to the dentist, I'm late. He picked up his books in a daze, and then he was out in the sun and running, running as hard as he could.

He came out on the sidewalk, sweating, gasping, the image of Bruce burning into his mind, the sight of him falling, his blood oozing onto the stone. And there in front of him like a mirage—was Meg.

"Hi, Jon. Where'd you get to last period?"

His mouth was dry. His lips seemed gummy, stuck. "I . . . had to leave early," he said. "—To go to the dentist."

"You already finished?"

"What? Oh, no, I didn't go yet. Had to run home first."

"I *guess* you ran," Meg said, "you're sweating like mad." The sun was bright on her golden hair; it dazzled him. "How come you didn't leave your books at home?"

Jon's mind was shattered, numb. "Oh. I thought . . . that maybe he couldn't take me right away and I'd have some time to do homework." He licked his lips. "Well, listen, Meg, I'd like to talk, but I'm late. I'll see you later."

As he hurried away he thought; What a fool I am! Why did I come out here? I should have taken the back way into Russelville! But criminals do those things. Their minds don't work right and that's why they get caught. He stopped and closed his eyes in the heat, the sun beating down on his head. It was an accident, he thought, an accident, I only meant to wreck the bridge! *They* are the criminals, not me!

He was fifteen minutes late, but it didn't matter, Dr. Chester was running behind. He sat in the waiting room and opened his history book. The words meant nothing.

All he could see was Bruce, his skull smashing into the rock, his broken body limp on the quarry floor. It was lying there now in the sun, the blood dried brown. His parents didn't know yet, nobody knew except Sonny. The question was, would Sonny tell anyone? If he did, they might hold him responsible.

When Jon was in the padded chair, the bright light shining on his face, Dr. Chester said, "This might hurt Jon. Do you want novacaine?" And Jon said, "No. I'll just relax the best I can." And just before Dr. Chester started to drill, Jon closed his eyes and flew.

He was out of the world of pain again.

If only he could stay out all the time! But he needed his body, he had to take care of his body, at least for now. Sometimes he thought: What if flying develops in stages—like the stages in a butterfly's life. Larva, pupa. . . . The day might come when his body would be superfluous. What a wonderful day that would be.

He flew out of the office and into the park at the corner of Main and Trask. He was perfectly calm again. He watched kids play in the little fountain, drifted on the breeze. He could think about the death of Bruce dispassionately now. An accident, and that was all. Unpleasant, yes, but he had seen far more unpleasant things than that on his travels at night. This was the first he had seen something happen to someone he knew, and that made a difference, but Bruce—he hated Bruce, and Bruce deserved to die that way—in his own evil trap.

Again that thrill went through him. Bruce would never torment him again. He thought; I could have killed him if I wanted to. I didn't, but I could have—easily.

When he got home, he ate lightly, went up to his room, and worked on his English paper. He was finishing up when his mother called through his door: "Oh Jonathan, something terrible happened. It was just on TV."

Jon went to the hallway. His mother was there in her robe, face blurred, a half-empty glass in her hand.

Eleven-fifteen, and local news was chattering out of

the TV set in her room. "What, Mother? What happened?"

"A boy at your school got killed this afternoon. He fell into the quarry. His name was Bruce Hodges. Did you know him, Jon?"

Jon nodded. "Yes. He was in my class."

"How *terrible*."

Jon blinked. "Yes. Terrible. How did he fall?"

"He was walking across a bridge he had made and it broke."

"Was anybody with him?"

"No, he was by himself."

"It must have been awful," Jon said.

His mother stared past his shoulder, eyes wet. "The poor child." She looked at him and said, "I hope you never go to dangerous places like that."

"Oh no, I stay away from there."

She smiled sadly. "Be careful, sweetheart. Always be careful, please?" She kissed his cheek.

The smell of alcohol, the wet of spittle. He tensed, pulled back. "I will be careful, Mother. Thanks for telling me the news. Goodnight."

He closed his door as she stood there staring crookedly, holding her glass. Once again he saw Bruce on the quarry floor and he said to himself with a smile: "*After life's fitful fever he sleeps well*."

CHAPTER NINETEEN _____

The next day Sonny was absent. School was quiet. Mr. Bondino let kids do what they wanted to in gym and nobody fooled around. At lunchtime Jon was standing near the fence, looking out at the baseball field, when one kid said to another, "Crushed his skull! Really *gross*!"

Jon thought, That's as much as they care. Not that Bruce was the kind of kid that you cared about, but what if Matt Wilson or Chuckie or Meg had died? Would it be any different? A little, maybe, but not much.

He shuddered to think of something happening to Meg. He wouldn't be able to bear it. He'd have nothing to live for then. He would probably kill himself, but these other kids? They would find it thrilling, something to talk about for a day or two, and then they'd forget it. If something terrible happened to him, they would joke about it. One last joke on Petrie. None of them cared about him at all—except Meg. And Chuckie, Chuckie cared.

Very few people cared about other people. They only pretended they did. That was the way the world was.

That afternoon as he walked home with Chuckie, Chuckie said, "I'm not sorry he's dead. That isn't nice to say, but I'm not."

"I'm not either," Jon said. To himself he said, I'm *glad*.

Over the weekend he finally completed his paper on

Macbeth and worked on his history paper, but most of the time he flew: to the quarry, peaceful now, the bridge mysteriously gone, a brown stain still on the rocks. He flew to Meg, to the Monarchs, saw his father with Joanna again.

Bruce's death had changed everything. His life was filled with new options now. The mind outside the body could spy and plan, while the mind inside the body could . . . arrange things. Untie ropes—little things like that which led to large effects. As he thought of it, he smiled: He would no longer be helpless against his enemies.

On Monday, everything was back to normal. It was just as if nothing had happened. English class was almost over; Jon was in a tired dream when Miss Robards called him up to her desk. He made his way to the front of the room, wondering what she wanted. He had turned in his paper, what more did she want? He was terribly glad to have finished that paper, it bothered him to think about *Macbeth*, it made him have bad dreams.

The class was noisy, joking, getting ready to leave. Miss Robards looked at him sternly and said, "This paper of yours—this wasn't the assignment."

Jon frowned and said, "What do you mean?"

"I asked you to write about the characters of Macbeth and Lady Macbeth. Your paper is called, 'A Study of the Criminal Mind.' "

"They had criminal minds," Jon said.

"You're an expert on such things, I'm sure," Miss Robards said sarcastically. She handed the paper back to him and said, "This may be fine for a sociology class, but it won't do for me. You'll have to write another one."

Jon stared in disbelief.

"Do it over or fail the assignment." She looked at him hard. "And, if you fail the assignment—you fail the term."

Jon flinched as if he'd been slapped. His jaw worked back and forth. He said, "You leave me alone, Miss Robards."

She frowned in surprise and shock. "*What*?"

Jon held the paper tightly, knuckles white. "You just better leave me alone."

Miss Robards's eyes flashed as she said, "I think you and I better go have another talk with the principal."

Jon shook his head. "That wouldn't be a good idea at all," he said, then turned and walked back to his seat.

The bell went off: chairs shifted, books slammed. Jon went to the hallway, books under one arm, the English paper tight in his other hand. His face was a mask, a sleepwalker's face.

At home in his room he said to Eeyore: "I won't let her do this to me. I worked hard on this paper, there's nothing wrong with it. I made her look bad in class, that's what it is, and she's out to get me. She thinks she knows everything, Eeyore, and what does she know? Nothing at all.

"I don't have *time* to do another paper, I have to fly. She's kept me from flying long enough with her stupid assignment—she won't hold me back anymore." He stared at the toy for a long time, lost in thought, then said: "We'll talk about her later, Eeyore." Then slowly, smiling oddly, he tore his rejected English paper to shreds.

Carlos opened the mailbox—the coffee can that sat on a beam in the cellar's dark hall. Jon watched him unfold the paper, read the note, and laugh. He said to Turk, "Hey, Felipe's got a good one. Dude does a three-card monte number, makes out fine. We take him at Mr. D's, Sixteenth and Masterson, at midnight."

Jon waited in the alley with the gang. From the shadows Felipe watched the door of the bar. "Hey, here he comes," he said, and everybody tensed. They heard the footsteps, watched the man, a black man, short and slender, hair shaved off, walk past. Then the four of them jumped from the darkness. Turk and Skiv grabbed the man by the arms and pulled him into the alley. Carlos held the knife to his throat and said, "One move an' you dead."

The knife blade creased the man's skin. His eyes were desperate, wild, sweat beaded his forehead and nose. Felipe searched his pockets quickly, came up with a fat wad of bills. He shoved them at the black man's face and said, "You like robbin' people, man? Hey, how's it feel?" The man didn't speak, didn't move. Turk and Skiv shoved him down, put a gag in his mouth, then Carlos did that horrible thing again, the thing he always did to the people they robbed: jumped hard on the man's left knee; the cartilage snapped with an audible pop. The black man jerked, groaned low behind the gag, and Carlos sliced his cheek with the shining blade.

Jon turned away. Carlos shouldn't have hurt the man like that. It was vicious, cruel, as bad as Sonny and Carl— No. No, he wasn't like them, he had to do it, had to punish evil, that was all. But it made Jon sick.

At the hideout they counted the money. "Five hundred an twenty-one bucks." Skiv said. "He do that much every day?"

"We gotta visit him again sometime," Turk said. "Five hundred an twenty-one tax-free dollars a day, hey, that ain't bad. Maybe I learn to play monte myself."

"Then we have to rob *you*," Carlos said.

Jon stayed as they drank and joked around. In his mind he saw the robbery, the look on the black man's face. He thought of Miss Robards, how nice it would be to see that knife at her throat.

He stared at the Seth Thomas clock in a trance, the voices dull in his ears. Two periods to go, he couldn't stay awake, he'd have to fly—

Suddenly he heard his name and blinked. The class was silent. Everybody stared. Miss Robards said, "Do you know the author or not? I'm not going to wait all day."

Jon's eyes were dim, his thoughts were buried, far away. In a dream he said, "Seth Thomas."

Everybody laughed, and Randy Hankins said, "No, man— he invented the clock."

Miss Robards's mouth was a hard, thin line. "I've had enough of your insolence!" she snapped. "You've been nothing but trouble for over a month! One more smart remark like that and you'll go to the principal!"

Jon squinted, thought, The principal. You mean your lover, Miss Robards. Your lover, why don't you say it?

"Did you hear what I said?"

"Yeah, sure."

"Answer me respectfully!"

Jon smiled. "Yes . . . Miss Robards."

Carol Washington gave the correct answer, Thomas Hardy. Randy Hankins mumbled, "Naughty-naughty, Pee-Tree." Jon ignored him, thought of Carlos, the knife at the black man's throat. Behind his eyes he saw the Monarchs' vests flashing orange and black. His mind went dim again, he dozed, head slumping on his chest. . . .

Then something was on his desk. He snapped awake, room bright, saw Randy's arm pull back. Cheap yellow sheets of paper, stapled, and he read: ". . . Plunged deeper. She moaned and raised her legs . . ." In shock he picked up the story and shoved it away as Miss Robards said, "All right, let's have it! Jonathan! Bring that up to my desk this minute!"

Jon walked up the aisle, the pages hot in his hand. His skin was flushed, his knees were quivering. If she tells my father, if she tells my father. . . . He handed the story over. Miss Robards thumbed through it coldly, looked at him, and said; "I'll meet you in Mr. Diedrick's office at two forty-five."

Jon's heart was dancing crazily. He took his seat again without a word. He saw Meg frown and he blushed, so embarrassed he wanted to die. He glanced at Randy, whose face wore a smug, snide smile. He saw the empty seat near Randy, Bruce's seat. Dark thoughts spread through his mind.

He told them the story was his. Miss Weller talked to him after Miss Robards and Mr. Diedrick finished. She asked about how things were going at home and about Dr. Schlosser, things he didn't want to talk about. Just leave me alone and let me fly, he thought, oh please, just leave me alone! He was sick to death of school and its stupidities. He didn't need school. He knew more than his teachers would ever learn in their lives.

She wouldn't call his father, she said. "She'd give him another chance. But he had to be sure to keep tomorrow's appointment with Dr. Schlosser. He squinted, half hearing, resentment bitter in his throat. Randy, Miss Robards, Mr. Diedrick—he hated them, hated them all.

He waited across the street from the garden apartments. They were in Oak Hill, a mile or so away from Evergreen Row. There were close-cropped lawns, a few young trees, some shrubs near the red-brick walls.

Kids played on a few of the lawns, little kids not old enough for school. Jon watched as the dusk came down and fireflies flashed. The kids shouted and quarreled and laughed, drove their Big Wheels and wagons, crashed into each other. He tried to remember what it was like to be that young. It was only ten years ago, but it might as well have been ten centuries, he felt so removed from that time.

The kids ran, yelled, chased fireflies. Once long ago he must have had fun like that: In a time before he went to school, when he didn't know his mother drank, when his father wasn't so mean. It must have been that way once, but he didn't remember.

Dark fell, the kids went in, the lights blinked on. A light was on behind Miss Robards's drapes.

Jon was ready to go inside, to fly through Miss Robards's door, when a car—a very familiar car— pulled into the drive. It stopped and its lights went off. Mr. Diedrick stepped out and closed the door and started up the walk. Jon followed him.

As soon as Mr. Diedrick went inside he kissed Miss Robards's neck, her ears, kissed her mouth for a long time. To think of kissing Miss Robards made Jon feel sick. She was horrible, ugly, a witch.

They had drinks on the couch. Mr. Diedrick talked

about school and Miss Robards said, "Stan, please—no shop. Let's forget the little bastards for a while." They had another drink and then Mr. Diedrick took off Miss Robards's clothes.

Jon watched as they did it clumsily and eagerly. He watched as Miss Robards got on her hands and knees and Mr. Diedrick did it like a dog. He thought, That pornography really shocked you, didn't it, Miss Robards. —Shocked you so much you had to send me to your lover. You know that story isn't mine, but you don't care, as long as you can torture me. Mr. Diedrick thrust hard and groaned, fell forward, clutching Miss Robards's breasts. Jon laughed bitterly, flew outside. Randy, Miss Weller, Miss Robards, his father—the images piled up, clashed in his jumbled mind.

The next afternoon he went to see Dr. Schlosser. He said nothing about the pornography and didn't talk about Bruce, just answered Maybe and I don't know. But I *do* know, he thought, know more than you ever will. Miss Robards and Mr. Diedrick are filthy, as filthy as you. And he pictured the woman, Marie, saw her bringing the whip down again and again on Dr. Schlosser's soft flesh.

CHAPTER TWENTY _____

The following week things got worse. Miss Robards came down hard on him again, he failed his math and history tests, Sonny gave him work to do, Carl and Randy said he'd better do their papers or else. On Thursday, haggard, weak, exhausted, he shut himself in his room and said to Eeyore: "Three more weeks of school, but that won't be the end. In the fall it will start all over again. Papers, homework, taunting, torture. . . ."

He held the toy in his hands. He felt its energy, its soul, its life force radiating hotly through him and he thought of Bruce lying dead on the quarry floor. A knot had given way, a bridge had broken, Bruce was gone. So fast. An accident, and one less evil person in the world. He thought about it, head tilted as if he were listening intently to something, then put Eeyore back on his shelf.

Dr. Schlosser talked to him for ten minutes, then asked him to wait in the waiting room and called his father in.

Jon went to the mens' room down the hall, locked himself in a toilet stall, flew back to the office again.

"He's very resistive. That's usually how it is with adolescents. According to what he says, things are perfectly fine, but I've had contact with the school, and I know otherwise."

Jon listened. So Miss Weller had told on him. Told Dr. Schlosser about the story, about his marks. She shouldn't have done it.

"He's a mixed-up kid, but he's not in a real bad way," Dr. Schlosser said. "I think a change of environment would do him more good than therapy."

Jon held his breath. His father said, "You mean Harrington, then?"

The psychiatrist took a brochure off his desk and handed it over. "No, this is the place I have in mind. The Slade School, in Ohio. It's a highly structured environment. The kids are constantly challenged—academically, physically, emotionally. There's a full range of extracurricular activities. I think it's just what Jon needs to help him become more assertive. They don't baby the kids at Slade, but there isn't any drill, inspection, all that business. Why don't you look this over and let me know what you think?"

Doug Petrie skimmed the brochure. "I'll go with your recommendation, Jack."

"Take it home, Doug, take your time. I'm sure Alice wants to see the material too."

Doug Petrie said, "He'll go to Slade."

The psychiatrist shrugged. "Fine. They have a waiting list, of course, but I know the admissions director pretty well and I don't think we'll have any problems."

Doug Petrie said, "I appreciate it, Jack. If it isn't Slade, it's Harrington. I've had it with the kid." He stood up.

Jon looked at him and thought: You've had it with me? No, Father, I've had it with *you*. He moved close to the calendar on the doctor's desk. Appointments Saturday morning and afternoon, and then, at the foot of the page: "Marie."

Jon quickly flew back to the mens' room. His body was still on the toilet. A man was using the urinal outside the stall. Jon flushed the toilet and opened the stall and hurried into the hall.

His father was there in the waiting room, sitting beside a heavy man whose mouth twitched wickedly.

"Where the hell were you?"

"Had to go to the bathroom."

They walked down the hall. "What did he want to see you about?" Jon asked.

"He thinks you should go to a different school, a place called the Slade School. It's in Ohio."

"Ohio," Jon said. He waited a minute and said, "A school for crazy kids."

"A school for kids who don't get along in the school they're going to," his father said, annoyance in his voice. "It's a good school, hard to get into. Dr. Schlosser will write a report on you, and then we'll visit the place."

As the elevator sank, Jon thought; A good school, yes, where you're constantly challenged. Where they smother your life with their stupid activities and you never have time to fly. I'll never go there, Father, never.

He narrowed his eyes and blinked and thought, Dr. Schlosser will write a report on me. Well, we'll just see about that.

It was seven-fifteen and the hideout was empty. The table was covered with beer bottles, cigarettes, stale scraps of food. Under the table Jon found what he'd come for—a note from Felipe.

He studied the note, absorbing its every detail. He flew home again and sat at his desk and wrote Felipe's message down on a sheet of paper. The look of the handwriting burned in his mind: its thickness, slant; he saw the crooked *r*s, the *o*s left open at the top, the circles dotting the *i*s. He saw the name Felipe, the ornate *F*, the way the tail of the final *e* turned down. He watched his effort with the image clear in his head, corrected, practiced, smiled.

He practiced writing new words in the script. Late at night when he'd finished the message he showed it to Eeyore, laughing quietly. "Look, Eeyore, what do you think?" He paused for a couple of minutes, head cocked to the side, a crooked grin on his face. "Exactly, Eeyore, exactly . . ."

He slept poorly, rose early. The day was humid, overcast. His father had gone to inspect the condominium site, his mother was in the family room staring out at the pool. He forced himself to swallow half a glass of orange juice and went back to his room. He studied the map of the city again, then got his wallet, asked Eeyore to wish him good luck, went out the door.

He walked up the hill toward the high school and caught the first bus. There were only two people on it, people he didn't know, but even so he felt strange as he asked where to transfer for Lincoln Street. The driver frowned oddly, then said he would need to take two more buses, not just one.

It took twenty minutes to reach the first transfer point. He caught the D bus, asked where to change for the H bus, tried to appear relaxed as the bus rattled down through neighborhoods he'd never seen before.

He waited on a desolate corner in front of a brownstone church that was covered with red graffiti. Glass and papers littered the streets, two men with gray stubbles of beard sat in front of a red-brick house with torn window shades. The air was very muggy now, a pearl-white sun bled through the haze, he waited, waited, waited. At last the H bus came, decrepit, glazed with soot, and Jon got on.

He told the driver what street he wanted and took a seat up front. He stared through the windshield, stomach tight. The smell of exhaust made him gag.

The driver said, "Okay, sport, here you go," and pulled up to the curb. Jon went through the doors and found himself in a dream. He had never stood on this spot before, yet he'd seen it many times: that empty house, that store with the signs in Spanish, that ancient garage. He felt the way he felt when he first saw the Statue of Liberty: Everything was so familiar and yet so different, so . . . unbelievable.

His heart sped up, sweat coated his skin. He saw the sign, JAMES MONAGHAN, THE BEST IN PAINTS SINCE 1888, and started off.

He went two blocks, turned right. And God it was real, he was part of it in the flesh. When he saw the factory, brown and grimy, screens across the windows, his mouth went dry.

An hour and forty-five minutes of riding, waiting on corners, walking—and he was *here*! One solid line of paving linked his home in Evergreen Row with this street *here*. It seemed fantastic.

The street was empty, desolate. Two blocks ahead, he saw a bus go by. In the distance, cars crawled on a rusted black steel bridge.

His legs seemed locked. He forced them to move. The factory came closer, closer. Face streaked with sweat, legs quivering, the stifling cotton sky pressing down, he glanced over his shoulder—then ran down the alley as fast as he could.

He stopped in front of the door to the cellar, heart crashing wildly. If they caught him they'd kill him. But no one is here, he told himself as he wiped thick sweat away from his forehead and chin. He had flown to the Monarchs on Saturday three times before, and no one had ever been there until well after dark. It was ten thirty-five in the morning, the building was empty. He steeled himself, nose twitching like a rabbit's, and went down the concrete steps.

The smell was much stronger than he remembered: a sourness that came from—what? Damp crumbling plaster, piles of rags—or maybe something rotting in the crates against the wall. He stood there at the foot of the steps, each nerve on fire. A car clanked over a manhole cover outside. He waited a moment, then started across the littered concrete floor.

His footsteps loud in the silence, his blood beating hard at his temples, he made his way across the space to the corridor. It gaped like a dragon's mouth, black, huge. He swallowed hard, throat stiff—and walked into the dark.

He stood there, letting his eyes adjust to the grimy light, the only sound his hot and ragged breath. And there on his left not more than twenty feet away—was the beam with the coffee can.

A jolt of urgency struck him. He had to act fast, get

out of here, he couldn't take this anymore! He groped for the coffee can, grabbed it, almost dropped it. Held it tightly, heart beating hard, and told himself to calm down. Cold sweat dripped off his chin as he took the lid off, felt inside. Nothing there. He set the can on the floor, reached into his pocket, and pulled out the note.

He dropped the folded paper in the can, put the lid back on, put the can in its hiding place on the beam. I did it! he thought exultantly. I did it, I did it, it's done!

Suddenly the creak of hinges—and the door to the hideout opened.

A bar of light hit the floor in front of him. His heart contracted violently. He jumped back, flung himself behind the post below the beam that held the coffee can. He pressed himself flat, stood rigid, terrified.

The hard, crisp click of footsteps on the floor. Closer, closer. . . . In utter panic Jon almost ran, but forced himself to stay there motionless, pressed up against the post. The footsteps stopped. Whoever it was stood only an arm's length away.

Jon's heart was deafening in his ears. Whoever was standing there could hear it, he was sure. He almost cried, almost threw himself on the floor in complete surrender. But he clamped his jaw shut hard, sweat stinging his eyes, its hot salt taste in his mouth.

The hard heels pivoted; Jon heard the crunch of grit. Three more footsteps echoed off the walls like radar probes. His mind was shrieking, screaming, wild, but he forced himself to stay still.

"Medrano, you hearin' things," a terribly familiar voice said softly. Jon thought he would faint. The sweat poured over him, coating his skin, bright noises rang in his ears.

"You crazy, just like Rita says." The voice banged into the vaultlike cellar, died. "You hearin' things, man. Bad sign. Nex' thing you know they'll be wheelin' you off." A silence, and then a shout: "Anybody here, I slice your throat! You hear me, man? Nobody gonna get Carlos Medrano—nobody!"

A cold white numbness seized Jon's chest. He was

fainting, dying, he couldn't hold out. But now he was frozen, paralyzed, he was one with the post, pressed into its hard abrasive dampness, feeling nothing.

Carlos spit. Jon saw the silver splinter shoot past and land on the floor. The hard heels turned again and Carlos said, "Yeah, Medrano, Rita's right—you a crazy dude." He laughed, went down the corridor. Jon heard the door bang closed.

He stood there shaking, cold as ice. Slowly he moved away from the post and crept toward the cellar, certain the door would fly open and Carlos would have him, would break his legs and slash his cheek and leave him to die and rot upstairs under piles of filthy rags.

All at once his mind exploded. In panic he ran, the world a blur except for the dull rectangular light across the room, the opening to freedom. He raced up the steps and down the alley, out onto the street. He ducked into a doorway and waited, lungs bursting, his heart pounding at his ribs. He waited, waited, and Carlos did not appear, and he ran again, turned left, was out on Lincoln Street.

Behind him the bus was coming. He ran as hard as he could and beat it to the stop. He went to put the change in the box and dropped a dime and nickel on the floor. He sat in the back and slumped into a seat. He gulped at the humid air, the sweat pouring down and soaking his shirt and hair. He held his face in his hands and softly cried. Nobody seemed to notice. Soon he was standing across the street from the brownstone church. Right before he caught the D bus, he vomited into the sewer.

He waited outside the apartment house. Invisible now, he was strong again. He had rested all afternoon, finally falling asleep after flying for half an hour to calm himself. Now he was the real Jon, powerful and confident.

He was worried, though. Dr. Schlosser would be here soon and there was no sign of the Monarchs. Maybe Felipe found the note in the can. He hoped with all his heart that didn't happen; hoped that Felipe had been scouting around as usual, and Carlos or Rita or Tiny or one of the others had found the note. But damn, they should be here by now.

He waited. Cars went by, a few pedestrians. —And then the green Mercedes pulled up to the curb, and Dr. Schlosser stepped out.

Jon watched the psychiatrist check to make sure that the door was locked. He checked and double checked, then started up the sidewalk. Jon watched him, impotent, sick to his heart. He had done all that planning, had risked his *life*, and the Monarchs hadn't come.

Then suddenly Skiv and Carlos jumped out of the shadows.

They grabbed Dr. Schlosser and dragged him into the alley beside the apartment house. Jon hovered over them. Skiv pinned the doctor's arms behind him, Carlos held the knife. Quickly Carlos frisked Dr. Schlosser, came up with the wallet. He laughed.

Now they would break his knee, Jon thought. A broken knee and a gash on the face would slow him down just fine. Surgery, a cast—and he wouldn't write the Slade report or anything else for a while.

Then Dr. Schlosser did something foolish—he kicked with all his strength and caught Carlos right in the ribs. Carlos staggered backward, clutching his side. A look of pure hatred on his face, he rushed forward again. Dr. Schlosser struggled against Skiv furiously, kicked again, but missed. And Carlos said, "Hey smart guy, look," and plunged his knife into Dr. Schlosser's neck.

Skiv let him go. Dr. Schlosser clutched his throat and made a hoarse croaking noise, his hands suddenly red. He staggered and slumped against the wall. Slowly, face going slack, he slid to the ground.

Jon watched in shock. He had wanted to hurt Dr. Schlosser, stop him from recommending Slade, but he'd never counted on this. But now Dr. Schlosser was lying unconscious, bleeding, badly hurt.

Jon flew down the alley and into the street. He looked back, saw the doctor slumped against the wall and told himself: It's not my fault!

He had written the note that told where Dr. Schlosser

would be, and that was all. Carlos had done the stabbing, not him, he was not to blame. How stupid Dr. Schlosser was! How stupid to try to fight back! He deserved to be stabbed.

He flew to the Monarchs' hideout, saw the blade plunge in, the blood spurt out, again and again in his mind. It was horrible, and yet. . . . He had finally used his power to protect himself. He had wanted Dr. Schlosser hurt and he'd made it happen. This wasn't any accident, like what happened to Bruce; without his note the stabbing would not have occurred. He was truly one of the Monarchs now. They'd never see him or know his name, but he was one of them, and would join their celebration.

Carlos and Skiv were already back at the hideout when Jon arrived. They were laughing and passing the wine around. "A thousand bucks," Carlos said. "The guy was walking around with a thousand bucks!" Jon watched as they joked and drank, then Turk and Felipe came in.

Carlos got up and slapped Felipe on the back. "Hey, what a tip!" he said. "The guy had a thousand bucks on him, man!"

Felipe lit a cigarette. "What tip you talkin' about?"

"That mark downtown, on Willow Street. He showed up right on time."

Felipe blew smoke out, frowning. "I didn't give you no tip on no mark on Willow Street."

Carlos reached in his vest and came out with Jon's note. He shoved it at Felipe. "Hey, this your writing or not?"

Felipe took the paper, held it to the light. He laughed. "Hey, man, what kinda joke you playin'?"

"Joke," Skiv said. He held up a fistful of bills. "You think this a joke?"

Felipe smoked thoughtfully, looked at the note. "I never wrote this, man."

Carlos said, "Hey, come on, man, don' fool around."

"I said I never wrote it, man." His face began to twitch.

Everyone was quiet. Carlos drank from the bottle and

said, "Felipe, you full of shit." He laughed. "We got a thousand bucks because of you an' you don' wanna take no credit."

"I never wrote no note."

"Hey, maybe in your sleep," Turk said.

Felipe dropped the note on the table, frowning. "This is weird, man. Gimme some wine."

Then Rita and Tiny and Manuel came in, and two other girls named Esther and Carmella. Soon they were on the second bottle of wine and the talk was loud. Tiny went off in a corner with Turk; Carlos had his arm around Rita's neck. Felipe sat at the table, frowning, staring at the note, then finally crushed it into a ball and threw it across the room. Carlos and Rita disappeared; Carmella went out with Felipe.

Jon watched and listened, pretending that Meg was there, that she was a Monarch too. Then he flew upstairs to where Carlos and Rita were.

Pale orange light came through windows across the room. Carlos had drunk a lot of wine and was talking loudly now. His voice was angry, echoed off the walls.

"No, Rita, it ain't gonna be like that! I'm gonna be free, understan'?"

"How you gonna be free if they catch you?" Rita said. Her face was hidden in shadows. "You stick this dude tonight an' what if he dies and they catch you? Then what?"

"He won't be the first one, Rita. There been other ones died an' they never got me, right?"

Then Rita was crying. "Carlos, you got to stop! They get you an' stick you away, an'—"

Suddenly Carlos slapped her. "Shut up!" he yelled. "You just shut up! Nobody gonna catch Carlos Medrano, never!"

Jon stood there, stunned. Carlos was wrong to hit her, very wrong. She wanted the best for him. She screamed out of the darkness, "You're crazy, Carlos! Crazy, cra—"

He hit her hard this time. Her head snapped back and she fell to the floor. "You think so, Rita?" Carlos shouted. "Yeah? A thousand bucks for fifteen minutes work, you think that's crazy? That bastard, why should he have a car like that an money like that an clothes like that an' I gotta live in a shithole? Huh?''

"Carlos, please, you're drunk, please, don't—"

He slapped her again. Jon couldn't look.

He flew outside. In the streetlight's pink-orange glare he thought, Carlos is just like Sonny, just as cruel. He didn't have to break the black man's knee, he did it just for fun. Rita loved him and he was beating her senseless. He was stupid, cruel, an enemy, not a friend.

He flew home quickly and entered his sleeping form. He took the shining donkey off the shelf and held it, feeling its power flow through him, and whispered: "He shouldn't have hit her, Eeyore. He shouldn't have done that, she loves him. He's cruel, he's cruel."

The house was still, the animal glowed. Jon got back in bed, still holding the toy. He lay there and the movie of the day raced by: the trip to the hideout, planting the note and hiding from Carlos, Dr. Schlosser being stabbed and Rita being hit. Around and around it went as the donkey glowed, all jumbled and rich in Jon's mind.

CHAPTER TWENTY-ONE _____

A shaft of sunlight fell on the sugar bowl. His father's face was dark. He looked at Jon and said, "Dr. Schlosser was murdered last night."

Jon caught his breath. The breakfast table swam before his eyes. He sank into his chair and said, "Oh no."

"The bastards stabbed him in the neck. Here it is in the paper."

Jon shook his head and turned away. Sun glittered on the pool. "I don't want to read it," he said.

"Bastards," his father said. "I've known Jack Schlosser for twenty-five years. You wouldn't want to meet a finer man." He looked at the paper again and drank some coffee. "Puts me in one hell of a fix," he said.

Jon looked at him. "What?"

"It's going to be tough to get you into Slade without his recommendation. Guess I'll have to find another psychiatrist. Christ, I don't have enough to do."

"Where's Mother?" Jon asked.

"In bed, where else? Not *feeling* well." He stood up, slammed the paper down, and said, "I hope they catch the sons of bitches and boil them in oil." He left the kitchen and went to the den.

Jon went to his room. He shut the door and put his hands on Eeyore and closed his eyes. He stood there rigidly, charging himself with Eeyore's stored-up power. When he felt strong enough, he walked to the window and looked out.

The sun on the pool hurt his eyes. He turned and looked at the toy again. A sadness came over him as he said, "I could have saved him, Eeyore. I could have called the police, but I let him lie there and bleed to death. He shook his head violently then and said, "No, no, it's not my fault! All I did was write a note, Carlos is to blame! He killed Dr. Schlosser, he beat up Rita, he's evil, he's cruel!" He narrowed his eyes and stared at the donkey as noises sang in his ears. "Carlos is a *murderer*," he said.

A noise outside his door. He stood there, silent, blinking. Suddenly his father's voice: "What's going on in there?"

"Just . . . practicing my French," Jon said. "I have a test tomorrow."

Silence. Then: "You talking to that goddamn toy again?"

"Just practicing my French, that's all."

"That better be all."

Jon waited, breathing shallowly, head cocked to the side. Just mind your own business, he thought. You have no right to criticize what anybody does. Stay out of my affairs.

He put his hands on Eeyore again and took some more of the charge. Then he opened his door, walked down the stairs, went out through the garage.

He made the call from the booth in Henderson, outside Gordon's Drugs. When they asked who he was he hung up, left the booth, and headed home. On the sidewalk near Evergreen Row he ran into Meg.

Sun sparkled in her hair. She squinted, shading her eyes. "Hi, Jon. What's new?"

"Oh, nothing much." He stared at her, bright noises in his ears. He said, "Can you go on dates yet? Are you old enough?"

She smiled, caught off guard. "Oh . . . no, not yet."

Jon blinked. He said, "Well when you are, I want to be the first."

She frowned. "The first?" she said.

"To take you to a movie." He stood there, staring.

"Oh." She smiled again. "Sure, that would be very

nice. Well listen, I have to meet somebody, I'll see you later.''

"See you later," Jon said. He stood there watching her walk down the hill to Russelville, and then he went home.

Chuckie came over while he was asleep. His mother called him, he went downstairs, he went to Chuckie's house. They messed around with his trains for a while but it was boring to Jon, so they walked back over to Jon's house and went for a swim.

Chuckie couldn't really swim, he just sort of splashed around in the shallow part of the pool, but he seemed to have a good time. Jon had always liked to swim, but now he found that boring too. Compared to flying, everything was boring.

Chuckie sat on the edge of the pool, his skinny body gleaming in the light, and said, "Boy, Jon, I just can't wait till school is out. We can swim anytime we want and go to the store anytime we want and sit around and read comic books all day. We can play Monopoly and watch TV!"

Jon stared at the pool, the angles, motion, sharp light.

"Hey Jon . . . what's the matter with you?"

Jon looked at him. "What?"

"You're so . . . different. What happened to you? You don't like to play with stuff anymore, you don't do your school work anymore. . . . You're always tired, you don't want to *do* anything."

"You just be quiet," Jon said. "Just shut your mouth and mind your business."

Chuckie's eyes went wide. His mouth curled into spasms. "The . . . that's another thing," he said, "you say mean things. You never used to say mean things, what happened to you?"

"Nothing happened to me," Jon said in a threatening voice. "I'm fine, I'm normal, there's nothing the matter with me." He stared at the depths of the pool: light, shadows, azure blue. He frowned and pressed his lips together, looked at Chuckie, said, "I'm sorry I talked to you that way, I didn't mean it. You're my friend. You'll always be my friend. It's just. . . . Yeah, I'll be glad when school's out too.''

Chuckie was quiet a minute, then said, "At least Bruce Hodges isn't around to bother you anymore.'' He frowned, face serious. "You think he went to hell?''

Jon looked at him. He smiled. "Hell,'' he said. "You're something, Chuckie.''

Chuckie laughed. He pointed to the water, said, "Look, Jon—there's a dime down there.''

Jon said, "I can't believe your eyes.'' He dived, swam deep. He came up gasping, laughing, handed the dime to his friend.

In the morning it was on TV. Jon watched it, mesmerized. There was Carlos, handcuffed, there were Turk and Manuel. And just before the film clip ended, there was Rita—and his heart felt aching and sad.

"They got the bastards,'' his father said, a wad of toast in his mouth. "Bunch of goddamn filthy spics. Scum like that attacking a guy like Jack. I hope they fry the sons of bitches.''

It was in the paper, too. An anonymous caller had told the police the location of the hideout. The Monarchs had been arrested Sunday night and were being held in the county jail until they could be arraigned. Murder, assault, armed robbery, stolen goods, drugs. . . . He read the names and ages: Carlos Medrano, twenty-one, Rita Ortiz, seventeen. . . .

Only seventeen. Two years older than he was, one year older than Meg, and she was a woman. He'd thought she was twenty-one or twenty-two at the least. He felt terrible about Rita. She'd tried to talk sense into Carlos, tried to keep him from doing those terrible things, and now she was going to prison too. Well, maybe not, maybe they'd let her go. He would follow the story in the papers and see how things turned out. In a way he felt bad about all of the Monarchs. He had liked them once and had learned from them. But killing Dr. Schlosser had been a cruel and senseless thing, and they had to be punished for that.

He had a horrible day in school. He couldn't concentrate at all and fell asleep twice in biology class. Sonny gave him a paper to do, an English paper already two weeks late. He hadn't done his second *Macbeth* paper yet, the term was drawing to a close, he still owed Carl and Randy papers too. At lunchtime he leaned on the chain-link fence and stared at the playing field and thought of what Meg had said that time: You can't let them push you around, you just can't live that way.

She was right. He had gone along with them all this time and where had it gotten him? Deeper and deeper in trouble. It was Hitler all over again, a little here, a little there, and maybe he'll stop but of course he wouldn't —till he had it all. He'd always given into them because he'd had no choice. But things were different now.

A hard dark rage began to build as he stared at the playing field. Bruce, Dr. Schlosser, Carlos—powerful people, yet he'd stopped them all. He squinted at the field, the distant figures abstract, meaningless. Yes, Meg was right, it was wrong for these others to run his life, it had to stop. And the sooner it stopped, the better.

He flew Monday night, and Tuesday in school he fell asleep five times. Miss Robards hassled him about his paper. He told her to shove it. She sent him to Mr. Diedrick. He squinted and blinked as Diedrick lectured him, his mind a movie screen: He saw Diedrick's thick flanks pump against Miss Robards's crotch and heard Miss Robards moan. In the locker room Sonny shoved him hard, sent him crashing into the garbage can, and as Jon walked home a blood-red haze of anger blurred his eyes. Sonny, Diedrick, Robards—he'd thought of a way to get them long ago. Back then it had been a fantasy, a dream. But now he knew the extent of his power, knew he could make the dream real.

CHAPTER TWENTY-TWO _____

On Wednesday he left the house early, hurried past the high school, and went to Henderson. He ducked into the phone booth outside Gordon's Drugs, looked nervously around, then dialed the number.

"Aronson High School." Miss Ellison, the secretary.

Jon's throat was suddenly dry. He swallowed, took a breath, and said, "There's a bomb in your school. It's set to go off at nine forty-five." He put the receiver back in the cradle quickly, as if it were hot. He picked up his briefcase, left the booth, and walked to school.

At nine twenty-five, during gym, the fire alarm went off. Jon was on the playing field, and he watched as the kids and teachers came trooping out of the building up above. They stayed out for nearly an hour. Half of second period, biology, was gone before things settled down.

So Miss Weller had won, Jon thought. She had won or the school board had met and decided to clear the building every time a bomb threat was received. Either way, his plan wouldn't work. But maybe, just maybe, Diedrick still called the shots. The only way to find out was to try again.

The next morning he called in another bomb threat from the same phone booth. The minutes crawled by on the Seth Thomas clock as he waited in art class, waited, waited. Nine forty-five finally came—and went—and the fire alarm did not ring. Another ten minutes passed, and no alarm.

On Saturday he was up with the sun. He dressed in the clothes he had worn the last three days, didn't bother to wash, got downstairs before everyone else, and ate his Cheerios. When his father came into the kitchen at seven, Jon said, "You going out to the condominium site?"

His father looked at him. He'd never thought Jon even knew there *was* a condominium site. "Yeah, that's where I'm going," he said.

"Can I come along?"

"To the condominium site?"

"Is that okay?"

"Sure, fine."

Doug Petrie spooned some coffee into the Mr. Coffee machine, thinking, Maybe Schlosser did some good after all. Hard to believe after only three sessions, but why the sudden interest in my work? "I've got one project nearing completion down in the south end," he said. "Twenty-six units. And they're just getting started on the condo in Westbrook. Hope to break ground for another development soon—another one like Evergreen Row. I'm going over to Westbrook this morning. They're still excavating. They've made one hell of a hole."

Jon stared at the pool with a curious smile. "I'd like to see it," he said.

Huge thunderclouds had gathered by the time they reached the site. The air was oppressive, humid, dense: far off, a heavy rumble.

While his father talked to the architect, Jon slipped past cranes and piles of beams and mounds of earth till he came to the foreman's shack. Behind the shack was a tarp-covered mound. He started toward it.

"Hey, you! Where you think you're goin'?"

He froze. The man was powerful-looking, with heavy tattooed arms, a huge protruding stomach. He had iron-gray hair and black eyes. The eyes bored into Jon. "What the hell are you doin' here?"

"Just . . . looking around," Jon said, breaking into a

sweat. "My father's building a condominium here, he brought me with him today."

The man spit. "What's your old man's name?"

"Doug Petrie."

The trace of a smile formed on the heavy man's lips. "So you're the big boss's son," he said. "Don't look like him. Don't look like him at all." He spit again. "All right, look around," he said, "but don't go over by that tarp. That area's off limits."

"Okay," Jon stammered, wiping the sweat off his forehead. He started back in the direction he'd come from.

He hid behind a stack of beams and watched the heavy man. The thunder broke closer, lightning flashed in the clouds. The man went into the shack, stayed there a while, came out again. He looked out at the excavation, shielding his eyes with his hand, then walked away.

Quickly Jon ran to the tarp-covered pile. Thunder rolled through the sky. Off limits, yes, it must be what he was looking for.

He hid behind the pile, peered out, made sure that no one was near—then lifted one end of the tarp.

The boxes were wooden, painted red. Stenciled in white on their sides were the words: EXPLOSIVES. DANGER. Jon trembled with excitement—then saw with dismay that all three of the boxes were locked.

He looked quickly around, then ran to the foreman's shack. The keys hung on a nail inside the door. Hurriedly he sorted through them, picked out the ring with three keys stamped REESE, the name he had seen on the locks, then ran to the boxes again.

Huge drops of rain began to fall, a jagged band of lightning cracked the air. Hands shaking, he tried one of the keys. It wouldn't turn. He tried the next key on the ring and the lock came open with a snap.

Quickly he ran to the shack again and replaced the keys, ran back to the pile in the rain. He was filled with a wild excitement now. He slipped the lock out of the hasp and opened the box.

It was only about half full, but what he wanted was there: the dynamite, the blasting caps. . . . In his mind's eye he saw the Monarchs at work on the wooden table, building the bomb. He didn't need much, not nearly as much as they'd used, he would only take—

Then he heard the voices. The heavy man was coming back and was bringing somebody with him. Jon froze. The voices were coming closer; he could understand some of the words. In desperation he climbed into the box of explosives, flipped the tarp down, closed the lid. Thunder crashed above him, rain splattered the tarp.

Then the voices were right beside him, the men were right there, and one of them said, "We gotta take about twenty feet of that bedrock out of the north wall there. We oughta be able to handle that this afternoon."

"You got enough stuff?"

His father's voice. His father was standing there, inches away. Jon lay in the total blackness, dynamite sticks and blasting caps jabbing into his ribs, his heart jammed into his throat. Then he thought of the book he had read on explosives: It said that electrical storms could accidentally set off dynamite. He pictured the box exploding, chunks of his flesh spraying into the sky.

The heavy man said, "If we need any more we can get it from Reston, can't we, Cliff?"

"Yeah."

Silence, then his father's voice again. "Where the hell did that kid of mine get to?"

"I seen him here a little while ago," the heavy man said.

"Here?" Doug Petrie said. "What the hell was he doing here? Jesus Christ, he's supposed to be smart, but half the time I think his brains are in his ass."

Everybody laughed. Jon smothered in thick hot air, salt sweat taste strong in his mouth. He couldn't stand it anymore, he had to get out, throw the tarp off, get air!

"You want to look and see if we got enough?" the heavy man said.

A pause. Jon's eyes went wide. Then Cliff said,

"Nah, we can always get more from Reston."

"Okay," Doug Petrie said, "I want to check with Borshack about those reinforcement rods. . . ."

The three of them moved away. Jon was shaking all over, drenched in sweat. He waited, lying on the dynamite, till the voices faded away. Then he lifted the lid of the box and gingerly climbed out, crept out from under the tarp. The sky was painful, blinding, wet, his glasses were totally steamed. He wiped them on his shirt and looked around. The rain came down.

His father and the others were not in sight. He tucked the dynamite and the blasting caps into his shirt and locked the box, replaced the tarp. Then he made his way back to the Eldorado and hid the explosives under the seat. He leaned back in the seat and closed his eyes and sighed, drained, enervated.

By the time his father came back to the car the sun was out.

"I thought you said you wanted to see the site. I bring you here and all you do is sit in the goddamn car!"

"Oh no, Father, I was walking around," Jon said. "But it started to rain."

"Afraid of a little goddamn rain?"

"There was lightning," Jon said. "But I saw a lot. I'm glad I came."

"Oh shut up," his father said.

He bought the timer that afternoon. He rode his bike to Henderson, found a fine one there in the Radio Shack, then went home and built the bomb.

His memory was so perfect it was almost like having Carlos there to help. When he finished, he put the bomb in his briefcase and sat on the bed. Staring at Eeyore through half-closed lids he said: "They should never have bugged me like that. I told Miss Robards to leave me alone but she wouldn't listen, and now I'll have to scare her—scare her good. And Sonny and Mr. Diedrick wouldn't listen either—so now they'll be going away. Diedrick is stupid, Eeyore, he shouldn't be principal of a school. And Sonny is cruel, he can't be allowed to live in freedom anymore.'' He sighed, lay back. It was ten o'clock and he was exhausted, but two more hours went by before sleep would come. Then he slept right through till one the next afternoon.

CHAPTER TWENTY-THREE _____

When school was over Monday, Sonny shoved him against his locker and said, "Where's my paper, Petrie?"

"I'm . . . working on it," Jon chattered. "I'll give it to you Wednesday."

"You goddamn well better," Sonny said. He chewed on his toothpick, sneered, banged Jon against the locker, then let him go. As he left, Jon stared through narrowed eyes and thought, Tomorrow. And tomorrow and tomorrow creeps . . .

When the hall cleared out, he hid in his locker and flew. Down all the halls and into the principal's office, the classrooms, until he was sure that everyone was gone except Mr. Stinson, the maintenance man. When Mr. Stinson went up to the second floor to check the jammed window in room 241, Jon entered his body again.

Quickly he went down the stairs to the gym, turned right, went down the hall to Mr. Stinson's room. He took the key to the front door off the hook and put it in his pocket, then went back to his locker, closed himself in, and flew. He followed Mr. Stinson around the building, watched the cleaning crew come in, watched as Mr. Stinson discovered that the key was gone. He cursed and tore his office apart, went through his desk and pockets repeatedly, finally gave up and told the head of the cleaning crew about the missing key. Still muttering to himself, Mr. Stinson left the building.

Minutes later, Jon sneaked out the east-wing door.

He hardly slept at all that night. The plan kept spinning in his mind. He was up before the sun, dressed,
went to the garage and took a multipurpose screwdriver
out of the toolbox there. He put it in his briefcase beside
the bomb and hurried off to school.

He took the stolen key from his pocket and let himself
in through the east-wing door. The building was deathly
quiet, strange with early morning sun. Quickly he went
down the hall to Miss Robards's room.

The heating duct was set in the wall behind her desk, a
foot or so off the floor. Jon took the screwdriver out of
the briefcase, unscrewed the duct's slotted cover. He
reached in the briefcase again and took out the bomb.

Fingers trembling, he set the timer. Nine forty-five,
just over three hours from now. He took a deep breath,
slipped the timer's cord through the heating duct's
cover, plugged it into the outlet beside the duct, and
slowly and cautiously lowered the bomb down the shaft.
He fitted the cover back in place and screwed it on
again, then picked up his briefcase and left the room,
closing the door behind him.

He stashed the briefcase in his locker, went down the
row, and opened Sonny's lock, the combination still
sharp in his mind from weeks ago. Sonny's jockstrap,
his sneakers, his gym shorts, a copy of *Gallery*
magazine, a few books—and way in the back of the
shelf, marijuana in a plastic bag. Jon shivered, half expecting Sonny to suddenly grab him and beat him
senseless. He reached in his pocket and took out the key
to the school, stuck it under the pile of papers on the
locker floor. He shoved one of the papers into his
pocket, an English test from a couple of months ago,
and closed Sonny's locker again. Then he hurried down
the hall and went outside.

He sat in the brush beyond the athletic field, exultant.
Everything was working perfectly. The bomb would go
off at nine forty-five. It would make a terrific noise,
tear a hole in the heating system, and scare Miss Robards to death. Mr. Diedrick—Jon smiled—Mr.

Diedrick would have some explaining to do. To receive
a bomb threat and not evacuate the building, what excuse could he give? What excuse would the school board
accept? He was finished at Aronson, finished in
education. Maybe he could be a janitor like Mr. Stinson. Or a short-order cook.

Jon smiled again when he thought of Sonny, because
Sonny would get the blame. The blame he deserved,
since he was the one who started the bomb threats, gave
Jon the idea.

He waited in the brush until eight-thirty, then hurried
to Henderson. After he made the call he tore a piece off
Sonny's English paper, dropped it on the floor of the
telephone booth. His paper in the booth and the key to
the school in his locker. Let's see him get out of *that*,
Jon thought with a grin. He hurried back to school.

Art class was two doors down from Miss Robards's
room. Jon bent over his paper, pretending to concentrate. An unbearable tension swelled in his chest. He
ached with it; he felt like screaming, running down the
hall. He couldn't keep his eyes off the clock; the second
hand seemed stuck in glue.

At last it was nine twenty-five, nine twenty-six, nine
twenty-seven. . . . Nine-thirty and no alarm. Diedrick
had decided to ignore the threat. The plan was going to
work!

He couldn't take the excitement, couldn't sit still
anymore. He raised his hand. Mr. Wallace arched his
eyebrows. Jon said, "May I be excused for a minute?"
and Mr. Wallace nodded, looking bored. Jon walked
past Sonny's desk and Sonny said, "Gotta pee, Pee-
Tree?" and kids laughed. Jon thought, Laugh, Richardson. Laugh while you can.

He went to the boys' room, relieved himself. When he
came out again it was nine thirty-seven. He stood in the
hallway and looked at Miss Robards's door. Eight more
minutes. He shivered, flushed with excitement. How
he'd love to be able to see her face when the heating duct
blew up. He bet she wouldn't look so superior then.

"Hi, Jon."

Jon turned. —And there was Chuckie. "Chuckie! What are you doing out here?"

"What are *you* doing out here?" Chuckie said with a grin. "Were you bad?"

"I'm coming back from the boys' room," Jon said. "Is that where you're going?"

Chuckie shook his head no. "I'm going to give Miss Robards a message," he said.

Hot needles jabbed into Jon's throat; his voice was stuck. He wet his lips, said hoarsely, "Chuckie, don't."

Chuckie smiled his sunny smile. "It's okay, Jon. I'm not going to stutter. I practiced with Miss Weller. See, first she had me do it with teachers I know real good— like Mr. Mucelli—and I didn't stutter at all." His eyes blinked slowly. "Then I did it with Mrs. Carter. I know her pretty good but not real good. The first time I tried it with her I stuttered a little, but the second time I did fine. Now I'm going to try Miss Robards. I don't know her at all and she doesn't know me."

Jon looked at the clock on the wall. It said nine-forty-one. A cold sweat coated his skin. "Don't go in there," he said.

"I won't stutter, Jon, honest, I know I won't. I'll do good." He started for the door.

"Chuckie listen, no, you can't—"

"I'll bet you a quarter," Chuckie said. "A quarter that I won't stutter."

"No, please—"

"I'll be back in a minute—and you'll owe me a quarter, Jon." He turned away and opened the door and entered Miss Robards's room.

The class was quiet. Miss Robards said, "What is it?"

Chuckie said, "The . . . the . . ." He wasn't looking at her. Something behind her desk had caught his eye, something in the heating duct. He stared at it. "The . . . uh . . ."

"Come on, I don't have all day," Miss Robards said impatiently.

"The . . . there's something in your vent, Miss Robards."

Kids laughed. Miss Robards said, "Don't tell me you came in here to tell me *that*."

Chuckie ignored her, intent on his find. He went to the duct, bent down, examined the cord.

"What are you doing?" Miss Robards demanded.

"Suh . . . see, there's something here!"

More laughter. "You're disrupting my class!" Miss Robards said.

"But see?" Chuckie said as he pulled on the cord. "Here it is!" And the cord was longer, longer, Chuckie's eyes were gleaming, enthralled, Miss Robards said, "What's your name? Who sent?—"

Then light and sound filled the world.

CHAPTER TWENTY-FOUR _____

School was canceled for the rest of the week. The police found the key in Sonny's locker, found the scrap of English test in the telephone booth, and Sonny was held in the Midvale Youth Detention Center to await his trial. Under threat of immediate dismissal, Mr. Diedrick resigned.

The doctors couldn't save Miss Robards's leg. They had to take it off above the knee. One side of her face was badly burned and rumor had it she might lose one of her eyes. Only one other person was hurt in the blast: Chuckie Palmieri, who died instantly.

When Jon came home from Chuckie's funeral he lay on the bed and sobbed. He cried and cried till his pillow was soaking wet. When he finally stopped he lay there and stared out the window at the dark green treetops, thinking of Lucifer. He washed his face, went back to his room, and sat on the edge of his bed and said to his donkey: "He isn't dead. We know that, don't we, Eeyore? People don't die, they just *change*. Their body falls away and their spirit flies. Chuckie is still alive —somewhere, on a different plane."

He sighed and held his head in his hands and said, "But I can't make contact with that plane. I've never seen the spirits of the dead. They exist in another dimension that I can't reach. But maybe things will be different with Chuckie, maybe I'll learn how to meet his spirit someday.

"What matters now is to treat that spirit well, to think good thoughts about that spirit, like the Indians and those tribes in Africa. You have to think good thoughts." Tears came to his eyes again as he said, "Oh Chuckie, I wish you the best."

He'd thought about the incident at least a hundred times these last few days. He had never wanted to hurt anybody, had only meant to scare Miss Robards, get Diedrick and Sonny in trouble. If they'd only let him alone the whole thing wouldn't have happened and Chuckie would still be alive. His best friend would still be alive. They had pushed him and pushed him until he just had to fight back.

Shadows covered the swimming pool. The sun was a copper ball on the western trees. Jon said, "He was just as good as anyone else and they called him a freak. He was born with a brain that wasn't right and he couldn't move right, so they called him a freak. What would his life have been? A horror, Eeyore. He's better off dead. No people staring, laughing, calling him Crip and Weirdo, all the names. . . . In his new life he can fly—the way I fly, but ten times faster, ten times higher. That's how it is for him now, I know it is."

His chest was shaking. He'd hardly slept at all the last few days and his eyes were circled with dark, his lids puffy and red. Strange images flew through his mind with bulletlike speed: the bomb going off, Chuckie's spirit soaring, the Monarchs, Miss Robards, Bruce falling, falling—everything whirling and blending and merging until there was only a feeling: a dark hard sadness soaking the sun in blood.

CHAPTER TWENTY-FIVE _____

"I say we hang the creep by his balls."

Jon watched, invisible, as Randy and Carl smoked. They were out in the park, behind the yellow-brick maintenance building, passing the joint back and forth.

"I been buggin' him for weeks about those papers," Randy said. "It's time to shake him up."

"All I need is a B in history and my old man gets me the car," Carl said. "The bastard better write it. He better write it soon."

"After we're through with him he'll do *anything* for us," Randy said. He grinned. "If Sonny was here we could get him to blow off his leg."

Carl sucked on the joint and said, "Sonny. What an asshole. The scuzzball really *did* it."

Randy's lids were heavy, half-closed. He sucked the joint with a hissing sound. "I guess that's enough to get me through Worthington." He offered the roach to Carl, who turned it down.

"So what time you want to go out there?" Carl said.

"Around two."

"You sure we still got dust out there?"

"Shit, yeah."

"We'll do the dust. And decide what to do about Petrie."

Jon flew back to his body, stepped out of the locker. He stood there, staring, in the empty locker room. So they still hadn't learned. Someone had lost a leg and someone had died, their friend was locked away—and they still hadn't learned. They'd pushed him until he had planted the bomb, they had killed his best friend and it wasn't enough, they wanted even more. Well they wouldn't get it. This was where it stopped.

The plan was a good one. So good that when the bell went off he didn't hear it, stood there mesmerized as kids swarmed by. Matt Wilson looked at him and sniffed and shook his head. Jon didn't see. His mind was on the plan.

The substitute English teacher's name was Mr. Kammler. He didn't know about Jon's assignment, the paper on *Macbeth*. All he seemed to want to do was tell stories till school was out, and that was fine with everybody, especially Jon, who slept.

The bell woke him up and he went to history, stared out the window as Mr. Worthington droned on about the greatest economic system in the world. Randy and Carl stared at Jon through drugged and sleepy eyes. He thought: The evil ones will pay.

As he went down the hill alone he thought of all the days he'd taken this walk with Chuckie—all those questions Chuckie had asked, that funny smile of his. Now there was no one to share his rocks and stamps and butterflies, no one to talk to about the planets. He thought of the look of amazement that crossed Chuckie's face when he heard that Mercury was blazing hot, four hundred degrees centigrade, that days on Saturn were ten hours long, that Jupiter was eleven times larger than earth. No matter how many times you told him the same things about the planets, he was always amazed.

He missed Chuckie terribly. The bitterness hardened in him and he thought; It's *their* fault he's dead. They wouldn't leave me alone and I had to fight back and things went wrong. They still won't leave me alone, they still want more and more. The plan went through his mind again.

A noise behind him—and there was Meg.

"Hi, Jon."

"Oh . . . hi." He walked beside her silently. He loved her so much, and now he suddenly felt unworthy of her, somehow unclean. They were halfway up the hill to Evergreen Row when she said, "You must feel really terrible about Chuckie."

"Yeah," Jon said. He looked at his feet as he walked.

"I can't believe that anyone would do such a horrible thing."

"Me neither."

"He's sick, don't you think? You have to be sick to do things like that."

Jon squinted at his shoes. He said, "Well maybe it was an accident."

"An accident? He put the bomb in the heating duct. It wasn't any accident."

"But . . . maybe he didn't want to hurt anybody, maybe it just happened."

She smiled. "You're too kind, Jon. Sonny wanted to hurt somebody all right. He hurt you, didn't he? Hurt you for no reason at all."

"But maybe he only wanted to scare somebody this time."

"I think he wanted to kill somebody," Meg said.

"I'm glad he's where he is, too," Jon said. He stopped and Meg stopped too. He said, "Do you need any help with your homework?" He blinked, and she frowned. "Oh . . . no," she said. "I'm doing fine."

"Oh," he said, his dark eyes staring, his lips in a curious smile, "I just wondered."

She was silent a minute, then said, "Jon . . . you're sweating so much. Do you feel all right?"

"I'm fine," Jon said, still smiling.

"You sure?"

"Oh yes, I'm positive."

They started to walk again. "Poor Miss Robards," Meg said. "What a horrible thing. Do you know how old she is?"

"How old?"

"She's twenty-six. So young."

"Young? Twenty-six is pretty old."

"You think so? I don't think you're really old until you're thirty." She shivered. "Losing your leg like that. . . . I don't know what I'd do if that happened to me."

Jon stopped and looked at her. "Oh no," he said. "Nothing bad will ever happen to you."

He stood there staring at her. Uncomfortable, she smiled weakly. "Well . . . I hope not, Jon. And . . . I hope nothing bad ever happens to you."

He smiled and thought: She loves me.

At home he said to his donkey, "We will always protect her, Eeyore. No evil will ever touch her."

He went to his desk and opened the bottom drawer. He hadn't looked at the bottles in weeks. He took them out and stood them on his desk.

Yes, this one here would do just fine. And this one, too, and this. . . . He mixed the substances together, stared at them. How light they were, just water and air, and yet. . . . He smiled. "Earth is the most amazing planet of all," he said to the toy on the shelf. "It truly is."

He flew that night: over trees, the swamp, the field, kept flying till he saw the tall oak tree against the inky sky; flew to it, went to Headquarters, dropped down close. The key was still there in its spot above the door. Good, good, he thought.

Randy and Carl would meet here tomorrow at two. To take their angel dust and plan his punishment. Well they would get their angel dust, all right—the dust of a very different angel from the one they knew.

Back in his room in the bright blue glow he looked at the substance again. His eyes were heavy, burning, as he looked at his donkey and thought, *We fail? But screw your courage to the sticking-place and we'll not fail.* We won't, we won't, the plan is excellent, nothing will go wrong this time. He put his hands on Eeyore, drank his power. Hours later, Macbeth and the witches and Lady Macbeth and blood-soaked Duncan whirling in his head, he dropped into fitful sleep.

CHAPTER TWENTY-SIX _____

The day was hot and dry. His father went to the condominium site and his mother drove into town. He sat in the kitchen and stared at the pool, time dragging by. He tried to read, dozed off, woke up with the sudden fear that he'd slept for hours. By noon he couldn't stand it anymore and left the house, the bottle in his pocket, and started down Evergreen Drive.

He walked down the path through the trees, along the swamp. He'd be early, very early, but that was fine, he'd have plenty of time to do the deed and find a good place to hide.

When he went through the field the sun was high and the air was completely still. The leaves on the trees hung limp, the tall grass didn't move. The first real scorcher of the year.

In the wavy heat ahead he spotted motion: something flying, tiny, brown. He stood stock-still as the butterfly came closer, dipped and dived erratically above the grass.

The metalmark again. He stood there holding his breath as it danced at his eyes and past his shoulder, every marking visible. All the years he had tried to catch the metalmark and now that desire was gone. Those years of innocent killing were past, belonged to childhood, a time forever lost. A sadness swelled in his heart as the metalmark flew to the trees, became a dot once more, then disappeared. He kept on walking through the field and entered the woods.

He'd never liked to kill the butterflies, but if you wanted a collection, well, it just had to be done. To achieve certain ends meant you had to do certain . . . unpleasant things. The main thing was to do them quickly, be efficient, fast.

> *Yet do I fear thy nature:*
> *It is too full o' the milk of human kindness*
> *To catch the nearest way . . .*

And was his plan the nearest way? he thought again as he walked through the trees. Maybe not, but it was a good way, a fair way. If anything terrible happened, it would be their own fault. Once again he would just . . . arrange things, and if others took certain actions that were wrong, illegal, evil—they'd get what they deserved.

At the clearing he stopped. There was the huge oak tree, and there the mound of brush that hid Headquarters, made it blend into the trees. He looked around quickly, nervously—then ran.

Down the steps, heart pounding. Grabbed the key above the door. Opened the door and then he was there—in the room where they'd nearly choked him to death. It seemed long ago, in another life, when he was young—and helpless. No one would ever hurt him like that again.

He crossed the floor and lifted the stone, took out the key to the cabinet. Opened the cabinet door and looked around.

It was dark and hard to see. He reached inside. Two bottles. He brought one into the light. Small squares of paper, that was the angel dust. He stuck it in his pocket, examined the other one.

The mushroom was dark and dry. He opened the bottle, poured half of the contents into his hand, stuffed it into his pocket. He took out the bottle he'd brought from home and hesitated, sudden sweat on his brow. He licked his lips. *"But screw your courage to the sticking-place . . ."* That made him think of Carl. Screw your courage. Carl had found that funny and had laughed.

Jon poured his mushrooms into the bottle belonging to Randy and Carl. He screwed the lid back on, shook the bottle. He stared at it. In the grimy dull light it looked fine, the same as before. No one would know the difference—until it was too late.

Quickly he put the bottle back in the cabinet, clicked the lock, put the key back under the stone. He locked the outside door and scrambled down the hill behind Headquarters, hid in the tangle of brush and waited, staring straight ahead.

He waited, waited, the heat pouring out of the sky. Two o'clock came and went and the woods were still. All he could hear was the songs of birds and the hot silver whine of cicadas and far in the distance the steady soft roar of the highway, mechanical surf. Even here in the shade of the trees it was sticky, sweltering. He waited, sweat coating his face, his glasses slipping, and then it was two-thirty, two forty-five. . . .

They aren't going to come, he thought. Everything perfect—and they aren't going to come! He waited another ten minutes, sick with despair, stood up to leave—and heard them on the path.

He left his body, flew, saw them head for the cabin. They opened the door, went through, Carl first. He followed them in.

Carl went to the table that sat near one wall of the dark musty room. He slumped onto one of the benches, set two cans of Coke on the tabletop, and said, "If I don't get a B in history, man, my ass is in a sling. I gotta do it, Hankins, or it's good-bye Camaro."

"You'll do it," Randy said as he crossed to the cabinet. He lifted the stone in the floor and picked up the key, slipped it into the lock. "Let's forget that school shit now and get happy." He opened the cabinet door and looked inside. He felt around. "It's gone," he said.

"What?" Carl said.

"I said it's *gone*. That fucking Richardson! Jesus, it's bad enough he fucked with that bomb, did he have to take all his shit?"

"Well how do you know it was him?"

"How do I know it was *him*," Randy said. "Nobody busted the front door open, nobody busted the cabinet open, they had to use keys—and who knows where we hide the keys except Sonny? —Unless you took it."

"Unless I took it," Carl said. "Get serious, Hankins. Jesus Christ, now what, I wanta do dreams. That mushroom still in there?"

"Yeah, that's still here." Randy picked up the bottle, shook it, held it up. "I didn't know we had this much. We oughta be able to get off fine on this."

"Let's do it, then."

"I guess we'll *have* to do it. It's just so slow, all that goddamn chewing, it's really *dry*."

"But it's good."

"Oh yeah." Randy grinned. "It's good all right." He opened the bottle and tapped it against his palm and out fell some of the wrinkled, leathery crumbs. He popped them into his mouth and said, "Here you go," as he handed the bottle to Carl. He sat at the table and opened his can of Coke.

Carl chewed on a few of the mushroom pieces. "Jesus these are tough."

Randy swigged his Coke. "Let me have some more."

Carl passed the bottle.

"Last time I did this shit it wasn't strong enough," Randy said as he put more mushroom into his mouth. "Salty! Jesus!" He drank more Coke.

As they chewed on the mushrooms and drank their Cokes, Jon hovered above their heads. He could almost feel sorry for them now. All the days they had wasted in petty pleasures and senseless cruelties, and chemicals—mind-bending drugs—were the closest they'd come to joy. If only just once they had tasted *true* exhilaration, if only they'd learned to fly, how different their lives might have been.

"Sonny is fucking *crazy*," Randy said.

"Jesus! Blew her leg off! The bitch deserved it, but Christ!"

Randy swallowed the last of his Coke and made a

face. "Were those last suckers *bitter*." He belched. "Too bad it wasn't Petrie got killed instead of Palmieri."

"Hey man, we need the fucker. What are we gonna do about him, anyway? Give me a smoke."

Randy laid his Marlboro pack on the table. "Grubber."

Carl shook out a cigarette and lit up. Randy took one and lit it with Carl's match. He looked at the ceiling, exhaled, and said, "What are we going to do about Petrie? Good question. I'll think of something, you better believe it, I'll get him good."

"Let's burn him at the stake."

"Not a bad idea."

"I need that history paper, man."

"You'll get it, don't worry. You'll get the biology paper too. We're gonna scare the shit out of the creep."

Jon watched. What poor pathetic fools they were. Still dreaming up torture and pain even now. He had made the right decision. These two were beyond redemption. He floated, watching them lazily smoke, and listening to their vicious lewd small talk. Randy's freckled face was complacent and smug, his eyes half closed. His head was nodding slowly back and forth.

Carl's grin was silly and wide. He squashed his cigarette butt out in the jar lid they used as an ashtray. "Getting anything?"

"Just a touch. Yeah, yeah, it's coming."

"Hey, it's *nice*," Carl said with a sudden laugh. "Hey, holy shit."

"This stuff is *good*," Randy said, "really *smooth*. It was never this good before, what happened?"

"The longer you leave it dry the stronger it gets. It musta been in there a month. You want to go walk around outside?"

"Let's just dig it a while. Let's see where we go."

Carl started to giggle, then shook with laughter; tears came to his pale blue eyes.

"What's funny, asshole?" Randy said, and then he

was laughing too. The laughter came faster, harder, he couldn't control himself.

"Blew her fucking *leg* off!" Carl said. "Blew—" He laughed so hard he was silent, shaking his head as tears rolled down his cheeks.

"Hey, look at your finger," Randy said.

Carl looked, laughed even harder.

"Did you ever see anything so *ridiculous*?"

They doubled up, hysterical; then after a few more minutes the spasms passed and they calmed down again.

"Wow," Carl said, "this shit is dynamite! Come on, let's go for a walk and mellow out."

"In a couple of minutes. I'm digging this."

Carl leaned back against the wall, his hands behind his head, his grin huge once again. Then all at once he winced.

Randy looked at him, frowning. "What the hell is the matter with you?"

"I don't know," Carl said. "I got some kind of cramp—" He winced again. "Ow, Jesus!" He clamped his hands on his stomach and doubled up.

"Try and fart," Randy said with a grin, and he started to giggle again.

Carl sucked in a hard sharp breath, jerked backward into the wall. Suddenly his arms began to twitch.

Randy stared. "Hey, what—?" Then suddenly his eyes went startled, wide. He clutched himself as if he'd been kicked in the solar plexus, grimaced as agony stabbed through his gut.

Carl's skin was a pasty yellow. Sweat beaded his forehead and ran down his face. His arms were jumping, jerking, trembling. "The mushrooms," he said. His voice was strangled, thin. "There's something—" he groaned and doubled up again.

Randy's hands were fists as the pain jabbed into his shoulders, raced over his arms. "We ate this shit a dozen times! It never—" he shuddered and gasped, grabbed his stomach, and closed his eyes. Carl's body was shaking violently, as if he were freezing cold. He opened his mouth to talk but his teeth clicked shut again before he could get out a word.

Jon calmly watched. It was perfect. It was going just as he'd planned. He stretched, he sighed, he kicked his legs and sailed through the roof of the fort, coasted down through the trees, and entered his body again.

Crouching low, he climbed the hill and hid behind the oak. Thumping and moaning sounds and a harsh loud cry rose up from the cabin's roof. The door burst open with a bang.

Randy's features were twisted, he gulped at the air, he gripped the sides of the doorway with shaking hands and pulled himself slowly up. Abruptly he jolted forward and fell to his knees on the dusty earth near the door. His shoulders jerked as if a live wire were grafted into his back. In the doorway behind him Carl's face appeared, then dropped into darkness again. Then Carl, too, struggled up out of the pit and lay violently twitching and writhing in dusty leaves, pine needles, and dirt.

Randy's mouth was purple. A strangled scream escaped his contorted lips. As if pulled by invisible cables from somewhere above, he shot to his feet, did a crazy palsied dance in the dust, then just as suddenly fell to his knees again.

Carl groaned and whined as he inched his way forward on stomach and elbows, his trembling fingers clawing at roots and leaves. He vomited: Pale yellow strands hung down from his chin, drooled onto the earth. He jerked forward, moaning, a spastic swimmer stranded on dry land.

Jonathan stepped from behind the tree. Randy's head snapped back, his eyes went wide. His foaming lips attempted to shape words, went slack. Then his body convulsed and he cried in a squeaky and almost comical voice, "Pee—" That was all he got out before vomiting down his shirt.

"Pee-Tree?" Jon said as he watched Randy quiver and heave. "Is that what you wanted to say? Pee-Tree? Come on then, why don't you say it?"

Randy's eyes were pleading, wild. He seemed to be trying to shake his head no, but his chin jerked up and back and then crashed to the ground. Shreds of leaves and bark adhered to his lips.

"Too much for you?" Jon said. "Well how about 'fuck'? You've never had any trouble saying that."

Groveling on his side, Randy retched again, his knees banging into his chest. What came up now was dark yellowish-green; it slid into and over his hands.

Carl was up on his knees again. He scurried in small frantic circles, squealing pathetically, scuffing the dust.

Jon watched. The scene began to sharpen, a tension grew in his gut. "So you're at a loss for words too," he said. "Not even 'shit'? I can't believe it. No 'shit,' no 'fuck.' Are you sure you're trying?"

A liquid rattling sound came from Carl's throat. He puked once more, jerking forward as if in a sack race. The vomiting noises were harsh and raw as he buckled and fell again.

"How I wish you could talk," Jon said as he stared, eyes narrow slits. "How I wish you could. There's so much I'd like to discuss with you. Like how I made Hodges fall into the quarry. And the bomb—how I built it and planted it in the duct, and best of all how I pinned the blame on Sonny."

Randy panted and moaned, his chest heaving. His eyes looked at Jonathan dull and unfocused, the lids flicking rapidly, crookedly.

"Do you understand what I'm saying?" Jon said. "*I* was the one who did those things, it was *me*!"

Carl's chin was sunk in the dirt; he retched convulsively. A dark stain spread through his crotch.

Jon's heart sped up. He licked his lips. *"Russula densifolia,"* he said, "that's why you're vomiting. And *gyromitra brunnea*—it poisons the blood, you see? It paralyzes the central nervous system, brings muscle spasms and loss of bladder and bowel control—and pain in the stomach and head." He was breathing heavily now, his thin chest heaving. "Even though the pain is quite severe, these mushrooms rarely kill."

Randy's eyes were watery, red; his tongue, a purplish black, protruded from his lips. Carl rolled and scrabbled in the dirt.

Jon licked his lips again; his skinny arms were trembling. "Rarely kill," he repeated. "But see, you wanted angel dust, so I gave you some of that, too. *Amanita virosa*, the Destroying Angel. And before the effects of *russula* and *gyromitra* disappear, the Angel of Death will seize you by the throat!" His heart was beating fiercely now; sweat beaded his forehead and brow.

A slow breeze sighed in the pines. Carl's head jerked backward violently; his ear banged into a stone and began to bleed. The fingers of Randy's left hand snapped into a twisted, gnarled fist and his foaming lips worked slowly, silently.

Jon forced himself to keep watching. The tension in his gut turned into nausea; he swallowed hard. The shock of what was happening was numbing, made things seem unreal. "The *amanita* has yet to begin its work," he said, and now the words came automatically, flat and dull, though his throat was tight. "The *amanita* will bring *real* pain, not just this mild discomfort you're feeling now. Incredible agony, and then—remarkably enough—the symptoms will start to subside. You'll think you're getting better, but no. Oh no," he said with a violent shake of his head. "For soon the Angel will wreak its vengeance, torture you and torture you— before mercifully putting you out of . . . of—" He choked. The look on Randy's face, the slime and vomit, it was too much to take. He forced himself to speak again but his voice began to crack.

"Tell me, Hankins, what do I look like now?" he said, voice rising hysterically. "Do I look like some kind of a monster? I'm only miserable, helpless Jonathan Petrie, that's all! No monster, just skinny, weak Jonathan Petrie! Remember when you smoked me out of your cabin over there? Remember what fun it was when I rolled on the ground here, choking and gasping for air? And you, Renniger—remember the time you threw the baseball at my head and broke my glasses? Do you? Do you?''

Dust clung to the froth on the puffy distorted mouths of both boys. Jon clenched his hands into fists. The sweat was pouring down his cheeks as he said, ''I warned you, didn't I? I told you to stop but you wouldn't listen! You had to keep teasing, had to torment me every way—'' His voice died out, nausea tightened his gut, he felt dizzy.

Randy inched through the dirt like a snake with a broken spine. Jon thought of the cecropia moth, the first one he'd ever killed, the way it had beaten its wings to shreds against the sides of the jar. Sweat dripped from his nose, from the fuzz on his upper lip. His words came in bursts as he cried, ''No, stop! Don't do it like this! Lie down and go to sleep! You don't have to die like this, all you have to do is lie still. Please, listen to me!''

Carl Renniger retched green drool. A dark horrendous groan escaped his throat.

''Lie down, lie down and sleep!'' Jon said in a shrill weak voice. ''Just sleep! Please! Why do you have to make it so hard? Why are you doing this?''

The moth had banged and banged against the jar and finally he'd let it out. It fell to earth like a stone and moved in feeble little circles, quivering, and tried to work its torn and faded wings. Jon watched it, horrified, then closed his eyes and squashed it, ending its pain. If only he could do that now. If only he could end this, end it, stop this agony.

Hit them both on the head with a rock, he thought. A heavy rock would make them both lie still. But then there would be no secrets, he would be found out. No, they had to die this way, the natural way, or he would be caught, would be trapped like a butterfly, pinned to a board.

In sickness and desperation he cried, ''I just wanted you out of my way! I didn't want you to go through this, I just wanted you to stop—''

He was suddenly down on his knees. "Randy!" he cried. "I'm sorry! I didn't mean . . ." His thoughts were ragged, buried in humming heat. "Why didn't you *listen* to me? Why did you have to be so *mean*? I didn't want to have to do this to you, but you *made* me. You *made* me!" He crawled over to Carl, who lay with his tongue in the dirt. "Was I supposed to put up with it all my life? You picked on me and picked on me till I just couldn't *take* any more!" He licked his lips, looked quickly around, then back at Carl again. "There isn't any help," he said. "I've read the books, a doctor can't help, there's nothing anyone—" His skinny chest heaved up and down, his heart was beating frantically.

Carl's eyes were glazed with gray film. He can't even hear me anymore, Jon thought, it's even too late for that. He looked at Randy, who retched and doubled up again. He got to his feet, he stumbled, caught his balance, looked around again. There was nothing he could do to help them now. This torture was the way it had to be.

Carl's palsied mouth clamped down on his chalk-white hand: Dark blood ran down his palm. In wide-eyed horror Jon stepped backward three slow steps, then turned and ran.

Looking back he saw Randy's tortured face in a shaft of sun, his twisted hand extended like a claw. The image blazed in his mind as he ran through the field, fell, got up again, and kept running through knee-high grass, his side in pain, his burning lungs screaming for air.

In his room he buried his face in his pillow and cried. The image of Randy's twisted face, that hand groping toward the sky, was burned in his mind like a brand. He rolled onto his side and looked at the things in his room: the string of planets, the globe in its stand, the poster of hot-air balloons in the bright New Mexico skies—but nothing would drown the image of Randy, the drool on his lips, the hand grasping wildly at air.

He wiped his face on the pillowcase, bit his lip, got up, took Eeyore off his shelf. He held the donkey tightly, trying not to weep again, and whispered into his ear; "It was horrible, Eeyore—so much worse than we thought it would be. I know it had to be done, it's just that . . . I wish you'd let me know how terrible—" He stopped. He looked at the toy and sighed, face futile and sad. "Then I wouldn't have done it. You're right. If I'd known how bad it was going to be I wouldn't have done it. Of course I'm glad, but . . ."

He closed his eyes and slowly shook his head. "It was just so *hideous*, I can't get it out of my mind." He looked at the donkey in earnest desperation, saying, "Help me, Eeyore. Please, help me forget. Take a shower, yes, and what else should I do? Look through my stamps. I will, I will. Is there anything else?" He was starting to shake. His stomach had turned to ice, and now in the air-conditioned room he was cold. He would take a shower, a long hot shower, get warm again—

"Jonathan?" His mother's voice, plaintive and thin, at the foot of the stairs.

He went to the door and opened it a crack, stared down at his dusty shoes. "Yes, Mother?" A roaring, rushing river was in his ears.

"We're eating now."

Sharp pains tore into his gut. "Oh . . . well, I think I'll wait a while. I want to take a shower and a rest."

"Are you feeling all right, sweethcart?"

"I'm fine. Just a little tired."

"Well there's soup on the stove when you want it."

"Thank you, Mother."

He closed the door. His pulse was thick in his neck. He put on his robe, went into the bathroom, ran the water, stepped into the shower. He sucked the warm soothing steam down his throat, let the water run over his face and his body, washing all the bad away and making him clean again.

Eyes closed, the water beating against his lids, the image of Randy returned—the outstretched hand. He gasped and opened his eyes and stared at the shower curtain—stared at the pattern, roses, blurred into blotches of blood. Quickly he turned his face to the showerhead, letting the water run into his eyes and blind and sting and burn. *A little water clears us of this deed* . . .

He turned off the shower, dried himself, combed his hair, and put on his robe. He tried to look at his stamps, but it didn't work. He got under his sheet, hugged Eeyore close, and told himself to sleep.

But fatigued as he was, sleep wouldn't come. He tossed and turned and a voice in his head kept saying, "*Sleep no more! Macbeth does murder sleep.*" He sat up and pressed his hands against his ears. "No, stop!" he whispered hoarsely. "Stop it, stop it! Eeyore, tell them to stop!"

CHAPTER TWENTY-SEVEN _____

Monday morning it was on TV. Cindy Atkinson's German Shepard had come home Sunday afternoon with a human ear in his mouth and the bodies were discovered that night.

"Stupid assholes," Doug Petrie said as he tossed off the last of his coffee. "Messing around with stuff like that." He stood up and put his jacket on. "They got what they deserved."

Jon squinted at the TV set and thought, They did, you're right, they got what they deserved. Bright dots of light sped away from his eyes as he watched the weatherman.

"Did you know those assholes?"

"They were in my class."

Doug Petrie picked up his attaché case. "They must have been idiots."

Jon continued to stare at the screen. "They were evil," he said.

Doug Petrie frowned and said, "Evil?"

"Yes, evil."

Doug Petrie stood there looking at his son's rapt face; the pale and waxy skin, dark circled eyes. He shook his head and said, "Evil. Well, see you later, Jon." As he left through the laundry room he muttered to himself, "Good Christ, that kid is weird."

They were standing out back of Fogle's Fountain, surrounded by trash cans and empty boxes, and Meg said, "What are you getting at?"

Matt pressed his lips together and shook his head. It's just goddamn *weird.*"

"Try not to use that language, will you?"

Matt stared at the ground. "I'm sorry. I'm just upset, I don't know what to think. I mean Bruce, Sonny, Randy, Carl—the four kids who gave him trouble—and three of them are dead and the other's in jail. Don't you think that's a little strange?"

"They could have been killed in a car crash too—they all hung around together. Would you think that was strange?"

"No, I wouldn't. I could understand that. But a rope bridge breaking, a bomb. . . . And you can't tell me Carl and Randy accidentally killed themselves. They've been doing that stuff for *years*."

"People make that mistake all the time," Meg said. "My uncle used to pick wild mushrooms with a guy at work, the guy didn't show up one day, he was dead from mushroom poisoning. My uncle never eats mushrooms now, not even the kind in the store."

Matt kicked at a Popsicle stick. "Okay, I guess it can happen," he said, "but . . ." He looked up and said, "There's something I never told you about. It's about Jon."

She frowned at him. "What's that?"

"One day a couple of weeks ago I got to school late, I was trying to open my locker, shaking it, and the door to Jon's locker came open. And he was in it. Just . . . sitting there."

Meg kept frowning and Matt continued, "He looked dead. His eyes were rolled up in his head and he was . . . *drooling*. I got Miss Weller, but when we got back he was standing outside his locker like nothing happened. And he told her it *didn't* happen. But it did. I saw it."

"But . . . what was he doing?" Meg said.

"I don't know. All I know is something's *wrong* with him. You don't go from being a straight-A student to flunking stuff in two months without something being wrong. He lied to me, Meg. And . . . just *look* at him—he's nothing but skin and bones, he looks like he never sleeps."

"I know it," Meg said. "He looks bad. And he really has changed so much. Talking back to Miss Robards—"

"Miss Robards," Matt said. "See, there it is again. Miss Robards was giving him trouble, and where is she now?"

"Matt, really."

"I mean it, Meg. Remember that time you told me you saw him coming out of the woods—how weird he looked? That was the day Bruce Hodges fell into the quarry."

"Oh Matt, come on."

"I'm *serious.*"

"Oh that's ridiculous. Jon wouldn't hurt anybody. He just isn't like that."

"He *lied* to me, Meg—like it was nothing. And I say he *is* like that."

Meg sniffed. "Oh Matt, that skinny little kid? He couldn't hurt anybody if he wanted to—and he *doesn't* want to. You think he made Randy and Carl eat poison mushrooms? Shoved Bruce into the quarry? I mean, really. Or maybe he killed his best friend with a bomb, does that make sense?"

"No, it doesn't make sense—but I think it's true."

Meg's mouth was a line. "You're really going off the deep end, Matt. If this is what working on that scholarship is doing to you, you better forget it."

Matt glared, his hands balled into fists. "It has nothing to do with that," he said. "I'm telling you, Petrie's behind these 'accidents.' I'm right and I know I'm right!"

Meg shook her head. "I think that's crazy, Matt."

Matt's eyes went wide. "Oh do you?" he said between clenched teeth. "I'm crazy, is that what you think?"

"I didn't say— Oh forget it!" She turned abruptly, walked away.

Matt yelled, "Like the rest of the Wilsons, right? Like

the rest of the crazy Wilsons. Is that what you think?''
He stood there, furious, shaking, rigid, as Meg went
down the street.

Meg felt bad about what she had said, but she didn't
speak to Matt for the rest of the week. She was on her
way home from school on Friday, walking up Evergreen
Drive, and up ahead was Jon, slouching, briefcase
weighing him down. He looked weary, frail. His hair
stuck up in a ragged tuft, his pants were baggy, his walk
was awkward, comical. Now that Chuckie is dead he
must be the loneliest person in the world, she thought.
He was walking slowly, staring straight ahead. Soon she
was right behind him and said, ''Hey Jon?''

He stopped, his head cocked to the side. He turned
and faced her, frowning. ''Meg,'' he said. ''Oh, hi.''

''Hi, Jon.'' She looked at him, his shoulders
slumped, dark circles around his eyes. To think of this
pathetic creature hurting anyone. . . . Why had Matt
ever said such a thing? He stood there pale, forlorn. Impulsively she said, ''Jon . . . my parents have said I can
date. Would you like to go to the movies with me
tonight?''

Jon's head was still cocked to the side. He blinked as
if he didn't understand; then he nodded slowly and said,
''Oh . . . yes. Yes, certainly, Meg.'' He just stood there,
holding the briefcase.

''Well . . . will you come and get me then—about six-
thirty?''

He blinked. ''I . . . I'm not old enough to drive.''

''Oh, sure.''

''So I guess we'll have to walk—or go on our bikes.''

Meg stifled her smile. ''I guess we'll walk,'' she said.
''Why don't you come over about ten after, then. That
should give us plenty of time.''

''Of course it will,'' Jon said. He smiled, a wan and
distant smile that made Meg frown. He just kept staring
at her, briefcase in his hand.

''I'll see you then,'' Meg said. She forced a smile that
quickly faded, walked up the drive to her house.

His mother was drinking and watching "General Hospital," and he went upstairs to his room. He showered and changed his clothes and combed his hair, pressing the cowlick down and putting some Brylcreem on it to keep it in place. So excited he couldn't sit still, he paced up and down talking softly to Eeyore for nearly an hour. Suddenly tired, he lay on the bed and flew to calm himself. A date with Meg. He couldn't believe it was true.

He entered his body again and went downstairs. Five thirty and his mother was still in the family room. Dinner would obviously be late, so he ate half a peanut-butter-and-jelly sandwich, forcing it down, then told his mother he was going out.

She looked at him, puzzled, her glass in her hand. "Now? We haven't had dinner yet. We're having pizza, your favorite, Jon."

"I ate something, Mother, I'm fine."

She drank, and smiled. "My, don't you look nice," she said. "I've always liked that shirt." She hesitated, said, "You look like you're dressed for a date."

He blushed bright red. "I . . . have to leave. I'm going to the movies. I don't want to be late."

"Enjoy yourself, dear."

His hand was shaking as he rang the bell at the Hales'.

Meg opened the door. She was beautiful, a princess out of a fairy tale: in a yellow blouse, blue shorts, her blue eyes sparkling. "Right on time," she said, stepping out and closing the door. The scent of her perfume hung in the soft warm air.

As they walked down Evergreen Drive, Jon felt both embarrassed and proud. He was struck by the terrible feeling that people were watching: All Evergreen Row was peering out from behind their drapes and blinds. The feeling was horrid, oppressive, he couldn't wait to be out of the street, and yet . . . he wanted them to watch. He wanted them to see him walking with Meg, the most wonderful, beautiful girl in the whole wide world.

He didn't know what to talk about, so he talked about all the old things that were once important: the planets, rocks, and butterflies, and Meg nodded and told him how interesting it all was. To Jon there was only one interesting thing—his flying. But he couldn't talk about that, just the other stuff, and he did, non-stop, mechanically, till they reached the theater.

He insisted on buying her ticket. The cashier gave him his change and he dropped a quarter, chased it down the sidewalk. When he opened the door for Meg he hit his foot, but it didn't matter. The movie was *Summer Dreams*, a long love story that Jon found boring, but that didn't matter either. All that mattered was that Meg was there. When she was there he could almost forget those terrible things, those nightmare things that wouldn't let him sleep. He stole glances at her beautiful face as the movie went on and on, admiring the gentle curve of her jaw, her perfect lips, her golden hair. Her hand was on the armrest and he almost touched it but drew back, afraid of offending her. He sat there, the movie meaningless, the screen a blur. Everything he'd dreamed about was finally coming true, and he was the luckiest boy on the face of the earth.

Outside again he said, "Do you want to go over to Fogle's and get a soda?"

"Not really," Meg said. "I mean, Fogle's is full of creeps."

He hesitated. "Well . . . I really don't know what else to do."

"We could get an ice-cream cone at the stand," Meg said, "and then we could just walk back."

"Okay."

Jon eagerly paid for the ice-cream cones at Lenny's, a hole in the wall that was only open summers, and Meg said, "Jon, I didn't mean for you to pay for everything. I thought we'd split it, you know?"

"Oh no," Jon said, quickly shaking his head, "I wouldn't think of it. I want to pay."

They turned off Main Street and walked past dark lawns. It was warm, and Jon's cone was dripping. He licked some melted ice cream off his hand.

Meg laughed. He stopped and frowned and said, "Do you think I'm funny?"

She smiled. "A little bit," she said.

He stood there, frowning, the ice cream starting to melt again and said, "Meg, I think you're great. You're just . . . the most wonderful person I've ever met in my life."

She smiled. She said, "Oh Jon, that's sweet." And then in the darkness she quickly kissed his forehead.

A tingling shock spread through him. He stood there, numb. She was smiling, he stood there open-mouthed, and then she said, "Jon—your ice cream!"

It was running over the back of his hand, dripping onto the sidewalk. "Oh, geez," he said, and licked the cone and the back of his hand, embarrassed, blushing. Meg laughed again and then Jon laughed too, confused, and they started to walk. He could still feel her kiss burning into his forehead, and now he was so excited he had to force himself to finish the ice cream.

As they walked up the hill to Evergreen Row, cars shooting past, the crickets chattering in the grass along the road, he said, "Did you ever have dreams about flying, Meg?"

She said, "I guess everybody's had dreams like that."

"Did you like those dreams?"

"They were fun. Except one time I dreamed I was falling. I didn't like that."

Jon shook his head. "No, falling dreams are bad. They mean something went wrong."

She looked at him. "Wrong? What do you mean?"

"Falling dreams . . ." He stopped. "They're, well . . . it's hard to explain—but you woke up before you hit the ground?"

"That's right," Meg said, "I woke up before I hit."

"That's how it has to be," Jon said. He was frowning now and blinking, looking straight ahead. They walked a while in silence and then he said, "Meg, how can you stand it?"

"Stand what?" she said.

"Oh everything. You're so nice, so good. How can you stand all the evil in the world?"

"I . . . don't see that much evil, Jon. I think most of the world is good."

He stopped and looked at her and said, "No, Meg, you're wrong. It's evil. Evil and filthy and cruel. I know. I've looked beneath the surface. I've been there night after night, I've seen it, Meg."

She looked confused. "But . . . how?"

He didn't answer, just started to walk again. He was silent, brooding, staring until they were near Meg's driveway, then stopped again and said, "We talked about God once. Remember that?"

"Sure I do. You said—"

"I was wrong. There were things I didn't know back then."

"So now you believe—"

He stared. His eyes were bright and hot. "The primitives were right," he said. "The images in dreams exist—on another plane. When you dream about someone who's dead, that person's spirit is visiting you. It really *exists*, you see?"

Meg hesitated. "Well, I never thought about it like that before. I know that heaven—"

"Yes, 'heaven,' " Jon said. He laughed, looking out at the darkness beyond Meg's lawn and said, "What counts is how you treat the spirits of the dead. The Pueblos arrange the bones of the slaughtered deer in a definite way, so the spirits will be at peace. The Crees hang the skulls of dead animals in the trees."

"Oh, gross," Meg said.

"No, not at all," Jon said. "It lets the spirits fly away to the west. You have to treat the spirits right, or they haunt you, stalk you in your dreams. And things go wrong, you fall when flying. *Macbeth does murder sleep*." He stared at her as crickets whirred in the lawns.

She shook her head. "Jon, I . . . You're going from one thing to another. I can't follow it all."

"It all fits," Jon said with a passionate gleam in his

eye. "Don't you see?" He bit his lip and said, "Macbeth. What do you think about Lady Macbeth?"

"What do I think about her?" Meg said.

"Do you think what I said to Miss Robards was right?"

"I . . . don't know. I guess I didn't really think about it all that much. I just read it and took the test, you know?"

"But you must have some opinion about her character. Do you have to do evil deeds to succeed, as she said? Is ambition—of any kind—always tainted with blood? I mean money . . . When you hold it in your hand you can *feel* the pain and blood oozing out of it."

Meg glanced at her house at the top of the driveway: squares of soft suburban light, the things she knew. She wanted to be back in her house, where nobody talked about these other things, away from confusion, safe. "I . . . don't understand," she said. It seemed suddenly dangerous here.

Jon squinted darkly. "This is the least important plane," he said. "The other planes revealed to us in dreams, in . . . other ways. . . ." He stopped. "We don't have to stay on the lowest plane, Meg, the plane of desire, of evil. We can live at another level, I know we can."

The crickets racketed against the dark; the spotlights shone on entrances and patios. "Jon, what are you talking about?"

He wet his lips. "About us," he said. "About you and me." He smiled crookedly. "I know things, Meg. I've made discoveries. I know we can be different, we can live where no one has lived before. Leave the others here with their gross material ways, their money, their ambition. You and I—"

She cut him off. "Jon, why don't we go inside and have a Coke?"

He stared at her, his eyes like coals. "Meg, listen. I know what I'm talking about. I can't tell you everything now, but one day soon it will all be revealed to you. It will all be revealed to you and you'll understand.'' He smiled distantly. "Just you and me, Meg. You and me.''

"I have to go in now," Meg said. "The mosquitoes . . .''

He stood there, staring in the darkness, smiling.

A sudden chill ran through her as she said, "I'm going in. Goodnight, Jon, I—'' He stared. She hurried up the drive.

"Someday you'll understand," Jon mumbled under his breath as he walked away. "I'll teach you, Meg. Now that I know you love me I'll teach you everything.'' He slowly walked up Evergreen Drive and just before he reached his house he grinned. She loves me! he thought. She kissed me, she loves me!

And suddenly he knew that things would be all right. His enemies were vanquished: No more slavery! No more torture! No more humiliation! He would not be afraid of anyone now; he knew he could handle them. And next year, school would be no problem. He'd learn to fly in class, just leave his body a minute and go to the teacher's desk and look at the answers to tests, then enter his body again and write them down. No more studying bleak details of the sordid material plane, this tale told by an idiot. Studying, learning, struggling, striving, and all of it lost to the grave.

What he had to do now was forget the past. It was over, finished, and after all what had he done? He had merely released some spirits—no, arranged to have spirits released—so that they would be free to soar to a higher plane. Murder, what a foolish concept, a fiction created by those who were mired in clay. There wasn't any murder, death—just change.

He wished he could tell Meg everything. But not yet, not yet, he had to work up to that. Little by little, and then he would teach her to fly. He pictured them flying together, living together forever on that high pure plane above the clouds. Bright bubbles of joy welled up in his chest.

As he walked through the kitchen, voices—the TV set in the study. He went there, saw his father asleep in his swivel chair, mouth open, snoring softly. What plane are you on now, Father? he said to himself. Do you still chase after money in your dreams? He turned the TV off and looked at his father's slack face. How harmless he seemed, cut off from the clatter of consciousness. He looked at the hands lying limp on the desk, the veins, the knuckles, the hairs. He looked at the blotter under the hands—and saw the note.

Call Slade to confirm, 6/14.

Jon stared at the paper with narrowed eyes. So his father was going through with it after all. On June fourteenth, just a week and a half away.

And why? Jon thought as he stared at the sleeping face. Now what have I done that isn't right? What excuse is there now for getting rid of me? I can take care of myself just fine now, Father, just fine.

He clenched his hands into fists and thought: How dare you! Meg loves me and my enemies are vanquished—and now this! Do you realize what I could do to you? Do you have any *idea*? He pressed his lips together, stared. *The sleeping and the dead are but as pictures*, said his mind, and then: No, Father, I'm not going to let you, I swear I won't.

CHAPTER TWENTY-EIGHT

On Monday he stayed out of school and flew to his father's office early, before his father arrived.

He went to the desk and checked the calendar. What he'd hoped to see wasn't there.

He waited. Soon his father was in the outer office saying hello to Mrs. Pelman, barking out commands; and then he was there at his office door, came in, sat down at his desk, made a telephone call.

Why wasn't the concrete delivered on time? Who the hell was running things down there? They better get on the stick and fast, goddamn it, or he'd look for another contractor. He hung up, lit a cigarette, and made another call. Yelled at somebody else. Hung up. Looked through some papers on his desk and muttered to himself.

Jon waited, bored. Finally his father reached for the calendar on the desk, and Jon moved close.

The fingers turned the pages. One day, two days—there it was, he saw it as Thursday flashed past: "J. 2:00." That was all he wanted to know.

That night as they slept he flew into their room. His father's keys were there in their usual spot on the bureau, next to the copper ashtray. He returned to his body, entered it, left his room, and crossed the hall. Slowly, scarcely daring to breathe, he turned his parents' doorknob.

The door came open silently. He broke into a sudden sweat. His mother would never hear him, he was sure of that, she had taken pills. His father was snoring soundly but that was deceptive: A restless sleeper, he could jolt awake any time. Jon crept across the rug, every muscle tense. He reached for the keys on the bureau. Slowly he picked them up. His hand shook. The keys hit the ashtray with a clink.

The pattern of his father's snoring changed abruptly. Jon stood there, throat suddenly thick, the keys in his hand.

His father did not wake up. Jon dropped to the floor. He opened the ring, slipped the key to Joanna's apartment off it, put another key in its place. Then he reached up, slid the keys onto the bureau again, crawled out of the room, closed the door.

He lay on his bed breathing heavily, sweating, the stolen key tight in his hand. He looked at the glowing donkey and whispered, "I got it, Eeyore. He'll never put me in Slade School now, I *got* it."

He took the key to school the next day. At lunchtime he hurried to Silva's Hardware in Henderson and had a duplicate made. That night he sneaked into his parents' bedroom again and put the original back on his father's ring.

On Wednesday he went right home. Nobody was there, and he went to his father's den, tore several sheets of his note paper off the tablet on his desk, and looked through his filing cabinet till he found what he wanted: a letter in his father's writing. He went to his room, painstakingly copied the letter over and over again till he got the writing perfect. Then he wrote the note on a sheet of his father's paper:

Alice. Meet me at 2:30 today at 54 East Third Avenue, Apt. 201D. Use this key—don't ring the bell.

Love, Doug

He compared the note to the letter. The writing was identical. He smiled and looked at his donkey and said, "After this she'll *never* listen to him, Eeyore. She'll *never* let him send me away after this. *He'll* be the one who goes." He tucked the note in his drawer and went downstairs. He had just put the letter back in his father's files when his mother walked through the door. He hurried out of the den and into the family room.

"Hi, Jon. Did you have a nice day at school?" She put her purse on the table beside the door and went into the kitchen.

Jon followed her. "Yes, Mother. Very nice." A pang of sadness hit him as he watched her mix the drink. The pain would be unbearable for her. He wished there was another way, but he had no choice. She'd learn about it anyhow someday, he thought, so the sooner the better.

But then he thought, No, she probably wouldn't. His father had probably been cheating for years, and yet she suspected nothing. Or if she did, she ignored her suspicions, denied they existed, muffled them with alcohol and pills. Tomorrow would hurt her terribly, but once she got over it life would be so much better. His father was crude, deceitful, brutal— It was wrong for her to live with a person like that. And anyway, he had to go through with the plan, he just couldn't go to Slade.

His mother sipped the drink and said, "What a day. I spent *hours* in Bloomingdale's and they just didn't have what I wanted. I finally found it at Bonwit's. Absolutely exhausting." She took another sip and said, "Would you like some Coke or anything?"

"No thank you, Mother." He hesitated, wetted his lips, and said, "Are you going out tomorrow too?"

"Never," his mother said. "Once a week is more than enough—especially in this heat." She smiled. "Why do you want to know?"

"Just . . . curious. You shouldn't run around all the time, you know, you'll wear yourself out."

She went to him and smoothed his hair. "So sweet," she said. He cringed involuntarily; a shiver went down his spine.

The next morning he waited behind the garage till his father went to work, then slipped back into the house and planted the note and key on the breakfast table. He sneaked upstairs to his bedroom and locked the door. He waited. It was after ten when he heard his mother go down the stairs. Quickly he left his body and followed her, watched her carefully read the note. She held it for a long time, looking out the window dreamily, then frowned and put it back on the table again.

She ate breakfast leisurely, then had her first Pernod. When she went upstairs to get ready, Jon felt anxious, sick. The time ticked by. Jon thought of school. Math class was ending now. With luck he would still pass math, but history, biology, he'd never get those papers done. One more week until school was out, oh God, he couldn't wait.

At last his mother was ready, left the house, got into her BMW. The garage door slid open, she backed down the drive.

He followed her into town. She went through two stop signs but nothing happened. She parked on Third Avenue, four cars away from the Cadillac Eldorado, trying four times to get into the space before she succeeded. Jon watched her open the door and get out, then quickly he flew to the second floor of the apartment house and waited for her to arrive.

Alice Petrie stepped into the empty elevator, her mind filled with hazy thoughts. She had drunk three Pernods and the world was mellow and soft. As the car began to rise she gripped her shoulder bag tightly, steadied herself against the motion.

Years ago, before Jon was born, Doug had often surprised her with bouquets of flowers and dinners out and invitations to lunch downtown, but that was so far in the past it seemed part of another life. She couldn't imagine why he had asked her to meet him here. Things hadn't been good at home for such a long time, but maybe. . . . The elevator stopped, the door slid open, and she stepped into the corridor. A muffled excitement coursed through her.

She stood there, hesitating, bemused and slightly

anxious, then nodded to herself and walked to the right.
The carpet was so beautiful, she thought—such a stunning red. She stopped in front of 201 D, read the note
again. "Use this key—don't ring the bell." She fished
around in her shoulder bag, came up with the key. She
slipped it into the lock and turned it.

Jon was there as the door came open. His shock was
so great he barely heard his mother's strangled gasp.

His father and Joanna were naked. She was leaning
back in a chrome and leather rocking chair, legs high in
the air, her heels on his father's shoulders. His father
kneeled in front of her, moved quickly back and forth,
his buttocks thrusting hard. Joanna's head was tilted
back, her eyes were closed, she moaned and bit her lip.
As his wife cried out, Doug Petrie looked up startled,
frozen in midstroke. Joanna screamed and covered her
breasts with her hands. Alice Petrie turned and closed
the door, face ashen, eyes unfocused, stunned. She
leaned against the wall, her right hand clutching at her
throat. And then she ran—past the elevator, down the
stairs.

Jon heard his father's wild shouts and curses behind
the door. He flew through the wall of the building and
into the street.

He watched his mother start her car. Oh God, he
thought, don't let her have an accident, *please* don't.
The car squeezed out of the space, sped down the street.
The traffic light turned red. The brakes slammed on
with a vicious squeal, the people on the sidewalk stared.
I'm sorry! Jon screamed in his head. I had to do it,
Mother, I had to, I had no choice! He was going to send
me away! The car pulled away from the light, turned
left, and Jon rushed home.

He waited there two hours. His mind was filled with
horrors, saw his mother's car smashed, saw her body
crushed, her blood oozing onto the street. He ached for
her to be safe, to come home, to be sitting here in the
family room where he could talk to her and make
everything right again.

He paced the floor of the family room, his stomach

knotted, his mind a jumbled chaos of worries and fears. The house was quiet, the phone didn't ring. Then a car on the driveway, the BMW, the garage door grinding open. She was home! Her footsteps in the laundry room, and there she was, in the kitchen.

Her eyes were red, her cheeks were stained with tears. Her hair hung over her forehead, limp and damp. She banged the cabinets open, made a drink. She stood there holding it, bleary, looking old.

Jon's heart rushed out to her. A wave of guilt tore through him. He went to her and said, "What's wrong? What happened? Mother, are you all right?"

She drank, set the glass down hard on the counter. She looked at him, eyes groggy, dull.

"Come into the family room and sit down," he said. "Please. Tell me what happened."

She shook her head and said, "No. No, Jon, I can't talk now, I just. . . . I want to sleep." She started toward the hall—and suddenly fell to the floor.

"Mother!" He ran to her, held her under the arms, tried to help her up. Her weight nearly pulled him down. "Mother, please, come sit on the couch, I'll call Dr. Goss."

"I don't want Dr. Goss," his mother said, voice thick. "I just want . . . sleep."

He helped her up the stairs and led her to bed. She lay there, skirt up to her thighs. He said, "Are you sure you don't want Dr. Goss? Can I get you anything?"

She nodded heavily. "A glass of water, Jon."

He went to her bathroom, ran the water, handed her the glass. She held it crookedly, then took a sip and said, "You're such a sweet boy, Jonathan. Now I have to sleep."

At the doorway he turned and said, "I'll be right here. If you need anything at all, just let me know."

She lay there, staring at the ceiling, skirt hiked up, eyes glazed. He closed the door.

His father did not come home and didn't call. The hours passed. He lay on his bed, exhausted, tense, unable to relax. It hurt so much to think of what he'd done. But the plan had worked. His father was finished, would have to live somewhere else, would have no power over him again. He would live with his mother, right here, and not have to go to Slade. He would stay with his mother and be near Meg and they'd love each other forever.

The sun went down, the light drained out of the sky. The house was quiet, totally still. His mother had slept for hours now. A small dark worry nagged him and he thought: I should have called Dr. Goss no matter what she said. She looked so *terrible*. What if she's really sick?

He crossed the hall and knocked on the bedroom door. No answer. "Mother?" He waited. Silence. "Mother, are you feeling better?" He stood there a minute, then turned the knob and opened the door a crack, looked into the room.

His mother was lying face down in the feeble light. Her left arm dangled over the side of the bed, the back of her hand on the floor. Jon went to her, frowning. "Mother, are you all right?"

He looked at the table and saw the pills, the empty water glass. A sudden panic struck his heart. "Mother!" She lay there, face in the pillow, features hidden. "Mother!" he cried again. Impulsively he pushed her shoulder. She didn't move. "Mother!" he screamed, and he shook her now, he lifted her arm and shook it hard. He let it go and it flopped to the floor again. "No, no!" he screamed. "Wake up! Wake up! You have to! Mother! No!" He buried his head in the bed and held her, racked with sobs.

CHAPTER TWENTY-NINE _____

For three days after that, he didn't eat. The funeral was a blur, a pale sick dream—the hearse, the coffin lowering into the ground with a little mechanical hum, the heat, his sobs, his father's hateful face . . .

The night of her death came back again, again, as he lay in his room. The frowning face of Dr. Goss, his father coming home after midnight, drunk, Jon screaming, "Go away! I hate you! Go away!" Over and over the mad dream played in his brain.

He left his body every day, hoping to fly beyond his pain, but the pain was solid, wedged like a stake in his soul. Sometimes he thought he heard his mother humming an off-key tune, heard her padding along the carpet in the hall. But it was a trick of the brain. She was dead, her spirit and flesh were separated forever. But how? he asked himself. What was it that locked the spirit out and made the flesh decay. He didn't know. Nobody did.

He only knew that she hadn't wanted to die. She had taken the pills to dull the pain, not to kill herself. And who had caused the pain? His father. Him and his harshness and neglect, his infidelity, his treachery. His father was the one to blame. Deep in Jon's heart the hatred gathered and grew.

The very sight of his father disgusted him. To live with him here in this house, day after day, would be unbearable. Yet the alternative was—Slade.

He was trapped. Again. In spite of all he had learned

and done, in spite of his marvelous powers, he was trapped. His mother, his poor good-hearted mother, had gone to another plane, a plane he could never reach. And before very long—unless he arranged things right—he would go to Slade.

Ten minutes to closing time. The pinball machines were dead. Meg poked at the ice in her empty glass and said, "I should never have done it. I just wanted to make him feel better, that's all, but he got the wrong idea. He was acting so . . . crazy."

"I wish you wouldn't use that word," Matt said. "People use that word and they don't know what they're talking about."

"But Matt, he *was*." She chewed her lip. "He was talking about the spirits of the dead, all kinds of crazy things."

Matt wiped the faucets behind the counter, slowly, thoughtfully. "That time I saw him in the locker. . . . There's something very weird going on. *Very* weird."

"I know there is. I'd like to help the kid, but what can I do? Now that his mother's gone he must really be bent out of shape."

Matt squeezed his sponge out, rinsed it in clean water. "You get over it," he said.

"I wonder," Meg said. Matt looked at her funny and she said, "Oh Matt, I don't mean you, let's not get into that again. There's nothing wrong with you. I mean Jon."

Matt sniffed and said, "His mother. Everyone who comes in contact with the kid—"

Meg shook her head. "Matty, no. He really loved his mother."

"Of course he did. It's just weird, that's all."

"Do you think Miss Weller could help?"

Matt drained the sink. "He's already seen her a couple of times."

"When he got in trouble. I mean every week—the way she sees Charles and Jan and some of the other kids."

Matt shrugged. "Yeah, maybe. But what do we do, suggest it to her?"

Meg poked at her ice. "I don't know. There must be a way."

Matt wiped the sink, put the sponge near the faucets, took his apron off. "Hey, time to go," he said.

Meg dumped her ice in the sink. Matt washed the glass and dried it, set it on the rack. He checked the front door and switched off all the lights save one behind the counter. The two of them made their way through the darkened back room.

Meg suddenly took his hand. In the darkness she said, "Matt . . . I'm *afraid* of him."

He held her tight. "Don't be," he said. "But stay away from him. Please. Stay away from him."

Meg and Eeyore were all he had left in the world. For days he had wanted to talk to her but didn't. He thought he might cry in front of her, he missed his mother so. He would wait until he felt better, was strong again, and then he would tell her his secrets, his plans—and would teach her to fly.

He ached to sit beside her, to see her face. He had stayed out of school since his mother's death and missed her desperately. Just to see her sweet smile . . .

He flew to her house. He looked all around, but she wasn't there. The only place she went on school nights was over to Sue Greely's house or down to Fogle's.

He flew to Russelville. As Fogle's came into view its lights blinked off. As Jon approached the store, two figures came out of the alley in back and started up the street. Matt Wilson—and Meg. He flew in close.

"If I work hard tonight I ought to be able to get it done by tomorrow or Thursday," Matt said.

"I'll type it as soon as you're finished," Meg said.

"That's great. I'll be glad when it's over, I'm really beat."

"You've been working so hard," Meg said.

They walked under the ring of lamplight and crossed the street. "You better believe it," Matt said. "I've been busting my tail. And I won't win the scholarship anyway."

"Of course you will."

He sniffed. "Hey, it's not only Betty I have to beat, it's the whole damn state."

"I bet you've worked harder than all of them put together," Meg said.

"I'm as *tired* as all of them put together, that's for sure."

Jon watched as they walked past houses, lawns, and started up the hill. Matt's house was on the other side of Russelville, so why was he walking toward Evergreen Row? A strange anxiety spread through Jon's chest.

Matt stopped in the shadows of tall lush trees. He smiled. "Chemical engineer," he said. "It still seems like a dream. But scholarship or no scholarship, I'm going to do it."

Then suddenly his arms were around her, he drew her close—and he was kissing her. The kiss broke and he said, "Again."

"Matt, please."

"There's nobody here, come on."

The kiss was long and slow this time. His hands caressed her back, she held him tight. Jon stared in disbelief. His stomach plunged.

They stood there holding each other and Meg finally said, "I have to go. And you have to work on your paper."

He ran his fingers through her hair. "I know. I'll see you tomorrow in school. Unless I don't do well tonight. Then maybe I'll stay out."

She took his hand and squeezed it. "You'll do well." She looked at his eyes and said, "I love you, Matt."

"I love you too. I love you so much, Meg." He kissed her again, just a touch on the forehead. "I'll see you tomorrow."

They separated, walked away. Jon stayed there, numb. Then sudden tears flooded his eyes and he wept in his silent voice. He would die, he knew he would. Not Meg; she couldn't do this. He would die. "*I* am the one you love!'' he yelled as he watched her go up the hill. ''*I* am the one! Forever!'' Then he covered his face with his hands and wept in the empty dark.

When the crying finally stopped he stood there sick and sad in the shadows and thought, No, Meg is not to blame. It's Matt. Deceitful Matt. Pretends to be your friend, and then. . . . She doesn't love him! She only said she does!

He drifted down the hill again and stared across the street at Fogle's Fountain. Matt. He should have known. The way he got Miss Weller after him that time in the locker room. . . . He was doing something evil to Meg. She had tried to keep him from kissing her but somehow he'd forced her into it, even forced her to say she loved him. He controlled her spirit somehow. Through deceit and evil ways he had conquered her soul. He pretended to be a friend and was really evil, like all the rest.

Even worse than the rest. The others had never pretended. You knew what they were, but Matt . . . Matt lied. Dissembled. Treated Meg as his father, Doug Petrie, had treated his mother. Cheated and lied for all those years until he had finally killed her. And what were Matt's plans for Meg? Why was he doing this to her?

He stared at Fogle's, dull, dim light behind plate glass. He thought of the way Matt had offered to help him, the way he had scared Randy Hankins that time. All a ruse. All a game to get him to think he was on his side. Enough to fool others, those tied to Earth, but his flying had taught him plenty about people's games: his father and Dr. Schlosser, Miss Robards and Mr. Diedrick, all those dozens of others whose names he had never known, all actors in a real *Macbeth*, a cruel, malicious play. Matt was the same as they were, exactly the same.

No, worse. He had captured Meg's spirit, had made her his slave.

Quickly he flew past Fogle's, past houses and trees, until he saw Matt up ahead walking briskly home. He followed him out of Russelville and up Brewery Hill.

He had been in houses like this before in his travels, but never dreamed that anyone he knew would live in such a place. The walls were covered with yellowed paper, a flowered print streaked with stains. The woodwork was dark and gouged, its paint having worn away years ago. In the kitchen a bare bulb hung from a cord; a scratched, chipped sink on legs stood crookedly against one wall, a small cracked mirror above it.

A girl of eleven or twelve was watching a small fuzzy black-and-white TV set in the tiny living room. The couch she sat on was bulky, sagging, covered with threadbare fabric. Matt came into the room and said, "Hey Jill, when'd the old man leave?"

"Half an hour ago."

"He say when he'd be back?"

"No." She stared at the set, entranced.

Matt looked at the mail that lay on the small round table at the end of the couch. He tossed it down again. "You better get to bed," he said.

"Oh why? School's almost over."

"Come on, you need your sleep. Anyway, that junk will rot your brain."

"Oh bull." Reluctantly she got up slowly, turned the TV off. "Goodnight, Matty," she said as she left the room.

"Goodnight, Jill."

Matt went back to the kitchen, looked in the refrigerator. It was small and old, with rounded edges and a door that snapped open loudly. He searched through one of its drawers, came up with an apple, washed it at the sink, then went upstairs.

The stair treads creaked, the banister was loose. At the top of the steps Jon paused, looked down.

That's where it happened, he thought. That's what the kids always said, at the top of the stairs, that's where she'd killed herself. The wood was spotted, stained. Jon tore his gaze away and followed Matt.

Matt's room was a surprise. The walls were white, the

woodwork blue, there were posters, everything was neat, the bed was made with a red and blue striped spread. Not a child's room, not a teen-ager's room: the room of an adult. A light with a metal shade hung over Matt's desk. He snapped it on, sat down, bit into the apple, looked through the papers there.

Jon looked at the papers too. They dealt with the synthesis of hydrogen gas from sea water. He wouldn't take chemistry until next year, but he'd studied it on his own and remembered the symbols perfectly. The paper was a good one; not brilliant, but respectable, quite good for a high-school student's. Jon watched Matt work, looking over his shoulder, reading, memorizing. He hated Matt with a passion, hated being with him in this room, but he had to stay if his plan was going to work.

Matt went over the paper again and again, checking and double checking all the formulas. It looked like he would finish the paper tonight. Jon smiled to himself, flew home.

He put his hands on Eeyore, drank his power, and said, "Right now. While it's fresh in my mind." Then he sat at his desk and wrote feverishly, long into the night.

He slept until one o'clock the next afternoon. His father had made no attempt to get him up. Since his mother's death, his father had left him alone, completely alone. It was almost as if he had ceased to exist, had died along with his mother.

Jon was exhausted in spite of the sleep and lay on the bed a long time. Then he dragged himself up, got dressed, and ate half a bowl of Cheerios. By then it was almost three o'clock, and he went to his room and flew.

As soon as Meg came home she went right upstairs. She set the folder on her desk, took her typewriter out of its case.

So Matt had finished last night, Jon thought. He had finished his paper and now he was making her type it. She was in his control and would work for him, would kiss him, might even—no, not that. No, never! He shuddered. Never that, but she would work for him. He'd forced her to, as Bruce and the others had forced him to work for them.

He moved close to the typewriter, stared, fixed the type in his mind. He was inches away from Meg, just inches away. Flushed with love, he gave her a phantom kiss. She rubbed her cheek and frowned, stopped typing a minute. He looked at her clear blue eyes, her serious face, those lips. . . . He forced himself away, flew back to his bedroom again.

Elite Rental was next to Silva's Hardware in Henderson. He checked the machines they had for rent and said, "Yes, this one here, the Royal. How much does it cost for a day?" He gave the man the deposit and hurried home.

He was not a fast typist and it took him eight hours to do the twenty-one pages. By then it was nearly one in the morning. He had eaten nothing, and he had a headache. His eyes were swollen and red, vague pains stabbed into his ankles and elbows and knees. But he smiled and said to his donkey, "Finished, Eeyore. Finished!" He laughed oddly, off-key. "Let's see what Matt Wilson makes of this!"

CHAPTER THIRTY _____

It was his first time at school since his mother died. Kids stared as if he had come from another planet. He ignored them and went to the locker room.

Soon Matt came in. And there was the paper in his hand, the paper Meg had typed. "Hi, Jon."

Jon nodded curtly, hatred burning in his heart.

Matt opened his locker. He put the paper on the shelf, then stood there. He took a deep breath and said, "I'm sorry about your mother."

"Thanks," Jon said. His voice was shaking. He looked at his lock, turned the dial. Matt closed his locker, left the locker room. Jon sighed a huge deep sigh.

Matt had chemistry sixth period; that's when he'd turn his paper in. The locker room cleared out. Jon waited. The bell rang starting first period and Jon stepped in front of Matt's locker. He turned the dial. 32-4-8, he still remembered that. He still remembered Sonny's combination, Bruce's, Randy's, Carl's. All those lockers were empty now—because of him.

The lock stuck. He yanked it. Yanked again. And suddenly Mr. Turnbull, vice-principal in charge of discipline, was standing there.

He squinted, gave a backward nod, red creases of fat at his neck. "Let's go, get a move on, Petrie."

Jon's hands were frozen on the lock—Matt Wilson's lock. "I'm sorry, Mr. Turnbull. I'm a little late."

"Well let's go."

Jon worked the combination, terrified that Mr. Turnbull would realize it wasn't his locker. The padlock clicked, he yanked again, the door came open this time. He grabbed the chemistry paper, stuck it in his briefcase, pulled out the paper he'd typed and put it in the locker. He closed the door and snapped the lock and hurried off.

He turned the corner, leaned against the wall. Sweat coated his skin as he thought: Good God, that was close. If Mr. Turnbull had caught me. . . . He started off down the hallway again, almost running, then stopped abruptly, opened his briefcase, looked inside.

Too good to be true: He had taken not only the finished copy that Meg had typed but the handwritten copy too. They were clipped together. Wonderful, perfect, he thought, it couldn't be better.

Matt handed the paper in at the start of the class. They were having a test, and Mr. Frazier looked through the paper as everyone worked silently. Every so often Matt glanced up nervously at Mr. Frazier, trying to guess his reaction to what he was reading, but he just kept frowning his usual steady frown.

Something was nagging at Matt, some vague unconscious worry. Just as the period ended, he knew what it was: the original draft of the paper. He didn't remember unclipping it before handing the typed copy in. But he must have—it couldn't be missing.

When the test was over and kids started leaving the room Mr. Frazier said, "Matt, I'd like to talk to you."

Matt stood there in front of the desk. Mr. Frazier straightened the test papers, frowning deeply, waited till all the kids were gone, then looked at Matt and said, "Your paper makes no sense."

Matt stared, incredulous. "What?"

"It makes no sense. It's completely confused. Look at this." He put down the tests and picked up Matt's paper and turned to the second page. "Read this," he said, "and tell me what it means."

Matt read the section, frowning. He looked up slowly

and said, "But I never wrote that."

Mr. Frazier said, "It's your paper, isn't it?"

"But I never *wrote* that." Matt thumbed through the paper quickly, disbelieving. Everything was different, everything was changed. It was just like his paper but . . . crazy. An odd flushed tingling spread through his chest and neck. "I didn't write it like this," he said. "I . . . had a friend type it for me. She must've gotten mixed up. His brain was racing, his skin was hot. Panic started to grow as he said, "Wait a second, I'll be right back."

He hurried out of the room and down the hall. The original copy. It had to be there in his locker. Doubt and confusion struck him as he spun the dial, cursed the lock and yanked it viciously. He threw the door open, looked inside, broke into a sharp cold sweat.

He cleaned out his locker, looked through everything. Not there. Not *there*! He'd had it this morning, he *knew* he had! He felt suddenly weak; the locker room seemed to shift behind his eyes.

Back in Mr. Frazier's room he said, "I brought the original copy with me this morning, but it isn't there."

"Maybe you just thought you did," Mr. Frazier said. "Maybe you left it home." His tone was kind.

"I *know* I brought it!" Matt said. His eyes were blazing, hard.

Mr. Frazier shrugged and said, "I'm sorry you can't find it, Matt. This draft is simply . . . nonsense." He handed it back.

Matt's forehead was soaked with sweat. He took the paper, trembling. "This isn't the paper I wrote," he said. "This isn't it! I know what I wrote, and this isn't it!"

Kids were filtering into the room. They stared with curiosity. Matt swallowed hard and said, "I'll talk to my friend. The one who typed it. I'll get this squared away, believe me I will."

Mr. Frazier regarded him coolly. "The deadline is Monday, Matt. If you can fix it by then you have a chance, but as it stands . . ."

"I'll fix it," Matt said. "I'll fix it one way or another, I swear I will."

"I hope so," Mr. Frazier said.

Jon waited in the locker room, invisible. Matt came in, face furious, the worthless paper tight in his hand. He spun the dial on his lock and pulled. It stuck; he cursed and slapped the locker door. He tried the lock again, yanked hard. It opened and the row of lockers shook.

He threw his locker's contents onto the floor: his sneakers, jockstrap, papers, books, two oranges, a tennis ball. . . . He stood there, red-faced, sweat trickling down his cheeks, his lips pressed tight. Then abruptly he crammed the stuff back.

Jon followed him to Mr. Worthington's class. Most of the kids were already seated and Mr. Worthington was at the board. Matt stood at the door and gestured to Meg, who sat near the center of the room. She frowned, then came to him.

"What do you want?" she whispered. "The period's starting."

"I have to talk to you."

"Now? Can't you wait—?"

"No, I can't."

He took her aside out of sight of the class and said, "I turned this paper in to Frazier and he gave it back. It's no good."

"No good? But that's impossible, you worked so hard."

"This isn't the paper I wrote. It's all changed around."

"But. . . . I don't understand."

He looked at her. "You're sure you typed it exactly the way I wrote it."

"Of course I did. Exactly."

He thrust it at her. "Look at this. Is this the paper you typed?"

She took it, turned the pages. "Well . . . yeah."

"Well it isn't the paper I wrote. Now look at it

carefully, Meg. Is it just the same as the handwritten copy I gave you?''

Meg stared at the pages, shaking her head. "I never had any chemistry," she said. "I didn't understand a lot of it."

"But look at it, look at it! Is it the same?" Matt's voice was strident, the veins in his neck were bulging.

"Matt, please—calm down, they'll hear you."

"I don't give a good damn if they hear me or not! I have to know what's happening!"

Meg shrugged. "I'm not sure if it's the same," she said. Her mouth was quivering. "It looks the same, but I'm not sure."

"It's *not* the same!" Matt said. "Somebody's changed it all around! Somebody's trying to mess me up!"

"Matt, stop it! Stop shouting, are you—?"

"Am I what?" His eyes bored into her, on fire.

"Nothing. I'm sorry. Nothing."

"Am I *what*?"

Then Mr. Worthington was at the door. He looked at them, his fat face bland, and said, "All right, let's knock it off. We're starting, Hale. Get moving, Wilson. And that's enough of that foul language, understand?"

Matt pressed his lips together, turned abruptly, and walked down the hall.

Jon flew to his body, entered it, and hurried to Mr. Worthington's class. He took his seat and looked at Meg. She seemed close to tears. He thought, Oh Meg, please don't feel bad. It's going to be all right. Just one more thing to do—and he will never cause you any pain again.

Meg waited for Matt outside his last-period class, but he didn't show up. The bell went off, the class began, and she stood there in the empty hall. A terrible apprehension seized her. She was supposed to be in hygiene, but she hurried upstairs instead.

"Miss Weller?"

Sue Weller looked up from her desk at the pretty blonde. She knew the girl, but the name wouldn't come. "Hi," she said.

"Can I see you a minute?"

"Sure. Come on in, sit down."

Meg sat on the edge of the little couch across from Sue Weller's desk.

The name came back. "Meg Hale."

"That's right."

"You worked on the athletic equipment drive."

"You have a good memory."

Sue Weller laughed. "Nobody's ever told me *that* before." Meg's face stayed serious. Sue said, "What is it you want to see me about?"

"Matt Wilson."

"Oh?"

Meg's voice began to crack. "That chemistry scholarship you had him try for. I typed the paper. I know I typed it right, but it—" Suddenly her face dissolved in tears. She cried, hand over her eyes.

Sue Weller sat beside her and gave her a Kleenex. Five minutes went by before she could tell her story.

"I'm worried," Meg said. "No, I'm *scared*. He worked so hard, you wouldn't believe how hard he worked. And now . . ." She shook her head. "His older sister . . ." She began to cry again. When she stopped, Sue Weller talked to her for more than half an hour. She called Matt at home but nobody answered the phone.

"I'll keep trying," she said. "If you hear from him, have him give me a call. This is my number at home." She wrote it down, tore the sheet off the pad, and handed it to Meg. "If you have any problems at all—or just want to talk—just call."

"Thanks a lot, Miss Weller. I really mean it."

"Hey, that's why I'm here."

Meg brushed her hair back, sighed, and forced a smile.

When she got home she tried Matt's number again. His little sister answered; he wasn't there. She went down to Fogle's. He hadn't come in. In her mind she pictured the staircase she'd never seen, the body lying there, the gun, the pool of blood. . . .

Jon flew beside her as she walked back home. He'd been to Fogle's Fountain too, hoping to find Matt there. He was disappointed, but he could wait. Tomorrow would be soon enough to do what he had to do.

As he went up the hill he said in his silent voice, "I love you, Meg. I'll always love you, always, forever and ever. And we'll live together forever in love, in our own special world, away from all this pain. You're sad right now, but soon I'll make you the happiest person on Earth. Once evil Matt is out of the way you'll be free—as free as the butterflies and birds, as free as me. He blew her a kiss, he waved, then flew up the street ahead of her, turned left, dipped down behind the houses, soared into the trees.

He flew down the path, past the swamp. He remembered that day that Bruce and Carl had shoved him into the water there and thrown his glasses away. Nothing like that would ever happen again. He knew too much, he was too strong now, he was safe forever. He had taken care of Bruce and Carl, and tomorrow would be Matt's turn.

He flew happily out of the trees and into the field. Then suddenly he stopped short.

There on the opposite edge of the field were three huge Caterpillar tractors, two backhoes. Their cabs read HELLER EQUIPMENT COMPANY, MIDVALE, NEW JERSEY.

He had seen that name before—that time he went to the condominium site. Heller Equipment, yes, that was the firm his father used. His stomach suddenly plunged, and he flew home.

"Father?"

Doug Petrie hung his jacket in the foyer closet, closed the door. He looked at Jonathan coolly. "What?"

Jon wet his lips. "I went to the field today. I saw backhoes and bulldozers there."

Doug Petrie walked into the kitchen. He took a glass from the cabinet and opened the freezer compartment of the refrigerator. "Twenty-eight units," he said.

"Bigger than Evergreen Row. We'll start clearing the site on Monday."

"But you can't!" Jon said with sudden passion. "The metalmark lives there!"

His father dropped ice in his glass. He steeped it in Jack Daniel's, tasted it. He frowned and said, "The what?"

"The metalmark. It's a butterfly. That's where it lives."

Doug Petrie sniffed. "You have to be kidding," he said.

"It isn't just *any* butterfly," Jon said. "It's special, it's rare. There's probably not another breeding ground for over a hundred miles."

Doug Petrie took a gulp of the whiskey and said, "You think I'm going to stop my development because of some stupid bug? Are you out of your mind?"

"No," Jon said slowly, "I'm *not* out of my mind."

Doug Petrie sucked his teeth. He drank again and said, "I'm starting on that site Monday."

Jon stared, his eyes sharp, strange. He blinked and said, "I'm not going to let you."

His father set his glass on the counter, looked at him. "What did you say?"

"I said I won't let you."

"Get up to your room!" Doug Petrie said. "Get out of my sight. Just get the hell up to your room!"

Jon kept on staring, noises in his ears. He clamped his jaw tight, slowly turned. He left the kitchen and started up the stairs. "You little bastard!" his father yelled.

He closed the door to his room and went to Eeyore, took him down from the shelf. He held him, blinking, felt the power flow. Circles of noise whirled into his brain, the donkey's fur seemed charged, electrified. He set the toy on the bed and said, "The only thing he understands is money. Beauty, love—they aren't a part of his world. The fields are full of beauty and the metalmark's only home in a hundred miles—and he's going to ruin them. If metalmarks sold for a million dollars he'd sing a different tune, you bet he would."

He paced up and down, his voice grew louder, the planets on the string above his head began to whirl. "What could I ever say to him, Eeyore? How could I ever make him understand? There was plenty that Mother didn't understand, but she understood beauty." He raved, his voice hysterical, face flushed. "He understands nothing important, nothing! He's narrow, vicious, stupid, cruel—"

A noise in the hall. And then, with shocking force, the door to the room flew wide.

Jon whirled. His father was in the doorway, red with anger, hands clenched into fists. "Talking to that toy again?" he said in a dark voice filled with rage. He was in the room, loomed powerful and huge. "Did I tell you never to do that again? Did I? How old are you? Three?"

"No, no!" Jon said. He cowered, shielding his face with his hands. "I was talking to myself," he said. "I wasn't talking to Eeyore, I—"

"You liar!" His father lashed out with the back of his hand. The blow caught Jon on the lower arm, glanced off his skull. Jon stumbled backward, crashed against the desk. He scrambled to his feet, eyes terrified. His father cursed, snatched Eeyore off the bed.

"What are you doing?" Jon cried. "Father! No!"

"This goddamn piece of shit!" Doug Petrie screamed.

He yanked at the toy and one of the legs came off. Pale stuffing flew through the air.

Jon screamed and clutched his arm as agony ripped into him. In desperate panic he lunged for the toy. With one swift stroke his father sent him flying and he crashed against the wall. Bright streaks shot through the black sky in his head.

His father tore another leg off Eeyore and Jon screamed again, a high, blood-curdling yell that made his father freeze, then narrow his eyes. "To think that I put up with this for all these years," he said. "I must've been a goddamn idiot!" He threw the torn-off leg at Jon and hit him flush in the face. Jon's eyes were wild, dazed. He cringed against the wall.

"You coward!" Doug Petrie said. "You sniveling, infantile coward! I'll make a man out of you yet! You'll go to Harrington tomorrow!" Still holding the mangled toy, he turned and walked out of the room.

Jon ran to the doorway, his shoulders and head racked with pain. His father went down the stairs, cursing under his breath. Jon ran to the stairwell faint with agony, crouched low. His right eye throbbed and stung. "If he burns you, Eeyore, if he burns you—" The tears were hot and wet and huge on his face, his heart was numb with fear.

His father walked through the laundry room and out of the house. Jon heard the back garage door slam against the wall. A silence: then the sound of the trash can lid crashing down. Jon breathed a heavy sigh of relief and swallowed, throat tight and dry.

Doug Petrie walked back through the kitchen and into the den. He slammed the door. Jon heard his curt, muffled voice on the phone.

He was calling Harrington Academy. He was going to send him away.

Jon sneaked down the stairs, his heart thick and hard in his chest. His right eye throbbed, was blurry, out of focus. He ran across the kitchen floor as if it were covered with blazing coals, slipped into the garage. Went out through the back, slowly lifted the lid off the galvanized metal can.

There was Eeyore, staring up, front legs torn off, his head cocked crookedly. His right eye dangled out on a thick dark thread. Jon poked it into place and winced. His vision cleared. He took the toy in his arms, hurried into the house, ran quickly up the stairs.

At the top of the landing he heard his father slam the phone down, heard the door to the study open, heard his father mutter something, walk into the kitchen. And then he was in the laundry room and in the garage again. Jon's heart beat wildly. If his father found out that Eeyore wasn't there . . .

Then the Eldorado roared to life, and Jon sighed and

staggered into his room, clutching Eeyore tight against his chest. He fell onto his bed and cried, "Oh Eeyore, look what he's done to you. You'll never be right again!" He laid the donkey on the bed, put his hands on the matted fur; the vibration was feeble, dim. Jon narrowed his eyes. "He nearly *killed* you," he said. He ran his hands across the fur and said, "I'll share my power with you, Eeyore. Please, don't worry, I'll make you better, I swear. I'll sew your legs back on and keep you safe."

He picked up the torn-off legs from the floor and laid them on the bed. The anger, rich and dark, flowed through him, masking his pain. He sat on the edge of the bed and stared at the wall as bitter thoughts dived and twisted in his mind. After a long time, after the pain in his head was no more than a tiny throb, he picked up the legless crooked Eeyore, stared at him sadly, and said, "He killed my mother, he tried to kill you, he's sending me away. On Monday he'll destroy the home of the metalmark." He stared, eyes dark, a hundred voices singing in his ears. "I have no choice," he said. "I've given him every chance, and I have no choice."

He bent close to the mangled donkey, whispered in its ear: "We'll do it together, Eeyore. You'll show me how."

CHAPTER THIRTY-ONE _____

Jon stood in the kitchen, the light streaming onto the counter, reflecting off pots and pans. His father was finishing his breakfast.

"Excuse me, Father."

"What the hell do you want?"

"I'd . . . like to clean the garage."

Doug Petrie sniffed. "I don't believe it," he said.

Jon wet his lips. "I'm sorry about what happened yesterday. It's just that the metalmark is very special to me."

Doug Petrie slipped his jacket on and said, "You're going to Harrington. It's too late to change that now. You're going."

"I understand that," Jon said. He stood there, pulse rapid. "Father, before you leave, would you move mother's car outside? It will give me more room to work."

"Be glad to," his father said.

The shop in junior high had been well equipped: with drill presses, bench saws, routers, planers, as well as a vast array of hand tools. Jon had made a storage cabinet, which was in his room upstairs, a bench, and a wooden planter that his mother loved and which now stood near the swimming pool. He was not really good with tools but he wasn't bad, and he had all the skills he needed for the job ahead.

His mother's car was parked beside the garage and he had a lot of space in which to work. He set up the horses, dragged out the first sheet of half-inch plywood from the rack against the wall. His father had a terrific assortment of tools: a circular saw, an electric drill, all kinds of hammers, screwdrivers, pliers, wrenches. . . . They had never been used and were new as the day he'd bought them. Doug Petrie paid others to do manual labor; he'd given up staining his hands years ago. But every garage should have tools, as every bookshelf should have books, whether anyone read them or not; and of course Doug Petrie bought the very best.

Jon wrestled the sheet of plywood onto the horses. He measured one of the windows, transferred the measurement onto the wood. Three panels—one for each window, one for the door that led out back—and after that two blocks and a hole drilled into the eaves. Not a whole lot of work, but his father often came home early Saturdays, and he'd have to move fast.

After she got home from Fogle's on Friday afternoon, Meg had called Matt's number twice while her parents were out by the pool. No one answered the phone. When her parents were sleeping she'd called once more. The angry voice of Matt's father came on the line and she quickly hung up.

She'd hardly slept all night. She forced herself to wait until eight o'clock before trying again. Again she got his sister and yes, she said, he was there, hang on a minute.

When she heard his voice she was so relieved she almost cried. "Where *were* you?" Her voice was tense, indignant, grateful. "Don't do that to me. Don't ever do that again."

He sounded tired, contrite. "I'm sorry, Meg. I had to get away by myself, that's all. I had to think things out."

"You *scared* me."

"I'm sorry." A long pause, then he said, "I'm not crazy, Meg."

"Of course you're not."

"I've gone over that paper four times and—I don't know how to explain it, but it isn't the paper I wrote."

"I gave you back the original," Meg said. "What happened to it?"

"I don't know. All I can think is that somebody stole it and typed this phony paper—to mess me up."

"But Matt, who would want to do that? And how could they do it so fast?"

"I don't know. But I have an idea."

She frowned. "You mean—? No, it *couldn't* be. I mean, *why*?"

"I don't know. All I know is I'm going to do that paper again. I still have the notes and original draft, and I'll be there when you type it so we'll know it's right. And we'll make an extra copy and hide it somewhere."

"Let's meet at the library this afternoon."

"I have to work this afternoon."

"Oh Matty, forget about Fogle's. We're talking about a scholarship."

"I didn't show up last night and didn't even call. Mr. Falcetti must really be ripped. I owe it to him, Meg."

"But when will you finish your paper?"

"I'll get it done. Tonight, tomorrow . . ."

"My parents are going up to the lake today," Meg said. "Why don't you work on it here tonight?"

"I don't think that's such a good idea."

"Why not? As soon as you're finished at Fogle's, come over here." Her voice turned plaintive. "Matty, I want to see you. I *have* to see you."

The line hummed hotly. Matt sighed and said, "Okay. I ought to be there between nine thirty and ten."

"I love you, Matt."

"I love you so much, Meg."

She set the receiver back in its cradle and sighed. Thank god, she thought. She would see him tonight and they'd work together and everything would be all right. She stared out the open window at the thicket of phlox by the swimming pool and thought of what Matt had said. Jon? No, impossible, he'd have no *reason* to do such a thing.

She thought of something else. Miss Weller had asked her to tell Matt to give her a call. But now she felt funny about having gone to Miss Weller. She'd made such a big deal out of things and he had been fine all along. He could see Miss Weller in school on Monday, that would be soon enough.

She looked at the cluster of phlox again. It was covered with butterflies: bright yellow ones and tiny white ones, flickering orange and silver ones. She looked at them and thought of Jon, and suddenly a chill went down her back. Not him, she thought again. It couldn't be.

Through the open window, somewhere not far away, came the whine of a circular saw.

Jon's arms and face and hair were covered with sawdust, and he dripped with sweat. He looked at the panels that covered the windows and door and thought: There are crimes so huge, so vile, that their perpetrators no longer deserve to exist on this earthly plane. Society had said this many times. Society made guillotines and scaffolds and electric chairs because of this. "Your eyes and mind are filled with money, Father. Let's see what good your money is in the other realm." He smiled, hot sweat pouring down his skin. He took the panels off the door and windows, hid them in the rack. Then he worked with furious energy, cleaning, straightening, till he saw the Eldorado's shiny hood far down at the end of the drive.

The sight of her car beside the garage made Doug Petrie's mind go through it all over again. He had thought about it a hundred times since it happened: How had Alice found out? How long had she known? To make a duplicate key like that, to surprise him like that—it wasn't like her at all. There was something *wrong* about it. Alice was the kind who would bring up the matter at breakfast one day as casually as if she were asking about a new rug or new set of drapes. That was her style. Out of it. Completely out of it. To surprise him like that, to *plan* like that . . . he just couldn't figure it out.

He pushed the button on the Genie control; the garage door slowly rose. He pulled in, turned the engine off, and looked around.

The kid had done a job all right and most of the place was neat—but there in one corner was a pile of scrap wood, paper, old milk cartons, all kinds of junk. Typical, he thought. Can't follow through on anything, not a goddamn thing. He stepped out of the car and the strong smell of gasoline hit him.

He looked at the concrete floor and saw the stain. He sighed and shook his head, went into the laundry room, closed the door behind him.

Jon was there at the breakfast table, drinking a glass of milk. He was covered with filth and sweat. He was pale as a ghost, his eyes were dark, and his hair was tangled wildly.

"Hello, Father. Do you like the job I did?"

Doug Petrie yanked at his tie and went to the freezer compartment. "Great," he said. "But why did you leave that mess in the corner? And how the hell did you manage to spill the gas?"

"I was moving some stuff around and knocked the container over. The cap came off. I got it up as fast as I could. I'm sorry, Father."

I'm sorry, Doug Petrie said to himself. Jesus, if he heard that one more time he'd slug the kid. He filled a glass with ice and opened the cabinet, took out the sourmash whiskey. "I'm going to bring the other car inside again," he said, "so get out there and air the place out."

Jon frowned. He looked at his milk and said, "Could you leave the other car outside for one more day? Till I get the rest of that mess cleaned up? It would really help."

Doug Petrie poured the whiskey in the glass and tossed it off. "Yeah, sure, whatever you say. But get out there and open the windows, I don't want the house to explode."

"Yes, Father, I will."

Jon got up, put his dirty glass in the dishwasher, and went to the garage. He opened the windows and the door that went out back. There Father, he thought with a smile, I carried out your request. Your last request. You're entitled to that, Father. Every condemned man is.

They ate TV dinners. His father sat in the family room and watched TV as he ate. ". . . Dressed as a security guard, lured the child into the alley and raped her." Tomorrow night may be *your* night on that screen, Jon thought. *Your* name may be in that announcer's mouth. He left most of his meal on the tray and went to his room.

He set the damaged Eeyore on his bed and kneeled before it, closed his eyes, and placed his hands on its fur. He stayed there several minutes in communion with the toy, then hid it behind his desk. After that he stood at the window and watched the crimson setting sun.

Tomorrow would be clear and warm, and his father would play golf. Everything was going to work out fine. He'd do the rest of what he had to do when he got home tonight. But now. . . .

He went to his desk and opened the bottom drawer, reached way in the back, and took out the bottle. Opened it, shook four of the tiny squares of paper into his hand. Stuck them in his shirt pocket, put the bottle away.

His father was in the family room, watching the Mets play the Reds. He remembered the time his father made him play with Carl and the rest of them, the terrible pain of the baseball hitting his face. I'll be so much nicer to you, he thought. You won't feel anything, Father, nothing at all. He went through the laundry room and out through the garage. The doors and windows were still wide open. He laughed to himself and started down the drive.

*   *   *

Two guys were at the pinball machine when he walked into Fogle's. They looked at him with superior smiles and went back to their game. A couple of girls were finishing sodas down at the end of the counter. When they got up to leave, Jon sat on the last stool and waited silently.

A flash of surprise was in Matt's eyes when he saw Jon sitting there, then his face went level, cool.

"Hi, Matt."

Matt ran some water onto his sponge. "Hi," he said. He wiped the counter slowly and deliberately, then finally came over to Jon. "We're closing now," he said.

"It's only quarter of," Jon said.

"We're closing early tonight."

Jon looked at him. "I have to talk to you. In private. It's important."

"Talk about what?" Matt said.

"About a lot of things."

"I have to clean up and close the place. I don't have time to talk."

"I said it's *important*," Jon said. He took a dollar out of his pocket and put it on the countertop. "I'll buy you a Coke and we'll sit in a booth and talk."

"I don't want any Coke," Matt said. He wiped the counter with firm, quick strokes.

"It's about the chemistry paper."

Matt stopped. He stared at Jon. The muscles in his jaw worked back and forth. "And what would you know about that?" he said.

Jon pushed the dollar at him. "Two Cokes," he said. "Then get those other kids out of here and we'll talk."

Matt put ice in two glasses, squeezed syrup in, ran the seltzer water. He rang up the sale and gave Jon the change.

"I'll wait in the booth," Jon said. He picked up the Cokes, stood up.

Matt told the guys at the pinball machine they had to leave. Jon took the squares of paper out of his pocket, dropped them in Matt's Coke. *I have drugged their*

possets . . . The insane root. . . . They floated and he
pushed them down with the straw. Matt was locking the
door as Jon picked out the papers, crushed them between his fingers, and dropped the tiny white ·vad on the
floor.

Matt went to the door of the back room and said,
"Mr. Falcetti, I'll finish up if you want to leave. I have
to talk to this kid for a couple of minutes."

"Okay, turn the lights off now so people won't think
we're open. When you leave, go out the back."

"Okay." Matt flipped some switches. All the lights
went off except the one behind the counter. He sat in the
booth across from Jon and stared at him. Jon drank his
Coke. Matt poked at his Coke with his straw then took
the straw out, drank from the glass. Mr. Falcetti kept
banging around out back. At last he said, "I'll see you
Monday, Matt."

"I'll see you, Mr. Falcetti."

The back door slammed. Matt glared at Jon and said,
"Okay, let's have it."

Jon stirred his Coke with his straw. He smiled and
said, "The paper that Mr. Frazier read is not the paper
you wrote."

Matt stared at him steadily, took a large swallow of
Coke, and said, "Yeah. How do you know that?"

"I wrote the paper Mr. Frazier read. I substituted it
for yours."

Matt narrowed his eyes. "You little bastard," he
said. "I knew it was you, I knew it." He breathed hard
and said, "How did you know what to write about?
How could the papers be so close? And how did you
open my locker? I never told anybody my combination—*anybody*."

"I have magical powers," Jon said.

Matt sneered. "You do, do you?" He shot up,
reached across the table, and grabbed Jon's collar.
"You little son-of-a-bitch, I ought to kill you!"

Coke dripped from the straw in Jon's hand. His
mouth began to twitch. He said, "I want to tell you
about it—tell you everything."

Matt let him go, sat back in the booth. "Go on," he said. "And make it good." He swallowed, resentment and hurt in his eyes. "Why the hell did you do that to me? What did I ever do to you?"

Jon looked at him, face haggard, pale, his sunken eyes aglow. "It isn't what you did to me," he said, "it's what you did to Meg."

"What do you mean, to Meg?"

"Making her kiss you. Making her say she loves you. You shouldn't have done that, Matt."

Matt stared at him, stunned. "How do you know about me and Meg? How do you know anything at *all* about that?"

"I told you, I have magical powers," Jon said. "I saw you kissing her. On Wednesday night, on Halsey Street."

"You sneaky little creep!" Matt said. "Hiding in the goddamn bushes!"

"No," Jon said. "Not that at all. I saw you . . . in a different way."

Matt's lips were suddenly dry. He drank some Coke and said, "What do you mean, a different way?"

"A special way. A magical way." He smiled. "Have I ever been in your house?"

"You know damn well you haven't."

"Then how do I know that your kitchen sink is old and stands on two legs? How do I know the house isn't painted, except for your room? The walls of your room are white and the trim is blue. It's a nice room. Cozy. Colorful."

Sweat beaded on Matt's forehead. "How the hell? . . . You *can't* know that."

"But I do," Jon said, eyes blinking, bright, "I obviously do." He grinned and drank some Coke. "And I'll tell you how I know." A drop of Coke hung on his lower lip as he said, "I read minds. I can tell what's in people's heads. I can see where they live, what they think, who they love, I can read their chemistry papers—and know anything I want to, Matt."

Matt stared in the semidarkness. His mind was

racing, his skin was slick with sweat. He nodded slowly, said, "You really can. You really *can* read minds." He shook his head. "That time in the locker room. You were in there, I saw you there."

"You did," Jon said. "I was reading minds then."

"I knew I wasn't seeing things," Matt said. He felt peculiar; everything seemed distant, foreign in the feeble light. "And you lied. You tried to make me think—"

Jon cut him off with a laugh. "That's how I took care of them," he said. He squinted, blinking, smiling crookedly.

Matt frowned. "How you took care of . . . who?"

"Well, Carl and Bruce and Randy and Sonny, of course. I took care of all of them."

Matt stared. A distant sound of bells was in his ears. "You *were* the one," he said. "I was right all along. The bomb. The poison mushrooms. It was you!"

Jon laughed again, an off-key cackle. "Yes," he said, eyes hot in the orange light. "They'll never bother me—or anyone else—again." He stared intently, said, "I did humanity a service, Matt. They would have given nothing to the world, they were parasites, vermin. They would only have taken, taken, taken, all their lives." He smiled vaguely. "Vermin must die. Vermin like them —and like my father."

"Your father?"

"My father," Jon said. "He will die in the morning. He's vermin. . . . And so are you."

The light was fractured, odd. Matt's heart was beating like a drum, it hurt his ears. He licked his dust-dry lips and said, "You're crazy, Jon."

Jon shook his head. "No, you're the one who's crazy, Matt, and everybody knows it—your classmates, Miss Weller, Mr. Frazier, they all know you're insane."

Matt banged his fist down hard. His hand felt doughy, dull. "You lying bastard!" he said. "Don't you ever say that to me!" His voice was distant, filled with static, flat.

"It isn't a lie," Jon said. "You know it's true. Your

mother, your father, your brother—and of course your sister Denise. She was very crazy, Matt. She was terribly crazy—almost as crazy as you." He laughed. "And what if I said you *did* write that crazy paper. What if I said you *didn't* see me in the locker, it was only a mirage. You wouldn't know what to believe, would you, Matt?"

Matt's breath seemed to clot in his throat. The light behind the counter was a rainbow, splintered shards. He started to stand up. His knees felt rubbery, thick, and numb. He sat again.

"You know I can read minds, Matt—and your mind is diseased."

"You know nothing!" Matt shouted. "Nothing!" His voice roared, echoed in his head, seemed far away.

"Oh but I do," Jon said, his dark eyes glittering. "I know you will kill yourself! Insanity is in your blood—and you will kill yourself!"

"Shut up, shut up!" But waterfalls were running through Matt's eyes, he heard a rush of music, light hung frozen in the room. "What did you do to me?" he screamed. "Oh God, Jon, what did you do?"

Jon stood up slowly, his face a mask. He went to the counter, turned, and said, "I liked you, Matt. You should never have enslaved Meg's soul. For those who do evil must pay." He walked out through the back, gently closing the door.

Matt pushed himself out of the booth. His body was a universe, gigantic, he weighed tons. On dream-slow legs he struggled to the phone. Call Meg, he thought; the words exploded like a bomb. He lifted the burning receiver and the dial was made of spider webs, the room was moving like a train, the numbers made no sense. He braced himself against the countertop; its surface felt soft and cold, like powdery ice cream. The room was sound turned solid; light shot painful splinters into his brain. He sank to his knees with a groan and lay there, gasping, helpless, as roaring bright rivers flowed.

Jon hurried home. He went through the garage and

laundry room, the kitchen. . . .

His father was asleep in front of the family-room TV. Two women in pink tights were singing a duet. Jon turned the TV off. As he looked at his father slouching there, mouth open, a blob of spit on his lower lip, a surge of hatred hit him. *The sleeping and the dead are but as pictures.*

"Father!"

Doug Petrie jerked awake, eyes startled. "What? Oh, it's you. What, what do you want?"

"Don't you think you ought to go to bed? You fell asleep."

His father brushed his hair back with his hand. "Oh. Yeah, I guess so," he said thickly. "Did you close up the garage?"

"Not yet. I will."

"Then open it up in the morning again. I want that place to air out good."

"I'll do that, Father."

Jon went to his room as his father got ready for bed, and he placed Eeyore on the window sill beside the desk. He propped the torn-off legs against the torso, looked out the window, and whispered, "I'll be right down there, in the garage. It's working perfectly, Eeyore, just as we planned."

He waited, listening, and soon he heard his father's rasping snores coming out of the bedroom. The bedroom where he murdered Mother, Jon thought, and he said to himself, "Sleep well, Father. It's the last sleep you'll have on this earth."

CHAPTER THIRTY-TWO _____

At ten thirty-five Meg Hale called Fogle's Fountain. Oddly, the line was busy. She called five times in the next twenty minutes and still got a busy signal.

Fogle's closed at nine. The latest Matt usually stayed was nine thirty. It took him fifteen minutes to walk up the hill to her house, and he certainly should have been there by now. Fifteen minutes late, okay, half an hour late, well maybe, but forty-five minutes late? It wasn't like Matt at all. Maybe he was on the phone with somebody else, she thought, but why didn't he call her first?

At eleven she had the operator place the call. The line was still busy. It wasn't right, even Mr. Falcetti wouldn't be there this late.

At eleven-ten she couldn't wait any longer and left the house. She didn't run into him on the way and her heart was in her throat as she neared the store.

As she'd feared, it was dark, locked tight. She squinted through the window at the phone. The receiver was out of its cradle, hung behind the counter, out of sight.

A numbing fear washed over her. She tapped on the door, a sudden desperation in her heart. She waited. Nothing. Tapped again. No reply.

She hurried around to the back of the store, went past the stacks of empty milk and soda cases—and the door was open, swinging in the soft June breeze.

Cautiously, frightened, she entered the store. She stood there in the darkness, listening, her breathing loud in her ears. "Matt? Matty?" Nothing. She crossed through the back room, went into the front. The phone's receiver hung there, dead, emitting a flat dull buzz. She reached for it, then stood there holding it, confusion flooding her mind. She looked up Mr. Falcetti's home phone number, dialed.

Six rings before he answered, groggy with sleep. Meg told him who she was and what she'd found, and Mr. Falcetti thanked her for calling, his voice sharp, irritated now. No, he didn't know where Matt was. He didn't know what had got into the boy. He hadn't shown up the night before and now he had left the store without locking up. Was he with anyone when you left? Meg asked, and Mr. Falcetti answered, Yes, some little kid with glasses, didn't know his name. He'd be right down to check things out. Would she lock the door for him? She said she would and he thanked her again.

She hurried back up the hill, her mind in a whirl. So he'd been with Jon. She thought of all the terrible things that had happened at Aronson High but told herself no, he had nothing to do with all that. He was different, weird, but he couldn't do things like that, he just couldn't! Then his talk about spirits and death came back, the talk about Lady Macbeth. She broke into a clammy sweat, hurried into the house. She dialed Matt's number again.

The gruff voice answered; his father. She hesitated, asked in a quavering voice, "Is Matt Wilson there?"

"No." That was all—the line was dead.

The receiver hummed in her hand. Slowly she put it back on the hook and sat at the kitchen table. Suddenly her fear welled up and she started to cry. *Matt, be all right. Please be all right. Please, call me, come here, come see me, please.*

She wiped her eyes and calmed herself and sat in the empty house. The second hand on the kitchen clock spun around with a gurgling sound. She thought of

Aronson High again, she thought of Jon. Impulsively she went back to the phone, looked up the number, and dialed. The kitchen clock said twenty after twelve.

Jon looked at the lumber rack, the tools. The light in the Genie garage door opener blazed down. He had closed the windows earlier as his father had asked him to, and the smell of gasoline had begun to build. *The container just fell over, Father.* How stupid his father was! Jon laughed to himself and walked to the lumber rack.

Suddenly he froze. He thought he'd heard—

My God, it was! The phone! It would ring in his father's bedroom too, and it would wake him up!

He tore open the door to the laundry room, raced into the kitchen, lifted the phone in mid-ring. He stood there in darkness, his pulse banging into his ears. "Hello?"

"Hello, Jon? It's Meg."

His heart jumped wildly. "Meg!"

A pause. "Jon listen, I'm sorry about calling you now, I probably woke you up, but I'm looking for Matt. You don't know where he is, do you?"

Jon's breath roared into the phone. "Matt?" he said. "How would I know where he is?"

"Mr. Falcetti told me he saw you together tonight."

Sweat beaded Jon's lip. "I went to Fogle's for a soda," he said. "Matt sat in the booth and had one with me."

"Did you stay until he locked up?"

"No. He was still there when I left." It's the truth, he thought. I'm not lying to you, Meg, it's true.

A pause on the line, then: "I'm worried about him, Jon. He left the back door open and nobody knows where he is."

Jon frowned. His voice turned thick. "Why should you be worried about him, Meg?"

Another pause. "He . . . has a book I need. For my history paper. He said he'd give it to me tonight, but he never stopped by."

"You shouldn't worry about him, Meg."

"Jon, please— Do you know where he is?"

Jon frowned at the darkness. "Don't worry about him. Don't let him control your mind."

Her voice changed pitch. "Control my mind? What are you talking about?"

"You know, Meg. You know."

"I *don't* know," Meg said. "Jon, please, if you know anything at all—"

"I don't know where he is. I'm sorry, Meg." The line hummed gently. "Goodnight, darling, sleep well, and don't worry. There's no need to worry at all. . . ."

He flicked the cradle, cutting her off, and let the receiver dangle there on the cord. The dial tone hummed at the dark. He went to the foot of the stairs and waited, thought of Meg and Matt. Dear Meg and evil Matt.

He waited till he heard his father's loud and rhythmic snoring in the room upstairs, and then he went back to work.

Matt Wilson stared at the streetlight. Ruby-red beacons bled into the blue-black sky. Then suddenly a shift, and emerald green, a luminescent green with depth, dimension, green that he could feel. It wormed its way into his eyes, slid down his throat, bored through his stomach, wriggled out his pores. It was poison, this green—a beautiful deadly poison, and it snaked through his veins and out through his pores and he fell to his knees and wept.

He had no idea where he was. He had no idea how long he'd been walking or where he was headed. One minute it mattered terribly and the next he didn't care at all, the crystal magic stunning his eyes and banishing all thought. The snow came down, a solid screen of tragedy and fear. He leaned against furry, rubbery walls, his feet a thousand miles below him, huge clown feet, bright comical balloons. Bright hours of ecstasy, and days of sheer insanity: when Jon returned, his body glowing blue, and told the Wilson history. His father, his mother, Pete, Denise. And even little Jill, who went to see the special teacher once a week. All this would come, then dissolve like smoke. The moment, *now*, the only moment ever, would roll up out of dark wheels and stare him down. He'd scream against the mad distorted splash and weep in empty streets with streetlamps showering needles of yellow rain.

CHAPTER THIRTY-THREE _____

Sue Weller took off her pantyhose and tossed them into the hamper. She took off her bra and sat on the edge of the bed.

She had gone to a movie with Gary Black, the ninth-grade social studies teacher. They'd had a drink at a bar and he'd asked her back to his place. She'd said no. The third date and the third refusal. They had gotten into a hassle then, and he'd turned sullen and driven her home. It wasn't that she didn't like Gary, he was all right, it was just. . . .

She sat there picking at her finger and the memory rose up. "You're turning down a ride in a Porsche 928? Hey Sue, come *on*." And Mark had smiled and said, "You'll be sorry, Sue." And she *was* sorry, sorrier than he had ever dreamed, and she'd never forget that smile.

She cut the memory off abruptly, picked at her finger, and thought, What a year. Three students dead and one in jail, a teacher badly hurt. . . . Common enough in a ghetto school, but for Aronson High, wow. Drugs, pregnancies, an auto accident, okay, but this kind of stuff. . . . Quite a switch.

She lay back on the bed, exhausted. More than a month to go before her break. She was going to work through July this year, take August off. Mostly administrative nonsense, tedious junk, but not too bad. One more week and the kids would be gone and that would help. She liked the kids, but Jesus, you needed a break.

She turned off the light. She had no air conditioner and the room was stuffy. The window shade flapped gently in the warm, dead breeze. She lay there, sweating, staring at the bar of light on the ceiling, and suddenly thought of Matt Wilson. He'd never called. She wondered—

The telephone rang.

Gary, she thought, and it rang again. Gary, leave me alone, I'm tired, I don't want to deal with it now! Another ring. Persistent S.O.B. Two more rings and she said aloud, "I'm not going to answer you, Gary, leave me alone!" In the middle of the seventh ring she couldn't take it anymore and picked up the receiver.

"Hello?"

"Miss Weller?"

A girl's voice, not Gary, a girl. "Yes?"

"This is Meg Hale. I have to talk to you."

Jon took the plywood panels out of their hiding place and screwed them over the windows and the door that led out back. He took the wooden blocks he'd made and placed them in the tracks of the overhead door, wrapping them firmly in place with strapping tape. Then he went outside.

He had cut the length of hose that afternoon. He pulled it out of the bushes beside the garage and taped its end to the BMW's tailpipe. He propped the ladder against the garage, grabbed the other end of the hose, climbed up, fed the hose through the hole he had drilled in the eaves. The hose fit snugly, but he packed it with rope caulk to hold it tighter and seal off any cracks.

He went back inside and carried out all the tools. All the tools and everything that could function as a tool: golf clubs, bottles, cans of paint, an old lawn chair. . . . He carried it all around the side, put it next to his mother's car.

Once that was done, he placed the screws in the holes he had drilled in the door that led out back, screwed them tightly into the jamb. He unlatched the hood of the Eldorado, lifted it, removed the ignition coil. He put it in his pocket and looked at the ceiling. There was the hose poking out of the hole in the eaves. He took the can of gasoline and splashed more gas on the floor, then put the can back again. He smiled. That was it.

In the morning he'd wait till his father was washing up, then he'd sneak outside and turn on his mother's car. The garage would fill with exhaust while his father was drinking his coffee and eating his toast. His father would finish his breakfast, eager for golf, go through the laundry room, enter the garage. He'd see the panels on the windows and would smell—just gasoline. Not exhaust, just gasoline. He'd hear the BMW idling outside, and confusion would enter his mind. And the door to the laundry room would slam behind him and lock.

And all at once he would know what was going on. He would run to the laundry room, try to open the door—but would have no key. He would not be able to break down the door because it was extra strong, a security door he'd installed to protect his precious property. He would try to get out through the back, but would find that the door was screwed shut. He would try to open the overhead door but the blocks in the tracks would immobilize it. By now he'd be dizzy, the world would be fading away. He'd see the hose between the eaves, but he wouldn't be able to reach it: no ladder or boxes to stand on, no rake or other tool to knock it down. No tool to smash his way through the plywood-covered windows and door. He would kick at them wildly, hurting his legs, but they wouldn't give.

In final desperation he'd think: the car! He'd start the car and smash his way out! Gasping, faint, he'd turn the key and press on the gas—and the motor wouldn't start. It would grind and grind and wouldn't start and that's where he would die—in the seat of the Eldorado, or maybe on the gas-stained floor, or scratching at the plywood panels, frenzied, tearing his hands to a bloody pulp as Jon had torn his hands on the clay walls of Headquarters so many long weeks ago.

And once he was dead, Jon would turn off his mother's car and take down the hose and take the panels and blocks away and unscrew the door and put the ignition coil back in the Eldorado—and it would look like suicide. ". . . Despondent over the death of his wife, the developer, who lived at 34 Evergreen Drive . . ." Jon could hear the TV announcer now, could see the phony face. ". . . Survived by one son, Jonathan, age fifteen . . ."

And he'd live with Aunt Edna, his mother's sister, and when he turned twenty-one he'd inherit his parents' estate. He would have all the money he'd ever need and would not have to work and he'd marry Meg and they'd fly together forever.

Jon stood there looking at the job he'd done, the smell of gas strong in his nose. He turned off the lights and went through the laundry room, crept up the carpeted stairs.

Just one more thing to do. One very important and dangerous thing to do.

Cautiously he approached his father's room. Through the open door he could hear the snoring, jagged and abrasive. He slipped through the doorway, stared at the dark. Could see his father's bulk in the bed—desecrating the bed where his mother had died. Jon quivered with hatred and fear as he crept toward the bureau.

This afternoon he had taken his mother's keys out of her bureau drawer. His father's keys were there in their usual spot. He picked them up, holding his breath. He snapped the ring open, slipped off the key to the laundry room, snapped the ring closed, put the keys down again. A slight jingling noise as they settled onto the bureau. He stood there breathing measured, even breaths and listened to the snoring and thought: Sleep well. Sleep well in preparation for your final sleep. For your trip to the other realm, the realm where you can't hurt me any more. He turned and took two steps.

And suddenly the snoring stopped. His father sat bolt upright in the dark.

A freezing fear exploded in Jon's chest.

"Who is it?" his father growled. "Who's there?"

Jon stood there, the key in his hand, skin slimy with sweat.

"It's you!" his father roared. "What the hell are *you* doing in here?"

Jon opened his mouth in a daze. His jaw moved slowly, thickly, and his tongue was paralyzed. A feeble whine escaped his lips. He was going to die.

"I told you to get those specs back by Friday!" his father said. "I'm not interested in your goddamn excuses, understand?"

A dream. His father was having a dream. The sweat poured over Jon in rivers as he stood there, shaking, clutching the key so hard it bruised his flesh.

Then his father turned, lay down again. Jon slipped from the room, his legs like water. In the hall he stood and listened in the dark, licked sweat off his lips, choked down his heart. Soon the snoring began again and he went to his room.

He went limp on the bed. He lay there staring at the ceiling, shivering, thoughts racing through his mind. The witches, Duncan, Banquo and, *Macbeth does murder sleep.* "No, no, another realm, that's all it is! *He* is the killer, it's *him*!"

He got up, took Eeyore down from the window sill, held him, sat down at his desk. He stared down at the spotlight shining on the garage. "Tomorrow," he said. "Tomorrow it will end, Eeyore, our troubles will end. We'll know peace. . . ."

CHAPTER THIRTY-FOUR

Sue Weller sat in Meg's kitchen, smoking, frowning, a headache pressing hard at the back of her eyes. When Meg finished telling the story they got in the car and drove to Brewery Hill.

It was two thirty-five when they pulled up in front of Matt's house. Sue Weller got out of the car and said, "You let me handle this. Stay here." She went up the three marble steps to the door and rang the bell.

She could hear it buzzing dully inside the house. She rang seven times and suddenly above her head a window shot up with a crash. A thin, dark, gnarled face with a sharp mustache. "What the hell do you want?"

"Mr. Wilson?" Sue said.

The man said nothing.

"I want to know if Matt is here."

The man cursed loudly, shouted, "No!" and banged the window shut.

Sue pressed the bell again. It rang another six times before the head appeared again. "You get the hell out of here, goddamn it, before I call the cops!"

"Mr. Wilson, your son never came home from work tonight. I'd think you'd be worried about him."

The man said sharply, "Who the hell are you?"

"Sue Weller. The guidance counselor at Aronson High. I've worked with Matt and I care about him."

"Then go find him," the thin man said, and the window slammed shut again.

Sue Weller got back in the car and whistled between her teeth.

"Matt told me he was bad," Meg said.

"He sure didn't exaggerate," Sue said. She drove till she came to the first phone booth and called the police.

Jon had been sitting at his desk for hours now, while strange bright images, touches of dream, paraded through his mind. He nodded off, then jerked awake again. No sleep. Not now. Not till after the deed was done.

The sky was growing light. He checked his clock: five after four. His father would leave for the golf course at ten, so six more hours to go. His lids began to close again, a dream flared bright as day, he snapped awake. He went into the bathroom, splashed cold water on his face. Looked out the window there. A gleaming band of sun so bright it blinded him pushed over the edge of the hills.

Matt Wilson had walked for years. Or maybe he had just begun to walk, he didn't know. Time made no sense, had disappeared, and all that remained was color, sound, and light.

A bar of gold burned into the edge of the world. He stared as the gold grew, thickened, filling the heavens, filling his soul. He wept, and the world wept too: It was crying and melting in huge golden blobs, and he knew all sadness, pain and hatred, knew all loss. He was one with the world, it lived within the borders of his flesh, he ached to the burning fires of his melted core. Crawling on the ground he cried, "Forgive me! Mom! Denise! Oh please, please!" Tears streamed down his cheeks as he crawled, kept crawling, found himself in air.

They had driven through all the streets in Brewery Hill, and after that they'd gone through Russelville and Henderson. When they checked with the Brewery Hill station again, it was after five.

The scanner in a flat and toneless voice said some-thing about an assault. The sergeant shook his head. "But we'll find him," he said. "Why don't you go on home and get some rest."

Meg stood there exhausted, face puffy, tears in her eyes. Sue Weller put her arm around her. "You won't stop looking," she said.

The sergeant shook his head again and smiled. "The kid is probably sleeping off a drunk somewhere, but—"

"He isn't like that!" Meg said in a passionate burst. "He wouldn't just go off like that! Something's *hap-pened* to him!"

She started to cry again. Sue Weller held her, said, "It's okay, Meg, they'll find him. He'll be okay."

"I'll stay here until they do," Meg said.

They sat on the bench, Sue's arm around Meg's shoulder. Cars passed outside the open door. Sue said, "You mind if I have a smoke?" Meg shook her head.

The scanner's voice described an accident at Tenth and Maple, then: "We found the Wilson kid. . . . He's out on the Ferry Avenue bridge. Looks like he might try to jump. We'll need a unit—"

The sun hung bright on the horizon, burned through haze with glaring spears of light, glowed dully on the girders of the bridge.

There were seven squad cars parked at the foot of the bridge, and Sue Weller pulled up behind them. She and Meg got out and ran to the barricade. The cop, white-haired and red-faced, held out his arm. "You can't go out there. We've got a possible suicide on our hands."

"I'm a guidance counselor at Aronson High," Sue Weller said. "I know the kid. I think I can help."

"Sorry, Miss, I can't let anyone through. The suicide prevention unit's here. They'll handle it."

"But I'm the one who started the search," Sue said. —And she saw Meg walking slowly across the road. She frowned and looked intently at the policeman's face. "Is Captain Miller here?"

"He's out on the bridge with the unit, Miss."

"If I could talk to him—"

"I'm afraid not, Miss, you'll just have to wait here."

Then Meg was on the narrow walk on the side of the bridge and running toward the orange van in the distance.

"Officer, look, Captain Miller knows who I am. I worked with him last fall, when we had a girl who threatened to jump off the roof of the gym."

The policeman sighed and took his intercom off his belt. "I shouldn't really be doing this, Miss, but . . ."

Matt stood at the gate to heaven. Around him the universe shimmered in thick, rich light. Far below he saw softness, rolling and lovely, a beautiful land of peace. He would go to that land and the terrible sadness would end.

He heard the voices saying, "It's okay, Matt, it's all right, Matt, just stay right there," and he knew they were demon voices, voices sent to lure him from the path. They wanted to drag him down to hell, but now he was face to face with heaven and it was too late. The demons were slow and weak and afraid and he had time, all the time in the world, and before they could grab him and take him away he would fly. He would fly to the land of peace, the soft land far below where sadness was banished forever, the land of dreams.

The voices kept on talking: treachery and lies, spoken softly and deceitfully. They faded as he raised his arms, stood high. The sun was bleeding now, huge crimson drops ran down its face and splattered on silver-blue scales. And now there was a different voice, a voice that cried out, "Matty, Matty!" and he frowned. The voice came spinning through layers of cotton, shattered behind his eyes. He knew that voice. He remembered it from long ago. He stood there, splinters of music stabbing his brain, and watched the silver ribbon far below. The ribbon was sound, the voice again, and then she was there beside him.

She shimmered, glowed in gold. Huge tears ran down

her face like lava as he stared. "I love you, Matt! Oh Matty, Matty, please!"

Bright shining stars rolled down his cheeks. They burned, they stung, he stared at her, his heart swelled hard with love. So she had come to find eternal peace—and he would take her there. He said her name. His voice exploded, rocked down marble halls. He smiled, reached to take her hand—

And the demons had him, locked him in their gray-blue arms. He thrashed and kicked and cried out "No!" but they had him, thousands of them. They dragged him down and held him hard against blazing asphalt and steel. . . .

CHAPTER THIRTY-FIVE _____

Jon woke up, stunned. The room was bright. In a panic, he checked his watch: twenty minutes to nine! All the nights that he couldn't sleep, and now when he wanted to stay awake . . .

He was still at his desk. He jumped up, went to the hallway, listened. Faintly, through his father's door, he heard the shower running.

Quickly he left his room and went downstairs. He went through the sliding door that led to the pool, went around to his mother's car. He jumped in, fumbled in his pocket for the keys. Put the key in the ignition, trembling, turned it, pressed on the gas.

The engine sputtered, coughed. He broke into a sweat and turned the key again. Again the engine ground away but wouldn't catch. He sat there, numb, hand shaking, the smell of gas burning his nose.

If he couldn't start the car he was finished, absolutely finished. His father would see the plywood panels, the blocks in the track of the overhead door, and he would be caught. He gritted his teeth and pumped the pedal, turned the key again. The starter ground away. Sweat poured down Jon's cheeks. Then suddenly the engine quickened, roared to life.

Jon pumped the gas, fed the engine until it purred. With a sigh he slumped back in the seat. When the engine was idling smoothly he left the car and went back into the house.

He closed the door between the kitchen and the laundry room, and still he could hear the muffled sound of his mother's car. He turned the TV on and drowned out the noise and thought, Soon it will all be over. Soon the deed will be done.

He got a bowl, the Cheerios, the milk. He poured the cereal into the bowl, poured the milk on, sprinkled it with sugar. He sat there staring at it, stomach knotted.

When his father came down he would eat. He would force himself to act normal and eat. His father would drink his coffee and eat his toast, and after that he'd go through the laundry room and out to the garage.

And Jon would jump out of his chair and slam the door shut behind him. His father would try to get back in, would reach for his key—and find it gone. And soon after that he would die.

Jon stared at the TV set. A preacher was saying, "Give yourselves to *Je*sus, and ye shall have life everlasting, ye shall enter the Kingdom of Heaven." Jon stared. There was nothing to do but wait.

At Midvale Hospital they gave Matt Wilson Thorazine and a sedative, and he slept. Meg sat beside the bed and held his hand. Sue Weller sat there too, exhausted, dizzy, smoking, drinking coffee. When she thought of her date with Gary Black it seemed far in the past.

Matt slept for three hours, then rolled over onto his back. He blinked, then jerked up suddenly and vomited hard on the floor. He gripped the side of the bed, shaking, retching and groaning. The nurse brought a pan, and the orderly mopped up the vomit. The nurse took his pulse as he lay there, stupified, eyes dull. Then he frowned, a pained expression on his face, and said, "Meg."

She wept. She held him and cried, her face on his chest. "Oh Matty, Matt."

He lay there limp, mouth open, skin pale. "It was Jon," he said. "He . . . put something in my Coke."

Sue Weller crushed her cigarette out and said, "My God." She got up, stood by the bed.

Matt stared at the ceiling. "I'm tired," he said. "I'm just so tired, I have to sleep. But everything looks okay again. I'll be all right." His eyelids drooped, his face went slack. Then suddenly he flashed awake and tried to push himself up. "His father!" he said.

"Whose father?" Meg said. "Jon's father?"

"He killed them all," Matt said. "Randy, Carl, he set the bomb, it was him, he did it all!"

"Oh no," Meg said. "Oh Matt—"

"He told me everything, and . . . his father. He's going to kill him! He's going to blow him up or . . . oh . . ." He winced, fell back again. "It's probably already too late."

Sue Weller put her hand on Meg's shoulder. "I'll be back," she said. "You stay with Matt." She left the room and ran down the corridor and through the sliding door that led outside.

Jon stared at the TV preacher, the choir, his mind going over the plan. His father would eat, go out to the garage, the door would slam, he'd reach for his key. He would try to break in, would fail, would get in the car, the engine wouldn't start—and he would be doomed, trapped, no escape, he would—

Suddenly he thought of something.

The car. In the trunk of the car was a jack. His father could use it to bash his way out of the garage.

Sharp needles of panic jabbed through him. The jack! He had to get it, get rid of it! In a flash he was out through the sliding door and back at the BMW.

The extra key to the Eldorado was on his mother's ring. He turned off the engine, grabbed the key ring, worked at it frantically. He cut his finger and blood oozed out. "Come on, come *on*!" he said. At last the ring snapped open and the key to the Eldorado was in his hand. He shoved the BMW key back in and started the car again. Gasping and drenched with sweat, he ran back to the house.

At the sliding door he stopped and listened. The TV set was saying, "For the Lord is merciful. For he who hath sinned shall find peace . . ." His father still hadn't come down. He left the sliding door open, ran through the laundry room, and opened the door to the garage.

The powerful smell of gasoline and a choking gray-blue haze. Hurry, he thought, my God hurry up or he'll smell it! He ran to the Eldorado, shoved the key into the lock on the trunk and turned it. It opened. There was the jack. He grabbed it, took it out—

At the edge of his vision, movement. —And there was his father, standing in the doorway.

"Jonathan!"

Jon stood there, nailed to the spot, the jack in his hand.

His father's face was red with rage. "What the hell's going on in here?"

"I . . . I . . ." Sweat flooded Jon's face.

"Good Christ, this smell!" What the hell is that shit on the window? Where *is* everything?"

Jon gasped. "I . . . put it outside. Until I could finish."

His father's eyes were puzzled, hard. "I told you to air this place out! It's worse today than it was last night, what's the matter with you?"

"I'm sorry, Father, I—"

"What! You what! What excuse do you have this time?" He pointed across the room. "What the hell have you done to the windows? What's that plywood doing there?"

Jon stood there, dizzy, dazed. The hose in the eaves poured out its poison, he coughed, he gagged, felt faint.

"And why is my trunk open? Why did you open my trunk?"

Jon gagged again. His eyes were burning, raw. In sudden desperation he cried, "Because that's where it is! It's in there!" And he pointed inside.

"*What's* in there?" his father said.

"Come quick and look! Hurry, Father, hurry, come here and look!"

His father started into the garage. "What's that noise

out there? Whose car is that?" He hesitated, frowning.
And the doorbell rang.

"For Christ's sake, who's that now?"

"Don't answer it!" Jon cried. A frenzied look came
over him as he said, "Come here! Your trunk!"

The doorbell rang again. Doug Petrie said, "You get
that shit off the windows and air this place out before I
get back!"

"But Father!"

"*But* shit—you heard what I said! The whole house
smells like gas, goddamn it. Now move your ass!"
Again the doorbell rang. "All right, all right, I'm
coming, damn it!" At the doorway he suddenly turned
and frowned and said, "You were in my room last
night. I saw you there!"

The bell rang again. Doug Petrie stared, then said,
"I'll deal with you in a minute. Stay right here!" He
turned abruptly, slamming the door behind him.

Jon stood there, paralyzed. Then in panic he ran to
the door and grabbed the knob. He twisted, pulled. It
was locked.

"Father!" he screamed. "Father, open the door!"
But his father was in the foyer now, too far away to hear
his voice above the rousing hymn on the TV set. . . .

Doug Petrie opened the front door, thinking, That
goddamn kid, I'll kill him, I swear I will!

A young woman was standing there. She looked
vaguely familiar. Her face was frightening in its urgency.

"Mr. Petrie, I have to talk to you."

It came to him. "Miss Weller," he said. "What are
you doing here on a Sunday morning?"

"I have to talk to you. Now."

Doug Petrie sighed and shook his head. "Okay, come
in," he said.

"No, not in the house," Sue Weller said with a
vigorous shake of her head. "In my car."

"In your *car*?"

"Please, hurry! There isn't time!"

Doug Petrie frowned and stepped outside. "What the hell is all this about?"

"Just come with me! And hurry!"

He followed her out to the street. A violent crashing came from the garage. You *better* work, he thought. Get that crap off that door and those windows or I'll fucking crucify you.

Sue Weller stopped and said, "What's that noise?"

Doug Petrie sniffed. "It's Jonathan," he said. "I told him to do some work in the garage, and he's a little ticked off."

"He's . . . here?" Sue Weller said.

"Why the hell do you say it like that?"

Sue Weller said, "Let's sit in the car."

Doug Petrie squeezed into the Pinto, sat there, sweat beading his lip. "Okay, Miss Weller, what's up?"

She told him everything: about Matt, the mushrooms, Bruce, the bomb. He stared through the windshield, shaking his head and mumbled, "No. You can't be right. Not Jon. He couldn't do things like that. You're wrong, you have to be."

"I only wish I were," she said in an exhausted voice. "But he told Matt Wilson he did those things—killed three of his classmates, and now he's out to kill you." Her face was earnest, tense. "I had every reason to think that he planted a bomb in the house, that's why I had to get you out of there. But I must be wrong. If he's still in the house, I'm wrong, he must have planned some other way."

Doug Petrie stared. Then suddenly the whole thing clicked. "My God!" he said. "No, not a bomb, my God!" He threw open the door of the Pinto and ran to the house.

Jon lay on the concrete floor, the jack beside his head. He was terribly weak, too weak to move; there wasn't any air. His mind was gray, dim yellow pinwheels spun behind his eyes. He thought of Meg as the darkness fell. Oh Meg, dear Meg. . . . His mind was a distant point of consciousness, he pictured Lucifer high in the tree—and then he flew.

He was standing there, invisible, when his father ran in crying "Jonathan!" Jon watched as he shook the crumpled body, lifted it and ran through the laundry room, ran outside through the kitchen's sliding glass doors.

He watched his father set the body on the grass and tilt its head back, breathe into its mouth. The lungs of the body rose and fell, but without any will of their own. Tears came to Jon's phantom eyes. So you cared after all, he thought. You yelled and bullied and threatened and never understood me, never at all—and yet you cared.

Suddenly the shade came down, and all was black.

CHAPTER THIRTY-SIX _____

He woke up floating. Dizzy, foggy, floating in air above manicured grass, chiseled stones.

The cluster of people came into focus, and he heard the voice say, ". . . Name of the Father, and of the Son, and of the Holy Ghost, amen," and the coffin was slowly descending into the cloth-draped hole.

His father was standing there in a dark blue suit. And Sue Weller was there, and some friends of the family, Aunt Edna and Uncle Lew. . . . And Meg. His beautiful, wonderful Meg. She was there holding hands with Matt on the edge of the grave.

A flood of tears rushed to Jon's eyes and he screamed, "I'm not dead! Meg, look, I'm here, right here! I'm not dead! It's supposed to be *us* together, not you and him, oh *no*!"

Everybody stood there calmly, watched the coffin disappear. In desperation Jon flew down, flew into the grave, through the polished wood, tried to enter the body that lay there cushioned in silk.

The waxen flesh was hard as stone, unyielding, as he banged against it time and time again. "Let me in!" he cried. "Let me back, let me in!"

At last he sighed, rose up again, and stood by the side of the grave. No use. No good. His body and spirit were severed forever, closed off from each other for good. He stood there invisible next to the grave and wept.

Slowly and sadly he flew as the small knot of

mourners walked off. "I never understood the kid," he heard his father say to his Uncle Lew.

"It still seems unbelievable," Meg said to Matt, and Jon could see tears in her eyes.

He flew up higher, choking, hurried back to his house. He felt weak and uncoordinated, odd, felt a horrible lack of control and a terrible urgency, flew faster, as fast as he could.

His house came into view. He flew lower, dropped down to his room. And there on the window sill below, he could see it, his Eeyore, ragged, forlorn, still sitting there. His father hadn't touched it; it was still right there.

"Eeyore!" Jon cried. "Look, Eeyore, I still exist! I was right about death, I was right all along!"

He tried to come closer, but his power was gone. And then he was being pulled back up again, was going higher, higher, quickly, so fast that the sky was a blur. His flying was not his own anymore. He was being controlled by other forces, powerful and huge.

The sky was racing, there was nothing but mist, a luminous blue that startled his wondrous eyes. He was on his way to that other realm, that plane he had thought about for so long now. He was immortal, yes. And so were all the others who had died—Chuckie, his mother . . . their spirits had not been extinguished either, he'd find them here, he'd search and search forever until he did. Their spirits would greet him. They knew that he'd wanted the best for them. And someday Meg would come here too. He would wait. He had eternity to wait.

He flew. The mist dazzled, amazed; and far in the distance he seemed to hear voices, a chorus of voices rushing closer, growing louder.

Suddenly a terror cold as ice coursed through him. If nobody died, if all spirits lived, then what about Randy, Bruce, and Carl? He trembled on the edge of nausea, horrified. The Indians, the Africans, their fears . . .

The time has been
That when the brains were out, the man would die,
And there an end. But now they rise again . . .

But surely the spirits here had been transformed, existed on a higher plane, surely they wouldn't seek revenge—

Ahead of him the mist thinned out—and there they were.

They stood there, staring at him, all of them. Randy and Carl had eyes like stone, bright stone that burned. Their mouths were warped and horrible, as if the agony of mushroom poisoning had still not died. Jon raised his hand to shield himself, as if their gaze was fire. "I only arranged things!" he said. "*Thou canst not say I did it*, I only arranged things. It was you!"

The faces stared. Jon looked away—at Bruce.

And Bruce's face was caked with blood, his hair was matted, dripping red.

"It was an accident!" Jon cried. "*Never shake thy gory locks at me*, it was an accident! You fell, I never meant—" His throat choked off.

The power rushed him closer and the mist blew hot; it seared his cheeks. The faces grew, detail clicked into focus sharper, sharper: the agonized stares, the clotted blood, the terrible grotesque mouths . . . Jon clutched his head and peered through his fingers, terrified.

And his enemies smiled, smiled, smiled, his enemies smiled. . . .

Bestselling Books for Today's Reader — From Jove!

___**THE AMERICANS** John Jakes	05432-1/$2.95
___**BURIED BLOSSOMS** Stephen Lewis	05153-5/$2.95
___**LONGARM AND THE LONE STAR LEGEND** Tabor Evans	06225-1/$2.75
___**NIGHTWING** Martin Cruz Smith	06241-7/$2.95
___**SHIKE: TIME OF THE DRAGONS** **(Book 1)** Robert Shea	06586-2/$3.25
___**SHIKE: LAST OF THE ZINJA** **(Book 2)** Robert Shea	06587-0/$3.25
___**A SHARE OF EARTH AND GLORY** Katherine Giles	04756-2/$3.50
___**THE ULTIMATE GAME** Ralph Glendinning	06524-2/$3.50
___**THE WOMEN'S ROOM** Marilyn French	05933-1/$3.50
___**YELLOW ROSE** Shana Carrol	05557-3/$3.50

More Bestselling Books
From Jove!

SF 0365